# Moment
# She Left

Susan Lewis is the bestselling author of thirty-six novels. She is also the author of *Just One More Day* and *One Day at a Time*, the moving memoirs of her childhood in Bristol. She lives in Gloucestershire. Her website address is www.susanlewis.com

Susan is a supporter of the breast cancer charity, Breast Cancer Care: www.breastcancercare.org.uk and of the childhood bereavement charity, Winton's Wish: www.winstonswish.org.uk

### Praise for Susan Lewis

'A gripping story of love, uncertainty and betrayal . . . a guaranteed tear-jerker that will keep you at the edge of your seat.' *OK!*

'A master storyteller.' Diane Chamberlain

'Spellbinding! You just keep turning the pages, with the atmosphere growing more and more intense as the story leads to its dramatic climax.' *Daily Mail*

'Utterly compelling.' *Sun*

'Expertly written to brew an atmosphere of foreboding, this story is an irresistible blend of intrigue and passion, and the consequences of secrets and betrayal.' *Woman*

'Sad, happy, sensual and intriguing.' *Woman's Own*

# Please return on or before the date below.

|  |  |
|---|---|
|  |  |

Non-loan returns

|  |  |
|---|---|
|  |  |

**Dearne Valley College Library**,
Manvers Park, Wath Upon Dearne, Rotherham, S637EW
**Want to Renew a book or book a PC?**
Telephone: 01709 513333 Ext: 1090
Email: library-dvc@rnngroup.ac.uk

1 3 5 7 9 10 8 6 4 2

Arrow Books
20 Vauxhall Bridge Road
London SW1V 2SA

Arrow Books is part of the Penguin Random House group of companies whose
addresses can be found at global.penguinrandomhouse.com

Penguin
Random House
UK

First published in Great Britain by Century in 2016
First published in paperback by Arrow Books in 2017

www.randomhouse.co.uk

A CIP catalogue record for this book is available from the British Library

ISBN 9780099586555
ISBN 9780099586562 (export)

Typeset in Palatino LT Std / 11.80 /15 pt in India by Thomson Digital Pvt Ltd,
Noida Delhi
Printed and bound in Great Britain by Clays Ltd, St Ives Plc

Penguin Random House is committed to a sustainable
future for our business, our readers and our planet.
This book is made from Forest Stewardship Council®
certified paper.

The Moment She Left

One of the most thrilling parts of having a secret – especially the sort Jessica Leonard had been savouring these last two months – was the way it made her feel so powerful and excited. Added to that was the way everyone seemed to sense something different about her, but couldn't quite decide what it was.

Her friend Sadie had asked outright. 'What is it with you?' she'd cried, her laughter edged with notes of puzzlement and envy. 'Are you in love, or something? You look like you are.'

Jessica regarded herself in the mirror, feline navy eyes sparkling with a tease, soft, creamy cheeks flushed with knowing. 'Is *this* how someone in love looks?' she countered, mussing up her wavy dark hair and twisting her beautiful singer's mouth into an awkward grimace.

'No, it can't be love, or you'd have told me,' Sadie decided.

Since she'd only known Jessica for a year Sadie wasn't yet aware of how secretive her flatmate in halls could be, or how loyal (loyal was not to be forgotten, for it was one of Jess's major qualities). And Jessica wasn't surprised that Sadie was putting the new Jess down to love, it was the conclusion anyone would jump to. She knew she would.

Electrified by the air of mystery she was creating, she blew Sadie a kiss and went back to rehearsing for a gig that night. She'd played at this particular ambassador's home before, but apparently tonight she was going to receive an even more fantastic sum for her services than usual. She guessed the event must be for more people, or perhaps they wanted her to do more sets. She'd find out when she got there. She had the kind of voice, throaty, sultry, mesmerising, that had made her one of the most sought-after young singers on this exclusive circuit, and the many contacts she was making were opening up the kind of doors she'd hardly even known existed.

One of these days she might share her secret with Sadie, but she was in no hurry. It would feel odd, she realised, to confide in someone other than her twin brother, Matt, who'd been her best friend and sharer of everything throughout their nineteen years. Not much had changed, in spite of them having been at different universities this past year. They were in touch every day, regularly went to concerts and exhibitions together, or parties, or sporting events (they shared a love of rugby with their father); they spent all holidays at home with their parents (Dad was definitely easier than Mum, especially these days), and whenever they could they performed together. Matt sang too, but usually he left the vocals to Jess and provided accompaniment on keyboard or guitar. Their parents – Dad mainly, but Mum could do it too – were constantly creating backing tracks for when she performed alone, making them easy to set up so she wouldn't have to rely on anyone to attend gigs with her. Her repertoire was growing all the time, and the number of hits she was getting on YouTube was phenomenal.

Right now, on this glorious sunny day in late June, Jess was making her way from the halls of residence in Marylebone across West London to Paddington station. Her tall, slender frame was weighed down by a monster backpack, a bag full of laundry, and a tatty old computer case containing vital laptop, both old and new tablets (latter still needed programming, Matt would do it), her precious music player and various chargers. Once on the train it shouldn't take much more than three hours to get to the quaintly old-fashioned seaside town that she and her family now called home. They'd moved there a year ago when her dad had lost his job (been robbed of his job, more like) and her mum – well, who knew what to say about her mum? One day she was her normal upbeat self working with Dad (she never sat for him now the way she used to), and the next she could be floundering about in the depths of despair. It wasn't that her mum didn't like their new home and the people they were getting to know, it was simply that it had never been a part of her plan to leave the north, and she couldn't seem to get her head around the fact that it had happened. As far as she was concerned they should never have had to pack up the lovely house where they'd lived since

Jess and Matt were born, and start new lives in a place they didn't even know. Worse than leaving, though, was the fact that there hadn't been anyone around to wave them off the day they'd departed, and if any of the neighbours had watched them drive away Jess had been unaware of it because she'd kept her head down until they were out of the street, and she was fairly certain the rest of her family had done the same.

Not that they'd had anything to feel ashamed of, it was just that everyone thought they did, and so that was how they'd behaved.

Stupid really. She bitterly regretted it now, but the time had long gone for them to be able to look anyone in the eye and challenge them; life had moved on, so must they.

Fortunately Jess and Matt had already sat their A levels and been accepted into their universities of choice by the time everything had imploded up north. However, the hurried move south, apart from what it had done to their parents (Dad was doing a better job of hiding it, but it had definitely badly affected him too), had completely changed the plans they'd made for a gap year. Instead of the fabulous world tour they'd had all worked out with a couple of mates, they'd decided they must stay close to their parents. Not so close as to keep them at home like a couple of nursemaids, but within easy striking distance if, for any reason, they were needed. So they'd taken up their places at uni a year earlier than planned.

As much as she loved her parents and would always be there for them, Jessica couldn't help feeling relieved that she was at University College London – in other words, a good two hundred miles away. Matt, on the other hand, was at Exeter and so felt that he had to go visit most weekends. Not that anyone expected it, her parents weren't like that, it was just how he felt and Jessica was in no doubt that she would too if she were less than fifty miles away. She knew it wasn't easy on her brother; they talked about it for hours on the phone, although he handled it much better than she knew she would. He was a different sort of character to her, totally laid back, always able to shrug stuff off, never making a big deal out of issues – not even all the crap that had happened to their dad had seemed to faze him much.

Of all the people in the world that Jessica loved most, her dad was top of the list. (Apart from Matt, but he didn't count, when it stood to reason he was up there just by being her twin.) At various times in her life her mother had held the honoured top spot, but these days it was always her dad. This was why she'd made a firm promise to herself that while she was at home for the summer she was going to spend as much time with him as possible, sitting for him if he was in the mood to paint, going to galleries, which he loved, and generally making him remember just how very special he was. Not that he was moping around feeling sorry for him-self. On the contrary, he actually seemed to be enjoying his new job, which was a big change to the old one, although still artistic in its way, for he was following in his father's footsteps working as a furniture and pic-ture restorer in a swanky antique shop in the middle of town. He'd made lots of new friends who Jessica and Matt had got to know during the last Christmas and Easter breaks, which wasn't surprising given how friendly he was. It was just a shame her mum preferred to keep herself to herself.

What had happened to drive them south was a secret so full of dark and negative stuff that Jessica just didn't need it in her life, especially now when she had so much to feel optimistic and excited about.

Starting as her mobile rang, she paused a favourite Sam Smith track playing through her earphones and clicked on. 'Hey, you!' she cried. 'What's up?'

'Everything's cool,' Matt told her in his usual laconic way. 'Just wondering what time to expect you.'

'You're already home?'

'Got here last night.'

'So how are they?'

'OK, I guess. Dad's looking forward to seeing you.'

Even though she knew it, it still pleased her. 'How about Mum?'

'Sure, she is too, she just forgot to say it. Dad's getting everything ready for our gig at the Mermaid tomorrow night, so we can go over there in the morning to check it out. Apparently the tickets have already sold out.'

'Wow!' Jessica exclaimed. 'It'll be all those groupies who keep following you around.'

'Yeah, right,' he said drily. 'I've added a couple of special requests to the songlist, but we can go over them when you get here. Are you up for an Italian tonight, Dad wants to know.'

6

'Deffo. Count me in. Will we go to the one on the promenade, what's it called again?'

'There are a few now, but Luigi's is still the fave. Mum's coming too.'

'Great.' That really was good news, for all too often it was just the three of them, and hard work as their mum could be at times it never felt right without her. 'I should be there in plenty of time . . . Oh, someone's trying to get through and my battery's nearly out, so I'll call you back from the train.'

'Jess!' Sadie cried excitedly. 'Get ready for the most amazing news. We've only got the flat in Vauxhall for next year. The four-bed one?'

Jessica immediately joined in Sadie's shrieks of delight, oblivious to amused glances from passers-by.

'I just had a call to say our offer's been accepted,' Sadie ran on, 'but we have to start paying the rent right away. Are you OK with that?'

Feeling a glorious charge of adrenalin lifting her skywards, Jessica declared, 'No problem.' They were going to pay rent for two months without actually living in the place, and it was *no problem*. Life was so cool.

Caught up in a great surge of affection for Sadie, Jessica let the line drop and her earphones once again filled with the sound of Sam Smith singing 'Lay Me Down'. More elation flooded her. She knew every word of the song, could feel every sentiment as though the music and lyrics were a part of her.

*She loved Sam Smith.*

She was about to descend into the depths of Goodge Street tube station when her mobile rang again. Seeing it was a voicemail, she held back to call it up, and when she heard the message her heart tripped to a fluttery halt.

She pressed to replay and listened with her head down, realising that if she did what was being requested she'd miss the train, but it didn't matter, she could always get a later one, or go in the morning if things worked out that way. She didn't want to miss the meal with her parents, but this was somewhere she had to go, and with no one around to try and stop her she wasn't going to fight it.

Twenty minutes later, after changing on to the Central Line at Tottenham Court Road and taking it through to Notting Hill Gate, she was walking through a part of London that she'd only come to know in the last couple of months. Until then she'd always considered South Kensington or Knightsbridge, or a few other areas around the West End, to be gobsmackingly amazing. Then she'd come to Holland Park and her mind had been totally blown.

As she turned from the main road, with her phone switched off to conserve what was left of the battery, the leafy residential streets became quiet, were practically deserted. After a couple of turns taking her deeper into the heart of the area, she entered a narrow, sun-baked alleyway that acted as a service divider between the backs of grand stucco villas on one side and elegant town houses on the other. Here there were only automated garages providing secure and spacious accommodation for rich people's luxury vehicles. The door Jessica approached, about halfway along on the right, had a digital keypad beside it, but even before she could press in the code the door started to rise.

By the time it was fully open and she could see who, and what, was inside, she was clasping her hands to her face.

'Oh my God, oh my God, oh my God,' she murmured, unable to believe her eyes. A flicker of fear flashed through her like summer lightning. This wasn't what she'd expected. Was it going a step too far? Even if it was, how could she not take it?

*Two Years Later*

# Chapter One

Andee Lawrence was staring through her reflection in the window, across the busy promenade below and over to the foamy waves lapping the seashore. The sun was dazzling, dancing in bright, sharp sparks across the blue-black waters of the bay, glittering on the grassy headlands that jutted far out to sea, burning the exposed flesh of its many worshippers below.

It was the beginning of summer: tourists were already piling into Kesterly-on-Sea, filling up caravan parks, campsites, hotels, B & Bs and holiday lets. Over on the beach they were taking hasty advantage of this rare sunny spell, setting up deckchairs and windbreaks, claiming their spot on the crowded sands while kids built sandcastles with moats, or splashed about in the muddy waves, kicked balls, tossed Frisbees and queued to ride the weary-looking donkeys.

From today this was going to be her view, the scene she would look out at each time she gazed or glanced from this window. It would change with the seasons, of course, but this small, seafront apartment with its neat Juliet balconies, open-plan kitchen-diner and allocated parking space, was her new home.

*Her new home.*

'So this is it then?' a voice said snappily behind her.

Flinching at her husband's tone, she forced herself to turn around.

Their eyes met, and it was all she could do to stop herself going to him to try to soothe away some of the hurt.

It wouldn't help. It would only complicate matters further, since pity, guilt, regret were the last things he wanted, or needed.

He wasn't a weak man, he wouldn't fall apart without her, although looking at him now, he was so tense, so pale, that it was as though his frustration might break right through his sun-weathered skin.

Perhaps she was wrong about how able he was to cope.

'You look beautiful,' he told her, unexpectedly, though the words came out roughly, resentfully.

She might not feel it, or even think much about it, but she was beautiful, in a forty-something, understated way. She had arresting aqua-green eyes, high cheekbones, and a wide, generous smile that was beguiling and infectious. Her hair, dark and full, was clasped in a bundle of curls at the nape of her neck; her slender body was partly disguised by baggy cotton capris and an old T-shirt top.

She rocked slightly on her bare feet, having kicked off her shoes at the door, a habit she'd been in all her life, thanks to her mother.

Martin, her husband, had done the same. His leather flip-flops and her thong sandals were bundled together at the end of the hall, overlapping one another, casually entwined, comfortable with each other, the way they, she and Martin, used to be. No doubt their shoes were expecting to leave together.

How strange she'd sound if she told him to take her shoes with him, if she said that they probably wanted to go so they could stay with his.

He'd be more convinced than ever that she was losing her mind, the excuse he was giving himself, and anyone who cared to listen, for her decision to leave him.

'You're losing it, Andee, you're not thinking straight,' he kept telling her. 'We need to sit down and discuss this, sort out what's really going on.'

He knew exactly what was going on and she truly didn't want to spell it out again. Once had been hard enough, repeating it wouldn't make it easier.

'I'm sorry, sorrier than you'll ever know,' she'd said when she'd finally plucked up the courage to tell him, 'but I don't want to be married to you any more.'

His shock, when he'd first heard it, had frozen him for a moment before he'd stumbled into uneasy laughter. She was joking, of course.

She wasn't and he could see it.

'Why?' he'd asked, genuinely bemused. His ruggedly handsome face had seemed so much younger all of a sudden, reminding her of how he looked in photographs his mother had of him as a child. He was lost, vulnerable, needing someone to show him the way. 'I thought we – you – were happy,' he said.

He could certainly be forgiven for thinking that, since she'd taken care to hide how she was really feeling, not wanting to hurt him, or their children, or the rest of their family. How she really felt was that she still loved him, and probably always would, but she was no longer *in love* with him.

She realised now that she hadn't been even when she'd agreed to marry him, three years ago, which was an awful irony – was that the right word, maybe mistake would be better – when they'd been together for over two decades by then and had felt no need to be married before. Actually it wasn't a *full* two decades, because he'd left her for a while. After seventeen and a half years of living under the same roof and bringing up their children together he'd suddenly announced one day that he'd had enough. He didn't want to be a house husband and stay-at-home dad any longer while she went about playing detective – that was how he'd put it – at all hours of the day and night. Apparently she was to ignore the fact that he'd managed to build a very successful Internet security business during the hours the kids were at school, and evenings when she was there to take care of them. For whatever reason he'd suddenly decided he needed to break loose of the home and travel the world, alone.

She harboured no resentment towards him for the desertion now; however, at the time, with her police career on an upward trajectory, and two young teenagers to cope with, she'd been devastated, furious, even murderous. She'd hated him, had sworn she'd never take him back, while all the time she'd longed for him to come.

He had, eventually, putting his aberration, as he'd called it, down to a midlife crisis that he was finally, happily, over. Wasn't that great? Actually, in a way it was, because life had moved on quite a bit during his two-year absence and punishing him was no longer a priority for her. They'd grown in ways neither of them would have been able to if they'd stayed together – he'd sold his Internet business and made a fortune, while she'd left the Metropolitan police to take up a promotion to Detective Sergeant with the Dean Valley force. What really mattered, she'd decided then, was the history they shared, the love that was still there, albeit altered, and most of all the children, Luke and Alayna, who were desperate for their parents to get back together.

'I never stopped loving you,' he'd told her on his return. 'You're the only woman I've ever loved, that I've ever even slept with, apart from Brigitte, and all that did was make me realise just how wrong my life was without you.'

Brigitte. He'd found someone else during the time they were apart, but she could hardly hold that against him when, eventually, she had too.

Maybe, if his beloved father hadn't just died (which in truth was what had brought him back from his travels), she'd have found a way to suggest that they just be friends. However, they'd all been deeply affected by Dougie's death, and at times like that it was normal, even necessary, for families to pull together. So, she'd asked him if he'd be prepared to stay in Kesterly-on-Sea, where she and the children had settled while he was away exploring the world.

He'd had it all worked out. He was definitely staying. His mother, like hers, lived in Kesterly, his father's property business was headquartered in the town and it was his intention, and his father's wish, that he should take it over. While she, if she was serious about giving up the police force, could do whatever she pleased. Work with him, study for a new career, she might even want to be a stay-at-home mum for a while.

The options were endless when money wasn't a problem, and the heady sums he'd made from the sale of his business, plus what he'd just inherited, had meant that the world truly was their oyster.

So she'd done what everyone wanted and married him while knowing, even as they were taking their vows, that she was making a mistake. It might be right for their mothers, the children, and presumably for him, it just wasn't right for her.

It had taken three years for her to decide she must stop living a lie. In spite of how many hearts it would break, she had to be true to herself, even if it was hurting her too.

'Are you *in love* with him?' he asked now, but not for the first time.

She looked away. 'I've already told you,' she answered, 'he has nothing to do with this.'

It was true; her reason for leaving had nothing to do with Graeme Ogilvie, the man she'd had a brief relationship with during the time she and Martin were apart. She wished now that she'd never mentioned him, and knew she wouldn't have, had Martin not kept on and on insisting she must have met someone.

Looking at Martin now was hard. His face was pinched, his dark eyes wide and hostile; fighting rejection never made a person attractive at a time when they most needed to be. 'Is he in love with you?' he demanded sourly.

With a flash of irritation, she said, 'How many times do I have to tell you it isn't about him?'

'Why don't you just answer the question? Is he in love with you?'

'Of course not. I've had next to no contact with him since we broke up three years ago . . .'

'But you're in touch with him now?'

She didn't argue, there was no point when he wasn't listening.

She wanted him to go, to leave her alone with her conscience so she could start deciding how best to handle it, and her children – and the rest of her life.

'If you leave, Mum, I'll never, *ever* speak to you again,' eighteen-year-old Alayna had ranted furiously down the phone when she'd found out about the break-up, thanks to her father calling her at uni to deliver the happy news.

Andee had wanted to wait until Alayna and her older brother were back for the summer before telling them, but it was too late for that now.

'Mum, you can't be serious,' Luke had protested when he'd rung from Exeter, where he was in his third year of Sport and Exercise Science. 'You need to think about this, because it sounds to me like you're doing what Dad did all those years ago, having a middle-aged meltdown.'

'I'm not in crisis,' she'd told him, although maybe quietly, underneath it all, she was. 'I just need to be on my own for a while. I'm renting a flat in Kesterly, so I'll see you every day when you're home, if you want to, but I know how busy you always are.'

'Every day could be overdoing it,' he agreed, 'but I just don't get why you have to hurt Dad like this. I know what he did when he left was terrible, but I thought you were over it. I mean you married him, didn't you?'

'I did, and I'm completely over what happened. This is something different. Something I have to do for me.'

She'd never told the children about Graeme Ogilvie, it had been too new a relationship at the time for her to share it with them, but as soon as she'd admitted it to Martin he'd clearly decided their children needed to know too.

In truth, she'd only run into Graeme a few times during the three years since she'd broken up with him. On the first two they'd been at the same function in town, and though they'd spoken, naturally, neither of them had referred to their past relationship. They hadn't mentioned it on the third occasion either, which was just last week when she'd gone to his antique shop, not to see him, but someone who worked there.

That was a whole other story, and perhaps one of the stranger ways in which fate had chosen to play its hand, at least for her and Graeme in throwing them together again. For Blake Leonard, the person she'd gone to see . . . God only knew what fate was trying to do to him.

Fixing her eyes on Martin now, she said, 'I don't want you to tell the children any more about Graeme. I only told you I went to his shop because I wanted to be

20

honest with you, but the reason for my visit had nothing to do with him.'

'Oh, just shopping for a few antiques, were you? Something you do all the time.'

Ignoring the sarcasm, she said, 'You're making this far more difficult than it needs to be.'

'Please excuse me for minding about you leaving me. Does he know? Have you told him you've rented your own place?'

'Of course not. It's nothing to do with him and for all I know he's met somebody else by now, so he wouldn't even be interested in where I'm living.' It wouldn't surprise her at all if Graeme had someone else. He was a good-looking man with a wickedly dry sense of humour, a love of the arts, most things Italian and – this would interest other women far more than it did her – he was pretty well off. A real catch, was how most would describe him.

Martin was that, too.

He started to speak, cleared his throat and ran a hand over his unshaven chin. 'So when do I next get to see you?' he asked gruffly.

She didn't know what to say to that. Anything would be wrong.

'You don't have to answer now,' he said, reaching for his keys. 'Call me when you've decided to stop behaving like a bitch.'

As the front door closed behind him, she turned back to the window and watched as he emerged into the street below and crossed to the van he'd hired to help move her in.

She was touched that he'd helped her, how could she not be when he was acting against his own interests?

He was kind; she'd always known that about him, it was a large part of why she cared for him so much – of why she *loved* him. She just didn't want to carry on pretending there was more in her heart than friendship. Perversely, she didn't want to lose him either, though she had to accept that she might, at least for a while.

As he pulled out into the slow-moving traffic she wondered where he would go after dropping the van and picking up his car. To his mother's, or to hers? Either would offer him a sympathetic ear, although, to be fair, both mothers had been understanding and patient with her too, which couldn't have been easy when they treasured how close they were as a family. So close that until today Andee and Martin had been living at her mother's in a craggy little hamlet up on the northern headland known as Bourne Hollow.

They should have moved into a place of their own long ago; perhaps this was another indication of how uncommitted she had felt to their future, that she had never been able to find the right house.

Martin was due to move over to his own mother's in the leafy suburb of Westleigh sometime in the next few days, where the children would join him for alternate weeks throughout the summer. They still had their own rooms in both grandmothers' homes, and no matter where life took them once they'd finished uni, Andee couldn't imagine that ever changing.

There was an extra bedroom here in the flat, and Andee was hoping that they might at the very least crash with her after a late night out in town.

Alayna was clearly still furious with her. She wasn't returning texts, or calling back after Andee left messages.

Andee would deal with that when the time came. For now she had a lot of unpacking to do, emails to send and a call to make to Helen Hall, the lawyer who'd asked her to try and help Blake Leonard, whose teenage daughter had disappeared without trace two years ago.

Andee remembered the case well, it had been all over the news at the time; that kind of story always resonated deeply with her.

When she'd first received Helen's call asking her to help, her immediate reaction had been to refuse. Trying to find missing children – and to her nineteen still qualified as a child – was one of the main reasons she'd ended up leaving the force. It wasn't that she didn't want to help these families, she longed to do so, knowing only too well what they were going through, but the emotional strain on her had become too great. She was no longer the right person to judge how best to handle panicked, shocked, terrified and even in some cases guilty parents, when she could never put her own parents out of her mind, and how it had been for them when her sister, Penny, aged fourteen, had disappeared from their lives.

If Penny had eventually come home Andee would almost certainly have put it all behind her by now. She might not even have joined the police force in the first place. As it was, no body, no trace of her at all, had ever been found. They'd received a letter though, sent around two weeks after she'd vanished, and the words were seared so deeply and painfully into Andee's heart that she knew she'd never forget them.

*Dear Mum and Dad, I probably ought to say sorry for leaving the way I have, but maybe you already don't mind very much that I'm not around any more, so instead I'll say sorry for always being such a disappointment to you. I know Dad wanted a son when I was born, so I guess I've been a let-down to him from the start, and I don't blame him for always loving Andee the most because she's much nicer-looking than I am and likes sports, the same as him, and is really clever so it stands to reason that he'd be really proud of her. I know I shouldn't say this, but sometimes I hate her for being so much better than I am at everything. No one ever seems to notice me when she's in the room. It's like I become invisible and I know she wishes I would go away. So that's what I'm going to do.*

*I don't know what else to say, except sorry again. I expect you'll all be much happier without me. Please tell Andee she can have whatever she likes of mine, although I don't expect she'll want anything at all.*

*Your daughter, Penny*

To this day they still didn't know whether Penny had committed suicide after sending the note, or if she'd gone off somewhere to make a new life. At fourteen it had seemed unlikely she'd make a new life, how would she, unless there had been someone to help her? No evidence had ever come to light of her being involved with someone who might have enticed her away. And surely, after seeing the news and realising how much they were all suffering, she'd have come back. With their father being a chief superintendent with the Met every imaginable effort had been poured into finding his daughter, and it hadn't stopped there because Andee herself had revisited the case several times over the years, but there was never anything new to be uncovered.

Almost as heartbreaking as losing Penny was their father dying without ever knowing what had happened to her.

It was like that for some families, Andee knew that better than most, not only because hers was one of them, but because of how many others she had watched suffering, while she, unable to give them the answers, or even the body, they needed, had felt every part of their helplessness and pain.

She hoped to God that Blake Leonard's family wasn't going to end up amongst those she'd been unable to help. No one, but no one, deserved to go through such interminable hell. However, two years was a long time in a missing person case, and going by the police files she'd so far been given access to, the search appeared to have been thorough and extensive. So she had to concede that the chances of finding Jessica really weren't good. Not that she was prepared to rule it out, miracles did happen, as the news occasionally showed, and who was to say that one wasn't waiting to happen here?

# Chapter Two

*'Daddy, you are totally amazing. I had no idea you could do that.'*

*Blake Leonard's hazel eyes sparkled with mischief. 'You'd be surprised at what I can do, young lady,' he teased, as she checked that the drawing really was exactly the same no matter which way up she turned it.*

*'Because you're magic,' she cried, and laughing delightedly she threw her skinny arms around him.*

*'Ask him if he can magic you off to your dance class,' Jenny called out from the kitchen.*

*Jessica's eight-year-old eyes grew round. 'Shall we fly there, Dad?' she whispered.*

*'Good idea,' he whispered back. 'I'll go and get my wings.'*

The joy, the comfort of the unexpected memory abruptly vanished as Blake's attention was snatched back to the present, where he was kneeling in front of a planter carefully tugging dead blooms from a fuchsia.

'So have you heard any more from the detective woman?' Matt asked, coming to stand at the back door of their terraced home on the edge of Kesterly old town. He was a tall young man with a lot of dark stubble hiding the delicate set of his jaw, long, spiked lashes around his deep navy eyes and an attitude that could switch from belligerent to vulnerable to frightened in the blink of an eye.

Before answering Blake glanced through the open French doors to the dining room where the white-washed walls were cluttered with some of the many paintings he'd done over the years, and the table was strewn with a number of books he was consulting for his work at Ogilvie's. Remembering that his wife had gone to stay with her parents, he felt a jolt of sadness, though it left him free to speak – it was rarely a good idea to talk about Jessica, or anything concerning her, in front of Jenny.

'She's an ex-detective,' he reminded Matt, 'and I'm seeing her tomorrow.' His once lively, handsome face, always claimed by Jenny to be too cheerful for an artist, had become creased and dulled by the blows life had dealt him, most particularly the disappearance of his daughter.

Matt sank his gangly frame into one of the canvas chairs in front of a rusting wrought-iron table. 'Is she coming here?' he enquired.

Blake wondered if Matt wanted to meet Andee Lawrence. Since the police had scaled back their search for Jessica they'd felt abandoned and helpless, frustrated to a point of madness, but then a friend of Matt's had said they should try talking to his mother who was Helen Hall, one of the town's more prominent lawyers. So Blake had called, and Helen Hall had put him on to ex-Detective Sergeant Andee Lawrence. 'I asked her to come to the shop again,' he told Matt. It wasn't that he didn't want to invite Andee to their home, he simply didn't want any of the neighbours recognising her and asking questions. They'd been subjected to enough attention at the time Jessica had vanished.

'So did she say if she'd found anything new yet?' Matt asked.

Blake shook his head, his heart aching with the torment they shared, the anguish and confusion that never went away. 'She's had no time, and anyway I don't think she would on the phone.'

It was so much easier to cope on the good days, and they happened from time to time. On the bad days it was so awful he felt like ending it all rather than carry on with the not knowing, the self-loathing and blame he heaped upon himself for what he'd done to his family. If he hadn't been forced to bring them here, Jessica and Matt would have taken their gap year and probably been thousands of miles from London on that fateful day. Jessica would never have known the person or persons who'd taken her, would even now be hanging out with her family here, or off somewhere with friends, maybe rehearsing for a gig, or writing new material with Matt.

Although the initial shock and disbelief, the sheer horror of her disappearance had eased some time ago, almost anything could make it feel present and terrible again. The crazy, unacceptable truth of it would creep up on him, catching him unawares, and he'd feel the panic, the debilitating helplessness and dread building all over again.

Thanks to counselling he could control it better now, but his imagination remained the very worst of his enemies. At any given moment it would conjure the sound of her screaming, shouting for him – *Daddy! Daddy!* – begging him to find her.

The media attention had dried up now, but in the early months it had been intense – and even welcome, for there was always the chance it would help to find her. The questions had gone on and on, creating ever more speculation and gossip. There had even been a time when they'd suspected him, though of what exactly he'd never discovered.

Matt had gone for counselling too, and they'd both clung to every word of advice they were offered, had tried every coping technique, breathing exercise, and support system that was in place for people like them. They'd prayed, meditated, run for miles, eaten recommended foods, written things down, spoken about them, and even drawn them.

Blake had wished with all his heart that Jenny would join them, but she'd always been nervous of strangers, and had started withdrawing from the world even before Jessica's disappearance. The way they'd left the north, what had happened to force their departure, had already been too much for her. Once she'd started to realise that they might not get their daughter back, it was as though the woman he loved, his muse, his passion his life partner, had disappeared too.

Jessica wasn't dead. He couldn't, wouldn't allow himself to think that, and no one had recommended that he should. If he did it would mean he'd have to give up searching for her, and he could never do that either. Nor could Matt, who looked, and felt, as though he'd lost a part of himself, which of course, as her twin, he had. What devastation this had wrought on his young life. He would never get over it.

Watching his son now, gaunt, good-looking, help-less, aimless, a shadow of who he should have been at twenty-one, Blake laid a comforting hand on his shoul-der. He felt the bones, the frailty. He was too thin. They both were.

Matt stared straight ahead as he said, 'I still keep hearing her, inside my head. It's so real I think she's there, or somewhere close by, I just have to work out where.'

Knowing exactly what he meant, Blake said, 'Maybe Andee Lawrence will be able to find something the police missed.'

'I forgot to tell you,' Matt responded. 'She's Luke Farnham's mum. You know, he was in the same halls as me during our first year at uni.'

'I remember him. Have you seen him lately?'

Matt simply shrugged.

It was unlikely that he had, since Matt had dropped out of uni after Jessica's disappearance and though he had friends around the area, most of them had flown the nest by now, or were managing to hold down jobs.

One of these days Blake would have to get on Matt's case about finding a job too, or going back to his stud-ies, but he could tell that the thought of going forward without Jessica was one his son still couldn't tolerate. It was as though he too had stopped on that fateful day. He was too locked into their closeness, their bond as twins, to be able to carry on with his life the way he'd planned. It would feel like the worst kind of betrayal when she couldn't do the same.

'He needs a girlfriend,' Jessica laughed, poking Matt in the ribs. 'That's what he needs. Someone gorgeous and sexy and who's ready to . . .'

'Yes, OK, we get the picture,' Blake interrupted, with a wink at his son.

'He shouldn't still be a virgin at his age. He's seventeen, for God's sake.'

'Who says he's a virgin?' Blake countered.

'And since when did I stop being in the room?' Matt protested.

Jessica's eyes were round. 'Don't tell me you've done it and never fessed up,' she cried. 'We made a pact, as soon as one of us did it . . .'

'I'm not saying I have,' Matt jumped in quickly. 'It's Dad. He's off in fantasy land again.'

'Well you were upstairs for a very long time with Amie Rice the other night,' Blake reminded him. 'And we all know she's just waiting for you to make the first move.'

Jessica laughed at Matt's blush and Blake crushed them both in a hug.

He could feel that hug in his arms now, bruising and absent, as he watched Matt walk back into the house. 'Are we going for a run later?' he called after him.

Without turning round Matt said, 'Sure, if you want to.'

'We should give Mum a call first.'

Helping himself to a drink from the fridge, Matt said, 'You mean to speak to Nan? Mum hardly ever comes to the phone.'

'She'll speak to you.'

'If she won't speak to you, I don't want to speak to her.'

Blake didn't pursue it. He understood Matt's frustration with his mother; it was something else they shared, though it was rare for Blake to express it in front of Matt.

It was its own kind of torture to think of what this was doing to Jenny, especially when she'd always been so fragile, so unsure of herself – except when she was with Blake and the children. He was her strength, her everything, she'd always claim, and she was his angel. Their family had meant everything to her, but now with Jessica missing, and the scars of what had happened in the north still raw, she could no longer cope. She'd gone to her parents unable to watch her husband and son's pain and know she could do nothing about it.

'I know I've asked you this before,' Matt said, coming back to the door, 'but do you think what happened with that scumbag Tyler Bennett . . . Do you reckon it could have something to do with . . .'

'No, I don't,' Blake interrupted gently. 'It doesn't make any sense to think it. He's in Manchester and Jess was in London when she disappeared – and we know the police have spoken to everyone up there. They don't know any more than we do.'

As Matt turned away Blake's mobile started to ring.

Seeing it was his boss he answered cheerfully. Graeme and his family had been a tremendous support to him and his family over the past two years, to a point that Blake really didn't know how he'd have got through it without them.

For a while they discussed the nineteenth-century gilt sofa that Blake had recently restored after Graeme had acquired it at auction in Italy. It had now been bought and the new owner was hoping it could be delivered to her home in Dorset the next day.

'With Dave being off on holiday this week,' Graeme said, referring to their regular driver, 'I was about to ask if you'd mind driving it down there, but I've just remembered, Andee's coming to see you?'

'At four,' Blake confirmed. 'I can easily get there and back before she arrives.'

'OK, if you're sure. I'd come with you to help carry it if one of my sisters was free to mind the shop, but apparently neither of them is tomorrow, and as of right now nor are my nieces. If that changes, I'll let you know.'

'Don't worry, I expect Matt's free. I'll get him to give me a hand. Are you sure you don't mind me meeting Andee at the shop? I can . . .'

'Of course I don't mind. You must do whatever works for you. What time shall I expect you in the morning?'

'Around eight?'

'Perfect. And you haven't forgotten you're invited for drinks at my sister's on Friday? She called earlier wanting to be sure you can make it.'

'Of course I can. I'm sorry I haven't got back to her yet. Thank you.'

After ringing off, Blake finished tidying the fuchsia and went inside to read through the notes he'd already made for his meeting with Andee. He was trying desperately not to invest too much faith in her, he didn't want to pressure her that way – nor did he want to face the wrenching disappointment when she ended up agreeing with the police that it was a mystery that might never be solved.

# Chapter Three

Rowena Cayne, middle name Zelda thanks to her father's passion for the Fitzgeralds, was affectionately known to her close friends and family as Rowzee. When she went about town she was more often greeted as Mrs C, and always fondly, since she'd been one of the most popular teachers at Kesterly High School for the past forty years. English and drama had been her subjects until she'd retired at the end of last term, so there weren't many children from the last few generations who hadn't studied or performed various comedies, tragedies, romances and even the occasional bloodcurdling horror on her stage, or in her lively classroom. And every single one of them – according to Rowzee's sister Pamela – had adored her. (Pamela rarely uttered this with pride or affection, in fact it was usually something closer to resentment, but that was Pamela for you and Rowzee knew better than to take offence.)

Pamela, being two years younger than Rowzee and quite unlike her in most ways, was generally annoyed with the world, including her daughters, now aged thirty-one and twenty-nine, for seeming to love their aunt even more than their own mother. While Rowzee and the girls vehemently insisted that wasn't true, Rowzee's late husband, Victor, had always insisted it was, though never in front of Pamela. He hadn't been a cruel man, though he'd confessed quietly to Rowzee on more than one occasion that her younger sister could easily drive him to violence.

Sadly Pamela had managed to achieve this with her own husband, for on the day he'd ended up leaving her for good he'd tried throttling her, and if Pamela and Rowzee's much younger brother Graeme hadn't heard the commotion and rushed to the rescue there was a fair chance Pamela's husband would have been behind bars now, and Pamela herself would no longer have been with them.

Happily for Rowzee, Pamela had survived. Understanding her sister in a way most didn't, Rowzee knew that behind the fierce façade and constant complaints there was a truly sensitive soul struggling to best her demons. Graeme also loved Pamela, and believed in her goodness, although he wasn't always as tolerant of her as Rowzee was, for he was firmly convinced that a piece of his mind did the younger of his two sisters – no matter that she was almost old enough to be his mother – some good from time to time.

Victor had been firmly of that opinion too. He'd tell Pamela, quite bluntly, that if she didn't have anything pleasant to say she should just shut up. This meant there had been many occasions when Pamela had flounced off in one of her famous huffs, only to return a day or two later, carrying on as though nothing unto-ward had happened at all.

What would Victor think, Rowzee often wondered, if he knew that not long after he died – two years ago of a sudden heart attack, and Rowzee still missed him terribly – Pamela had decided to move into the Coach House that had been Rowzee and Victor's home for over thirty years? Actually, Rowzee knew what he'd think, but since it was a little too savoury for her to dwell on, she generally sailed on past it, reminding herself that at least living under the same roof pre-vented her and Pamela from feeling lonely.

'You'd never be that! Everyone always wants to come here,' her niece, Katie, had protested when Rowzee had explained why she was allowing Katie's bossy mother to take up residence in the treasured retreat. Although it wasn't really much of a retreat, since it was only a few miles from town on the edge of the Burlingford Estate, and part of a staggered little hamlet of other smaller cottages. However, it was where Victor had written all fifteen of his successful children's adventure books, and he'd always insisted on peace and quiet while he was working.

The place had changed a good deal over the years, and was now, thanks to Victor's interest in interior design, much lighter and brighter than when young Charles, the most recent owner of the Burlingford Estate, had offered to let them buy it. Its last trans-formation had been completed only months before Victor died, when they'd opened the place up to cre-ate a much more modern and hospitable interior while careful to keep all the original features. So now the rambling old stone property, with its smart thatched roof and quaint front porch, boasted a big open-plan kitchen-cum-dining-cum-sitting room that occupied most of the back of the house, with a black glossy Aga, limed oak beams, and lovely fancy French doors opening on to a large covered terrace. The masterful inglenook fireplace was as grand as ever, though a little sprucer now, and Victor's study, at the front of the house, remained snug and sheltered from the sun during the morning, which was when he'd done most of his work. Upstairs Rowzee had a simply splendid en suite bedroom complete with dressing room, cosy reading corner and window seat where she could sit and watch the sun go down over the estuary. Across the landing Pamela had turned the largest guest room into her own private space, and had, with Rowzee's permission, knocked through to the spacious bathroom next door. The other rooms, for when they had visitors, were at the end of a further galleried landing that overlooked the hallway below on one side, and the back garden on the other.

It was in this garden that Rowzee was standing now, her floaty dark curls, threaded with silvery strands, lifting gently in the breeze as she waited on the phone. She might be sixty-five and retired, but inside she felt closer to thirty-five, and although her honeyed complexion was softly lined these days, and her twinkling green eyes didn't have quite as lively a sparkle as they used to, she hardly looked her age either. There was an air of gentle inquisitiveness about her that merged perfectly with an inherent impishness – as her brother often remarked, 'she's a bundle of goodness all tied up in mischief,' which was undoubtedly what had so appealed to her many students throughout the years.

According to Pamela Rowzee and Victor were both hopelessly gullible and naïve, prey to anyone wishing to take advantage of them, and Rowzee thought this was probably true. However, they'd bobbed along very happily in their own sweet way for plenty of years without coming to grief – or not much, but Rowzee didn't like to dwell on the things that had gone wrong.

Still waiting for someone to come back on the line, she gazed across her sprawl of lawns and flower beds, looking so lusciously colourful thanks to all the recent rain, to where the adjoining estate's chief gardener, Bill Simmonds, was careering about on his quad bike clearly having the time of his life. This was a machine Rowzee wouldn't mind having a go on herself one of these days, it looked such fun.

Something to add to her bucket list.

'Yes, I'm still here,' she told the voice that burst in to check she hadn't rung off.

'I'm so sorry to have kept you, but I'm afraid we haven't had anything back yet.'

'Oh, I see.' Rowzee couldn't be sure whether she was disappointed or pleased. 'Well, not to worry,' she said, brightening. 'I can always ring again. Thanks for your help,' and after wishing the girl a good day, she waved to Bill Simmonds who'd just spotted her before padding, barefoot, back into the house.

'Ah, there you are!' Pamela puffed, bustling in from the hall with half a dozen bags of heavy shopping. 'I thought you might have come out to help me.'

'I didn't hear you pull up,' Rowzee replied, going to take some of the load and setting it down on the kitchen's centre island.

'Who were you on the phone to?'

Rowzee started with surprise. 'How did you know I was on the phone?'

'Because I heard you ringing off. What, do you think I have some special powers or something?'

Rowzee's eyes narrowed. 'I'm never too sure with you,' she confessed, and felt the joy of making Pamela smile.

Pamela was the taller of the two, with lots of fluffy curls, much like Rowzee's, and the same heart-shaped face, only larger. In fact, almost everything about Pamela was larger, from her slightly protruding green eyes, to her extravagant mouth, to the voluptuous figure that she often tried stuffing into clothes a size too small for her. As a result she was generally too hot, especially at this time of year, and managed to look bothered, or stressed, or thoroughly annoyed even if she wasn't, although she usually was.

Rowzee only half listened as Pamela chuntered on about some woman at the supermarket who hadn't known how to wait in line, and so had had to be told, by Pamela of course, where she was going wrong. Apparently the woman had proceeded to call Pamela a bossy old cow who ought to mind her own effing business.

40

Having witnessed many such scenes while shopping with Pamela, Rowzee said, 'Are you going out again? If you are . . .'

'Of course I'm going out again. One of us has to find a job. We're not all lucky enough to have inherited from our husbands, or to be able to boast a healthy pension from the state. I've got things to do like . . . Like . . .' She was clearly struggling to remember what the demands on her time were, but Rowzee kindly refrained from mentioning Alzheimer's, the way Pamela usually did with her when she couldn't immediately call something to mind. 'Don't expect me back until eight at the earliest,' Pamela declared.

Rowzee gently prompted. 'Wanting supper?'

'Probably, if it's not too much trouble.'

'I'll do salad.'

'Again? Well, I suppose it might help me to lose weight, just don't overdo the dressing. Have you made a list of who you want to invite to the party on Friday?'

*You mean who you want to invite,* Rowzee didn't say. 'I have,' she confirmed.

'And have you rung them yet? They won't come if they don't know it's happening.'

Wanting to laugh, Rowzee said, 'I'm still waiting for a few calls back, but it could be they're away on holiday. Bill Simmonds dropped a very nice acceptance card through the door earlier.'

Pamela came to a stop, a purplish flush creeping up from her neck. 'You didn't tell me you were going to invite him,' she protested.

Amazed, Rowzee said, 'He's been to every other party we've given over the years, so why would I not invite him to this one?'

Apparently not having an answer for that, Pamela went crossly on with what she was doing.

'He says in his card,' Rowzee continued, 'that he'll come and cut the grass during the afternoon so everything's looking lovely for the evening. Isn't that kind of him?'

'If you say so.'

Rowzee eyed her carefully. 'OK, so what's Bill Simmonds done to upset you?' she challenged.

'Who says he's upset me?'

'I can tell. Oh no, did he try flirting with you again?'

'Let's drop the subject, shall we? If you want to invite the gardener, you go right ahead and invite him.'

'Now you're being a snob.'

Pamela ignored the charge, so Rowzee said, 'You were going to speak to the girls. As your daughters, and therefore I presume social equals, I think they should be here.'

'You consider yourself so droll, don't you,' Pamela shot back. 'I've left messages for both, and we know they'll come, because they always do, complete with husbands and children who, I hope, aren't going to charge about the place making blasted nuisances of themselves the way they usually do.'

'It would make a change from being *frightful* nuisances,' Rowzee commented lightly.

'Ha ha, very funny. Where are your shoes?'

Blinking, Rowzee looked around. 'I'm not sure, why?'

'I just wondered. What's happened to your toe?'

Rowzee looked down. 'You mean the black mark on my little toenail? It's from where you trod on it.'

Pamela eyed her in amazement

Rowzee grinned. 'It's always been there,' she reminded her. 'You just haven't seen my nails without polish for a while.'

'Which reminds me, if you've still got some of that Blueberry Pink I'll borrow it if I may.'

'You may. Apparently Blake Leonard can make the party, isn't that lovely?'

Pamela frowned. 'It's good for him to get out,' she agreed. 'I don't know if it'll help take his mind off things, but it has to be better than staying at home tearing himself to pieces. Is Jenny coming with him?'

'I believe she's away in Devon with her parents.'

'She's always away – and often with the fairies, if you get my meaning. What shall we do if he starts going on about his daughter? I mean, I wouldn't blame him, in his shoes I wouldn't be able to think of anything else, but it'll be a bit of a downer on the . . .'

'I'm sure he won't, but even if he does, it's our job to be sympathetic and supportive, not to treat him, like some people do, as if he's in some way to blame for what's happened.'

Pamela's eyebrows rose. 'I've never done such a thing,' she retorted.

'I'm not saying you have.'

Pamela eyed her meaningfully. 'For all you know he is to blame.'

'Pamela . . .'

43

'I'm just saying, that's all.'

'But it's not what you think, so stop pretending you're a cold-hearted, ungenerous old bag and take a copy of the guest list with you when you go. If I've missed anyone out send me a text.'

Minutes after Pamela drove off she rang. 'I thought you were going out today,' she declared.

'I was, but things changed.'

'Where were you supposed to be going?'

'Why?'

'What do you mean, why? Is it a secret?'

Rowzee laughed, for they'd had this very conversation the night before last when she'd tried to find out where Pamela was going. She never had got an answer, come to think of it. 'I had a meeting in town, but it got cancelled,' she lied, although it was sort of true, she decided.

'So you could help Graeme at the shop?'

Rowzee froze. She'd completely forgotten that their brother had asked if one of them could stand in for him today. The things she was forgetting lately, maybe Alzheimer's really was catching up with her. 'I'll call him right away,' she stated, and ending the call she scrolled straight to her brother's number.

The line was busy, but he rang back a few minutes later to assure her that he had everything covered.

Ten minutes later Rowzee was at her desk answering the emails she regularly received from ex-students updating her on what they were doing these days, or telling her about something that had reminded them of her, or, more often than not, showing her photographs of new babies as they came into the world.

She enjoyed them all and was meticulous about replying to each one, as well as careful in the way she declined the honour of becoming a godparent. There weren't so many of these requests, but they happened from time to time, and she was always touched, but firm with herself about not giving in. She really didn't need any more children in her life. She had plenty with Pamela's daughters, Graeme's two sons, and the great-nieces and nephew that had already started to swell the family numbers.

It was wonderful to be a part of the joy that came with a new life, especially in her own family, whom she loved above all else in the world. Her only sadness, which ran deeper than she could ever express, was the loss of her own dear little boy, Edward, to meningitis when he was a mere five years old. Such a cruel and contrary world it could be at times. After so many years of miscarriages and failures to conceive, along he'd come, all nine deliciously healthy pounds of him, when Rowzee was almost forty-five, and it simply couldn't have been possible for a baby to be more wanted. She'd felt from an early age that she was born to be a mother, so when it finally happened it was as though the years had rolled back and she was in her twenties all over again. Everyone adored him, Victor was besotted and her nieces, both much older by then, had spoiled him terribly, while her nephews, closer to Edward's age, had been more like brothers than cousins.

It had been a bleak and terrible time for everyone when he was taken, with a sense of shock and disbelief gripping the family that it had been almost impossible to move on from. Rowzee had never stopped grieving for him, and knew that she never would.

It was the most heartbreaking thing in the world to lose a child, but at least she knew what had happened to Edward. She couldn't begin to imagine what it was like for Blake and the families of children who simply disappeared and were never found. That had to be its own special kind of hell.

## Chapter Four

Andee had spent the best part of the day familiarising herself with every aspect of the Jessica Leonard case. Each police force that had been involved, which had included the Met, Greater Manchester, the Transport Police and her ex-colleagues here in Kesterly, had been extremely helpful in taking her calls and providing information. However, it was clear that they were as mystified now by what had happened to Jessica as they'd been at the start of the investigation. None of the calls Andee had made so far to Jessica's friends in London had in any way contradicted what they'd told the police two years ago. In fact nothing had come to light to make her think that anything had been over-looked, misconstrued or covered up – and considering some of the guest lists of the parties Jessica had performed at, that had surprised Andee.

There was only one anomaly, which had always been there and was still not yet resolved. It was the call Jessica had received just before going into Goodge Street station. Apparently there was CCTV footage of her taking the call – Andee hadn't seen that yet – which had lasted less than a minute before she'd continued on her way. No trace had ever been found of her mobile, computer or tablet, but the phone company's records showed that the call had come from a cellular number registered in the UK to a Kim Yoder. An extensive search had been carried out to try and locate this person, both domestically and internationally, but he – or she – had never used the phone again and the address given to the server turned out not to exist.

So all they knew was that after taking the call from Kim Yoder Jessica had entered the station, apparently turned off her phone, and instead of going to Paddington, which was where she'd been heading when talking to her brother minutes before, she'd gone to Notting Hill Gate. Video of her emerging from that station hadn't come to light until two days after she'd disappeared, for the simple reason that nothing had come to light to direct the investigation that way. She had no known connection with the area, hadn't, as far as any of her friends knew, ever been there before, and there was no resident, business or business owner using the name Yoder. However, further viewings of the station's CCTV prior to that June day showed Jessica coming and going on a regular, though random basis, over a period of two months. After leaving the station, she'd cross the road towards Holland Park, only then to disappear apparently into thin air. With no cameras monitoring the streets she was heading into it wasn't possible to track her movements, and, disappointingly, no private security cameras had produced anything either.

Nor had any footage been found of Jessica returning to Notting Hill Gate station on that day, or any other day afterwards.

Having Googled the name Yoder herself, Andee had discovered that it had Swiss origins, was common amongst the Amish communities in the Midwest, and was also the name of a barbecue grill company in Kansas. Naturally police inquiries had extended in all these directions, with considerable help from local law enforcement agencies, but none had yielded any positive results.

Andee also knew now that Jessica's bank account had not been accessed since that day, though it contained an impressive sum for a girl her age. The deposits had all coincided with the gigs she'd carried out at various embassies, hotels and private homes. No evidence had been found of any other kind of service being offered to warrant such generous fees. These people were simply very rich and apparently didn't mind throwing it around. Or that was what they'd have the police believe, and with nothing to contradict it that line of inquiry had eventually closed down.

Now, as Andee weaved her way along the crowded promenade heading towards the old town and her meeting with Blake Leonard at four, she'd have liked to remain focused on Jessica, but her own teenage daughter was not allowing it. Since arriving back from uni yesterday Alayna had refused to answer Andee's calls or emails, but she was on the phone now tearing into her mother as though they'd undergone some kind of role reversal.

'. . . he's really upset, I hope you know that,' Alayna cried angrily. 'You should be ashamed of yourself. He doesn't know what it's all about so I think you owe him an explanation, don't you?'

Stifling a sigh as she dodged a balloon, Andee said, 'Alayna, this is between me and Dad . . .'

'You're my parents. I think that entitles me to an explanation. And what about Granny?'

'Is Granny there?'

'No. Why?'

'I thought not. We wouldn't be having this conversation if she were. Is Luke at Granny Carol's yet?'

'He arrived about an hour ago.'

Stung that he hadn't called or texted to let her know, Andee was about to continue when Alayna said, 'You know Dad thinks there's someone else, don't you?'

'Yes, I do, but there isn't. Now, I'm sorry, but I have to go. I'll ring later, or maybe we can meet tomorrow for lunch, or a coffee?'

'If you're breaking up with Dad, then I'm sorry, but you're breaking up with me too,' and with that return to her own age, she ended the call.

Sighing, Andee clicked off her end and tried to re-focus her thoughts on what lay ahead. She was almost at Graeme's shop by now, and the last thing she wanted was to see either him, or Blake Leonard, while she was feeling as distracted as she did by Alayna's call. Graeme would sense it right away, since he was intuitive that way, and Blake just didn't deserve her mind to be elsewhere.

She was in the heart of the old town, crossing the cobbled square towards the antique shop, when her phone rang again. Knowing from the ringtone that it was Luke she decided she had to take it, even if it made her late.

As she clicked on she managed to bump into a denim-clad young man with razored red hair and a bullish attitude.

'Sorry,' he said, surprising her, for he didn't seem like someone who'd apologise.

Gesturing an acceptance, she said into the phone, 'Luke, hi. Are you OK? Alayna tells me you're at Granny Carol's. How was the drive back?'

'Cool. Loads of traffic on the M5, but OK coming across the moor. So you're definitely going through with this?'

Steeling herself, she said, 'Yes, I am, but I'm afraid now isn't a good time to discuss it. Can we meet? Just us, tomorrow?'

'I've got stuff on tomorrow. I'll call, OK?' and he rang off.

'Great,' she muttered as she disconnected at her end. This really wasn't going well.

Reminding herself once again that the next hour or so wasn't about her or her family, she took a deep breath to try and clear her mind, turned off her phone, dropped it into her bag and headed over to the shop.

The first thing she noticed as she opened the door was the extremely attractive young woman sitting at the mahogany desk Graeme normally used. She was clearly very comfortable there with her feet propped up on an open drawer as she turned a wave for Andee to come in into a sweep of invitation to have a browse, while continuing to chat merrily down the phone.

Determined not to listen too closely, although it was apparently a business call and the lovely blonde seemed to know her stuff where antique mirrors were concerned, Andee looked around at the predominantly art deco and oriental display. She'd noticed the last time she was here, a week ago, when she'd first come to see Blake Leonard that Graeme seemed to have changed his stock from when she'd known him before, but there hadn't been the time to ask him about it then. She wondered if the change was a result of the beautiful young woman's influence, and decided it almost certainly was, given how comfortably she seemed to blend in with it all.

'Andee, you're here.'

Andee turned and broke into a smile. 'Blake, it's good to see you,' she said, holding out a hand to shake. She'd taken to this man on sight, and so was finding herself genuinely pleased to see him again, even if she regretted the reason she was here. 'How are you?' she asked.

His expression was wry, showing that he didn't want to lie, but the truth wasn't going to get them anywhere either. 'Will you come on through?' he offered. 'Graeme's had to go out, but he asked me to pass on his regards.'

Refusing to ask who the woman was, Andee followed him through the door marked Private, trying not to wince as the young woman burst into a gale of loud laughter.

'I made us some tea,' Blake said, leading her into his cluttered workshop where the pieces he was restoring appeared more traditional than those in the shop. Victorian, Chippendale, Arts and Crafts Revival. Not that she knew much about antiques, but they looked to her to be from those sorts of periods. 'I remembered that you like peppermint,' Blake added, glancing over his shoulder.

Sensing the anxiety in his effort to please, Andee put real warmth into her smile. 'Sounds perfect,' she said. '*And* you have biscuits?'

'From the bakery next door.'

As he poured she took out a slender file containing the notes she'd made during her examination of the police files, and perched on a tall stool next to a workbench. Sun was streaming in through the open back doors, casting dusty bands of light over the dozens of crowded shelves and piles of furniture waiting to be polished, or restored or reunited with missing pieces, in much the same way as Blake was waiting to be reunited with his own missing piece. The air was curdled with the scent of old wood, turps, paint, glue and probably a dozen other ingredients essential to his trade. She found it quite pleasing, she realised.

After setting down the tea and sweeping a mound of stained rags aside, he pulled up a stool the other side of the bench.

'So what do you think?' he asked, coming straight to the point.

Putting a hand on the file as she spoke, and wishing she wasn't about to crush his hopes, she said, 'What I

53

think is that the police have done a thorough job. You know the case isn't closed, of course?'

He nodded. 'But the search has been scaled right back. I realise it has to happen when there are no leads, I just . . . It's hard to sit there doing nothing when it's your child.'

Understanding better than he knew, she said, 'Did you, personally, feel, during the height of the search, that every avenue was being explored? Looking back, do you think something might have been missed?'

His eyes drifted around the many objects in the room, clocks, dolls, musical instruments, cabinets, tables and chairs, and it was a while before she realised that he was caught in a memory, perhaps he was even hearing Jessica's voice. She knew how it happened, how incredibly real it could feel, so she said nothing, simply waited for him to return to the present.

In the end he said, 'I'm sorry, what was . . . Oh yes. Actually, my head was so messed up back then that it's hard to know how I felt, apart from scared out of my mind. I still am, it's just not always on the surface.' He looked down at his tea. 'I can't think of anything that wasn't covered,' he admitted quietly, 'but she has to be somewhere. People don't just vanish.'

Knowing that they did, and knowing that he knew it too, Andee sipped her tea, giving him a moment to recover from a build-up of emotion.

'Four police forces have been involved in the search,' she reminded him. 'Presuming everyone interviewed was telling the truth, and there's nothing to suggest otherwise, the only questions that remain, apart from the obvious one of where is she, is why did she go to Notting Hill Gate station that day when she'd only just told Matt that she was on her way to Paddington? And was the reason for the change of plan connected to the call that came as she was going into Goodge Street station? I think we can assume that it was.'

He stared at nothing in silent despair. How many times must he have gone over this already, and he was still no closer to an answer than he'd been at the start. No one was. 'People always think there are cameras everywhere,' he said. 'I've even heard that they can track mobile phones when they're turned off . . .'

When he didn't continue, Andee said, 'There are a lot of mistaken beliefs out there, and it's true to say that cameras often aren't where we want them to be.'

He nodded absently. 'If we had her phone,' he said, 'we might be able to find out more, like who was texting her, did she turn on her GPS, but I'm sure you already know that they've never found it. Or her laptop, or anything else she had with her that day.'

Yes, Andee did know that. It was largely why the search had proved so difficult. With no Internet search history to guide them, no emails in or out of an account that her friends and family hadn't known about, no social media memberships she might have kept to herself . . .

'A trace on the mystery number,' Blake went on, 'showed that it's registered to a Kim Yoder, but no one's ever been found with that name, so we have to assume it's false.'

Deciding to change the subject slightly, Andee said very carefully, 'The incident that forced you to leave Manchester, can you think of any reason why . . .'

'It's not connected,' he assured her. His face was taut, his hands clenched tightly together. 'Do you think it was?' he asked, suddenly not seeming quite so sure.

From what she'd read she didn't, and clearly the detectives who'd interviewed everyone associated with the incident didn't think so either. Of course their reports would have influenced her thinking, but there really didn't seem any logic to it. 'Are you ever in contact with any former friends or colleagues from those days?'

'No one. Jenny's mum and dad had already moved to Devon by the time we left, both mine have already departed this world and neither of us has any brothers or sisters. So when we left we severed all ties.'

'Did Jessica do the same?'

'As far as I know. She'd have told Matt if she was still in touch with anyone.' His eyes came bleakly to hers. 'You think it's hopeless, don't you?' he said, clearly making an effort to keep his voice steady.

The awful truth was, she did, but there was no way she could bring herself to admit it, so what she said was, 'There are a few calls I still need to make.' This was the truth, there were, but at this stage she didn't want to go into detail just in case the police had already been there and she hadn't yet found it in the files.

Rowzee's eyes were taking a while to open. She knew where she was – on the floor next to her desk – but she didn't know yet how long she'd been there, or how badly she'd hit her head in the fall. It was definitely hurting, but not unbearably. It was just making it difficult to get a full grip on her senses for the moment.

It didn't matter. There was no rush. She was quite sure she wasn't expecting anyone, so she could take her time getting up. She mustn't go too fast or she'd end up making herself dizzy again.

When at last she was on her feet, she righted the chair that had tumbled with her and took several breaths as she brushed herself down. How very silly of her to go and black out like that without realising it was coming. She must have been concentrating so hard on the email she was sending to Victor's agent about a rights issue that she hadn't spotted any little black tadpoles swimming about in front of her eyes, or connected with the light-headedness that made her feel as though she was floating out to sea. Those were the usual signs of something untoward occurring, although they didn't always come to anything. However, just in case, when she realised they were there, a bit like putting an umbrella in her bag on a stormy day, she could take precautions, such as sitting on a sofa, or going to lie on the bed. Today she'd gone and toppled right off her chair, clunk, bump, out for the count, straight on to the wooden floor.

Checking the clock she saw to her relief that she'd only been out for a couple of minutes, hardly any time at all. And she really didn't feel any the worse for it. In fact, she was feeling absolutely fine, she decided, apart from the little headache that was already passing.

She'd just get herself a drink of water, or maybe a nice cup of tea, check there were no visible injuries to her face or head then carry on with what she'd been doing.

To her delight, when she returned to her computer, she found four emails accepting the invitation to the party on Friday evening. She was especially thrilled to discover that Charles Stamfield, owner of Burlingford Hall and the whole of the estate, and their local MP until a spell of bad health had forced him to resign, was 'happy to attend'. She frowned. Maybe he'd lost his seat in the last election and that was why he wasn't in Parliament any more? Yes, she was sure that was it, but he'd been ill as well, so hopefully this acceptance meant he was on the mend. They hadn't seen him in far too long, or his lovely wife Gina. It was such a shame that he was no longer representing their community; everyone was agreed that he'd done a splendid job as their champion. Well, clearly not everyone, or they'd have voted him back in again.

Disappointingly, there was no mention of Gina coming with him. She was one of Rowzee's favourite people and not because she was such an accomplished actress, though Rowzee was naturally impressed by her talent, but because she was such good company and had always been so generous with her time. Over the years she'd often helped stage school drama productions, had even taken a cameo role in a few. She'd done the same for the local am-dram society, of which Rowzee was president; and on several memorable occasions she'd brought famous guest speakers to town for the WI to ooh and aah over.

Could it be true that she hadn't seen Gina since the last election? Time flew by so quickly these days that it was hard to keep track of everything, but now she came to think of it she felt sure that the last time Gina had been in Kesterly was for Victor's funeral. The election had been just after that, although Rowzee couldn't remember much about it now, she'd been in such a fog of grief at the time. Oh, now it was coming back to her. Gina had called a while after the funeral to find out how she was, and to let her know that she was flying to the States to sort out some family business. Yes, that was right, so maybe she was still there. It seemed a very long time to be away; however Gina and Charles's daughter, Lydia, was in New York, so maybe Gina was with her. She'd ask Pamela when she came home if she'd heard from Gina lately, then she'd patiently endure Pamela's snipes about her Alzheimer's setting in.

As if Pamela's memory was any better.

It wasn't, for she had to remind Pamela of things every bit as often as Pamela had to remind her. That was age for you: so depressing when even a look in the mirror showed two women who surely couldn't be considered anywhere close to mid-sixties – or not in the way Rowzee thought of sixty-year-olds, all fusty dry skin, grizzled grey hair and frumpy clothes. She and Pamela had, in her opinion, still-youthful complexions, soft bouncy hair, and the fashionable clothes they wore often came from Zara and Next.

Where had Pamela said she was going, again?

Oh yes, that was right, she hadn't said, but apparently she wouldn't be home until late. That meant Rowzee still had plenty of time to sneak a little nap without Pamela knowing and accusing her of getting old, before applying herself to the secret research project she'd recently started online.

It was quite exciting in its way, although frightening too, and she couldn't imagine for one minute that any of her family would approve if they were to find out about it. The point was not to let them find out.

*And take upon 's the mystery of things . . .* That was from *King Lear*, Act 5, Scene 3 – proving that her memory wasn't as rusty as she sometimes feared.


'Andee, you're still here,' Graeme Ogilvie stated in cheerful surprise as she and Blake came through from the workshop. 'I was hoping I wouldn't miss you.'

Appreciating his friendliness, Andee smiled as she noticed that the blonde from earlier was nowhere to be seen. 'It's good to see you again,' she said, glancing curiously at the bags that he was loading on to his desk, full of what looked like acres of foaming lace, ribbons, pink satin and – was that a sword sticking out of the top of one?

'I can explain,' he promised with a twinkle. To Blake, he said, 'Is everything OK?'

Blake turned to Andee, apparently wanting her to answer.

'I'm going to talk to some of Jessica's friends again,' Andee told them, keeping the plans for her next step to herself for now.

Evidently pleased with the reply, Graeme said, 'It never does any harm to go over things with fresh eyes. You know how sometimes you can't see for looking, so there's a chance something might have been missed somewhere.'

Andee couldn't deny his reasoning, nor could she feel quite comfortable with the way his dark eyes rested so easily, yet intently on hers. She knew he couldn't help it, it was simply the way he looked at a person, but it was that look, combined with the proximity of him, that had made her realise, the last time she was here, that she was still attracted to him. She'd even been ready, at the time, to believe the feeling was mutual, but that was before she'd come across his new partner, assistant, whoever she was, who'd just appeared from a storeroom with a giant roll of bubble wrap.

'Ah, have you met Lucie?' Graeme asked, turning to hold out an arm to the younger woman. 'She's been holding the fort for me this afternoon. Lucie, I'd like you to meet Andee Lawrence.'

'I recognised you the minute you came in,' the gorgeous Lucie declared, coming to shake Andee's hand. She looked so friendly and happy to be there – and clearly saw Andee as no threat to her position at all. 'I think it's wonderful that you're going to help Blake,' she ran on. 'We all do. We've come to think of him as family now. We did, even before Jessica disappeared, but I think it's true to say that this dreadful time has brought us closer together?' She was looking at Blake for confirmation.

'I sometimes wonder how I'd have got through it without you all,' he admitted. 'You've been so kind and supportive.'

Touching an affectionate hand to his cheek, Lucie went to investigate the bags Graeme had left on the desk and immediately began chuckling as she pulled out what looked like children's party costumes.

'They're going to look so cute,' she cried. 'Two princesses and a little knight in shining armour. I'm guessing Katie chose them?' she asked Graeme.

'Of course. I just collected them.' To Andee he said, 'My sisters, one of whom is Lucie's mother, are having a little get-together on Friday evening, and the children have decided they want to dress up for it.'

Instantly warming to Lucie, Andee smiled.

'They're seeing themselves as the stars of the show,' Lucie confided, 'and knowing Rowzee she'll make them feel that they're nothing less, in spite of it being an adult affair.'

'Are we talking about Rowzee Cayne?' Andee asked, feeling certain they must be. To Graeme she said, 'I had no idea she was your sister.'

Before he could respond Lucie said, 'The whole world knows Rowzee, or that's how it seems at times. Were your children in her class – presuming you have children, which you might not, but if you do . . .' She broke off as Graeme's hand gently silenced her.

Laughing, Andee said, 'Both my children were students of hers and they absolutely loved her. In fact, she's the reason Alayna, my youngest, is studying English Lit. and Drama at Bristol. I believe it's where Rowzee went.'

'It is,' Lucie cried excitedly. 'Does Rowzee know that?'

'Oh yes,' Andee assured her. 'She took Alayna out to celebrate when Alayna was accepted.'

'That is so Rowzee,' Lucie laughed. Rashly, she added, 'I know, why don't you come to the party on Friday? Rowzee would absolutely love it if you did.'

Stunned, Andee said, 'I'm sure your aunt doesn't even remember me . . .'

'Of course she does. Rowzee never forgets anyone, and anyway, you're quite famous around here. Please don't say no. Your husband is invited too, of course. My mother will be beside herself to meet him, the old mayor's son, but I have to warn you, she'll probably get on his case about following in his father's footsteps. I expect he gets that a lot?'

'From time to time,' Andee admitted, still feeling bedazzled by the invitation and wondering if she ought to be turning it down.

'Lucie, you're almost as bossy as your mother,' Graeme chided. However, to Andee he said, 'They really would love it if you came.'

Lucie was regarding her with such eagerness that Andee threw out her hands as she laughed. 'It's very kind of you, and if you're sure Rowzee won't mind, I'd love to come, but I don't think my husband . . . He'll have other . . .' She was making a mess of this. 'I'm not sure what he's doing on Friday, but I guess . . . Speaking for myself, I'd love to come. Thank you.'

With a whoop of joy Lucie exclaimed, 'They are going to be so pumped when I tell them. They'll probably roll out the red carpet, knowing them.'

'I hope not,' Andee laughed. 'Is it a special occasion?' she thought to ask. 'Someone's birthday?'

'My mother's,' Lucie replied, 'but she's pretending it's Rowzee's. Don't ask me why, because I don't have a clue. My mother's just weird like that.'

'Actually, I can explain,' Graeme stepped in. 'Pamela – Lucie's mother – always says it's Rowzee's birthday when they're having a party, because she's convinced that the sun only ever shines on Rowzee. If she owns up that it's her big day she's sure it'll rain.'

Andee and Blake both laughed.

'I swear my mother gets madder as she gets older, in all senses of the word,' Lucie told them, checking her watch. 'Oh my God, I have to pick Alfie up at five, so I need to go. I'll take the costumes,' she said to Graeme, scooping up the bags. 'Katie's got a free day tomorrow, she said, so if you need her to cover, just give her a call.'

As the door closed behind her Graeme turned back to Andee and Blake.

Andee was on the point of saying that she should go too when she realised Graeme was regarding Blake curiously. Turning, she found Blake staring hard at something outside in the square. Following his eyes she tried to spot what it might be, but everything seemed normal to her.

'Excuse me,' Blake muttered, and moving swiftly to the door he tugged it open and ran towards the Victoria fountain where a crowd of tourists were cooling hands and feet in the water.

Graeme said to Andee, 'Do you think he spotted someone who looks like Jessica?'

Almost certain that was the case, Andee said, 'It's cruel, the way your eyes and ears can play tricks on you.'

His expression softened as he turned to her.

Realising he was remembering Penny, she gave a little shrug and changed the subject. 'I feel I should have known that Rowzee Cayne was your sister. Did we never talk about her when we . . . were seeing each other?'

'There was a lot going on back then,' he reminded her. 'In fact, you were heavily involved in another case of a missing girl, as I recall.'

Remembering only too well, Andee's insides churned. Sophie Monroe, aged fourteen. The outcome hadn't been good, in fact it had been nothing short of terrible, but at least they had found a body.

'I'm sorry,' Blake said, coming back into the shop. His face was pale, his voice rough with emotion. 'I thought . . . It looked like someone . . .'

'It's OK,' Graeme said gently, putting a hand on his shoulder.

Blake looked at Andee. 'Thanks for coming,' he said, 'I really appreciate you giving this your time, but we still haven't talked about money. I don't have much, I'm afraid . . .'

'There's no fee involved,' Andee interrupted. 'Helen, your lawyer, will explain if you give her a call.'

Apparently overcome, Blake muttered a thank you and disappeared back to his workshop.

'How well do you know Jessica's mother?' Andee asked quietly.

'Jenny? Fairly well. She's taken this very hard. I guess any mother would.'

He was certainly right about that. 'I probably ought to talk to her at some stage. Do you think she'll be willing?'

'I don't see why not, but you know she's in Devon?'

Andee nodded, and glanced at her watch. 'I should go,' she said, remembering a call she wanted to make before five.

Walking her to the door Graeme said, 'So it looks like I'll see you on Friday.'

Feeling both embarrassed and pleased, she said, 'It would seem so.'

'I'm sorry your husband can't make it.'

Not at all sure he meant that, she simply smiled and left, taking out her phone and turning it on as she reached the other side of the square.

Connecting to Leo Johnson at Kesterly CID, she said, 'I know you can't make this a priority, but I'd like more information from the Met if you can get it.'

'Fire away,' he invited.

After giving him the details, she said, 'I couldn't find the answers to this in the files they sent, but they should exist. If they don't . . . Well, let's find out first if they do.'

'Mm, something smells good,' Matt commented, coming into the kitchen and dropping his keys and mobile on the table.

Blake read from the recipe card he was using. 'Chilli chicken with ginger and udon.'

Matt pulled a face. 'What the heck's udon when it's at home?'

'Japanese noodles. There was an offer on at the supermarket with free recipes thrown in, so I thought I'd give it a go.' He could hear both Jenny and Jessica telling him that of course the recipes were free, they wanted to sell the product, so he wasn't sure why he'd said it. 'Where have you been?' he asked, as Matt slumped at the table and stretched out his long legs. He wondered if the smoke he could smell was just plain cigarettes, or something a little more flavoursome.

'Out with some mates. So how did it go with Andee Lawrence?'

Putting the chicken on to grill, Blake gave his hands a quick rinse and took a couple of beers from the fridge. Handing one to Matt, he said, 'She's going to make some more calls.'

Matt nodded, and continued to nod as he cracked open the can. 'Did she think anything had been missed?'

'Not that she said, but she probably won't know for certain until she's carried out her own enquiries.' He was making it sound a lot more hopeful than Andee had, but Matt needed the boost to get him past this two-year anniversary. They both did, and if a little self-delusion on his part was necessary, well, bring it on, as Jessica would have said. 'I forgot to tell Andee that you know her son.'

Matt shrugged and picked up his phone to read a text. 'I saw him today,' he said.

'Luke Farnham? To speak to?'

'Yeah, to speak to. He came down to the beach with his sister where we were all hanging out. She's pretty hot these days. I don't remember her being like that before.'

Blake cast him an interested look.

Matt's eyebrows rose. 'You don't have to read something into everything I say,' he protested.

Grinning, Blake let it drop, though a summer romance would be a godsend for Matt right now, it might just focus him in a direction that was a whole lot healthier than the place he was in at present. However, getting involved with Andee's daughter? What would Andee think of that?

'What?' Matt prompted. 'Nothing's going to happen, if that's what you're afraid of.'

'I'm not afraid. I wish it would. Maybe you need a refresher on the birds and the bees. We could sit down after dinner if you like.'

'Yeah right, I'm definitely up for that.'

Blake laughed past the memory of Jess teasing her twin for being a virgin. Those days were a long way behind them now, but there had been no steady girl-friend since Jessica's disappearance.

A few minutes later they were tucking into large bowls of steaming noodles topped with delicious oils, spices, chicken and veg. After agreeing that it was one of his better culinary efforts, Blake said, 'Something else happened today. Or I thought it did. I'm not sure now.'

Matt scowled. 'Duh! Riddles.'

Blake had thought hard about whether or not to go down this route, especially when it was probably going to lead nowhere, or at least nowhere helpful. In the end, it was the pact that he and Matt had made almost two years ago, that they should have no secrets from each other, that persuaded him to speak up.

'There was someone on the square outside the shop,' he said, reaching for his beer. 'He looked just like Tyler Bennett.'

Matt stopped eating as his expression turned sour. 'Was it him?' he asked quietly.

Blake shook his head. 'I'm not sure. By the time I got outside he'd disappeared into the crowds.'

Matt sat back in his chair, his face hard with loathing. 'What would he be doing here?' he demanded.

Blake shrugged and shook his head. 'He could be on holiday, or maybe it wasn't him at all.'

'If it is, and he's looking for trouble, I'll be ready for him.'

'No, Matt. If you see him I want you to turn around and walk the other way. He's caused this family enough grief for one lifetime, we really don't need any more.'

Though Matt didn't argue, Blake could tell that it was going to be almost impossible for him to ignore the caution.

'Did you tell Andee Lawrence that you saw him?' Matt asked.

'If it was him – and no, I didn't, although I probably should, just in case I was right. The build and hair colour were definitely the same, and he was staring across at the shop when I spotted him next to the fountain. I don't know how long he'd been there, maybe he'd

69

just stopped to check his phone. All I know is that he'd vanished by the time I got out there.'

'What would he want?' Matt growled. 'What the hell else does he think he can do to us?'

Blake had no idea, so he simply shook his head.

'He can't have had anything to do with what's happened to Jessica,' Matt stated angrily. 'The idiot's so thick he'd never be able to pull off something like that.'

'Like what? We don't know what happened to her, but I'm inclined to agree. She'd never have gone near him, but even if she did . . .' He broke off as Matt's mobile started to ring. 'Do you want to take it?' he asked.

Matt checked the caller and shook his head. 'It's only Zac. I can ring him back.' His dark, injured eyes returned to Blake. 'If he is here, do you think we can get him arrested for harassment?'

'Not unless he harasses us and so far he hasn't.'

'But standing across from the shop, staring in . . . That's got to mean something.'

'He has nothing to gain from coming here and being associated with us again. Anyway, just because he had razor-cut red hair and tattoos . . .'

'Are you going to tell Andee Lawrence?'

'If either of us sees him again and feels convinced it's him, I will. Otherwise, there doesn't seem any point.'

## Chapter Five

'So where were *you* until after ten last night?' Rowzee demanded, intrigued to know, and enjoying the tease.

Pamela was at her dressing table, studying her reflection with deep interest.

'It's you,' Rowzee assured her.

Pamela's eyes flicked to hers in the mirror. 'I don't think I heard you knock,' she remarked smoothly.

'The door was open. Can I ask why you're pulling your face about like that?'

'I'm thinking of getting it lifted,' Pamela admitted, raising and tugging the loosened skin on her cheeks and neck, apparently trying to work out how much younger it would make her look if she could be rid of the baggy bits.

'I see.' Rowzee was amused. 'Will that be before you have liposuction, or at the same time?'

Pamela's eyes narrowed.

'I just thought,' Rowzee said innocently, 'if you're going to have a general anaesthetic to reduce your hips and thighs, which is what you were talking about last

71

week, then why not get the whole lot done at once? They might even give you a discount for bulk.'

Pamela winced at the last word. 'I'm fed up with dieting,' she sighed, sitting back in the chair. 'I've been doing it all my life and I'm bigger now than I've ever been.'

'You're not big, you're just curvy, and most men love curvy women.'

Pamela's eyes sharpened. 'If you're about to mention Bill Simmonds . . .'

Rowzee's hands shot up. 'He never even crossed my mind,' she lied. 'Anyway, they say dieting makes you fatter, so maybe you should just give it up and enjoy life? You're looking very lovely in that dress, by the way. Coral suits you, and it's a good idea to wear something that fits, you should try it more often.'

'And you,' Pamela spat back, 'should cover your arms. A woman your age never has good arms and whether you like it or not, you're no exception.'

'I'm sixty-five, not twenty-five. No one expects me to have good arms, or a young face, or a girlish figure. You need to try and be happy in your own skin, Pamela . . . No, don't shout at me, it wouldn't be a good way to start the evening and the caterers will be expecting us downstairs any minute.'

'I need to make a phone call first.'

'Who to?'

'What do you mean, who to?'

Trying it in French, Rowzee said, *'A qui?'*

'Why do you want to know?'

'Because I do.'

'I don't ask who you're calling all the time, so why are you bugging me? Now, if you'll excuse me . . .'

As Rowzee turned for the door she glanced along Pamela's bookshelves, a habit of hers, and spotting a paperback with a torn spine she took it out, intending to glue it back together. To her amazement it turned out to be the most unlikely addition to Pamela's collection. 'What's this doing here?' she asked, holding up a copy of *The Satanic Bible*.

Pamela looked round and almost shrank in horror. 'You must have put it there,' she accused. 'And now you can take it away again. I suppose you thought it was funny, putting something like that in my room?'

'Nothing to do with me,' Rowzee assured her. 'I thought you'd thrown it out when you found it in Victor's library.'

'I did. I mean, I thought I did. You must have rescued it.'

Rowzee laughed.

'I think it's disgraceful that he even owned it,' Pamela snorted. 'I know you say it was for research, but I used to wonder about him . . . He was always far too interested in the dark arts . . .'

Still laughing, Rowzee kept hold of the book and continued to the door. 'By the way, it seems the little trick you tried playing on nature hasn't worked. It's raining.'

'No doubt because you told everyone it was my birthday, not yours.'

Rowzee didn't deny it, although she hadn't told anyone. Graeme probably had though, and Pamela's daughters certainly would have. 'If someone brings me a present, I'm keeping it,' she warned, and with an airy little wave she crossed the landing to her own room, still enjoying the memory of Pamela accusing Victor of being into black magic.

'I always knew there was something strange about you,' she'd cried heatedly. 'And don't try passing it off as research to me. I'm not as gullible as my sister.'

Assuming his best astonished manner, Victor had said, 'It's not a secret, you know. Would you like to become a member of our cult? We're crying out for vampires.'

He'd teased her mercilessly, until in the end she'd stomped off in high dudgeon vowing never to set foot in their ungodly house again. Rowzee couldn't remember exactly how long she'd stayed away on that occasion, but she was fairly certain that it was Graeme who'd brought her back, insisting there was nothing to fear.

As if anyone could ever have had anything to fear from Victor. He'd been the gentlest, sweetest, most generous person alive – his irrepressible roguish streak notwithstanding. He'd also been very fond of Pamela in his way, and Rowzee knew Pamela had felt the same about him – she'd seen her wiping away tears at his funeral. However, it was true that he'd had secrets, well one, anyway, that Rowzee knew about, but it was nothing like the nonsense Pamela had accused him of. Devil worship, as if! No, the part of his past that he had been hiding was nothing at all to do with an unsavoury cult, but it could still make Rowzee anxious, even nervous, today.

Deciding this evening really wasn't the time to dwell on the awful day that Victor had come home all bloodied and bruised, which was when he'd been forced to reveal his secret to her, she skilfully swept it aside and went to fluff up her hair.

A few minutes later she was about to go and check on the caterers – her birthday present to Pamela – when she heard someone knocking on Pamela's door and Graeme calling out for the birthday girl.

'Don't come in! Don't come in!' Pamela squealed. 'I'm on the phone.'

Able to imagine exactly how her brother would respond to that – with as much amusement as Rowzee had – Rowzee threw open her own door and was immediately treated to a cheery wink as he crossed the landing to sweep her into an embrace.

'You look terrific,' he told her. 'In fact, I do believe I could eat you all up.'

Laughing at the threat she used to make to him when he was small and she and Pamela already in their teens, Rowzee said, 'You look rather dashing yourself, young man. Are the boys able to make it? It would be wonderful to have at least one of them here.'

'I'm afraid they're in Turkey with their mother and stepfather,' he reminded her, 'but they send their love.'

'Oh yes, I've had emails so I know that. Such a pity they're missing the party.'

Tucking her arm through his, Graeme walked her towards the stairs. 'So who's her ladyship on the phone to?'

'Heaven knows, but it sounds as though she's taken her clothes off to make the call.'

Laughing, he stepped back and gave Pamela's door another playful knock.

'Who is it?' she called out grandly.

'Beelzebub,' Rowzee called back, astonishing her brother.

'You're very funny,' Pamela declared, coming on to the landing. 'Darling, lovely to see you,' she cooed at Graeme, wrapping him in her floaty chiffon sleeves. 'Did you bring the champagne?'

'Of course. Everything's sorted, you don't need to worry about a thing. You look . . . amazing. New dress?'

'As a matter of fact it is,' she admitted, giving him a twirl. 'I had it delivered from a very upmarket Internet company who only sell designer clothes. It came by courier from London and they'd have had it picked up for free if it turned out not to be suitable, but I rather think it is.'

It was, in fact, the loveliest dress Rowzee had seen Pamela in for some time, and she rather regretted her jibe about it fitting now, as it would have been much kinder to tell her how very glamorous she looked in what was undoubtedly a very expensive creation.

76

After righting her wrong, she promptly dropped herself in it again by telling Graeme about the plans for a facelift.

'Can't you keep anything to yourself?' Pamela sighed as Graeme regarded her darkly.

'As a matter of fact, I'm very good at secrets,' Rowzee informed her, 'and you didn't say that this was one. Tell her she doesn't need it,' she instructed Graeme.

'You don't need it,' he repeated obediently.

'You would say that,' Pamela retorted. 'Are the girls here yet?'

'We'd know if they were,' he replied, gesturing for his sisters to go first down the stairs.

'Oh my goodness, look at that rain,' Pamela cried as they reached the busy kitchen with smartly clad caterers darting about all over the place, and the French doors wide open to the terrace. 'It's torrential.'

'But rather lovely,' Rowzee declared, enjoying the scent of wet grass and cooling air that was drifting in from the garden. 'We can still use the covered part of the terrace, and there's plenty of room inside if we move some furniture.'

Apparently remembering something, Pamela turned to Graeme. 'Lucie tells me Andee Lawrence is coming,' she declared excitedly. 'That's marvellous news, especially if her husband comes too. We can try to persuade him to run for mayor,' and spotting her daughters arriving with their husbands and children she sailed off to greet them.

Holding him back as he made to follow, Rowzee whispered, 'Am I right in thinking that you and Andee Lawrence . . . Weren't you seeing her for a while?'

With an ironic grimace Graeme said, 'Nothing ever gets past you, does it, Rowzee Cayne? You're right, we had a bit of a thing about three years ago. Nothing serious, and in case you're wondering, she wasn't with her husband at the time. In fact, it was before she was married.'

'I don't sit in judgement,' she assured him, although she would have if he had been involved in that sort of deceit, for she'd always considered cheating to be an unforgivable crime. 'Will you find it awkward if Martin does come tonight?' she asked.

His eyebrows rose. 'I shouldn't think so. We're all grown-ups, I hope.'

'I confess I'm looking forward to seeing Andee to find out how her children are getting along at uni, especially Alayna. I do hope they don't decide to go and live abroad when they graduate, the way yours keep threatening. I miss those boys terribly as it is – if they were so far away . . .'

'Life would be more peaceful,' he assured her, turning to catch Katie's little princesses as they came flying down the hall shouting his name. Scooping them up, one in each arm, he allowed himself to be showered in royal kisses.

'Oh, Alfie, look at you,' Rowzee cried delightedly, as Lucie's two-year-old knight in shining armour came toddling in through the door. 'You're the most handsome little dragon-slayer I've ever seen.'

Slashing his sword awkwardly from side to side, Alfie made to stab her as she went down to his height. She never said so to anyone, but he reminded her so

78

much of her own little soldier when he was the same age that it was sometimes hard to look at him without welling up.

'Rowzee? Rowzee? Are you all right?' she heard Graeme asking.

Looking up at him, she blinked blearily as she said, 'Of course. Why do you ask?'

'Are you dizzy?' He sounded anxious.

Belatedly realising she was slumped against the wall, she said, 'What do you mean? I was playing dead, wasn't I, Alfie?'

Clearly not sure what was happening, Alfie the Lionheart stabbed her again, and she gave a gulp of pretend agony before allowing Graeme to help her to her feet.

She was fine, no harm done, just a little fuzziness in her eyes that would go away in a minute.

What a quick thinker she was! *I was playing dead*.

Within an hour the house was bursting at the seams with all their guests, and Rowzee was on tipsy-top form as she floated amongst them, loving them all for coming and hoping that Pamela was enjoying herself too. She certainly seemed to be, the way she was laughing so heartily at whatever Charles Stamfield was saying, and since Graeme was with them and Rowzee hadn't said hello to Charles yet she was just starting in their direction when someone touched her arm.

To her delight it turned out to be Andee Lawrence, looking supremely elegant in a lemon knee-length shift dress and shiny gold pumps. And such glorious hair, all dark curls tumbling around her lovely face and shapely shoulders. 'I'm so pleased you came,' Rowzee cried warmly, embracing her. 'When Lucie told us she'd invited you I wanted to kiss her – and would have if she hadn't been at the other end of the phone. How are you? You're looking quite stunning.'

'Thank you, but I can't hold a candle to you,' Andee informed her affectionately. 'Retirement is obviously suiting you a lot better than I'm sure it's going to suit the school.'

'Oh, tosh,' Rowzee exclaimed modestly. 'They'll get along just fine without me, but tell me about Alayna. I was so proud when she got into Bristol. Is she enjoying it? From her emails I'm thinking she is.'

'You probably know more than I do,' Andee admitted, 'but yes, I think it's working out. She asked me to send her love this evening and was wondering if she could pop in to see you sometime over the summer.'

'Tell her I'd be honoured, if she can spare the time,' Rowzee enthused. 'I know how busy young people are. I shall want to hear all about everything she's up to, including the boyfriends. Most especially the boyfriends.' Leaning a little closer and lowering her voice, she said, 'Before anyone interrupts us I'd like to say how relieved we all are that you've agreed to help Blake. Please don't take that as pressure, I understand how difficult it is – well, I probably don't, but it's just too awful, what he's going through. I know the police have done their best, but with all the budget cuts over the last few years . . . Oh, ssh, here he is . . .'

As Andee turned to greet Blake Rowzee took his arm, showing how very fond she was of him, but before a greeting could take place someone called out, 'Andee Lawrence? Can that really be you?'

Recognising the voice immediately, Andee's eyes lit up. 'Charles Stamfield! How *are* you?' she cried, returning the ardour of his embrace as he swept her into his arms. 'I haven't seen you in so long.'

'Far too long,' he admonished, drawing back to look at her. 'As gorgeous as ever,' he decided. 'Actually, even more so.'

'Look at you,' she grinned, giving him an ostentatious once-over. 'Still a heart-throb, I see.' He was indeed an exceptionally handsome man in his mid-forties with deep brown eyes, a shock of dark wavy hair and the kind of smile that had always made women's hearts melt. 'Did you get my message after the last election?' she asked. 'We were all crushed in our house, but the region's got what it deserved after voting in the twit we've got now and turning its back on you.'

'I'll second that,' Graeme interjected, adding drily, 'I take it you two know each other.'

Laughing, Charles slipped an arm round Andee's shoulders. 'Andee and I go way back,' he answered. 'In fact, we were at school together, in London, before her family moved to Kesterly . . .'

'Where yours already were,' she put in.

'Right next door to here,' Rowzee added, 'in Burlingford Hall. Your dear parents, how we all loved them . . .'

'In spite of them sending their kids off to college in the States,' Charles teased.

'Probably because of it,' Rowzee insisted. 'Charles went to Princeton,' she declared proudly, for the benefit of anyone listening who might not already know.

'But I came back,' he reminded her.

'You did indeed and with the most beautiful American wife – and you've made such a marvellous success of your life, in spite of the silly election thing.'

'All started by my great-grandfather,' he reminded her, referring to the financial institution of which he was joint chairman and managing director, as well as the Hall, purchased by the same great-grandfather at the beginning of the last century and completely restored. To Andee he said, 'So you and Martin finally got married. Is he here? I don't think I've seen you guys since his father's funeral.'

Realising that it had indeed been that long, Andee said, 'He couldn't make it this evening, but I know he'd love to see you if you're going to be around for a while.' She was searching for signs of the ill health she'd heard about, and finding them well hidden in the slight grey pallor of his skin and unusual dullness of his eyes.

'I need to be around for a while,' he told her. 'I've been neglecting my affairs in this part of the world and I intend to make good over the summer.'

'Is Gina with you?' she asked, looking around.

Charles's expression turned grave. 'I'm afraid not. It's a long story, for another time, but she'll want to know that I've seen you. As will Lydia, who's turning twenty-five next month. I can hardly keep up with the time, it passes so fast.'

Becoming conscious of Blake standing awkwardly to one side, Graeme put an arm round his shoulders and pulled him in. 'Blake, have you met Charles Stamfield? Amongst his many other claims to fame he's my sisters' next-door neighbour. Blake Leonard,' Graeme said to Charles. 'He's working with me at the shop.'

'I feel I know your name,' Charles said, shaking Blake's hand, and glancing at Andee. 'Have we met before?'

'I'm sure I'd remember if we had,' Blake told him.

Since now wasn't the occasion to remind Charles of how or why he might recognise Blake, Rowzee said, 'We must get you a drink, Blake. Did Matt come with you?'

'He had other plans,' Blake replied, taking the glass Rowzee swiped from a passing tray.

Turning back to Andee, Charles said, 'This is such a wonderful surprise, but you know, I was intending to call you later this week. There's something I'd like to get your thoughts on, if you can spare the time.'

'Always for you,' she assured him. 'I can come up to the Hall if you like. It's an age since I was last there.'

'It doesn't change,' he chuckled. 'Still costing me a fortune in upkeep, but Lydia's idea to open the gardens to the public at weekends is lessening the burden.'

'How is Lydia?' Rowzee asked. 'Is she still running the UN?'

Laughing, Charles said, 'Not quite running it, but yes she's still there, doing her best for human rights. Katie, Lucie,' he declared warmly as Pamela's daughters, elbowed their way in.

'Charles, it's so good to see you,' Katie beamed. 'How are you? You look fantastic, so I'm hoping all the health issues are behind you now.'

'I'm happy to say they are,' he confirmed with a smile. 'And how are the children? You know, I haven't even met your little one, Lucie. Is he here? I hope you're going to introduce me if he is.'

'Come this way,' Lucie responded eagerly, taking his hand.

As they moved off through the crowd with Pamela and Katie following on, Andee turned to talk to Graeme and Blake, while Rowzee seized another glass of champagne as it passed and went to greet some new arrivals.

Minutes later Pamela was whispering urgently in Rowzee's ear, 'You have to rescue me. That blasted man keeps grinning at me.'

Knowing immediately who she was talking about, Rowzee hid a smile as she looked over to where Bill Simmonds was clearly engaged in chat with Charles. 'He's got his back to you,' she pointed out.

Pamela peered over her shoulder and grunted, grudgingly, 'How rude.'

As she laughed Rowzee managed to disengage with a breeziness she was far from feeling, and headed for the stairs. Her vision was starting to blur, brought on no doubt by a little too much champagne, so she needed to go upstairs for a few minutes to allow it to pass.

Outside on the terrace Andee was saying to Graeme, 'If I remember correctly, the last time we met you'd found a house in Umbria you were interested in restoring.'

His grey eyes shone with surprise. 'You've a good memory,' he told her. 'The place is now mine, but still in need of some serious work.'

'Is it habitable?'

'Only in a very basic sense. My boys and I manage to have a great time while we're there, but everything leaks and we're often not the only residents.'

Andee frowned.

'Think wildlife,' he grinned. 'Nick and I, that's my eldest, are hoping to get over there sometime this summer to make a serious start on the renovation.'

Remembering how he'd once asked her to come and view the place with him, and how very much she'd wanted to go, she said, 'Is he still at uni? No, he must have left by now.'

'He has and is taking a gap year before deciding what he wants to do with his degree. I have a feeling, as international law is his thing, he's going to end up in Paris, or possibly New York.'

'Such a high-flyer.'

'That's certainly how he likes to see himself. How are your two? Both at uni by now, I'm sure.'

'They are. They seem to be doing quite well, but you never know for certain until the results come in.'

With a wry smile he said, 'Isn't that the truth? My youngest hasn't done anywhere near as well as he'd hoped so far, but I don't know what he expected when he doesn't do the work. He'll have to knuckle down a bit harder for his final year if he wants to get through.' He turned to Blake as he came to say goodnight.

'I need to get back.' Blake shook Graeme's hand. 'It's been a lovely evening, please thank your sisters for me.'

'Of course,' Graeme assured him, looking around for Rowzee who he knew would want to say good-night, and spotting only Pamela apparently giving Bill Simmonds a good telling-off. Leaving her to it, he said, 'Have a good weekend, won't you, and see you on Monday.'

'Bye,' Andee said softly, giving Blake a hug. 'I'll be in touch soon.'

As he walked away, Andee noticed Charles on the terrace, watching him, either absently or with peculiar intensity, she couldn't be sure. Catching her eye, he waved and came to join them.

'You know, I haven't seen Rowzee for a while,' Graeme said, putting down his drink. 'If you guys will excuse me I think I'll go and find out what she's up to.'

## Chapter Six

Charles Stamfield was alone in Burlingford Hall – the magnificent home he had inherited from his father over twenty years ago at the age of twenty-six. He was standing at one of the wide, limestone-framed windows gazing down at the beech and lime avenue where, legend had it, medieval virgins used to exercise their unicorns – a beast visible only to pure damsels.

. In spite of the house not dating from those times, making the legend even more unlikely, he was wondering about those virgins now, or more accurately the real women who'd lived here down the centuries and what lives they must have led, what joys and hardships they'd have known, what secrets they might have kept or shared. Whatever their unspoken dreams, or whispered confessions, they were all lost to the world now, forgotten, vanished like unwritten words in the mists of time. They no longer had the power to injure or please, to tantalise or terrify, or destroy.

*That was what time did. It rendered everything powerless in the end.*

The inherent kindness in Charles's eyes was clouded by the troubling nature of his thoughts; the easy smile that was so infectious for many had yielded to a mask of quiet but deeply felt strain.

If he took his own secret to the grave would it finally set him free, or send him straight to a Dante-esque hell?

Wasn't he there already?

But to that second circle of sad hell,
Where 'mid the gust, the whirlwind, and the flaw
Of rain and hail-stones, lovers need not tell
Their sorrows. Pale were the sweet lips I saw,
Pale were the lips I kiss'd, and fair the form
I floated with, about that melancholy storm.

John Keats, imagining what Dante never revealed, the thoughts of the errant Paolo Malatesta: the Second Circle of Hell, especially for those who'd allowed their appetites to sway their reason.

Would the burden of his secret be any easier to bear if he alone knew it? Would it have had the power to break him the way it had over the past two years, rendering him incapable of normal human relations? Who, looking at him now, would ever guess at what he was hiding, could even begin to imagine that he was still broken, damaged beyond any possible repair?

He'd never felt cut out for the life he led; it wasn't money that excited him, though thanks to his forebears he had plenty of it, it wasn't business or property or any amount of material assets, all of which were his in abundance. He wasn't like the Stamfield men who had gone before him, yet he could play the part – or he had been able to until his weakness had been exploited and he'd been moved aside in the company and voted out of Parliament. He lacked the drive and ambition of those around him, the killer instinct that kept men in his position at the top. He was too gentle, too ready to see the other side of an argument, too appalled by the ruthlessness of cutting a deal that might put hundreds out of work, or destroy their investments, or take away their homes.

After the breakdown his old self had finally stepped forward to carry him through each day the way it always had, but the torment of his conscience, the knowledge of what he'd done, continued to do, was always waiting to fill each unguarded moment.

There was a note in his hand, arrived that morning; a single page of instructions that only differed from the others in the postmark it had been sent from. The amount required to keep his secret safe remained the same.

Pamela was Internet dating. Rowzee was sure of it. All this business about cosmetic surgery, new dresses coming by courier and costing heaven knew how much – two more had arrived that morning and very lovely they were too, though considerably more casual than the first one. Then there were the curious phone calls ('Don't come in, I'm on the phone,'), the mystery of where she'd been for the entire day yesterday, coming home in a worryingly good mood. Rowzee hadn't dared to comment on that, she knew if she did she'd get her head bitten off. And apparently Pamela was going to be late home most evenings this week so Rowzee wasn't to worry about supper for her.

If Rowzee were the sort of person to take a sneak peek at someone's computer she'd be surfing her way around Pamela's laptop like an electronic Poirot right now. It was sitting there on the centre island, seeming to taunt her with its secrets; however Rowzee only had to think of what she was hiding on her own computer to know how upset she'd feel if anyone invaded her privacy that way.

Maybe she should follow Pamela, shadow her, as they called it, like Sam Spade. After all there were some very strange people out there, and a lot of them came disguised as very normal men.

'What are you going to do if she spots you?' Graeme had wondered, clearly torn between amusement and concern when she'd rung to ask for his advice.

What indeed? Pamela's wrath would be unholy, Rowzee could be sure of that, and the likelihood of her being spotted was so high she might as well fly a kite to pinpoint her movements.

Maybe she could hire a detective. Not Andee, she was helping Blake and that was much more important, but there was a good chance Andee could put her in touch with someone.

Did she have Andee's number? Probably not, but Graeme would.

Starting as the phone rang, she put aside the vase she was washing and quickly dried her hands.

'Rowzee, it's Jilly Ansell.'

Rowzee's insides performed a dramatic somersault. Jilly had been one of her star pupils back in the nineties; these day she was her GP. 'Hello Jilly, how are you?' she asked cheerily.

'I'm fine, thank you. Your second lot of results are back, and rather than go through them on the phone, I wondered if you could come to the surgery.'

Rowzee's mouth turned dry. She didn't want to go. How could she get out of it? 'Is it urgent?' she asked. 'Should I start cancelling my subscriptions?'

Wryly, Jilly said, 'I don't think you need to do that. I've made a slot for you at the end of the day on Wednesday. Does six o'clock work for you?'

'Yes, that'll be fine.' She could always cancel whatever else she was supposed to be doing – a meeting of the local history society, she thought. Seeing Jilly was obviously more important.

'If you want to bring someone with you,' Jilly said, as though it was going to be a bit of a social.

Rowzee became very still. There was only one reason Jilly would suggest she didn't come alone . . .

After ringing off Rowzee went to sit at her computer, still too shaken to turn it on, or to think of anything beyond the feelings that were rising up inside her. She knew they were all rooted in fear, for it had been lurking for weeks now, a bit like a niggling ache that sometimes flared up in a shooting pain, only to fade away again. When it was at its worst she usually managed to settle it down with platitudes and scornful admonishments. 'You're getting everything out of perspective as usual,' she'd tell it. Or: 'You're jumping to conclusions

91

without knowing what on earth you're dealing with.' It was like giving directions to a cast that wasn't listening, but she usually got through to them in the end.

She could find no words for the fear now, or nothing that would soothe it and make it go away. It was far more likely to become worse, even turn into some sort of horrible inferno, and tears weren't going to drown it out so she really ought to stop that silly little flow right now.

*Keep your fears to yourself,* Rowzee, *but share your courage with others.* Dear Robert Louis Stevenson; she hadn't read anything by him in far too long. She must put that right straight away, for already just recalling his words was making her feel strong.


As Andee let her children into the flat she was listening intently to what Blake was telling her on the phone.

'So have you seen him again since?' she asked him, waving Luke and Alayna towards the sitting room and ignoring Alayna's pointed look at her mobile. *We've come to see you, as requested, and you're on the phone!*

'Actually, I think I might have spotted him today,' Blake was saying, 'which is what prompted me to call. He was on the square again, over by the florist so further away, meaning I didn't get a good look. He was standing there, staring at the shop, or he seemed to be, but when I went to the door he shot off through the arcade.'

'Remind me of his name,' Andee prompted.

'Tyler Bennett.'

'And can you think of any reason why he'd follow you here now, three years after you left the north?'

'No. Unless he wants to make trouble again.'

It was hard to imagine what sort of trouble when the boy had already caused so much, but Andee guessed he could always try doing the same again should he, for some warped reason, feel inclined to. However, Blake wasn't a teacher now, so nowhere near as vulnerable, and besides, she couldn't see Graeme swallowing any of the boy's nonsense.

'OK, I'll get on to it,' she told Blake. 'If he comes back at all let me know,' and ending the call, she put the phone on the table and tried to decide whether or not to attempt an embrace with her children.

Since they didn't appear to be inviting one, she decided to give it a miss and attempted a smile instead. Though this wasn't an encounter she was looking forward to, it had to happen, and the fact that they'd come she'd decided to view as a promising start.

'It's good to see you,' she began, reminding herself that they were her children, not strangers she had no idea how to reach. 'I know you're both busy . . .'

'You don't need to patronise us,' Alayna interrupted tartly. At eighteen she was all wild blonde beachwaves, impossibly long legs and, today at least, supercilious attitude.

Swallowing a reprimand for rudeness, Andee tried again. 'You're looking good, both of you,' she said, attempting another smile.

With a weary sigh, Alayna flopped down on the sofa and took out her phone. Luckily she didn't look at it, saving Andee the trouble of telling her to put it away again. Luke, fortunately, had stuffed his into a pocket. In contrast to his sister he was as dark-haired as Andee, with his father's arresting blue eyes and raffish good looks, and he was fast reaching Martin in height and build too. Though his manner seemed no friendlier than Alayna's, at least he wasn't coming over as entirely hostile.

'I asked you here,' she said carefully, 'because I want to try to explain what's going on between Dad and me.'

'We kind of know that already,' Alayna retorted. 'You're screwing him up big time, and he's got no idea why.'

Wishing Alayna would just listen, Andee said, 'He knows why I've left . . .'

'But it's not like he's cheated on you,' Alayna interrupted. 'You just upped and went and now there's some bloke you're getting involved with . . .'

'I'm not involved with anyone,' Andee came in forcefully. 'It's not the reason I left. I will admit that there was someone, when Dad and I were apart, but it ended when Dad and I decided to get married.'

'So you dumped him too?' Alayna snorted.

Annoyed, but letting it pass, Andee said, 'I wish I had the same feelings for Dad that I used to when you were growing up and we were all together as a family, but I'm afraid I don't. I still care for him, very much, and that'll never change, but I've come to realise that I don't want to spend the rest of my life with him.' There, so now they had it. It hadn't been so difficult

94

really, just shattering for them and in truth not so good for her either.

'So why did you marry him?' Luke wanted to know. 'You didn't have to. No one forced you.'

'I thought, at the time, that I still loved him, or that we could get back what we'd had before he left . . .'

'That's what this is really about, isn't it?' Alayna interjected. 'He left you, so now you're getting your own back and leaving him.'

Suspecting Martin had planted that suggestion, Andee said, 'Do you really think I'd do something like that?'

'I never thought you'd leave him at all,' Alayna countered sharply, 'so how do I know what you'd do?'

'He was crying last night,' Luke told her. 'I've never seen him cry before.'

Realising how hard that must have been for her son, to see his strong and beloved father in tears – and again wondering if it was all a ruse on Martin's part to get them on his side – Andee tried to think what to say. But what else was there? She'd told them the truth, that her feelings had changed. There was no more.

Suddenly welling up, Alayna wailed, 'Don't do this, Mum, please. He's really upset, we all are, and we want you to come home.'

Going to her, Andee said, 'I'm sorry, sweetheart. I know this isn't easy for you, it's not easy for me either, but please try to understand that feelings, emotions, can be incredibly complicated and most of the time it's as though they have a life of their own. I promise you,

95

if I could bring mine back for Dad and make you two happy, I would, but it just doesn't work like that.'

As Alayna sobbed into her shoulder Andee watched Luke, wishing she could think of a way to reach him too, but he wouldn't meet her eyes, and she knew he wouldn't want her to try and comfort him. He was too grown up for that now.

'I hope you understand, both of you,' she said gently, 'that it doesn't change the way I feel about you. You'll always matter more to me than anyone else in the world . . .'

'Apart from yourself,' Alayna sniffed. 'You're putting yourself first . . .'

'Why shouldn't she?' Luke interrupted harshly. 'She's got as much right to her own life as anyone else, and it's not like you're a kid any more. You don't even live at home . . .'

'Why are you having a go at me?' Alayna cried. 'I'm just saying, if we matter so much, why is she breaking up our family?'

'Stop,' Andee said gently, before Luke could hit back. 'Your brother's right, sweetheart, you're both at uni now, and before too much longer you'll be off living your own lives, probably a long way from here . . .'

'But this is our home.'

'Of course, and that's not going to change. Both grannies will always be here, and I'm sure Dad and I will too, just in different places.'

'Which means you'll be making us choose who to go and stay with and that's not fair. It's not like we're trying to make you choose between us . . . I mean, how would you like that . . .'

'Alayna, try growing up,' Luke muttered angrily.

Alayna glared at him. 'I thought you didn't want them to break up either,' she growled.

'I don't, but if it's going to happen, it's going to happen, so chill, for God's sake.'

'God I hate you sometimes,' she seethed.

'You hate everyone who won't do what you want.'

'Enough,' Andee came in firmly. 'Falling out with each other isn't going to get us anywhere . . .'

Luke got to his feet. 'I need to go,' he said, checking the time on his phone.

'No, I'm going,' Alayna declared, leaping up too. 'You're the mummy's boy, so you stay,' and before Andee could stop her she'd run down the hall, slamming the front door behind her.

Andee turned back to Luke, and saw to her relief that he didn't seem about to follow, at least not right away. As his eyes came to hers she sensed how hard he was struggling with this and reached for his hand.

'We'll get through it,' she promised.

'I know that, but I just can't stand seeing Dad so upset.'

'He should be talking to me, not to you.'

He nodded, keeping his head down, until eventually he looked at her again. 'I want you to do whatever's right for you,' he said hoarsely.

Surprised and touched, she said, 'Thank you.'

He shrugged and started for the door.

'Thanks for coming,' she said, 'and thanks for trying to understand.'

After he'd gone she stood at the window watching the street below until he came out of the building and started off towards the old town. She was so close to tears that her vision was blurred, and by the time she'd cleared it he'd turned a corner and disappeared.

Taking a breath to steady herself she reached for her phone to call Martin, but before making the connection she clicked off again. Venting her anger at him for burdening the children with his feelings and using them to guilt-trip her wasn't going to help the situation. Right now, she couldn't think of anything that would, apart from time, so deciding to try and refocus her thoughts she opened her computer to check if there were any emails from Leo Johnson yet.

Finding nothing, she deliberately didn't try to read anything into it, since she knew very well that he had other priorities, and moving on she called up the names of the lead detectives who'd conducted the Manchester end of the search for Jessica. Maybe one of them could throw some light on Tyler Bennett's whereabouts, just in case it was him hanging around the shop.

# Chapter Seven

Blake was sitting on the edge of Jessica's bed staring at the project she'd put together, aged twelve, after he and Jenny had taken her and Matt to an Edvard Munch exhibition in London. She hadn't done it for school, she'd done it for him because of his interest in the artist, carefully choosing Munch's works and words in a way that had impressed him then, and could just about break his heart now. His mind, his very soul, were in the blackest depths of despair. He tried so hard not to go there, had learned over time that there were ways to avoid it, but there were other times, such as now, when it sucked him in like a helpless victim and there was nothing he could do to stop it.

She was dead. He was never going to see her again. He'd never hear her laughter, her anger, her tears, her beautiful singing voice. There would be no more pride or fatherly fear for his girl; no more plans for the future, jokey reminiscences of the past, setting up for gigs, or arranging a wedding. They'd never paint pictures together again, or visit galleries or get excited about new talents, or share opinions, or spring surprises on each other. The fear of her never returning to his world, the dread of it, was so consuming it stole the air from his lungs, crushed the very beat of his heart.

He was asking himself if he'd been guided by some inexplicable fatherly instinct today to come and pick up this project, with its postcard of *The Scream* on the front, because she was trapped somewhere, screaming for him to come and find her.

*Jess, Jess, Jess,* he cried silently, desperately, as though he were answering her desperate plea.

There was no answering cry. There was only a voice from the past, hers, apologising for some silly falling-out they'd had. 'I'm sorry I got so mad,' she said tearfully. 'I didn't mean any of what I said. Please don't be hurt. You know I love you all the way round the world and back again.'

*All the way round the world and back again.*

It was how far he'd go to find her, as many times as needed, but where, dear God where, should he look along the way?

Forcing his head up, he dried the wretched tears from his face and looked around the room. It hadn't changed. It was still hers in every way. Her concert and fashion posters were pinned randomly to the walls amongst the portraits he'd done of her – Jess as Picasso's *Woman in a Green Hat*; Jess as Jawlensky's *Girl in a Flowered Hat*; Jess as Van Gogh's *Peasant Girl in a Straw Hat*. There were other paintings they'd done together, photographs they'd taken and books they'd read. Nothing had been moved, not the soft toys she'd collected over the years, nor the dressing gown hanging on the back of the door, nor the mess on the dressing table, nor shoes stuffed into a collapsing rack. Even the pile of fresh towels Jenny had put on the bed ready for when she got home were still where Jenny had left them.

They couldn't clear anything out yet; if they did it would be giving up, and he wouldn't allow himself to do that. She might be dead, but until someone could tell him that for certain he had to find a way to bring her back to her mother and brother, to him. They weren't complete without her and never would be. It felt as though all the purpose had been stripped from their world, that every thought had to be about her because it was the only way of keeping her with them.

But she wasn't with them, and today, because it was a bad one, he felt sure in his broken heart that she was dead. If it were true, if she was lost to him, it would be better to know than to endure this never-ending hell of wondering where she was, what might be happening to her. Tomorrow he'd probably feel differently. Tomorrow he might hear her so clearly in his mind that he'd know beyond a doubt that she was out there somewhere. And of course she was, she had to be, because people didn't just disappear. They might not come back, or ever be found, but they were still somewhere . . . Which led him to the small, but horrific comfort that could be found in the stories of girls who'd returned to their families after being imprisoned for months, even years, by some sick maniac whom no one had even suspected. They were hidden in cellars, or sheds, or bunkers far from anywhere they could be heard if they called for help, or screamed out in fear or pain.

Did someone have Jess in captivity? Had they tied her up, locked her into a windowless space, drugged her, done whatever was necessary to put her beyond the power of escape? Were they even now using her, abusing her . . . He inhaled sharply and closed his eyes, as if the image, the obscenity, could be shut out so easily.

Why didn't he know? As her father he should have some kind of instinct, or telepathic connection that would help lead him to her.

'We should consult a psychic,' Jenny had said when it started to become evident the police weren't getting anywhere. 'Anything's better than sitting here waiting and trusting people who don't know any more than we do.'

He hadn't argued, nor had Matt, because like Jenny they'd considered anything worth a try. A neighbour had recommended someone in Cornwall, so they'd taken Jess's first teddy, a photograph, a track of her singing, and her diary aged nine, to try and help the woman to pick up some vibes.

Either she wasn't very good, or they'd taken the wrong things, because they'd come away knowing no more than they had before going.

'We should never have come to Kesterly,' Jenny had wept when they'd got home. 'It wouldn't have happened if we hadn't.'

She'd known that made no sense. Jess had disappeared in London, but Jenny had felt compelled to say it anyway, and Blake understood that it was her way of trying to blame him for the way their lives were imploding.

Usually he let her, because he blamed himself. On that occasion he'd hit back in an outburst of frustration and self-loathing. 'You think I did it, don't you?' he'd accused. 'In your heart you believe I molested that boy.'

She'd turned away, shaking her head. It was Matt who'd raged, 'No one believes it. We all know it was about revenge.'

Tyler Bennett was a tough, cocky kid from a highly dysfunctional family on a notorious estate, an unpleasant thug who, when at school which wasn't often, had done his best to disrupt lessons, goad and humiliate teachers and ridicule those who wanted to learn. Everyone was nervous of him; there was never any knowing who he'd turn on next, no way of guessing what sort of punishment he was planning for a victim who had no idea they'd even committed an offence.

The last person anyone had expected him to turn on was Mr Leonard, the art teacher. Everyone liked Mr Leonard; his lessons were fun even for those who weren't much into the subject. He had the ability to make trips around galleries and museums interesting, and if some of the girls had a crush on him, which invariably happened, he always pretended not to notice. The same went for the boys, though Blake couldn't remember suspecting any of them of being gay, only of some misplaced hero-worship.

Though Tyler Bennett would never have admitted it, he was one of those boys. He didn't tend to act up in Blake's class in the aggressive way he did in others, although he was often loud and argumentative, or did his best to put down the more talented students. But he was rarely difficult with Mr Leonard himself. It was only when Blake had one day shouted across the art room, 'Tyler, leave it alone if you can't get it to stand up,' that the trouble had begun. In spite of the students knowing he'd been responding to Tyler's noisy and fruitless efforts to erect an easel the entire class, with the exception of Tyler, had exploded into laughter.

*Tyler Bennett can't get it up* appeared scrawled on the art-room blackboard the next morning. By the end of the day it had made its way on to just about every black- or whiteboard in the school.

Two weeks or more went by and there was no sign of Tyler. Calls to his home from the secretary's office elicited no reply, and none of his regular gang was forthcoming about where he might be. Then out of the blue he was back, not for assembly or classes, but for a visit to the art room where Blake was still clearing up after school. He said he was looking for one of his mates, and Blake half expected a posse of them to come piling in behind him to teach him their own kind of lesson. Instead, Bennett closed the door, stayed for ten minutes or so chatting about Man United's game the previous Saturday, and then left.

In spite of finding the visit odd, Blake hadn't thought much more about it until the Head called him into his office the following day. Tyler Bennett was waiting with his mother and uncle and Blake sensed right away that this wasn't going to be good. Apparently the boy had made some very grave allegations, and though the Head told Blake privately afterwards that he wasn't inclined to believe them, he was sorry, he had no choice but to suspend Blake while the matter was investigated.

So the police and social services came to interview Blake, as well as questioning other teachers and students, Jenny, his neighbours, and parents of other students, some of whom were, like Tyler, from the notorious Ordsall Estate. Exactly what the authorities were told Blake never found out, he only knew that in spite of no charges being brought it was no longer possible to go on teaching at that school, or living where they were. Tyler's gang had already targeted their house several times with paint bombs, packs of dog poo, fireworks, and the kind of threats that Blake couldn't afford to ignore. He knew, because everyone did, that Tyler had been involved in the beating of a man whose only crime was to ask the boy to pick up the litter he'd tossed into his garden. The man's injuries had been extensive, and might have been even more serious had a neighbour and his Rottweiler not come to the rescue.

Then came the shock of discovering that many of their friends and neighbours seemed to think there was no smoke without fire. Other rumours started that had no basis in fact, but that didn't seem to matter. He could hardly believe that people he'd known for years, who'd socialised with him and Jenny, whose children had played with his, were prepared to doubt him.

So he'd turned his back on teaching altogether and on the town he, Jenny and the children had lived in all their lives, and moved them all south to Kesterly. Graeme had offered him a job on interviewing him, and in spite of knowing his story Graeme's family had taken him and his family to their hearts.

'Is that you, Dad?' Matt asked, pushing open the door to Jess's room.

'Yes, it's me,' Blake replied, knowing, feeling, Matt's moment of blind hope that Jess had come back.

Clocking his father's distress Matt hung his head and Blake went to embrace him. They stood together, silently, painfully, asking themselves the same questions over and over – was she still alive? What more could they do? Who was holding her, if she was being held? Where was her body if someone had killed her?

'Any news from Andee Lawrence?' Matt asked as they started down the stairs together.

'When I spoke to her earlier,' Blake replied, 'she was still waiting for some information she's asked for from the Met.'

'Have you told her you thought you saw Tyler Bennett?'

'Yes, I have.' Blake was checking a text on his mobile. It was from Graeme about a card-table delivery they were expecting tomorrow.

'I don't get it, if it is Tyler Bennett,' Matt said, going into the kitchen. 'It's not his MO to stalk. He intimidates, bullies, beats people up, threatens them with knives, he doesn't lurk about like a closet psycho on turf he doesn't know, because there's nothing closet about that tosser, apart from his gayness.'

Whether Bennett really was a closet gay, Blake had no idea, nor did he care. All he knew was that, like Matt, he was having a hard time working out why

Bennett might have gone to the bother of tracking him to Kesterly.

It wasn't that Rowzee had been expecting anything different. Ever since she'd first gone to the doctor, several months ago, she'd had a feeling the outcome wasn't going to be good. Because of how often the headaches were recurring, especially in the mornings, and the odd little blackouts – absence attacks she now knew they were called – she'd been sent off to see a specialist at the Kesterly Infirmary. In turn he'd recommended she see a colleague of his at St Mary's in London. So, off she'd popped for a biopsy, telling her family she was meeting some old friends to catch a couple of shows and do a spot of shopping. She hadn't enjoyed the procedure much, but who would enjoy having a drill buzzing through their skull?

Anyway, there had been so many comings and goings over it all that she'd lost track now of how many tests, inconclusive results and call-backs she'd been through. Throughout it all a horrible sixth sense had kept on warning her that the outcome wasn't going to be good, so as though to wrong-foot it, or to show it who was in charge, she'd started looking into a one-way trip to a Swiss clinic.

That was all very well when the threat was still fiction; now the worst had been confirmed she was in a state of total shock, fear and disbelief.

'I'm really sorry, Mrs C,' her doctor Jilly had said yesterday evening, 'but this tumour in your brain is a secondary cancer.'

'Secondary?' Rowzee had echoed, stunned. 'So where's the primary?'

'We don't know that yet, but it's showing as a melanoma and obviously we'll be trying to find the source. What's important for now is that the tumour we know about is treated.'

Rowzee stiffened. 'But it's a secondary, so that means there's no cure?'

Jilly didn't deny it, but she did go on to say quite a lot of things Rowzee hadn't fully taken in. Something about checking for moles to find the primary, further tests, different treatments . . .

Having no idea how she'd got through the night without alerting Pamela's suspicions, or without going to pieces, Rowzee had started today by summoning every last acting skill she possessed to help her go forward. She still wasn't sure what her plan was – Dignitas would obviously have to play a part at some point, though she hadn't gone back to their website yet. In truth she could hardly even think about them without wanting to sob like a child and beg God to turn it all into a horrible dream she could wake up from.

For no particular reason she'd brought herself to the Seafront Café this afternoon, where she now sat drinking a cup of tea while gazing absently out at the glorious summer day. She was reflecting on what bad luck it was that her cancer had started out life as a melanoma when her sun-worshipping days were decades behind her. Was it possible it had flared into early action during those crazy times when she'd coated herself in olive oil to catch as many rays as the hot sun

108

could provide? It was scary indeed to think that the slow burn might have been going on all these years without any bleeding or unsightly moles to give itself away. Of course, she could be wrong, it might have started much later, but even so, it had managed to secrete itself away somewhere around her body and they still didn't know where it was – apart from in her brain, of course.

Apparently she was lucky not to have suffered more severe symptoms by now such as seizures (the absence attacks were a mild form of seizure), loss of balance and cognitive confusion . . . She couldn't remember what else, but not to worry, she had it all to look forward to, and Jilly would no doubt provide reminders if she asked. She remembered Jilly telling her that the neurosurgeon's team were working on a treatment plan for her, even though it had already been decided that the tumour was inoperable. So what she was most likely facing was a dose of radiotherapy and maybe chemo further down the line, by which time there was every chance she'd be gaga.

Jilly hadn't actually said that, of course, but Rowzee wasn't stupid, she knew what 'a certain degree of mental incapacitation' meant, most of her year nine students would know that, some even had it. Even if she wasn't completely doolally, she was likely to have speech difficulties, hearing and sight impairment, and her motor skills were also going to suffer. Once again Jilly hadn't gone into that sort of detail, Rowzee had found it all online last night before Pamela had come home from one of her mysterious dates.

So she was going to die. (She had to say it to herself like that, because beating around the bush wasn't going to get her anywhere.) Anyway, everyone was going to die, sooner or later. However, for her it was definitely going to be sooner – in fact much sooner than the medical team knew. This was because, once she'd summoned the courage, she was fully intending to contact Dignitas and take matters into her own hands. After all, what was the point of dragging this out, getting her head fried and zapped and whatever else they were planning, making her family miserable and scared, putting them to the trouble of ferrying her about for treatments she didn't want to have when they had their own lives to be getting on with? And she didn't even want to think about the kind of a nurse Pamela would make, giving injections and changing pooey pads. She'd do it, of course, and with a great deal of love, because Rowzee didn't doubt for a minute that Pamela loved her, but fear of losing Rowzee would be certain to turn Pamela into a jabbering monster.

Besides, she didn't want to get in the way of Pamela's Internet dating. (Rowzee didn't actually know for certain it was happening yet, but given the evidence so far she'd stake what was the rest of her life on it.) It would be a great weight off her mind if Pamela were to meet a lovely man of around sixty, with a lively sense of humour and very thick skin, to enjoy her twilight years with.

*Bill Simmonds was just that man, if only Pamela could see it.*

Pulling her notebook and cup of tea closer, Rowzee began jotting down reminders – forgetfulness was one of her symptoms, so she'd just bought this rather smart leather-bound book as her aide-memoire. After writing 'Open Pamela's eyes to Bill' she turned her thoughts to Graeme.

Of course, he was a very capable man with a successful business, a healthy outlook on the world and, at forty-eight, plenty of years left in his allotted span. He certainly wouldn't want her worrying about him. In fact, it would probably make him quite cross, but for her own sake, if not for his, she'd like to see him settled with a lovely, deserving woman before she, Rowzee, turned up her toes. Andee Lawrence would fit the bill perfectly if she weren't married to someone else. Such a pity that, because when Rowzee had first heard about Graeme's relationship with the detective, as Andee had been back then, she'd had very high hopes of it. After all, he was a bit of a detective himself, searching out antiques for clients and putting together the history of the piece or pieces. So they had that in common; they also spoke the same language, which wasn't to be sneezed at, they lived in the same town and their children were around the same age. Added to that Rowzee couldn't imagine Andee, or indeed any woman, not loving the idea of spending time in Italy over the coming years with someone as splendid as Graeme. He'd promised to take Rowzee and Pamela to stay at his villa when it was fully renovated – they'd seen the ramshackle place it was now when he'd flown them over for a viewing, followed by a fortnight's holiday in a lovely hotel. It saddened Rowzee immensely to think that she probably wasn't going to see the finished version, but she tried bolstering herself with the reminder that in the grand scheme of things it was hardly important.

What was very important was how she moved forward from here, and since the Dignitas brochure was already saved (unread) in a secret file on her computer, she should probably start giving some thought to her will. It should all be very straightforward – the house to Pamela, who would of course make sure it was passed on to Katie and Lucie when she fell off her perch (so many euphemisms for dying, and she expected she was going to learn a lot more before she bought the farm, ha ha). Victor's desk to Graeme, according to Victor's wishes, and all royalties from Victor's books to Katie and Lucie, again Victor's wishes. Rowzee's investments, jewellery and cash in the bank would also go to the girls, and various other bits and pieces to dear friends such as Gina Stamfield, Charles's wife.

That was how it should go; however nothing was ever quite as straightforward as a person would like it to be, and this was no exception, because she felt duty bound to sort out Victor's unfinished business before she hopped the twig. She'd better make a note of that too lest she should forget.

'Victor's unfinished business', she wrote.

'Rowzee?'

Rowzee blinked and looked up. She'd been so absorbed in her little world that she'd completely forgotten she was at the Seafront Café.

112

'Andee,' she exclaimed, shocked, confused, as if she were in a dream, but finally managing to put on one of her brightest smiles. 'How lovely to see you. Do you have time for a cuppa?'

'As a matter of fact I have,' Andee replied, sliding into the opposite bench. She peered at Rowzee closely. 'How are you?' she asked carefully.

Feigning surprise Rowzee cried, 'Me? I'm fighting fit, top form, never felt better.' She was overdoing it, needed to calm down. 'And how are you?' she asked gently.

'I'm fine,' Andee assured her. 'I was passing and saw you in the window and thought, wouldn't it be lovely if you were looking for company.'

Imagining herself through Andee's eyes (blotchy face, hair on end), Rowzee the actress declared, delightedly, 'I certainly am, and we've got the place more or less to ourselves, thanks to the sun coming out at last. Everyone's on the beach I expect, and who can blame them? My oh my, all the rain we've had these past few days. Let's hope that's it now for the rest of the summer.'

'Indeed. Peppermint tea,' Andee told the waitress.

'And a cake?' Rowzee suggested mischievously.

Andee looked about to say no, but thrilled Rowzee to bits when she offered to share one.

'Oh yes!' Rowzee enthused. 'You choose.'

'Coffee and walnut?'

'Perfect.'

As the waitress disappeared, Rowzee leaned forward and spoke quietly, in spite of there being no one close enough to overhear. 'This is quite a coincidence,' she confided, 'because I was just thinking about you.'

Andee's eyebrows rose. 'What can I have done to deserve such an honour?' she asked drily.

Realising she couldn't spill out the truth without embarrassing them both, Rowzee quickly rethought. 'I was wondering,' she said, 'if you've been able to give Blake any news.'

Sighing, Andee said, 'I'm still waiting for a couple of calls. Hopefully I'll have more to tell him then. Can I take it you know Jessica's mother?'

'Oh yes, we got to know the whole family quite well very soon after they moved here. Jenny used to help out in the shop from time to time. She was a quiet little thing, even then – what happened up north, I'm sure you know about that, had affected her badly. She told me once that it was the way some of their friends had reacted that had hurt the most. She felt betrayed, she said, and horribly belittled and didn't feel she could trust anyone afterwards. And she was angry with Blake for getting them into such an impossible situation, even though she knew it wasn't his fault.'

'Did she ever believe the boy's claims?' Andee ventured.

'No, I'm sure she didn't, nor did the children. I'm afraid I've come across plenty of youngsters like that over the years, and there really isn't any controlling them. You try, of course, but at the same time you have to be very careful not to end up on the wrong side of them, as Blake found out to his cost.'

'I guess,' Andee said gravely, 'that he's lucky they didn't attack him physically.'

Rowzee said, 'Yes very lucky, but it still . . . It stiiiill, still . . .' The words had got jammed.

Andee was watching her closely. 'Rowzee, are you all right?' she asked.

Rowzee nodded.

Andee was speaking again, but Rowzee couldn't make out what she was saying.

Then, as though she'd risen up from under the water, everything cleared. 'I'm sorry,' she said breathily. 'It was just one of my funny turns.' She was dabbing her mouth with a napkin in case she'd dribbled.

'But are you OK? I thought you were going to pass out on me.'

'Or have a stroke?' Rowzee grinned, wondering if both sides of her mouth had made it. It felt as though they had so she was going to trust to it. 'Please don't mention anything to Pamela or Graeme if you see them,' she urged. 'They'll only worry and there's really no need. It's just a little dizzy spell that comes and goes.'

'Have you seen a doctor?'

'Yes, yes, and I'm being prescribed a course of treatment. Now, where were we? Oh yes, I was thinking to myself before you arrived what a shame it was that things didn't work out between you and Graeme. Am I allowed to ask why that was? You strike me as being very well suited.'

The way Andee regarded her seemed slightly bemused, causing Rowzee to wonder if she'd said something awry, but in the end Andee said, 'Martin, my children's father, came back and I, as mothers often do, put my children's needs first.'

Rowzee sighed as she thought of Edward and how she still longed for him to come first. 'Oh yes, mothers often do that,' she agreed. 'Came back from where?'

'The Middle East, and actually it was for his father's funeral, not for me, although he insists it was. He'd taken some time out of our relationship. He wanted to explore another kind of world that didn't involve being a father and live-in partner, so for two years we were left to fend for ourselves while he went off to find himself. Then he decided it was us he wanted after all, and like a fool I took him back and married him.'

Encouraged by the sound of that, Rowzee echoed, 'Like a fool?'

'It was the wrong thing to do, and now I'm upsetting everyone, including myself, by trying to break away. I don't want to be with him, but I don't want to hurt him either.'

'Oh dear, I can see that's not easy. Does he know about Graeme? I mean, is there anything to know? I'm sorry if I'm being nosy, you don't have to answer if you don't want to.'

Andee smiled. 'He knows I was seeing Graeme while we were apart, but there isn't any more than that to know now.'

Though Rowzee was sorry for Martin, the children too, because they'd obviously be upset about their parents breaking up, she couldn't help feeling pleased for Graeme, since there could be a chance for him and Andee after all.

The question was, how could she make it happen?

'Will you excuse me?' Andee said as her mobile rang. 'I ought to take this. Actually, it's Charles, your neighbour.'

'Oh do send him my love,' Rowzee insisted, and waving her on she opened up her notebook, needing to record what she'd just learned to make sure she didn't forget it.

By the time Andee's call ended Rowzee's book was closed and a pot of tea had arrived with a giant slice of cake and two forks. As they began tucking in, Rowzee said, 'How is Charles? You know, we haven't seen him since the party. Did he go back to London?'

'No, apparently he's in Dartmouth visiting Gina, but he's coming back tomorrow.'

'Dartmouth? So that's where she is. I wonder what she's doing there? Maybe she's in a play. Let's hope she comes back with Charles tomorrow, it's been a long time since I last saw her.'

'Me too,' Andee responded. 'Alayna spent some time with her back last year when she was doing some work experience at the Royal Court.'

'Oh yes, I remember that. Gina does a lot there. It's one of her favourite theatres. We did a play together once, you know?'

Andee's eyes sparkled. 'You and Gina? I'd like to have seen that. What was it?'

Rowzee frowned as she tried to remember. 'It was a two-hander,' she said, 'and she played the charac-ter of Ruth who's a successful writer, and I was her protégée . . . No, it was the other way round, of course,

117

because I'm the eldest. Goodness, what was it called? It started out in America, but it was on in the West End for a while. Helen What's-her-name . . . Mirren, was in it then. Gina and I had such fun doing it here in Kesterly, and we couldn't have been bad because we ended up doing a mini-tour of the West Country. Of course it was her everyone came to see. We even did three nights at the Bristol Old Vic. *Collected Stories*, that's what it was called. Imagine me forgetting that. Imagine me on the stage with Gina Stamfield! It's an experience I shall never forget.'

*Well not yet, anyway.*

Andee was smiling fondly. 'Have the last piece of cake,' she insisted, pushing it towards her. 'And maybe we can do this again sometime.'

'I'd like that very much. Let's be sure to make it soon.'

A little while later, after hugging each other goodbye in the street, Rowzee remained on the corner watching Andee walk off down the promenade. Only when Andee had disappeared from view did she cross over to the taxi rank.

No one had suggested taking her driving licence away yet, but she knew it would happen, so she'd decided to start getting used to doing without her car. Her family were probably going to find it a bit odd that she wasn't driving, but they didn't have to know too much about it. She could do the grocery shopping online, walk down the hill to get the bus into town, and insist on taking taxis whenever they went out so she could have some wine. Of course, they weren't stupid, they'd soon realise something was up and if she was forced to tell them she knew they'd never let her refuse treatment, much less even consider making a one-way trip to Zurich.

Was she really going to do that? Was she absolutely serious about it?

Yes, she was. How could she not be if the alternative was being sentenced to the misery of chemotherapy with no chance of a cure, turning slowly and humiliatingly into a vegetable, becoming a terrible burden on her family? Faced with those choices the decision wasn't hard to make, it was only the courage to see it through that she had to find. And time wasn't exactly on her side – Dignitas wouldn't take her if they considered her mentally incapacitated – so if she wanted everything properly sorted before she went over there, she'd better start getting on with it.

Blake was standing between two art nouveau cabinets, hidden from outside view, watching Tyler Bennett pretending to look at a collection of bronze and silver statuettes in the window. The collar of his denim jacket was turned up against the sudden downpour, and his head was down, but the razored carroty hair, the stance, the piercings in one ear, gave him away.

What the hell did he want?

Blake's eyes went briefly to Graeme's niece Katie, who was busy with a collector of walking canes; Graeme himself had popped out.

Keeping an eye on Bennett who seemed to be watching Katie and her client, Blake sank more deeply into the shadows, skirted a triform harpist's seat and disappeared into the workshop. He moved quickly, out into the cobbled lane cluttered with dustbins and parked cars, along to Marsh Street, and up around the block on to the square.

Bennett was still outside the shop, his back half turned towards Blake's casual approach.

There were plenty of people about, in spite of the rain. Music was blasting out of a café, a human statue was giving up and heading for the arcade.

Blake was only inches from Bennett when the boy caught his reflection in the window and took off like a hare.

'Stop him! Stop that boy!' Blake shouted, sprinting after him.

Several people looked, startled, but no one stepped in.

Blake pressed on. He was close, so close. His hand closed around Bennett's shoulder, grabbed his jacket, pulled him back, almost to the ground.

'What the . . .!' Bennett spluttered, as Blake tried to spin him round.

Seizing the boy's arm, Blake wrenched it behind his back so hard he almost had him off the ground.

'Get off me! Get off me!' Bennett howled.

Looking at no one, Blake shoved the boy's head down and marched him back towards the shop, too fired up to feel surprised at the lack of fight.

'You're a nutter, you are,' Bennett cried. 'I haven't done nothing to you. Tell him to let me go,' he shouted at an elderly couple who'd stopped to scowl in their direction.

'Blake? What's going on?' Graeme asked, about to enter the shop himself.

'It's him,' Blake said breathlessly. 'The scumbag who screwed up our lives.'

Frowning, Graeme looked at the boy and back at Blake. 'What's he doing here?' he asked.

'Good question,' and shoving Bennett in through the shop's front door Blake spun him around roughly, ready to lay into him again if he as much as attempted an escape.

'I don't know what your problem is,' Bennett muttered, brushing himself down.

Blake blinked in confusion. It was like an optical illusion. He had no idea who this youth was, only that he wasn't Tyler Bennett. 'Who the hell are *you*?' he exploded.

'It's me what should be asking you that,' the boy retorted testily.

'This isn't him?' Graeme asked Blake.

'What's going on?' Katie wanted to know.

'This . . . This *person*,' Blake said angrily, 'has been hanging around the shop and I want to know why.'

'I haven't done nothing wrong,' the lad protested. 'It's a free world. I can look in any shop I want.'

'Then why did you run away every time you saw me coming?'

The boy's rugged face turned crimson. 'I wasn't running away,' he argued. 'I was in a hurry.'

Wondering if excuses got any lamer, Blake said, 'We both know you were running away, so what's going on? Did Tyler Bennett send you? Are you related to him?'

121

'Who?'

He looked so gormless, so completely mystified, that Blake turned to Graeme in despair.

Realising he needed to take over, Graeme asked the boy if he was looking for something or someone in particular. 'Is that why you're watching the shop?'

The way the boy shrugged surprised both Blake and Graeme, since it seemed to suggest that Graeme wasn't far off the mark.

'What's your name?' Graeme ventured. 'I'm Graeme, by the way, and this is Blake.'

Scowling at Blake, the lad said, 'My name's Jason.'

'OK, Jason,' Graeme responded, putting a friendly hand on the boy's shoulder, 'are you from around here?'

'No.'

'Then what brings you to Kesterly?'

'That's my business.'

'Where are you from, Jason?' Katie asked kindly.

He regarded her warily, but his manner wasn't hostile as he said, 'It doesn't matter.'

She seemed to mull that for a moment. 'No, I don't suppose it does,' she agreed, 'but I've seen you out on the square a few times lately, and you definitely seem to be focusing on this shop. Do we have something of yours, maybe? Something that might have belonged to one of your family?'

He shook his head.

'OK, so why don't you tell us who or what you're looking for?' Katie encouraged. 'We won't be able to help you if you don't.'

Seeming to acknowledge that, Jason wiped his mouth with a sleeve as he said, 'It's not any of you.'

'I think we've managed to work that out,' she murmured. 'Is it someone who used to work here, maybe? If you give us a name I'm sure we'll be able to help you find them.'

Looking at Graeme, his cagey, light brown eyes glistening with uncertainty, he said, 'Are you the Graeme what owns this shop?'

'I am,' Graeme confirmed.

'So you're her brother?'

Graeme frowned.

'Does the name Sean Griffiths mean anything to you?' the boy asked.

Graeme shook his head. 'Should it?'

'Yeah, as a matter of fact it should, but if you haven't . . .' He shrugged and looked at the others. In the end he said to Graeme, 'I'll tell you, all right, but no one else.'

As Graeme led the boy into his office for some privacy Blake and Katie watched, as intrigued as they were wary, until finally Blake returned to the workshop to call Andee.

'I got the wrong person,' he told her when she answered. 'The boy who's been watching the shop? It's not Tyler Bennett.'

'No,' she replied. 'I've just heard back from the Manchester police. Bennett's serving time for aggravated assault.'

123

Not surprised, only relieved, he said, 'Sorry for wasting your time. It seems it's not only Jess I'm seeing everywhere . . .'

'It's OK, no need to apologise. Everything's always worth following up. I had another long chat with Sadie this morning, Jess's friend from uni. She still wasn't able to tell me anything we don't already know, but I'll ask you the same as I asked her. When you gave the police a list of Jessica's friends are you absolutely sure you didn't leave anyone out? Maybe there's someone she mentioned only once, in passing . . .'

'I'll talk to Matt again,' he said, 'but we've been over it a hundred times. We told the police everything we know. I swear there's no one else.'

'OK, but keep thinking and we'll get together tomorrow. I'd like to talk to your wife as well. Is she due back any time soon?'

'I don't think so, but I can text you her number in Devon.'

After ringing off Blake picked up his tools and returned to work. He was still thrown by the events of the past half-hour, though grateful that the boy hadn't turned out to be Tyler Bennett. Thank God that part of his life was behind him now; he just hoped with all his heart that one day soon he'd be able to say the same about Jessica's disappearance.

It was early evening by now and Andee was walking into the flat as her mobile rang. Seeing it was Graeme she didn't hesitate to click on. 'Hi, what can I do for you?' she asked, feeling guilty for sounding more upbeat than she'd have managed had it been Martin or Alayna. They wouldn't have wanted her to sound in good spirits, of course, they'd far rather think she was suffering for what she was doing to them – which she was.

'If it's not too much trouble,' Graeme said, 'there's something I'd like to run past you.'

'Of course, be my guest.' She pulled open the fridge, saw a bottle of chilled wine and felt her spirits lifting even higher. Just what she needed.

'Actually, it's a slightly delicate matter,' he confided, 'so I was hoping we could meet.'

Immediately intrigued, she said, 'Would you like me to come to the shop?'

'Would you mind coming to my home?'

Remembering the nineteenth-century town house backing on to the Botanical Gardens, she said, 'Are you still in the same place?'

'I am. I'm sure you already have plans for this evening, so would sometime tomorrow suit?'

Though she didn't have any plans for this evening at all, she said, 'That should be fine, but it'll have to be later in the day, if that's OK.'

'You tell me a time.'

She suggested five and said, 'Is it about Jessica, by any chance?'

'No,' he replied, 'it's about a young lad called Jason and my sister, Rowzee.'

# Chapter Eight

Charles was in the spacious, high-ceilinged library of Burlingford Hall waiting for Andee to arrive. A table was set on the veranda with a flask of hot coffee, a pitcher of chilled lemonade and a plate of home-made biscuits. The veranda on this, the north-west side of the hall, offered a stunning view of the parterre, a feature of the gardens that did as much to pull in the week-end visitors as the many gazebos, follies, footbridges, lakes and orchards. It was where Bill Simmonds was currently busy trimming borders.

Charles felt deeply indebted to the man for staying on after his retirement. They'd known each other for a very long time, more than thirty years, since Bill had worked for Charles's father, starting out as an apprentice gardener, and going on, over time, to become chief landscaper. It was Bill and his son, Micky, who'd restored and expanded the magnificent parterre before Bill had taken over as estate manager, a position he'd held for the last ten years prior to his retirement.

In many ways Charles still saw him as that, though Micky and his hard-working crew were running the place these days, and doing a grand job of it too. Bill just popped in now and again, which seemed to be most days as far as Charles could tell, to tidy things up, mow the lawns, inspect the trees and keep a general eye on things. Charles had long realised that these sixty-two acres spreading widely and ruggedly at the outer reaches up to the moor probably felt as much like home to Bill as they did to any of the Stamfield family. Perhaps even more so, for Bill would certainly know them better, considering how well he'd taken care of them over the years, and it was obvious that he enjoyed eavesdropping on the visitors' admiration of the gardens at the weekends.

Noticing Andee stopping her car to have a quick chat with the old fellow, Charles strode out on to the veranda ready to greet her. 'Andee,' he smiled, pulling her in to an embrace as she came up the steps to join him. 'May I say how wonderfully fresh you're looking on this dreadfully humid day?'

'You may,' she twinkled, 'but I can assure you I don't feel it.' She stepped back to get a good look at him. 'Is everything all right?' she asked cautiously. 'I didn't want to say anything at the party, but you seemed tired, or worried? And I've heard through the grapevine that you haven't been well.'

'I'm fine,' he assured her, waving her to a chair, 'but I will admit to having had a few issues with the old ticker over the past year or so, which managed to keep me away from Burlingford.'

He knew she must be thinking that Burlingford would surely be the perfect place for convalescence, but she was too polite to say so.

'Is everything sorted now?' she asked.

'More or less.' He suddenly realised that asking for her help was going to be even harder than he'd imagined, and now he wasn't sure he could go through with it. In fact, it was starting to feel like a crazy idea even to have considered it. 'Tell me about you,' he said, pouring two glasses of lemonade and passing one over. 'How's Martin? I'd like to catch up with him while I'm here.'

'He'd like that,' she replied. 'I know you two always got along, but I guess now is as good a time as any to tell you that we're no longer together.'

Charles felt genuinely sorry, but perhaps not as surprised as he might have expected. 'Please don't tell me he's gone off to find himself again. I thought he was over that.'

'No, it's me who's left this time. It only happened a couple of weeks ago, so it's still early days, but I won't be going back.'

Realising this was probably harder for her than she was allowing to show, he said, 'You know, if there's anything I can do . . .'

'Thank you. We'll be fine, eventually, I'm sure.' Smiling, she raised her glass in a salute and took a sip. 'What about you and Gina?' she prompted. 'Is she still in Dartmouth?'

'She will be for a while. A friend of hers, Anna Shelley, I expect you've heard of her, has an art gallery there and Gina's agreed to look after it while Anna's touring the Middle East with a production of *King Lear*. Actually, we popped over to the Isle of Wight for a couple of days which I think she enjoyed.'

'Only think?'

He smiled. 'No, I know she enjoyed it. We went to a special exhibition of Julia Margaret Cameron's work. The Victorian photographer?'

'I can't say I've heard of her, but I can see it's something that would appeal to Gina. So how is she?'

Charles found himself nodding before answering. 'Good, in herself,' he finally replied, 'but I guess not so good either.'

Andee frowned. 'Please don't tell me the cancer's come back. I thought she'd been given the all-clear.'

'She was, yes, almost six years ago now, so that's certainly something to feel thankful for. She misses Lydia, our daughter.'

Andee blinked in surprise. 'I remember who Lydia is.'

He laughed. 'Of course. She's currently kicking up a storm over Syrian war crimes and making quite a name for herself with the media because of how passionately and eloquently she presents her cases, I quote. Not her, the *New York Times*. We can't help feeling proud of her.'

'You and Gina have done a lot for human rights yourselves over the years, so it's not hard to see where Lydia gets it from. It's OK,' she said, glancing at her phone as it rang, 'I don't need to take it.'

'If it's urgent . . .'

'It's not, I promise.'

As she turned it off, he changed the subject with a gentle sigh. 'So you and Martin are no more.'

'Please don't let's talk about that,' she protested. 'I want to hear about you and whatever it is you'd like my thoughts on.'

His insides tensed. He shouldn't have mentioned it at the party, should never even have considered involving her when no possible good could come of it, for either of them. 'Actually, it's nothing really,' he said dismissively. 'I don't need to bother you with it.'

'It won't be a bother. Why don't you try me?'

He was certain he wouldn't, and yet was so desperate that maybe he had to. After all, what else was he going to do, who else was there to turn to?

As his eyes went to hers he found her regarding him in the way that had always made him wonder if she was reading his mind. Taking a breath, he made sure to keep his tone light as he said, 'I know when someone talks about a friend being in trouble that they're almost always talking about themselves . . . Well in this instance it really is a friend, but because of who he is, his connections, his position . . .' He glanced down at his glass. 'He's being blackmailed and I was wondering if there might be some way of finding out, very discreetly, who's behind it.'

She appeared neither shocked nor suspicious, but he knew better than to assume that he'd convinced her they weren't talking about him.

'My first question,' she said carefully, 'has to be, what is your friend being blackmailed about?'

His smile was brief. 'And you know I can't tell you that.'

She nodded. 'OK, so let's begin with how this blackmailer is making contact.'

'By Royal Mail, I'm told. No emails or texts, I guess because they're traceable.'

She didn't disagree. 'Have you seen any of the notes? Are they typed, cut-out newsprint, handwritten even?'

'Typed, I believe.'

'And has your friend met any of the demands?'

'He has.'

'And how is he getting the funds to the blackmailer?'

'In cash, to a Post Office box number. Apparently the town or city has changed each time.'

'I see. Then I'm afraid that tracing this person without knowing the full story is going to be extremely difficult.'

Though he'd expected this answer, he felt crushed by it anyway.

'Tell me,' she said, 'has your friend confided in you? Do *you* know what it's about?'

He nodded. 'I had to know.'

'*Had* to know?'

His head was starting to spin. 'It doesn't matter,' he replied, dabbing his face with a napkin and watching Bill take off across the south lawn on his quad bike. 'Gosh, it really is humid today.'

She was still watching him in that knowing way of hers. 'Charles, I surely don't have to remind you that you can trust me,' she said softly.

He attempted a smile. 'Of course not, but it isn't my secret to share.'

'Then why don't you have a talk with your friend and see if you can persuade him to talk to me himself?'

'What on earth are you doing?' Pamela demanded, finding Rowzee on the terrace trying to attract Bill

Simmonds's attention as he emerged from the estate's apple orchard that bordered their garden.

'I want to have a go on his mower,' Rowzee informed her. 'It looks such fun.'

Pamela regarded her askance. 'I sometimes wonder if you're right in the head,' she commented.

Rowzee laughed. 'Wonder no more, it's official, I'm absolutely not right in the head.'

'Mm, that is definitely true if you're fancying *him*.'

Rowzee's eyes widened. 'Who said anything about *me* fancying him?'

'Well I certainly don't, if that's what you're implying, and if you ask me, it's the real reason you want to have a go on his mower. You ought to be careful he doesn't think it's a euphemism and start thinking you're after his body.'

Finding that hilarious, Rowzee went to hug her.

Laughing too, Pamela said, 'Ssh, he's on his way over.'

They watched as Bill Simmonds strode unhurriedly across their lawn looking, Rowzee decided, a bit like John Wayne in *The Quiet Man*. Or maybe he was more like Gary Cooper. Whoever, he was a very striking man in his all-male, rugged sort of way; he just needed a gun on his hip and spurs on his boots to make him the complete film-star package.

'Hello ladies,' he called out in his gruff West Country accent. 'Inviting me over for a cup of tea, are you?'

Rowzee cried, 'Absolutely.'

'Not,' Pamela finished. 'We'll never get rid of him,' she muttered to Rowzee.

'Who wants to?' Rowzee muttered back. 'I'll go and put the kettle on.'

Clearly not wanting to be left alone with her unwelcome admirer, Pamela followed her inside.

'Pretty hot today, innit?' Bill sighed, removing his battered hat as he came to the open door.

Here was someone with all his own hair and teeth, Rowzee was thinking, if Pamela could just get over herself. 'Would you rather have a cold drink?' she offered.

'As you like,' he responded, fixing his arresting blue eyes on Pamela. 'So what were you waving out to me for?' he asked her.

Affronted, she snapped, 'It wasn't me. It was her.'

With a wink at Rowzee, he said, 'Oh and there was me thinking me luck had changed.'

Pamela blazed as Rowzee choked on a laugh.

'She wants to have a go on your mower,' Pamela told him haughtily, and the next instant she and Rowzee erupted into laughter.

Clearly enjoying their amusement, he said, 'Of course she can have a go. You both can, any time you like.'

Afraid they might be getting out of control, Rowzee managed to gasp, 'I'm sorry, Bill. We're being very silly. It must be the sun getting to us.'

'Nothing wrong with that,' he told them, taking out his mobile as it rang. 'Micky,' he said into it, 'your timing's not great, son. I'm with two lovely ladies who are about to give me a cup of tea. You're right, I am talking about Rowzee and Pamela. No, I haven't asked them anything yet . . . You just mind your own business and get on with whatever you're ringing about.'

As he listened he wandered outside, leaving Rowzee to make the tea and Pamela to say, 'I wonder what he wants to ask us.'

Amused by her sister's intrigued tone, Rowzee said, 'I'm sure we'll find out when he's ready.'

Turning away sharply as Bill caught her looking his way, Pamela said, 'You'll be far more interested than I am. Now I need to get going or I'll be late for my next appointment. By the way, I should be finished early tonight if you feel like going out somewhere.'

Rowzee thought about it and decided that, yes, she did. 'Shall I book Luigi's?' she suggested, following Pamela to the front door. 'We always like their penne arrabiata.'

'OK. Let's meet there at seven.'

Remembering that meant she'd have to drive, Rowzee said, 'I think I'll spring for a taxi so we can travel home together.'

'You mean so you can have that extra glass of wine. OK, do as you like. Just don't bring the gardener,' and picking up her briefcase and handbag she went off to the car.

'I won't mind if you bring a date,' Rowzee called after her.

'Where am I going to get a date?' Pamela called back. 'And please don't . . .'

'The Internet?' Rowzee cut in quickly. 'Everyone's doing it these days.'

'Ah, so that's what you've been busying yourself with lately. You need to be careful, there are all sorts of weirdos signing up to meet people that way. And

I know what you're like, you'll end up on some big mean daddy website featuring whips and masks and God only knows what else without even realising what it is.'

'Is there such a site?' Rowzee asked, fascinated. 'What do big mean daddies do with all that stuff?'

Refusing to rise to it, Pamela got into her car, blew Rowzee a kiss and drove away.

Finding Bill sitting in the shade of the terrace, fanning himself with his hat, and no longer on the phone, Rowzee put down a tray of tea and sank into another chair. 'It's a beautiful day, isn't it?' she murmured, enjoying the warmth of the air as it wafted in from the distant sea.

'It is that,' he agreed, swiping away a fly.

They continued to sit in companionable silence, soaking up the gentle sounds of nature, until Rowzee remembered what he'd said to his son on the phone. 'What haven't you asked us yet?' she prompted.

He grinned and laughed, and she noted that yes, he definitely had all his own teeth, and very nice they were too. 'That's between me and Micky,' he replied, 'but I reckon I could tell you too. I'm after asking that lovely sister of yours out on a date.'

Thrilled by the idea, Rowzee was about to give a cheer of delight when a wave of dizziness swooped over her.

'Mm, you don't think she'll go for it?' he grunted, as she put a hand to her head.

That wasn't what she wanted to say. She wanted to encourage him, tell him he was right to pursue Pamela, that she thought they were a great match even though

135

Pamela might be playing hard to get, but the words wouldn't come.

'Are you all right?' he asked worriedly. 'You're looking a bit . . . strange.'

'I'm fine,' she mumbled. The garden, the sky seemed to be swaying, and nothing sounded right.

'I'll get you some water,' he decided, and kicking off his boots he tramped into the kitchen.

He was back in moments with a large glass filled to the brim and a cool, wet towel to put on her forehead. 'Sit back,' he instructed. 'Take it easy. A little bit of sunstroke, I expect. Nothing to worry about.'

'No, nothing to worry about,' she croaked, relieved to have got the words out. 'Thank you,' she added as he handed her the water.

He returned to his chair and gazed quietly out at the garden where butterflies were hovering over the wildflower borders and a pair of great tits with splendid yellow chests and busy beaks were pecking away at a feeder.

She loved the way he wasn't fussing her, while clearly knowing she wasn't herself; it made him seem so capable, and *there*, while she felt more strongly than ever that she should get him together with Pamela before she went.

However, for the moment, afraid this little episode might get worse before it passed, she said, 'If you don't mind, Bill, I think I'll go and have a lie-down.'

'Of course not,' he replied, and getting to his feet he held out a hand to help her up. 'Is there anything I can get you before I go?'

'I'll be fine,' she assured him, hearing the musical notes of a text arriving in her phone.

'OK, well you know where I am if you need me, and any time you want to have a go on the mower, it'll be my pleasure.'

Smiling, she watched him walk down the steps to the lawn.

'If you get the chance,' he said, turning back, 'maybe you'll put in a word for me with Pamela.'

With mischief in her heart, she said, 'Happily. If you tell me what it is that attracts you to her, maybe I could start with that.'

His head cocked to one side as he thought. 'Well, I guess I'm taken by the way she sometimes seems to miss her mouth with her lipstick. You know, when it goes all smudgy. It makes her very kissable.'

Unable not to laugh, Rowzee decided she might not repeat that.

'Oh, and there's the way she doesn't quite fit her clothes, like she's going to burst right out of them and give us all a splendid surprise.'

Knowing she wouldn't be repeating that either, Rowzee waved him off and went inside to check her phone. There turned out to be two texts waiting: the first, from her niece Lucie, lit up her world. *Would it be possible for you to take care of Teddy when we go to Spain?*

Rowzee didn't even hesitate. Looking after Teddy the Wheaten Terrier, taking him to the beach for long walks, or around the Burlingford Estate, or even into town to dog-friendly cafés, was one of her greatest pleasures.

The message saying *Yes, yes and yes* had already gone before she saw the reminder of her appointment at the doctor's tomorrow.

Was she going to be fit enough to take proper care of Teddy? And how was she going to ferry him around if she couldn't drive her car? He was very boisterous and inquisitive and loved nothing more than to go off exploring or to meet other dogs. What if she had one of her absence attacks while they were out and she ended up losing him? She simply couldn't bear that to happen, but she'd already said yes now, so how was she going to get out of it without raising suspicion and causing concern?

It was a blasted nuisance, this tumour. If she knew how to cut it out herself she jolly well would, but apparently even the experts couldn't do that. So instead of whingeing to herself about it, she decided that she'd better go and prepare for her appointment with Jilly. It probably wasn't going to be easy convincing her dear ex-student, now marvellous GP, that all she wanted from here on was something to help ease the symptoms for a while, so she could get done everything that needed to be done while she still had the marbles to do it.

'So, how much do you believe in the friend?' Helen Hall was asking Andee as their pre-lunch drinks were served.

Andee shook her head slowly as she went back over her conversation with Charles, trying to fathom where her instincts had been then, and where they were now.

She and Helen were seated at a window table of the grandly named Palme d'Or restaurant, newly opened on the first floor of the Kesterly Royal Hotel overlooking the bay. Since it was lunchtime, and the day was hot, tempting everyone on to the beach, it was less crowded than it might have been, but there were still several people around that both women knew. Helen, a petite, pale-skinned woman in her late forties with a shock of dark red hair and shrewd green eyes, was one of the town's more prominent lawyers so was particularly well known. She was also a good friend of Andee's and, in a sense, her employer, since she'd lately taken Andee up on an offer to help out with cases that should have been qualifying for legal aid, but thanks to all the cutbacks weren't.

'It's hard to imagine Charles doing anything that he could be blackmailed for,' Andee said, once the waiter had gone, 'which sounds naïve, of course, but you know him as well as I do. How easy would you find it to cast him in the role of a villain?'

Sipping a cranberry soda, Helen said, 'He doesn't have to be a villain to be blackmailed. It can happen for all sorts of reasons, as you well know. Oh dear, don't turn around now, but I'm afraid Martin's just walked in.'

Feeling her insides knot, Andee kept her eyes on Helen. 'Is he alone?' she asked, praying the children weren't with him, or his mother, whom she adored, but wouldn't want to meet in a situation like this.

'As far as I can tell he is. Ah, there he goes, working the tables in typical Martin fashion. Is there anyone in this town he doesn't know?'

Since the question didn't require an answer, Andee picked up her own cranberry soda and took a sip. She wondered how many people he'd told that she'd moved out, and guessed, or at least hoped, that he hadn't gone public yet, in the hope that she might change her mind.

'So how *are* things there?' Helen asked quietly.

Andee inhaled deeply. 'Don't ask,' she murmured.

Helen's eyebrows rose. 'That bad, huh? How are the children taking it?'

'Not well. They're not communicating with me much at the moment.'

Sighing, and speaking from experience, Helen said, 'Breaking up is hell, that's for sure.'

With a half-smile, Andee said, 'Don't worry, I'm not feeling as sorry for myself as I seem to be sounding. I'm just frustrated by how in limbo I feel. It's like I need to make some decisions, to get a sense of moving on with my life . . .'

'Hang on, it's only been two weeks since you took one of the biggest decisions of your life, so give yourself a break. Take a breath, let things happen *to* you for a while, instead of trying to force yourself into some sort of plan that hasn't even got on to the drawing board yet.'

Andee smiled. How good it was to have a friend to confide in, especially one so rational and supportive. 'I know you're right,' she said, 'but I can hardly believe I took this step without having at least some idea of what I want to do next.'

'That very step was what you wanted to do next. You had to free yourself from your marriage in order to find out what your options might be. Or that's how

140

you put it to me before you left. OK, brace yourself, he's coming over.'

Wishing herself a thousand miles away, Andee turned to greet Martin, and found herself feeling both sad and annoyed about how cheerful he was pretending to be. Or perhaps it wasn't a pretence. Perhaps he'd discovered that he didn't want to be married any more either.

She could always hope.

'So how's my darling wife today?' he chirruped, stooping to kiss her cheek in a brittle, almost aggressive way. 'Looking as lovely as ever, I see. Helen, always a pleasure to see you, but I hope you're not trying to talk my wife into joining the gay divorcee club.'

'Martin, for God's sake,' Andee muttered, hoping no one had heard.

Helen said, 'Long time no see, Martin. How are you?'

*Apart from bitter, angry and humiliated,* were the words that shot to Andee's mind.

'Just great,' Martin declared with a slick, self-satisfied grin. 'A lot of projects on the go, so busy, busy, busy. And how are you when you're not defending the town's lowlife?'

Tensing with fury, Andee was about to respond when Helen put up a steadying hand. 'No point rising to it,' she cautioned, as though Martin were no longer there. 'It's really not worth it.'

Laughing, Martin said, 'One to you, Helen. So, can I send some drinks over for you girls?'

Wanting to call him a patronising bastard, Andee said, 'We're fine thank you.'

'And I guess you're not inviting me to join you?'

'I presume,' Andee retorted, 'you're here because you're already meeting someone, so please stop this and go away.'

Putting a hand on her shoulder, he gave it an unpleasantly hard squeeze. 'Anything you say, my darling. Just don't let her pay the tab,' he warned Helen, 'she can't afford it,' and before either of them could respond he went off to his own table where a suited businessman was already waiting.

Helen took a breath, waited for Andee to do the same, and said, 'I don't remember him being so crass.'

'He isn't usually,' Andee replied, still furious, but determined not to let it spoil their lunch. 'Shall we just try to forget he's here and go back to where we were before he came in?'

'Closing the gap as if he never was. I'm all for that. So, I believe we were talking about Charles.'

'We were. So what am I to conclude about the friend?'

Helen was thoughtful as she sat back in her chair. 'Well, given who Charles is, the head of a financial institution, ex-MP with friends in very high places, there's a good chance the friend could be real.'

Andee nodded. 'I won't argue with that.'

'However, if Charles is actually talking about himself, now he's broached the subject with you he might be more forthcoming the next time you meet. How did you leave it with him?'

'I told him he should persuade his friend to talk to me.'

'And he said?'

'That's he'd mention it to him and get back to me.'

Since they could go no further with that for the moment, Helen changed the subject to Jessica Leonard. 'The last time we spoke,' she said, 'you were waiting for Leo Johnson to come back with some information from the Met. Have you had it yet?'

'Only in part,' Andee admitted. 'I wanted to know, because it wasn't in the files I received, how thorough a search had been carried out on the transient population of Notting Hill and Holland Park from around that time. On the face of it, everything that should have happened seems to have, but digging deeper I'm not so sure.'

Helen frowned.

'I'm trying to find out whether someone called Yoder was renting a house or flat in either of those areas, and right now I'm not getting a satisfactory answer.'

Helen looked intrigued. 'That would be a hell of an oversight if no one checked at the time,' she commented. 'Or maybe a cover-up?' she suggested, clearly intrigued by the notion.

Andee shrugged. 'You tell me.'

'So what are you going to do?'

'If need be I'll call all the estate agents myself,' Andee replied, 'but if this Yoder character borrowed the place from someone, or is hiding behind a company let, chances are I won't get very far. I need there to have been a proper police investigation at the time to be able to rule it out.'

Understanding, Helen said, 'And meanwhile?'

'Meanwhile, I'm thinking of taking a drive down to Devon to talk to Jessica's mother.'

'Do you think she might know more than she's telling?'

Andee shook her head. 'I doubt it, but it would feel remiss not to see her in person.'

After waiting for their seafood salads to be set down and pepper to be ground, Helen asked, 'And what about Blake Leonard? How's he holding up?'

Andee sighed sadly. 'About as well as you'd imagine. Some days good, other days not so good.'

'Was I wrong to ask you to do this?' Helen said worriedly.

'No,' Andee replied. 'I want to help him, and the situations aren't that similar. In my sister's case we know it's very likely she committed suicide, but a body has never been found, so we can't be entirely sure. With Jessica there's no suggestion at all that she might have taken her own life. As far as anyone can make out she had everything to live for, and was looking forward to getting on with it. She had all sorts of plans for the summer, and for when she returned to uni for her second year. Nothing I've heard has contradicted that. She was obviously hiding something though, because no one's ever been able to find out why she was visiting Holland Park on quite a regular basis.'

It was the middle of the afternoon and Rowzee was at her desk trying hard not to get upset as she read through the brochure from Dignitas. She hated self-pity, she really did, but it seemed she was awash with it today.

It was all very well to be certain about a decision, she was discovering – and she *was* certain, she really,

really was – but that didn't make it any easier to carry through. She kept telling herself that she wasn't afraid of dying; it was a natural part of life and was going to happen to everyone sooner or later, but then she'd imagine herself going to Switzerland on her own, knowing she'd never come back, and she didn't feel quite so committed any more.

From what she'd read so far in the brochure, the staff at the clinic all sounded very helpful and supportive, and if she wanted someone to hold her hand at the end apparently she had only to ask.

She expected she probably would want that, but then she thought of Pamela and tears welled in her eyes all over again. It should be Pamela's hand she was holding, and Graeme's.

The trouble was, she couldn't ask them because she was sure they'd never agree to her going in the first place. They'd want her to stay where she was so they could look after her to the end, but much as she loved knowing they cared so much, it wasn't what she wanted. She needed to take charge of her life – and death – in a way that felt right for her, and that was by bringing it to a quick, gentle and dignified conclusion.

Oh dear, there she went, crying again, was there no end to it? But it was only to be expected, she kept reminding herself, because no sane person would enjoy doing this. What she had to try to hang on to was the feeling of empowerment it gave her, and once that had returned she was able to continue following the instructions on the website on how to proceed.

First she must take out a membership.

Once that was done – it was surprisingly inexpensive, she discovered, and apparently she didn't have to pay anything until they'd confirmed she'd been accepted – she moved on to the other prerequisites. She needed to be of sound judgement, tick, and have a minimum level of physical capacity, tick, although apparently this last was so she could give herself the termination drug. She hadn't reckoned on having to do it herself, so she just had to hope it came in tablet form and not some kind of injection, because she wasn't sure she could stab herself with a needle at the best of times, never mind to send herself off to the next world.

The next world, where Victor and Edward and her beloved parents were waiting. Or they would be if she believed in the afterlife, which she always had, but to her dismay she seemed to be losing confidence in it now she was aiming to go. Maybe she should get some spiritual counselling to help things along. That seemed a very good idea, so reaching for her notebook she jotted it down to make sure she didn't forget.

Next on the list was the requirement that she should have a terminal illness. Tick. She must provide copies of her medical reports to prove she was definitely on her way out and there was no turning back. She would need to get those from Jilly, probably Mr Mervin, the neurosurgeon, too. What was she going to do if they put up a fight? Even if they did they still couldn't tell her family about the tumour, being bound, as they were, by the Hippocratic oath.

If they tried to talk her out of it she'd just have to make them see it her way. After all, it was her life, not theirs, and wasn't that what this was all about?

Next. Apparently she had to write a letter to Dignitas explaining why she wanted their help. She could do that; in fact it shouldn't even take very long. Dear Sir or Madam, I don't want to lose my marbles, become a vegetable, or a locked-in victim, or turn into somebody my family doesn't know and who can't even go to the bathroom or eat food without disgracing herself. She wouldn't put it quite like that, of course, but that was about the measure of it, and while she was with Jilly tomorrow she ought to ask about pain. Just how much physical pain was there going to be, because the headaches were already pretty intolerable in the mornings and she couldn't imagine them getting any better as time went on.

Oh, she'd just got to the bit where it was saying the end-game drug could be taken with water, provided she was still able to swallow. Now there was something she needed to find out. Was this tumour going to affect her ability to swallow? *Oh God, this was awful, she was going to end up with food dribbling down her chin, snot dripping from her nose, while all sorts of other bodily fluids went in for their own style of free flow.* She'd better find out about this, because it was starting to look as though she might be on a flight to Switzerland even earlier than she thought.

Black squiggles were floating in front of her eyes by now, and there was a tiredness creeping through her that might just manifest in a blackout if she didn't go and lie down. Before she went anywhere though, she must turn off her computer and hide her notebook – she just hoped she didn't forget where she'd put it because it was full of questions for Jilly tomorrow.

Without thinking she picked up the phone as it rang.

'Rowzee? It's Jamie Flood. How are you?'

Jamie Flood was the lawyer she and Victor had always used.

Pleased with herself for remembering, she said, 'Hello Jamie. I'm fine. I hope you are too.' She needed to get through this before her words dried up or consciousness drained. 'I'd like to come and see you to talk about my will.'

'So you said in your email. When is a good time for you?'

'What about tomorrow at three?'

'That soon? Let me look at the diary. You know, as it's you, I think we can squeeze you in. Are you all right? You don't sound your usual cheery self.'

'I'm fine,' she assured him. 'Just getting old.'

'Oh Rowzee, you'll never be old. Even when you're a hundred you'll still be young.'

Rowzee was still smiling past the thump in her head as she rang off and went to lie down on the sofa. A few minutes' rest and she could go back to her task, and she must remember to put in a word for Bill Simmonds with Pamela when they got together later.

# Chapter Nine

Graeme's home was on Amberton Square, a smart, leafy quadrant of mostly Regency town houses with communal parkland at its heart and the grandly arched entrance to Kesterly's botanical gardens at the far end. Andee was on her way along the south walk where the Clarendon Hotel blended discreetly with the elegant residences when, to her dismay, she saw Martin coming towards her.

'Twice in one day,' he declared chirpily as he reached her. 'How lucky am I?'

Having remembered that his family owned a property converted into three luxury flats on the north walk, she said, 'Is this where you're living now?'

'No, I was just checking on some updating we're having done. I'm living, as you put it, at my mother's for the time being, but I'm looking at a house over on Westleigh Heights tomorrow morning. As a matter of fact, I was hoping you'd come with me. I think you're going to love it.'

Suspecting he was trying to tempt her back with one of the area's more desirable houses, or maybe he was trying to prove something else, she said, 'I'm afraid I can't tomorrow.'

He cocked an eyebrow.

Close to ignoring the prompt, she said, 'I'm doing some work for Helen. You behaved appallingly at the restaurant today. I hope you're going to apologise to her.'

'If she was upset, I will. Would you like me to apologise to you too?'

'There's no need.' She glanced at Graeme's glossy black front door a mere few yards away and realised it was open, possibly for her to go in. 'I have an appointment,' she said, 'so I should . . .'

Snapping her off, he said, 'Don't just brush me aside like I'm someone you don't know or even care about. You're my wife, for God's sake. I at least deserve some good manners.'

Tempted to remind him of lunchtime again, she said, 'I've called you several times this past week and you've chosen not to call back. When you're ready we can talk again, but it's not going to happen here in the street.'

'Then come with me, back to your place . . .'

'I've just told you, I have an appointment.'

'So cancel it.'

'I can't. Actually, I don't want to. Martin, what the heck has got into you? I've never known you to behave like this before.'

His eyes glinted angrily. 'Maybe it has something to do with my wife leaving me.'

'Please keep your voice down.'

'Why? Am I embarrassing you?'

150

'You're embarrassing yourself.'

He stood glaring at her, clearly not ready to let her pass.

'What do you want?' she asked.

'You know what I want. For us to be a family again.'

'And this is how you're going about it? Trying to intimidate me, insulting my friends, crying in front of the children . . . Why would you do that to them? What on earth did you hope to gain?'

'Their understanding that I'm not at fault here. It's their mother who's walked out, not me . . .'

'You shouldn't be making them choose sides. It's not fair and they don't need to be worrying about you, or me, or anyone else while they're going through uni . . .'

'That's rich, coming from you who chose to go when they're right in the middle of it . . .'

'I chose now because I didn't want to go on living a lie. It's time for me to put myself first, much like you did when they were young teenagers and needed you badly. I could have tried turning them against you then, and I'd have succeeded, but you're their father, I didn't want there to be a rift between you any more than I want one between us now. I'm just sorry that you seem so intent on creating one.'

Red with anger, he said, 'And I'm sorry that you still can't get over something I did . . .'

'Believe me, I'm over it. And if you want to know the truth, I'm sorry you came back because I'd never have married you if you hadn't, and if we weren't married we wouldn't be going through this now.' That had been a cruel thing to say, and seeing the hurt in his eyes she already regretted it.

'You're such a bitch,' he told her. 'I don't know why I ever bothered to waste my time with you.'

Glancing at her watch, she was about to force her way past him when he suddenly grabbed her.

'Martin, let me go,' she said quietly.

'Look at me,' he urged, shaking her. 'Look at what you're doing to someone whose only crime is to love you.'

'I said, let me go.'

'Is everything all right?'

Andee tensed at the sound of Graeme's voice. She desperately didn't want him involved in this, wished it wasn't happening at all.

'Is there something I can do?' he offered.

'Yeah, mind your own business,' Martin spat rudely.

Graeme glanced at Andee.

'It's fine,' she told him. 'I'll be right there.'

Martin's eyes moved suspiciously between them. 'This is who you're meeting?' he demanded of Andee.

'Martin, I'll call you later . . .'

'Do you know who I am?' he shot at Graeme. 'I'm her husband. So make a habit of trying to run off with other men's wives, do you?'

With truly admirable calm Graeme said, 'I think you need to let her go.'

Andee was already wrenching herself free. 'Pull yourself together,' she muttered at Martin.

'You're going to regret this,' he told her. 'I was prepared to stand by you, to help you to sort yourself out . . .'

To Graeme, Andee said, 'Shall we go inside?'

With a glance at Martin, Graeme stood aside for Andee to go ahead of him. As she went she was certain Martin would try to prevent her, or even make some sort of assault on Graeme, but moments later she was stepping inside Graeme's front hall and he was closing the door behind him.

Feeling wretched for just leaving Martin, but relieved to be away from him, she said to Graeme, 'I'm so sorry. I had no idea . . .' She'd have liked a few moments to collect herself, but it was OK, she'd be fine.

'There's nothing to apologise for,' he assured her, gesturing for her to go through to the back where both sets of French doors in the kitchen-diner were opened on to the patio garden, and a jug of Pimm's was set between two glasses on a mosaic-topped table.

'He isn't normally like that,' she insisted. 'I haven't known him behave so . . .' What words could she use that wouldn't degrade Martin any more than he'd just managed for himself?

'People constantly surprise us,' he said gently. 'But please reassure me that he isn't normally a violent man.'

'Not at all,' she said earnestly.

His eyes held hers for a moment, as though seeking the truth. Apparently satisfied, he asked, 'So, will you have a drink?'

With an arched eyebrow she said, 'I think so.'

After filling two glasses he passed one to her and clicked his own against it.

'To you,' they chorused, and their like minds broke through the tension, taking them to an easier place.

'I'd forgotten how pretty it is here,' she declared, taking in the giant urns of velvety hibiscus on the patio, vivid climbing roses, multicoloured clematis and one entire wall of white hydrangeas. She hadn't forgotten at all, though she hadn't allowed herself to think of it often, there had been nothing to be gained from that. 'You're right on the botanical gardens, and yet completely private.'

Drolly he said, 'I do sometimes spot the odd face peering through the bamboo border, and of course voices carry, but so do the fragrances, and the jasmine is particularly lovely right now.'

Inhaling its warm, sweet scent, she sipped her drink again and thought how heavenly it would be to sit here for hour upon hour doing nothing but listen to the occasional burble of people, the drone of a bee, the trundle of a wheelbarrow passing by, the distant rumble of a mower and chomp of a spade. The only company would be the colourful, mesmeric butterflies dancing around the blooms, and birds chirping in the trees. No one would know where to find her, and she wouldn't have to go and find them until she was ready.

'I'm sorry,' she said, realising Graeme had spoken.

'It was nothing,' he assured her, and pushing a dish of olives her way he said, 'I feel you've rather a lot on your plate at the moment, what with helping Blake, and your own situation, so perhaps now isn't a good time to burden you with more.'

'If it's about your sister Rowzee it won't be a burden,' she promised, thinking of the odd turn Rowzee had had at the café the other day, although he'd mentioned another name when they'd spoken on the phone, so this probably wasn't going to be about his sister's health.

'It's an odd situation,' he began pensively. 'I'm not sure what to make of it, but a young lad by the name of Jason Griffiths told me something extraordinary yesterday, and before I go any further with it I'd like to find out if he's who he's claiming to be.'

Intrigued, Andee waited for him to continue.

'He's saying he's Victor Cayne's grandson – I'm sure you know that Victor is Rowzee's late husband – but Rowzee has never mentioned anything to me about Victor having another family. Apparently the boy's father – Victor's putative son – was born before Victor and Rowzee married, so it's possible that Rowzee knows nothing about him. Before I discuss it with her I'd like to be sure that Jason Griffiths really is who he's claiming to be, because I certainly don't want to involve my sister in any unnecessary upset if it turns out to be a scam someone's cooked up to try and get money out of her.'

Andee's mind was working fast, sorting through all kinds of scenarios and motives and comparing the situation to others she'd come across of a similar nature. She began by asking the boy's age.

'I'd say early to mid-twenties.'

'And where's his father?'

'Unwell, apparently.'

Andee frowned. 'Does his father know that his son is here, talking to you?'

'I'm not sure about the father, but I got the impression that the grandmother knows.'

'The grandmother being the woman Victor had a relationship with?'

'Indeed, if we're to believe the boy.'

Andee nodded thoughtfully. 'Do you have any idea if Victor knew he had a son?'

'Jason says Victor did know. Apparently they met once, a few years ago, which is the main reason Jason wants to see Rowzee.'

Baffled, Andee said, 'Did he elaborate on that?'

'Not really. He just said it's something he has to do for his nan.'

Andee was thinking hard, knowing already what she was going to do, but she still needed more detail about the family, such as the grandmother's and father's name and address, and where the boy was living.

Having already got the information from Jason, Graeme handed over a folded sheet of paper.

Andee read aloud, 'Grandmother, Norma Griffiths, father, Sean Griffiths and Jason . . .' She glanced up at Graeme. 'They all live at the same address in Devon?'

'Apparently,' he replied. 'Jason also tells me that he's got no problem with being checked out.'

Impressed by that, but by no means taken in by it, Andee said, 'OK, I'll pass this on to someone at the station. With all the necessary resources at their fingertips we should have an answer quite quickly.'

With a smile Graeme said, 'Thank you.'

Still concerned, Andee said, 'Have you thought about how Rowzee might take it, if it's true and she doesn't know Victor has a son?'

He nodded slowly. 'I've thought about it a great deal, which is why I want to be absolutely certain before I say anything to her.' After a moment he added, 'I'm not sure if you know that she had a son herself, who died when he was five. Edward. He was a late baby, and would be around Jason's age by now if he'd lived. When he went it was a terrible blow to the whole family.'

Seeing how moved he still was by the loss, Andee said, gently, 'What happened?'

'Meningitis. He was a lovely boy, only a couple of years younger than Ben, my youngest. It's been very hard for Rowzee watching my boys grow up, but they couldn't have had an aunt who loved them more.'

Feeling deeply for Rowzee, Andee said, 'Apart from Pamela?'

He smiled. 'Of course, but Pamela has a different way of showing things.' He glanced at his watch.

'I should go,' she said, putting down her glass.

'Please, there's no rush,' he insisted. 'I'm meeting a client for dinner at eight . . .'

'I should get this information to the police,' she interrupted, and reaching for her bag she got to her feet. 'Before I go,' she said as they started back through the house, 'did Jason Griffiths give you any idea of why he's looking for Rowzee now?'

'No. All he'd tell me was that he wanted to see her in person to explain things.'

Andee frowned. 'Well, let's find out if he's really who he's claiming to be, and if he is, we can decide how to take it from there – with Rowzee's best interests at heart, naturally.'

Rowzee was watching her doctor's pale, tense face as Jilly carefully read the notes in front of her. It would be easy for Rowzee to engage with the anxiety trying to overwhelm her, or to start scaring herself with all kinds of horrific scenarios, which she'd become quite accomplished at lately. Instead she was encouraging her mind to flit back over the years to when Jilly had played Rosalind – and many other roles that Rowzee wasn't quite remembering right now. As a young girl Jilly had shown a very real talent for acting, had possessed a remarkable feel for the language and nuance of the Bard and many other playwrights too, and Rowzee had done much to encourage her to pursue a career on the stage. How many years had passed since Jilly had listened to her parents and taken her place at Birmingham University Medical School? Probably as many as twenty, and dear Jilly, as gifted and dedicated a doctor as she was, didn't seem to be wearing well. Was it any wonder, when she had such a stressful job? It couldn't be easy dealing with sick and needy people every day, especially those who were frightened, or difficult, or thought they knew better than their GP.

Realising she might be falling into the latter category, Rowzee said, 'Please understand that I respect everything you've told me, it's just that I feel it's better if I do things this way.'

Fixing her with kindly but tired eyes, Jilly said, 'I know what you're like when your mind is made up

158

about something, it's how we got budgets for our plays, outings to theatres and even a memorable weekend in Paris as I recall. And I can see it's made up over this, which is why I'm reading your notes again. We need to be absolutely sure . . .'

'We are,' Rowzee came in gently. 'Mr Mervin was very clear when I went to see him for the results. He didn't use any terminology I couldn't understand, and nor did you the last time I was here. We know the cancer is secondary, so we know it's not curable . . .'

'Which doesn't mean it isn't treatable. And we've yet to find the primary.'

'Oh, I think I've done that. There's a black mark under my toenail that's never gone away, and I think it's bigger now than when I first noticed it. I expect it's a guilty mole.'

'I'll take a look,' Jilly said.

'OK, but whether I'm right or wrong, it's not going to change anything, is it? I still have a tumour in my brain and if you give me treatment you'll be keeping me alive simply to slide into a condition I'd rather not be in, and that will cause a lot of heartache and stress for my family, not to mention inconvenience and . . .'

'Mrs C, they love you. They'll want you here for as long as they can have you, no matter how sick you might be.'

'But it isn't their decision, it's mine. I want to go to this clinic to have it over and done with as soon as possible.' She didn't, in fact, want to go at all. She wanted desperately to carry on living the life she had now, or the one prior to this cancer, so she could grow old slowly, perhaps not always gracefully, but with all her faculties intact and her family around her. However, nature, God, fate, had other plans, and she had no way of altering them.

'Rowzee . . .'

'Please Jilly, I need you to give me the medical certificate they require.' Could Jilly sense how anxious she was feeling? She thought not; after all, she was managing to sound very pragmatic and in control, so it would seem her thespian skills were still cooking, even if her marbles were under attack.

Pushing her hands through her hair in a way that made her appear more drained than ever, Jilly replied, 'I'm not saying I won't give it to you, I'm only saying that you mustn't do this without telling anyone. Can't you see how cruel it would be? How on earth are Pamela and Graeme going to feel when they get a call from the clinic asking them to come and collect your body?'

Trying not to wince, Rowzee said, 'Ashes. I'm arranging to be cremated right after it happens.' A distantly placed part of her was feeling shocked by the words she was speaking, could hardly believe they weren't in a script that could be cut, or rewritten if necessary.

Jilly swallowed as she looked at her.

'I've been reading all about it,' Rowzee told her.

Sighing, Jilly said, 'I can tell that you have, and I know you have to satisfy the Swiss doctors that you are of sound enough mind to take the decision, but please don't rush this. If you take the drugs you've been prescribed, your symptoms will virtually disappear . . .'

'For a while, and meantime the tumour will grow and before we know it I won't be deemed of sound enough mind any more. Even if I am, I could well be in a wheelchair by then and I wouldn't be able to get into town without help, never mind to Switzerland.'

Shaking her head in dismay, Jilly said, 'Please, *please* talk to Pamela and Graeme. They have a right to know, surely you can see that?'

'They won't let me do it.'

'How do you know if you don't ask them?'

'I know them.'

'You mean they're against assisted dying?'

'No. Actually, they might be. We've never had the conversation.'

'Then you need to. Let them be a support to you. It's what they'd want, and what you're going to need if you're determined to go through with this. You can't do it alone.'

Certain that she could, but not willing to argue any further, Rowzee asked, 'Will you give me the certificate?'

'I'm not saying no, but I'll have to discuss it with Mr Mervin.'

'What if he turns out to be pro-life?'

'I happen to know that he isn't, but I can't see him being any happier than I am about you doing this without involving your family.'

Trying hard to sound sweet and reasonable, Rowzee said, 'But it isn't about making you and Mr Mervin happy, is it?'

Unable to argue with that, Jilly regarded her sadly. 'Please think about it,' she implored, 'and please take the dexamethasone.'

'How long will it take to kick in?'

'About three days.'

Rowzee was already on her feet when it occurred to her to ask, 'If I take these steroids . . . did you say my symptoms, the dizziness and headaches and everything, will disappear?'

'They should. Come and see me again in a week. We need to talk about radiotherapy . . .' She stopped as Rowzee's hand went up. 'It's here, in Mr Mervin's notes,' she told her. 'You need to see an oncologist . . .'

'I don't want all that sort of messing around.'

Letting it go for the moment, Jilly said, 'OK, make an appointment on your way out. We'll have another chat next week to discuss the situation again.'

As the door closed behind Rowzee, Jilly sat back in her chair and covered her face with her hands. Rowzee Cayne had to be the dearest, most selfless and most maddeningly stubborn woman in the world. Not that Jilly blamed her for wanting to take control of her life, who wouldn't in those circumstances, she just couldn't be allowed to do it alone. For a fleeting moment Jilly wondered if she should offer to go with her to Zurich, but it would most likely be the end of her career if she did.

Pulling Rowzee's notes forward again, her eyes fixed on the words that she'd not yet spoken to her, and because Rowzee hadn't asked she wasn't sure when, or even if, she should.

Life expectancy: Six–nine months.

If Rowzee knew she only had that long, surely she wouldn't see herself as burdening her family. It was going to be over almost before it began. On the other hand, if she told her she was going to die so soon there was every chance Rowzee would add an even greater urgency to her end-of-life plans.

With it being such a warm, but not overly hot day Rowzee decided to walk to the old town rather than take the bus for three stops along Primrose Lane and into Sidley Coombe. The exercise and fresh sea air were doing her good, and maybe even helping to clear her head, if such an achievement were possible these days.

One thing she'd decided on without too much trouble was that she was going to take the steroid, if only to get her through the next week or so. A respite from the headaches, not to mention the absence attacks and occasional blackouts, should mean no more fears of raising her family's suspicions and, with any luck, she might even be less forgetful. She wondered if the drug was supposed to help her memory, and suspected it probably wasn't or surely they'd give it to people with dementia. Maybe they did. How would she know?

Remembering she hadn't turned her phone on since leaving the surgery, she stopped outside the pharmacy on Sidley Coombe Way to check for messages. To her dismay there was one from Jamie, her lawyer, asking if she was all right as she'd missed her appointment today.

Annoyed and upset, she rang him straight away to apologise and ask if she could come now.

'I'm sorry, I'm chock-a-block for the rest of the week,' he told her. 'I'm sure we can squeeze you in somewhere next week though. I'll get my secretary to give you a call with some times.'

After collecting her prescription from the pharmacy, Rowzee headed on into the old town feeling wretched and foolish and despairingly frustrated with herself. She just hoped Pamela didn't get to hear about the missed appointment. As it was, she wouldn't stop going on about how Rowzee had stood her up at the Italian the other night.

'What do you mean, you fell asleep?' Pamela had snapped crossly when she'd got home. 'You look perfectly awake to me. So what *have* you been up to? And please don't tell me you've been riding around on Bill Simmonds's mower, because I won't laugh and I won't believe you either.'

'He's very keen on you,' Rowzee told her, seizing the change of subject. 'He asked me to put in a good word.'

'Well you can save your breath. I'm not interested. All I want to know is why you didn't even call the restaurant to let me know you couldn't make it.'

'I told you, I was asleep.'

'You mean you forgot.'

'That's not what I said.'

'You don't have to. It's written all over you. I want you to ring the doctor first thing and make an appointment. No, don't argue. I'm starting to get worried and you should be too.'

'Thanks for trying not to scare me.'

164

Pamela's face immediately softened. 'I don't want to scare you,' she promised, 'I just want to get to the bottom of what's making you so scatterbrained. It's probably nothing more than an iron deficiency, or low blood pressure, it can have a strange effect on you. I know, maybe I should have a check-up too. Keep you company. I'd just better not turn out to be the one with Alzheimer's, that's all I can say, or there'll be trouble.'

Fortunately, ironically, Pamela seemed to have forgotten the doctor by the next morning, possibly, Rowzee decided, because she was too distracted by Bill Simmonds turning up to mow their lawns.

'For someone who's not interested,' Rowzee commented, 'you're spending a lot of time at the window watching him.'

'I'm checking he's not making a mess of it,' Pamela retorted.

'He never has before.'

'There's always a first time.'

Rowzee looked her up and down. 'Where are you going all dressed up to the nines?' she demanded.

Tapping her nose, Pamela said, 'That's for me to know and you to find out.'

'So what's his name?'

Ignoring her, Pamela mistakenly returned Bill's wave and scowled to show she hadn't meant it. 'Time to go,' she declared, picking up her bag. 'Things to do, people to see.'

'I don't understand why you're being so secretive,' Rowzee grumbled, following her to the door. 'If you're Internet dating I think it's wonderful.'

'I'm *not* Internet dating,' Pamela assured her. 'But if you want to, I'm happy to help. It could be fun.'

'You're up to something,' Rowzee told her. 'All these new clothes and talk of surgery.'

'Well, you can't take it with you when you go,' Pamela replied breezily.

Dear God, was Pamela hiding a similar secret? Was that what was happening here? She was spending all her money (money Rowzee had always thought was tied up in investments) before some dastardly disease kicked in and felled her? No, it wasn't possible. She was the picture of health, and besides no ailment had ever struck Pamela, big or small, without her complaining to the world about how much worse she had it than anyone else ever had.

Dropping a kiss on Rowzee's cheek, Pamela said, 'You'll find out everything soon enough. I just need to make some more progress first.'

Rowzee watched her go, trying her best to work out what was going on, but apart from Internet dating she was fresh out of ideas.

'There's sure to be a man involved,' she confided to Blake over a cup of tea in his workshop. Having arrived with no clear memory of why she'd come, she'd left Graeme to the client he was busy with in the show-room and wandered through for a back-room browse. 'And I hope there is,' she continued, 'because she could do with some romance in her life. She deserves it after what she went through with her marriage.'

'And she's still an attractive woman,' Blake added helpfully. 'In fact you both are, so maybe some romance for you too?'

Rowzee smiled ruefully. 'I've had my share,' she assured him. 'I really don't want any more.' Her eyes went hesitantly to his. 'How's Jenny?' she asked gently. 'Will she be coming home soon?'

He shook his head dismally. 'I've no idea. She's not in good shape, that's for sure. Her mother's trying to persuade her to see a doctor to help with the depression, but she won't.'

'Did she ever suffer from depression before?'

'You mean before what happened up north? Sometimes, but it was never like this. Well, nothing like this ever happened to us before.'

'No, of course not. I don't suppose there's any news?'

He shook his head. 'I'm still waiting to hear from Andee. However, on a more positive note I think Matt's got himself a girlfriend.'

Rowzee's eyes brightened with interest. 'Anyone we know?'

'I can't tell you that, because he hasn't actually admitted there's someone, but I heard him on the phone to one of his friends last night saying he couldn't make some event or other because he was seeing Ellie.'

Impressed, Rowzee said, 'If it's Ellie Sandworth then I'd say they're very well suited, because she's as excellent a guitar player as he is, and if you've heard her sing . . .' Realising what she was saying, she came to a sorry stop.

Blake gave her a reassuring smile. 'I wasn't sure a time would ever come,' he confessed, 'when I'd want to hear Matt playing without Jess, but I think I could, if only to reassure myself that he was getting over it.'

Understanding that, Rowzee squeezed his hand in a vain gesture of comfort. She wondered if she should start talking to him about the collaborative art project they'd been discussing before Jessica had disappeared. It might help to distract him – or it might just remind him that his life had come to a standstill, and that wouldn't be good. *'He who would search for pearls must dive below,'* she recited softly.

He regarded her curiously. 'What makes you say that?'

She shook her head. 'I don't know, it just came to me. It's from the prologue of John Dryden's *All for Love.'* It was strange the things she remembered, how they came floating up from places she'd long forgotten. She hadn't read Dryden since she was a student.

After a while, Blake said, 'Do you think she's dead?'

Keeping her hand on his, Rowzee said, 'I wish I knew how to answer that. Better still, I wish I could tell you where she is, but at least you're doing everything you can to find her.'

His smile was weak. 'It doesn't feel like much when I'm sitting here, day after day, repairing treasures from down the years, bringing them back to life in a way that makes them seem to breathe again, and yet I can't do the same for my wife or my daughter. I keep thinking if only Jess was as easy to find as a missing chair from a pair, or the lost bow to a precious violin.' His eyes drifted around the watchful clocks and cabinets, the silent dolls and damaged paintings. 'Some missing parts can take years to trace,' he said, 'but they're usually found in the end, and the odd thing is how often they turn out to be not so very far from home.'

Another letter had arrived. This one was postmarked from a town in Cornwall; the previous one, which he'd received only days ago, had come from somewhere in Berkshire. It was as though his persecutor was getting greedy, couldn't wait to get his – or her – hands on even more money, in cash, unmarked, so untraceable and ready to be spent.

*Send £40,000 in cash to the PO Box below. If you don't you know what will happen.*

It was much shorter than previous notes; the sender didn't need to go into detail any more, he or she had convinced him in the first note that they knew enough.

At least this time he hadn't been asked how he was living with himself.

He read the two short lines again and felt a vacuum of horror opening up inside him, one so black and powerful it could have swallowed him completely, and he almost wished it would.

Did this person have any idea how complicated the situation was, how impossible it was for him to do the right thing and tell what he knew? His and his family's lives would be completely destroyed if the truth were to get out, especially now.

He wanted desperately to talk to Andee again, to ask for her help in any way she could give it, but she'd confirmed his fears the last time she was here: unless he told her everything there was nothing she could do.

And would finding the blackmailer really put an end to it?

He'd started seeing the face again – the woman's face, stark as a moon, circled by a fiery halo in a forest of night-blackened leaves. It kept coming to him like a warning, a threat, a terrible damnation. The first and only real time he'd seen her she'd appeared out of nowhere, suddenly she was there, and it had happened so fast, quicker than the blink of an eye or the gasp of a breath. He had no idea who she was, or how she'd come to be there. Was she the blackmailer? If so, how had she found out who he was? Who had told her, when there was no one to tell?

There was no doubt in his mind that he'd send the money. He was ready to, and could do so without raising questions at the bank. A long time ago his father had advised him always to keep large sums of cash in the safes of both houses, Burlingford Hall and Bede Lodge in London. 'If someone breaks in and holds you or your family to ransom, you must have something to give them,' he'd cautioned.

As Charles went to the safe, sensing the strange woman's face lurking behind him, he was wondering if Andee believed in the friend he'd told her about. There was a friend, though he wasn't a victim, as Charles had made it seem. In fact, for all Charles knew he was the blackmailer, for he was the person who'd invited Charles to the gathering the night it had all begun. Apart from the ghostly woman this man was, as far as Charles was aware, the only other possible suspect in this unending nightmare. Yet it made

170

no sense at all, for he was an ex-Cabinet minister with a wife who had her own aspirations in that direction and a son who was rising fast through the ranks of the Party. Why on earth would someone like that resort to blackmail? He had no need of the money, and if he suspected for one minute that his friend and colleague, Charles Stamfield, knew anything at all about the disappearance of Jessica Leonard he'd surely have gone straight to the police.

# Chapter Ten

Andee was driving behind Graeme through Kesterly's affluent suburb of Westleigh Heights, across Moorland Park where hikers and tourists set out on their explorations, down through the Valley of Streams and finally up Lidditon Hill to the Burlingford Estate. It was a gloriously sunny day, with endless views of the estuary stretching out like dreams to the west and the dramatically rugged rise of Exmoor to the south.

She had heard this morning that Jason Griffiths did indeed live in Totnes with his grandmother and father, that he'd never been in trouble with the authorities, and was currently working as a groundsman for the local council. His father, on the other hand, had been arrested a number of times for drunk and disorderly offences and had also, several years ago, received a suspended sentence for attempted robbery. All she'd been told about the grandmother was that she worked part-time at a local arts and crafts boutique, which she part-owned.

After relaying all this to Graeme, Andee had agreed to visit Rowzee with him, taking two cars in case Rowzee decided she wanted to meet Jason, at which point one of them could drive back into town to get him. He was staying at one of the caravan parks, apparently, with an old schoolfriend who was doing a summer stint as a security guard.

As Graeme pulled into the hamlet where Rowzee and Pamela's coach house dominated the smaller cottages like a dowager duchess with a loyal band of attendees, Andee came to a stop behind him and checked to find out who was calling her. Seeing it was Martin she decided to let it go through to messages, and turned to the texts from Alayna.

*Why did you have to be so mean to Dad when you saw him? He just told me about it and he was really upset.*

She was clearly referring to the incident in the street outside Graeme's house. No doubt Martin hadn't mentioned anything about manhandling her, or about the embarrassment he'd caused at the restaurant earlier in the day.

The next text said, *Are you avoiding me too? Really grown-up of you.*

And the next, *Has Luke told you he's going to Cornwall with some of his mates? Lucky him. Wish I could get out of here too.*

Andee did know that Luke was heading south for a couple of weeks, it had always been in his plans for the summer, and besides he'd rung last night to remind her.

'Can I see you before you go?' she'd asked.

'Oh Mum, I don't really have time. Everyone's going to the Mermaid tonight to watch Ellie Sandworth.'

'Paul and Lucy Sandworth's daughter? The singer?'

'That's right, and apparently Matt Leonard might play keyboard. If he does, it'll be the first time he's done anything since his sister disappeared.'

Moved by that, Andee said, 'Then of course you must go, and I hope he does play.'

Whether Matt had she still didn't know, because Luke hadn't replied to her texts yet today, probably because he was still in bed or too busy getting on with the journey to Cornwall. She could ask Blake, of course, and probably would when she spoke to him later.

'Everything OK?' Graeme asked, as she got out of her car.

'Just fine,' she assured him. 'Is Pamela at home?'

'Her car's not here, so I'd say not, which is a good thing, because if neither she nor Rowzee know anything about this we'll have a job getting a word in once Pamela finds out.'

With a smile, Andee said, 'But Rowzee is expecting us?'

Graeme nodded for her to turn around and Andee found Rowzee at the front door, beaming with pleasure to see them.

'This is such a lovely surprise,' she enthused, wrapping Andee into a fond embrace. 'When Graeme called to say you were both coming for coffee – well, I wondered what I'd done to deserve such an honour, and in the middle of the working week too.' There was a roguish twinkle in her eyes as she peeked up at Andee. 'Do you have something to tell me, maybe?'

'We do,' Graeme interrupted, 'but it isn't what you're thinking. Shall we go inside?'

Taking Andee's hand Rowzee led her through to the kitchen, where coffee was already made and the heady aroma of summer grass and honeysuckle and something a little riper from a nearby farm was wafting in through the open doors.

'I should have told you,' Rowzee said to Graeme, 'to bring some of those lovely shortbread biscuits from the bakery next door to you. They're to die for,' she informed Andee. 'If you haven't already tried them . . . Oh, you brought some,' she laughed as Graeme held up a greaseproof bag. 'You're such a mind-reader, I could feel quite exposed if you weren't my brother. Now, shall we sit on the terrace? It could be a little hot while the sun's still on it . . .'

They decided on the dining table, and once the coffee had been poured and the biscuits duly praised, Graeme fixed his sister with tender eyes.

To Andee's surprise Rowzee seemed to pale and become nervous, as though expecting bad news. 'If this is about what I think it is,' she began.

Curious, Graeme said, 'What do you think it's about?'

Rowzee shook her head. 'Nothing. I mean, go on. You tell me. I shouldn't jump to conclusions.'

With a glance at Andee, Graeme took a breath and said, haltingly, 'I've recently learned . . . Well, it came as a bit of surprise to me to find out that . . . I'm not sure if it'll be a surprise to you too.'

Rowzee frowned.

Though Andee wanted to offer some help, this really had to come from him.

'Is it a nice surprise?' Rowzee prompted. 'You look so worried that I'm beginning to think it isn't.'

'Did you know,' Graeme said, 'that Victor had a son?'

Rowzee's eyes flew wide with astonishment, though her next words belied Andee's understanding of the shock. 'How on earth did you find out?' she exclaimed. 'Have you seen him? Oh dear, please don't say he's treated you the way he treated poor Victor.'

Astonished in his turn, Graeme said, 'So you've met him?'

Rowzee shook her head, and twisted her fingers. 'No, never, but I keep wondering . . .' She put a hand to her head, clearly trying to establish the order she needed to follow. 'I didn't find out about him until Victor did,' she began, 'which was about ten years ago, maybe less, I'm not sure. He turned up out of the blue. It was a complete shock, no one had ever told Victor he had a son. He was born before Victor and I met.' She shook her head regretfully. 'What that boy did to Victor – he wasn't a boy of course, he was a grown man. I shall never forget it.'

As her eyes closed Graeme reached for her hands and held them. 'Rowzee?' he prompted after a moment or two. 'What did he do?'

She seemed not to hear the question, or if she did, she apparently wasn't ready to answer it.

Andee said quietly to Graeme, 'Perhaps I should leave you two alone.'

'No, don't go,' Rowzee said hurriedly. 'If he's been in touch again . . . He might have changed, of course, but if he hasn't . . .'

'It's not him who's been in touch,' Graeme told her gently. 'It's his son, in other words, Victor's grandson.'

'Victor has a grandson?' she gasped, seeming amazed, even entranced by the idea. 'How old is he?'

'I'd say early twenties.'

Her gaze drifted towards the garden and Andee found herself imagining the faces, dreams, past scenes, that only Rowzee could see. 'The same age as Edward would be,' she murmured, 'if he were still with us.'

Still holding her hands, Graeme said, 'He wants to see you, but obviously if you'd rather not . . .'

She didn't answer, simply continued staring into her memories.

In the end, Graeme asked, 'Do you want to tell us what happened between Victor and his son?'

Rowzee slowly started to nod, and continued to do so until finally she was ready to put her long-held secret into words.

'I got home from school at my usual time that day,' she began distantly. 'I remember being excited because I'd managed to track down a translation of a play we'd been to during our recent trip to Argentina. I couldn't wait to tell Victor, but his car wasn't there when I pulled up, and there was no note inside to tell me where he was.

'I made a cup of tea, intending to start on some marking, but I couldn't settle to it. I felt worried without knowing why. I rang his mobile and went straight through to messages. After half an hour of the same thing I rang Charles at the Hall to find out if Victor was there, but Charles hadn't seen him that day. I rang you next,' she said to Graeme, 'but you hadn't seen him either. So I called his agent and publicist, in case he had an engagement he'd forgotten to tell me about. They could throw no light on his whereabouts, but as I hung up the phone I finally heard his car pulling up outside.'

She took a breath and her eyes seemed to glaze as though she was waiting for a wave of discomfort, even pain, to pass.

'I went to the door having no idea what I would find, but I knew instinctively that something wasn't right. When I saw him . . .' She sobbed on a breath. 'It was terrible. If it hadn't been for his dear, shaggy thatch of hair – matted in blood though it was – and his dark-rimmed spectacles, smashed as they were, I'd have thought it was a stranger. His poor face was a mass of cuts and swellings and he could barely walk.

'I helped him inside, trying to stay calm. I kept asking what had happened, if he'd had an accident, but he didn't answer. He couldn't, his mouth was too swollen. We got as far as the hall when he collapsed. I rang 999 straight away and he was rushed to A & E.

'He turned out to have three broken ribs and a punctured lung, there was damage to his pancreas and kidneys, and he was also concussed. These were the injuries we couldn't see; there were so many visible ones that it was hard to look at him without wanting to cry.'

Andee glanced at Graeme's grim expression, wondering if he remembered the incident, but had believed it to be about something else at the time.

'They kept him under close observation for five days,' Rowzee continued. 'I stayed with him, of course, but he was so dazed by pain and shock and the drugs they were feeding him that it was hard for him to speak and make much sense. The police came, wanting to know who had beaten him so severely, but he would only mumble that he didn't know, it must have been a case of mistaken identity or a random mugger.

'It wasn't until I got him home at the weekend that he finally told me the truth. Apparently the call had come out of the blue during the afternoon of the attack, from someone claiming to be his son. His first thought was for Edward, naturally, but that was nonsense. It couldn't possibly be him, so he told the caller that he must have a wrong number. The caller insisted he didn't. He said that his mother was Norma Griffiths, and that she'd told him all about his father, the famous Victor Cayne.

'Victor remembered having a girlfriend by that name, but their relationship hadn't been serious and they'd had no contact at all from the day they'd broken up. Naturally this didn't mean that he couldn't have fathered a child with her, but it begged the question why had she never told him, if he had? In the end, because the caller sounded so urgent and needy Victor agreed to go and see him. You remember how kind-hearted he was,' she said to Graeme. 'He said he kept thinking, "If he is my son then the very least

I owe him is a chance to talk to me, maybe there's even something I can do for him, and his mother." It turned out that Sean – it was only later that we learned his name – didn't have much talking in mind. He wanted money. They weren't even inside the pub, they were still in the car park. He said he wanted a hundred thousand pounds and that was just for starters. Victor asked if he had any proof that they were related, and that was when the attack began. Victor tried to defend himself, but Sean was a large man and he didn't seem to care how much injury he caused. He was full of anger and hatred, Victor said. He only managed to get away when Sean staggered and fell against a bollard, hitting his head. Victor stumbled to his car and just managed to drive off before Sean tore open the door.'

Tense and horrified, Andee watched Rowzee's face, the twitching blink of her eyes, the clear distress of reliving that time.

Graeme said, very gently, 'Why did you never tell me any of this? I remember the incident, of course, when Victor was in hospital, but I thought it was a mugging.'

Rowzee nodded distractedly. 'That's what he wanted everyone to think, because he felt – and this was Victor for you – that if Sean did turn out to be his son then he needed to protect him.'

Andee and Graeme exchanged glances. 'And he did turn out to be Victor's son?' Andee prompted.

Rowzee nodded. 'We tracked down Norma and she confirmed it. She also agreed to a DNA test. As soon as we had the results Victor got in touch with

180

her again to ask what he could do to help her and Sean, but she said there was nothing, that they were fine and really didn't need his help. She didn't sound bitter, he said, just matter of fact. He told her that Sean had asked for money, but she advised him to ignore it. We didn't hear from her again, but Sean rang a few times. He was always drunk and abusive, I'm afraid.'

'Did he ever try to see Victor again?' Andee asked.

'No, I don't think so. I'm sure Victor would have told me if he had. It had a terrible effect on him though. He found it very hard to come to terms with being a dad who had no relationship with his son. If he'd known earlier, while Sean was growing up, there's no doubt he'd have been there for him. We'd have embraced him into our family, done everything we could for him, but it wasn't possible by the time Sean was a man. The poor thing was riddled with hatred, all he wanted was money and Victor was afraid to send it because he was sure he'd just spend it on booze or gambling or drugs, whatever he was into.'

'Did he ever threaten Victor again?'

The frown between Rowzee's eyes was so deep Andee could almost feel the pain of it. 'Not that I know of,' she murmured. 'If he had I'm sure Victor would have gone to the police.'

Graeme said to Andee, 'I don't think we should bring Jason here.'

Andee was about to agree when Rowzee interrupted. 'Jason? Is that Victor's grandson?'

Graeme nodded.

Her eyes drifting slightly, Rowzee said, 'He's been on my mind a lot lately – not him, of course, his father, but . . . do you know where his father is?'

'Apparently he's in Totnes,' Graeme replied. 'Jason says he's not well, which, by the sound of it, is very probably alcohol related.'

Rowzee nodded and stared down at her hands. After a while, in a shaky voice, she said, 'I want to see Jason.'

Glancing at Graeme, Andee said, 'Why don't you take some time to think it over?'

Rowzee's eyes were bright as she said, 'Time isn't . . . I . . .' She took a breath. 'I want to see him. You'll be here, won't you? So if he does turn out to be like Sean . . . Where is he?'

'I can go and get him,' Andee offered.

Rowzee stopped her. 'Let Graeme go,' she said. 'Is that all right?' she asked her brother.

'Of course,' he replied. 'But I think Andee's right, you should take some time . . .'

'I don't need it. I promise, I'm fine and if Victor has a grandson I want to meet him.'

As the door closed behind Graeme Andee was regarding Rowzee closely. 'I'm not going to ask if you're OK,' she said, 'because I can see that you're not. So what can I do?'

Managing to speak past the nausea swirling inside her, while hardly able to see through the swarm of tadpoles in her eyes, Rowzee said, 'I'm fine. I'd just like to have some time to get used to this, if you don't mind. If I said that to Graeme he'd worry and refuse to bring the lad.'

'Maybe you're not up to it today.'

Rowzee struggled to her feet. 'I'm sorry to leave you alone. If you . . .' Words were crowding around her thoughts, trying to turn them into sounds, but she was finding it hard to speak.

'Don't worry about me,' Andee interrupted. 'If you need some time to yourself I'll pop over and see Charles.'

'Yes, yes,' Rowzee mumbled. 'He'll like that,' and praying she wouldn't lose consciousness before she was alone she stood watching, but hardly seeing Andee leave.

To Andee's surprise, when she got to the Hall she found the doors and windows firmly closed, in spite of the heat, suggesting that no one was at home. However, Charles's car was outside.

'He was there a few minutes ago,' Bill Simmonds told her, as she wandered over to admire his topiary skills. 'He'll be on the phone, I expect. Daisy, the housekeeper, should be around if you fancy a cup of tea.'

'I'm fine,' Andee assured him, turning to look up at the Hall. Spotting Charles at an upstairs window with a phone pressed to one ear she waved out and beckoned for him to come down. He spanned a hand, presumably meaning five minutes, and disappeared.

Though she was happy to pass the time with Bill, whose humour mixed with his vast knowledge of all things horticultural could be very entertaining, today she was distracted by her concerns for Rowzee. Not

183

only that, she was worried about Alayna and how low she sounded, and in spite of being angry with Martin she was troubled by him too. She wasn't making a good job of things with her family; even her mother, not usually given to criticism, had said on the phone last night that she seemed to be cutting them all off. This wasn't true, she simply didn't know what to do for the best, or at least what could be done to make them feel better – unless she was prepared to sacrifice herself again and give them what they wanted.

There was so much going round in her head, not to mention tearing at her conscience and confusing her heart, that she might have missed Charles hastening to his car if Bill hadn't tipped her off.

'Charles, wait!' she cried, running up to the drive. 'I need to speak to you.'

'I'm sorry,' he replied, lowering the driver's window to speak as she reached him. 'I'm in a tearing hurry. Can it wait?'

'I guess so. I just wondered if your friend had decided to . . .'

'Forget about him,' he interrupted. 'He needs to sort out his own issues. I'll give you a call . . .'

'OK, just tell me, is Gina still in Dartmouth? I'm heading down that way sometime in the next couple of days, so I thought I might drop in to see her.'

'Yes, she's there, as far as I know, and I'm sure she'd love to see you. Call first to make sure she's at home. Sorry, I really have to go . . . Oh, Bill, you're hedging and ditching too close to the Valley Woods. I was over there yesterday. We need to keep the terrain as impenetrable as possible or the next thing we know we'll have poachers or hikers trying to break their way through.'

'Aye aye,' Bill responded, with a salute. 'Wouldn't find nothing, even if they could,' he added under his breath. 'They don't go anywhere and there's nothing in there anyway.'

As they stood watching Charles's car speeding down the drive, Andee said, 'If I didn't know better I might think he was trying to avoid me.'

'If I didn't know better,' Bill grunted, 'I'd think he was trying to avoid us all.'

Andee turned to look at him.

'He's not himself,' Bill commented, and planting his panama back on his thick mop of silvery hair he left Andee to answer her phone.

'I'm at the Hall,' she told Graeme, starting back towards Rowzee's. 'Have you got Jason?'

'Yes, he's with me. We should be there in ten. Was she OK when you left her?'

'I'm not sure. You could see it was hard for her, talking about that time. Am I on speakerphone?'

'You are, and if you're wondering whether Jason knows what his dad did to Victor, he does.'

'OK.' Was that a good thing, or a bad thing? Probably good, since no one would have to tell him. 'I'll see you soon,' and clicking over to the next call, she said to Blake, 'You got my message?'

'Just. You've had some news from the Met?'

'Yes and no. They haven't given me what I asked for, but my contact in Kesterly is saying that more enquiries are happening as a result of my request.'

'You never told me what the request was,' he reminded her.

'I wanted to know if all the letting agents in the area had been contacted. Certainly the estate agents were, but there are some companies that specialise in rentals, and I couldn't find anything in the files about them.'

Sounding aghast, he said, 'So they're only contacting them now?'

'Possibly. I don't know anything for certain yet, but I'll let you know when I do.'

Not until she was arriving back at Rowzee's did she realise she'd forgotten to ask Blake if Matt had played at the Mermaid last night. She hoped he had, for it would be encouraging to hear that he was finding heart again, starting to move forward.

If anyone knew how difficult that was, it was her.

# Chapter Eleven

Rowzee's hands were clasped to her cheeks, trembling slightly, as she watched Jason Griffiths getting out of Graeme's car. The awkward young man wasn't how she'd imagined Edward would be by this age, mainly because she'd never envisaged her son with tattoos and piercings, or such a nervous expression. He'd have had Victor's red hair though, and the same summer-sky blue eyes so like Victor's that she couldn't doubt for a second that this lanky youth with his pallid complexion and tender shyness had Victor's blood running through his veins.

Clearly embarrassed, Jason glanced uncertainly at Graeme, waiting to be told what to do.

'She won't bite,' Graeme promised.

Unable to stop herself, Rowzee reached out to the boy and pulled him into a grandmotherly embrace. 'Thank you for coming to find me,' she whispered emotionally. 'You mustn't be nervous. I'm very happy to see you.'

'Thanks,' he managed to grunt. 'I wasn't sure . . . I mean . . .' He kept his head down as he stepped back. 'I thought you might not, you know . . .'

Taking his hand, she said, 'Let's go inside. I'm sure you'd like a cold drink, and I've got some delicious biscuits that Graeme brought with him this morning. Oh goodness, look at me,' she laughed as she stumbled against the wall.

Jason was quick to catch her and held on until she was steady again.

'It's all the excitement,' she confessed, and because he was so obviously Victor's she went on smiling at him.

'Kitchen,' Graeme reminded her.

Obediently she continued on down the hall, still holding her step-grandson's hand.

'Is Andee here yet?' Graeme asked.

'Is she coming?' Rowzee replied. 'How lovely,' and turning back to Jason she watched him looking around the kitchen and sitting room, taking in the paintings and books, old stone fireplace and glossy black Aga.

'This is where your grandfather lived,' she told him. 'I can show you his study if you like, and his books. Have you ever read any of the ones he wrote?'

Jason nodded. 'All of them. I read them to my dad sometimes.'

Rowzee wasn't quite sure what to say to that.

'Ah, here she is,' Graeme declared, as Andee came in through the back door. 'Andee, this is Jason Griffiths, Victor's grandson. Jason, this is a good friend of the family, Andee Lawrence.'

'How lovely to see you,' Rowzee smiled, clasping Andee's hands in both of hers as Andee turned from Jason. How fond she was of this woman who felt like a dear old friend, even though she wasn't. 'Do you have any news for Blake?' she asked.

With a swift glance at Graeme, Andee said, 'Not for the moment. How are you feeling now?'

'Oh, I'm fine, never better,' Rowzee assured her, picking up on the glance and realising that she must have lost part of the plot. Never mind, she wouldn't worry about it now.

After making sure everyone had lemonade, or in his own case a beer, Graeme said to Jason, 'Perhaps you can tell us what prompted you to come and find Rowzee now?'

Rowzee watched the lad's pale cheeks flush crimson as he turned towards his step-grandmother. 'I've wanted to come for ages, but I kept thinking you wouldn't want to have anything to do with me. Anyway, I didn't know where you lived. I knew you taught at the school, but by the time I got up the courage to come you'd broken up for the summer. Then my nan told me she was sure your brother had an antique shop in the old town.'

Rowzee said, 'So your nan knows you're here?'

He nodded. 'She'd have come with me if she could, but she can't leave Dad, so I had to come on my own.'

Puzzled, Rowzee said, 'Why can't she leave your dad?'

He shrugged. 'He's not all that well, so she takes care of him. Anyway, it was cheaper for me to come on my own. Only one rail ticket and I had somewhere to stay with my mate Ryan. I have to get back tonight though, they're expecting me at work tomorrow.'

Rowzee looked at Graeme as he said, 'When we talked you told me you wanted to speak to my sister and only her, so would you like Andee and me to leave you alone for a while?'

'It's OK, I don't mind saying it in front of you. I mean, I get that you probably don't feel right about leaving her on her own with me after everything that happened before, but I promise she's safe. I wouldn't never harm her, or anyone. I'm not like that. I know I might look like a bit of a ruffian, that's what my nan always says, but it's my way of trying to stop people having a go about the colour of my hair and everything. They still do it, but not as much.'

'You have beautiful hair,' Rowzee assured him. 'Just like your grandpa's. Well, he had more of it, but I'm sure you would if you let it grow.'

Seeming to like the advice, Jason began, 'The reason I wanted to talk to you . . .' He was blushing again, so hotly that it was all Rowzee could do to stop herself taking his hand. 'Well,' he stumbled on, 'it's to tell you how sorry I am, my nan is too, for what my dad did all those years ago. I only found out about a year ago, when my nan started telling me things she thought I should know. It was terrible, the way my dad beat up his own dad. He should never have done that. He probably wouldn't have if he hadn't been drunk. He was always drunk back then.'

He looked so dismal and saddened by this memory that Rowzee couldn't help patting his hand in an effort to comfort him. 'So he doesn't drink any more?' she asked hopefully.

He shook his head. 'Not the hard stuff, anyway. Sometimes he has a beer, you know, on special occasions and that. My nan blames herself for the way he is, but it's not her fault. She didn't make him go on the booze, any more than she pushed him under the car that nearly killed him.'

Rowzee felt a tremor of shock, and wished she'd started her medication days ago, as she tried blinking away the tadpoles. 'I didn't know about that,' she said softly.

Jason shrugged, as if to say why would you? 'The driver never stopped,' he went on, 'but he owed some people, big time, so it's pretty certain that's who did it. We realised that when someone came to my nan for money after, and the only way she could raise it was to sell her shop. She still works there, and has a share in it, but it's not completely hers any more.'

Rowzee said, 'Is this why your dad's unwell? He's never properly recovered from the accident?'

Jason nodded. 'He can't walk, or anything. He doesn't even talk.'

Overcome with pity, Rowzee turned to Graeme. 'We have to help them,' she told him earnestly.

'No, it's all right,' Jason insisted before Graeme could respond. 'It's not why I came, I promise. We're doing OK. It's just that my nan thinks it might help our karma if we said sorry to you. She believes in all that.'

'And who can say she's wrong to,' Rowzee responded warmly. 'Please tell her that I accept your apology and that I'm very glad you came to find me. Do you think there's a chance she'll see me if I go to Totnes?'

'Rowzee,' Graeme warned.

Ignoring him, Rowzee kept her eyes on Jason.

'I expect she would,' he replied. 'She works on Mondays and Thursdays, but any other day should be all right.'

'That's fine,' Rowzee assured him. How soon would her medication kick in? She daren't drive until it did. 'How about this Friday?' she heard herself saying. 'I could get the train, the same as you.'

'Or I could take you,' Andee suggested.

Rowzee turned to her in surprise.

'I'm going that way to see Jenny Leonard,' Andee explained. 'She's with her parents in Dittisham, which isn't so far from Totnes. So if Friday works for Jenny and Jason's nan, it'll work for me too.'

'Thanks for offering to take her,' Graeme said as he walked Andee out to her car, leaving Rowzee showing Jason photographs of his grandpa. 'I'd change things around and go myself . . .'

'You don't have to,' Andee came in gently. 'I'm more than happy to be her chaperone.'

Humour sparked in his eyes but was quickly gone. 'I'm worried about her,' he confessed.

Understanding that he wasn't just referring to the sudden appearance of a step-grandson, Andee waited for him to continue.

'You won't have missed what happened in there,' he said, his expression stiff with concern. 'She seemed to have forgotten that she'd already seen you today, and yet she hadn't forgotten that I was bringing Jason. That seems strange to me, remembering one thing and not the other. And the way she keeps blinking . . . I hadn't really noticed it before today. Did you notice it?'

Andee nodded.

'Pamela thinks she should see a doctor, and I'm inclined to agree.'

Carefully, Andee said, 'Has Pamela suggested it to Rowzee?'

'Yes, and Rowzee says she will, but I don't think it's happened yet.' He glanced back inside as he said, 'I've always worried about her. So has Pamela, mainly because she always seems to need protecting, though I'd never tell her that. She wouldn't like it one bit, she likes to consider herself completely capable and fiercely independent, which she is, of course, but there's no getting away from the fact that she's very trusting, and that's not always a good thing. Victor was the same. A sweeter, more generous and loving couple you'd never find anywhere, but being that way hasn't always served them well. A good example of that is Victor getting into his car to go and see a complete stranger who calls him up out of the blue claiming to be his son. If he hadn't been so trusting he wouldn't have ended up being beaten half to death.' He shook his head as though still trying to absorb it. 'You have to wonder what was going through their minds back then – and since. I mean, imagine not telling anyone the truth, or feeling ashamed of it, as if that dreadful attack were in some way Victor's fault.'

'I'm sure Rowzee didn't think that.'

'You're right, I'm sure she didn't, but being the way she is she'd have found a way to pity this lowlife – I'm sorry, even if he's Victor's son, if you'd seen what he did to him . . .' He took a breath. 'It would be Rowzee's way to try to understand him, rather than report him to the police. She misses her own son so much, is still grieving for him in her way, so she probably saw this Griffiths fellow as someone who could replace him.'

Easily able to believe that, given the tortured workings of a bereaved mother's mind, Andee said, 'Do you believe that he never came to see them again after?'

His eyes came to hers. 'Do you?'

'I'm not sure. Rowzee said he made some abusive calls, but I can't help wondering if they tried to reach out in some way and . . .'

'And what?'

She didn't know. 'I just have a feeling there's more, and maybe even Rowzee doesn't know what it is. Do you think Victor always told her everything?'

'My instinct is to say yes; however, if he thought something would hurt or frighten her, I'm sure he'd have kept that back. Unless, of course, she needed to know for her own safety.'

Andee nodded slowly. 'I guess we might find out more on Friday,' she said, 'if there is any more to find out.'

Graeme looked up and waved as Bill Simmonds drove out of the estate in his truck. 'So, you're going to see Jenny Leonard?' he said, seeming relieved to change the subject.

'I thought I should. Tell me, if she and Blake were as close as everyone says they were, why do you think she's avoiding him now? And her son, who presumably means as much to her as Jessica does.'

Looking surprised, and baffled, he said, 'Is she avoiding them? I guess you could see it that way, but I'm more inclined to think that she simply couldn't cope and has gone home to her mother.'

Accepting that, since she'd done the very same at a time of crisis in her own life, Andee said, 'The missing link in this case, as we've known all along, is the person who made the call as Jessica went into the station.'

'Kim Yoder.'

'That's him.'

'Or her?'

'Indeed, or her, and of course we can be pretty certain that it's not a real name. The question is, did he or she use it for anything else? Obviously it's a question that was asked at the time, and all attempts were made to answer it – at least, we think all attempts.' Curious, he waited for her to continue.

'I've asked for some information from London that I hope is going to prove, or disprove, an oversight in the investigation,' she told him. 'The fact that it's taking so long to come through is concerning me. It could be that they're shutting me out as they try to rectify the mistake – that's the best-case scenario. The worst case – and this bothers me a lot – is that we've managed to stumble upon some kind of cover-up.'

*'Don't worry, Dad, I've got it all worked out.' Jessica's deep brown eyes were shining with laughter – and secrecy and something else Blake couldn't quite define. She was growing up too fast, getting away from him in ways that worried and*

saddened him, but also made him proud of her independence and brave young spirit.

He looked at Jenny, who appeared as secretive and amused as their daughter. 'Do you know what she's talking about?' he demanded, trying to sound fierce though he never quite managed to pull it off.

'Of course not,' she replied. 'You're the one she confides in, not me.'

Knowing that wasn't true, at least not for everything, Blake turned to Matt. 'Are you in on this?' he wanted to know.

'No way,' Matt laughed, pushing back from the table to take his plate to the sink.

'You're up to no good,' Blake accused Jessica with a menacing glower.

Laughing, she cried, 'What's "no good" about sorting things out for myself? I thought you'd be dead chuffed to know I was getting my act together.'

'Well, that could happen if I knew how you were going to do it.'

Leaning forward so her nose was almost touching his, she said, 'Think of your worst nightmares, and guess what, that won't be it.'

'Stop teasing him,' Jenny chided. 'You can see he's worried.'

'I don't understand why.'

'Because that's what fathers do, worry about their daughters.'

'Are you worried?' Jessica wanted to know.

'Not today,' Jenny replied. 'Ask me again tomorrow and I might be.'

'Oh God, you're not going to go all silent and weird on us again, are you?'

'It's not something I plan in advance. It just happens.' Jenny's soft hazel eyes went to Blake.

He said nothing, only reached for her hand and held it as he wondered by what alchemy did fantasies and insecurities occasionally blend in her mind to close her down. He'd read enough about depression to know that the problem was more chemical than emotional, but that didn't make it any easier for them to deal with. He just wished there was more he could do; it made him feel so helpless and responsible when she disappeared inside herself and kept him shut out.

He was experiencing that same desperate frustration now as he explained to Jenny, on the phone, that Andee Lawrence would be coming to see her.

'Why does she want to speak to me?' she asked, her quiet voice falling softly into his ear. He'd never loved anyone – apart from their children – as much as he loved her. He'd never felt such a sense of closeness or understanding, or as much happiness as when they were together as a family and life was good. There'd been so little good since he'd been falsely accused at the school – and how much worse it had become since losing Jess.

'She's trying to help us find our girl,' he told her.

When it seemed she had nothing to say he decided to change the subject for a while. 'Matt played guitar at the Mermaid the other night,' he said, trying to sound upbeat in spite of how traumatic it had been for them both when Matt had come home and Blake had held him for hours as he'd sobbed with guilt and longing, and the same terrible frustration and helplessness that affected them all. 'Ellie Sandworth sang,' he continued. 'You probably remember Ellie.'

Jenny was silent again, but not for long. 'Were you there?' she asked.

'No.'

'Why not? You always go.'

'He didn't want me to this time. I think he was afraid I'd get upset.'

'Did he?'

'Not in front of anyone. We sat up half the night talking when he got home.'

'About Jessica?'

'Of course. Surely it's better than bottling it up.'

'You mean the way I do? But letting it out doesn't make it go away. It just fills you up all over again.'

She was right, of course; in fact there were times that talking about it made it feel even worse, for sharing memories had the power to bring Jess to them in a way that seemed so real that when they stopped the emptiness, the reality were insufferable.

'Will you see Andee Lawrence?' he asked, needing to be sure.

'If that's what you want.'

'Isn't it what you want, to carry on looking for her?'

After a beat she said, 'Of course I want to find her, I'd do anything to make it happen, but at the same time I keep trying to give up hope. I think it would be easier if I could.'

Understanding her feelings, and in a way sharing them, he said, 'I was remembering just now the time Jess told me not to worry about giving her an allowance. She said she had it all worked out. Do you know what she meant by that?'

'I assumed she was planning to do more gigs. What did you think?'

'The same, I suppose, but would it have been enough to cover all her expenses?'

'You saw her bank statements. She was in London, remember? People pay more for their entertainment there, and she managed to get a lot of very exclusive events. They've all checked out. The police spoke to everyone; her earnings were legitimate.'

It was true, they were. Even so, he said, 'But where did all the bookings suddenly come from?'

'Where they always come from, word of mouth. People who were at other events. You know all this, so why are you asking?'

'I'm not sure,' he replied truthfully, for he hated allowing his mind to explore other avenues of suspicion. The police had checked all the sugar daddy websites, escort agencies and gentlemen's clubs, and nothing had ever come up to show Jessica as a member, or even a one-time visitor. 'Maybe it's because I want to keep you on the line,' he said softly.

She stayed silent, but he knew she was still there. He could feel the need for her building inside him, the love that made him strong, gave him purpose, trying to connect with her.

'I miss you,' he told her.

'I miss you too.'

'Then why won't you come home?'

'I want to, I just can't right now.'

'Why?'

'I don't know. Maybe spending this time apart will help us both,' and before he could say any more she rang off.

As he hung up Blake looked around the workshop, his eyes skimming over all the damaged and neglected goods. They seemed to be watching him, waiting for him to make them whole and worthy again. It was as though everything, everyone, needed him to put them back together, and he just wasn't up to the task.

'Is everything all right?' Graeme asked, coming into the room.

Quickly pulling himself together, Blake assured him that it was.

Seeming uncertain, Graeme eyed him closely as he said, 'Andee's going to talk to Jenny on Friday?'

Blake nodded. 'I didn't know which day, but Friday should be fine. I'll let Jenny know.'

Graeme said, 'Have you spoken to Andee today?'

'Only briefly, this morning. Apparently she still hasn't heard anything from London.'

Graeme was about to say more when the phone rang and the shop door opened. 'This could be the call I'm waiting for,' he told Blake. 'Do you mind finding out who's just come in?'

Going through to the showroom, Blake closed the workshop door behind him and was surprised to see a young girl with long, wavy blonde hair and very long legs looking awkwardly around.

'Can I help you?' he asked.

Though she started to speak she seemed unable to find any words. In the end, she said, 'You're Matt Leonard's dad, aren't you?'

Frowning, Blake said, 'That's right. Are you looking for him?'

She shook her head. 'No, I came . . . I'm here to see Graeme Ogilvie.'

'OK. He's on the phone at the moment, but I'm sure he won't be long if you'd like to wait.'

She took a step back. 'No, no, it's fine,' she stammered. 'It doesn't matter,' and pulling open the door she almost collided with an elderly woman who was on her way in.

By the time the passing tourist left with a fine fieravino vase Graeme was back in the shop checking emails on his laptop.

'You had a visitor just now,' Blake told him. 'A young girl, late teens I'd say, long blonde hair . . .'

Graeme regarded him curiously. 'Did you get a name?'

Blake shook his head. 'She said she was here to see you, but then she decided not to wait.'

Baffled, Graeme returned to his computer. 'I tried ringing Andee again a moment ago,' he said, 'she must have her phone turned off.'

Without really thinking, Blake said, 'Are you worried?'

Clearly surprised, Graeme said, 'You mean about Andee?'

Unsure what he'd meant, Blake excused himself and returned to the workshop. He didn't make a habit of listening to gossip, but it was hard not to at times around here. This meant that he knew Andee had left her husband, and that the general consensus was that Graeme might be the reason. However, it wasn't his place to comment on it, much less ask inane questions, so he'd be better off focusing on Andee's fear that the police in London had either not carried out a full investigation, or they were covering something up.

Andee had been watching CCTV footage of Jessica exiting Notting Hill Gate station for so long now that her eyes were starting to blur. There was no doubt the girl had been in good spirits as she'd crossed the road towards Holland Park, but with no further footage showing where she'd gone from there it was impossible to say whether she'd entered a house or apartment, gone into a shop, or maybe she'd got into a car.

This video had arrived from London that morning, presumably in answer to Kesterly CID's request for more information on the transient resident search, which was disingenuous to say the least, since there was nothing new in the footage and not a word had been mentioned about rental agents.

After leaving the tech suite she went to talk to DI Gould about putting more pressure on the Met to give them what they were asking for, and an hour later she was at her flat on the seafront holding her own teenage daughter in her arms – though Jessica of course would be twenty-one by now. Had she been able to celebrate, wherever she was? Or had she never actually reached that glorious age?

'I know I shouldn't have,' Alayna sobbed, 'but I went to see him.'

'To see Dad?' Andee said curiously.

'No. Him. Graeme Ogilvie.'

Andee's insides folded as she said, 'When?'

'Before I came here. Don't worry, I didn't say anything. I didn't even get to speak to him, because I chickened out and ran away.'

'Oh Alayna,' Andee murmured, drawing her back into her arms.

'I wanted to ask him to leave you alone and let you come home again . . .'

'But Alayna . . .'

'I wanted him to know that he had no business breaking up other people's families, and he ought to give more consideration to others.'

Endlessly thankful that her nerve had failed her, Andee said, 'Alayna, you need to believe me when I tell you that I'm not having a relationship with Graeme. He's a friend, that's all, and I'm seeing a little more of him at the moment because I'm helping Blake Leonard, as you know, and Graeme's sister, Mrs C, has a few issues that I'm helping with too.'

Alayna's head came up. 'Mrs C is his sister?' she echoed, confused.

Andee nodded.

Apparently not sure what to make of that, Alayna said, 'What's wrong with her? Why is she having issues?'

'It doesn't matter, what does is that you . . .'

'So you're helping everyone except us?'

'Don't do this,' Andee chided. 'I'm trying to help you now by being honest with you, and by being here so you can tell me how you feel and we can discuss it.'

'But you're not listening.'

'I am. I'm just not willing to be pushed into doing what you want me to.'

With a growl of frustration Alayna fell back against the sofa and pushed her hair from her face. 'I can remember when I felt like your best friend,' she said miserably. 'It's like you don't want to be that any more. You're shutting me out.'

Realising they were coming close to some sharp words being spoken, mostly by her, Andee got up to open the window and stood for a moment gazing out at the busy promenade and beach beyond. The sea air was fresh and salty, the burble of voices was cheerful, and as she watched the people coming and going she thought of how many personal dramas were playing out right now, not just here in Kesterly, but everywhere. Lives were in turmoil for any number of reasons, health, marriages, careers were in jeopardy, but a casual glance at a passer-by would reveal nothing. People went about their days with their stories locked up inside them, their struggles and angst carefully hidden from strangers.

She remembered her father telling her once, after Penny had gone, that they weren't the only ones. They hadn't been singled out for this much suffering and heartache while the rest of the world continued untouched, unharmed. 'No one's immune,' he'd said, 'any more than they're gifted with special powers to endure the challenges life throws their way, or to overcome a loss – and it's almost always a loss of some kind that plunges blameless lives into chaos and despair.'

As those words resonated with her all over again, Andee heard Alayna say, 'You could come back with me now. I know Dad wants you to.'

Turning to her, Andee said, 'Alayna, I realise that Dad and me breaking up is a big thing for you, but you're not a child any more, you need to face it, and while you're at it you could spare a thought for how it feels to be Matt Leonard, or anyone else in his position. He has no idea where his sister is, what's happened to her, or whether he'll ever see her again. When compared to something like that, can you see how important it is to gain a proper perspective on your own issues and deal with them as bravely and considerately as you can?'

Alayna's eyes were wide as she looked at her mother, and filled with the kind of tenderness Andee was used to seeing in her. 'I think about that family quite a lot,' she admitted tearfully. 'It must be so awful for them, I can't begin to imagine, but I know you can.' Getting up, she came to put her arms round her mother. 'It's bringing it all back for you, isn't it?' she said softly.

'In a way,' Andee replied, 'but you're my main concern now.'

'No, Jessica should be. I can see how selfish I'm being, and I shouldn't be, because we have so much compared to Matt and his family.'

Stroking her hair, Andee said, 'This is the girl I know and love.'

'Is there anything I can do?' Alayna offered. 'I'd like to help if I can.'

Surprised, and touched, Andee was about to let her down gently when she suddenly realised that actually there was something Alayna could do.

# Chapter Twelve

It was Friday morning just after nine o'clock, and Rowzee was checking she'd packed everything she needed for her trip to Devon as she took a call from Jilly. 'It's very kind of you to offer me an appointment today,' she was saying chattily, 'but I'm afraid I have something important to do.'

'But this is important,' Jilly scolded. 'We have to talk about radiotherapy . . .'

'We will,' Rowzee promised, 'just not today.'

'Then when?'

'I'll call you early next week to see when you can fit me in, but my position hasn't changed. I still don't want it.'

'Why don't you just let me tell you more about it?'

'I already know, and I don't want it.'

Apparently deciding to park that for the moment, Jilly said, 'How are you getting along with the dexamethasone? Please tell me you're taking it.'

'I am, and I'm happy to report that it seems to be working. I woke up without a headache this morning, and I didn't feel nauseous or dizzy either.' This was true, and she couldn't feel more relieved.

'That's good, but remember, it's a steroid so you won't be able to stay on it for long. However, it'll be even more effective if you combine it with radiotherapy.'

'Do you have the certificate for me yet? The one I need for the doctors in Switzerland.'

'I've discussed it with Mr Mervin and he'd like to see you.'

Having expected as much, Rowzee said, 'OK, but I hope you told him that my mind is made up.'

'I did, and I don't think he's intending to try and change it. He just wants to be sure you've thought everything through. He'll also want you to discuss it with your family. Have you given any more thought to that?'

'Of course, but I'm afraid my position hasn't changed on that either. I'm very sorry, Jilly, but I have to go now. I promise to call next week,' and replacing the receiver she went to make sure that what she'd heard was Andee arriving early, and not Pamela returning for something she'd forgotten.

Seeing it was Pamela she braced herself, just in case their earlier discussion still wasn't over.

'I can't let you do this on your own,' Pamela declared the instant she came through the door. 'I'm sorry, I just can't.'

Getting slightly muddled by her recent conversation with Jilly, Rowzee said, 'How on earth did you find out? Who told you?'

Startled, Pamela replied, 'You did, last night. For heaven's sake, please don't tell me you've forgotten already. We were only discussing it ten minutes ago.'

Quickly catching up, Rowzee said, 'I really don't need you to come with me. Andee's going to be there, and I keep telling you, Jason is the sweetest young lad, and I have a feeling his nan is the same.'

'It's so typical of you to say that, but I'm not a pushover like you. They're after something . . .'

'Please don't let's keep arguing about this. Even if they are, I'll be able to make a decision . . .'

'I don't want you making any decisions while you're there, do you hear me? You're to come back and discuss them with me and Graeme first, and if that dreadful beast who claims to be Victor's son – the monster who put Victor in a hospital bed – as much as looks at you funny you're to get Andee to flatten him with one of her police moves.'

Breaking into a laugh, Rowzee said, 'I'm beginning to wish I hadn't told you . . .'

'You didn't until it was forced out of you. I still can't believe you'd keep something like that to yourself. Not to tell me, your own sister . . . That man should have been prosecuted for what he did and I'd have made sure he was if I'd known. So would Graeme.'

'Which was why we didn't tell you. He's Victor's son for heaven's sake. Now, if you don't mind, Andee'll be here any minute and I need to be ready.'

Grabbing her suddenly, Pamela smothered her in a bruising embrace.

Rowzee gasped, trying to get some air. 'What was that for?' she demanded when Pamela, just as abruptly, let her go.

'I'm trying to let you know how much you mean to me,' Pamela told her, this rare confession of feeling making it hard for her to meet Rowzee's eyes. 'I want to be there for you, but I understand that all three of us can't go in, so I'm happy for Andee to go in my place. She'll be less likely to say something offensive.'

Rowzee blinked in amazement. 'You? Say something offensive?' she repeated, seemingly aghast. 'That would never happen.'

'I know you're mocking me, but I mean it, I don't want to do anything to ruin this for you, just in case the boy's on the level, but I don't want you taken advantage of either.'

Smiling, Rowzee drew her back into a gentler embrace. 'I promise to call as soon as I have some news,' she told her.

'Good. What time do you expect to be back?'

'I'm not sure because Andee's arranged to see Jenny Leonard while we're down that way, and we might drop in on Gina Stamfield as well.'

'Sounds like a busy day. Are you sure you're up to all this gallivanting about? You know you haven't been yourself . . .'

'I'm perfectly fine, thank you, it's only you who thinks I'm not. Now, please stop worrying about me and go and do whatever you're supposed to be doing. You're looking very nice again, by the way.'

Enjoying the compliment, Pamela said, 'I'm told if you look nice on the outside it'll make you feel nice on the inside.'

Rowzee frowned. 'Isn't that supposed to be the other way round?'

Pamela shrugged.

Deciding that in some instances it could work either way, Rowzee said, 'That sounds like Andee arriving. Quickly, before she comes in, do you think there might be something between her and Graeme? I hope there is, but I can't quite tell.'

'Stop being such a matchmaker,' Pamela chided. 'First me, now Graeme. What's wrong with us being single?'

'Nothing, if it's how you want to be, but I don't think it is. Are you still Internet dating?'

'I told you, I never was, but I'm almost ready to divulge what I have been doing. In fact, I'd hoped you might have noticed a bit more than you have by now, because I'm told I'm making great strides.'

Left to stare after her as she swept back down the hall, Rowzee racked her brains to think of what she might have noticed a little bit of, but not enough to have come to a conclusion. Apart from how well Pamela was dressing . . . Was she studying for some sort of fashion diploma? It must have something to do with beauty because her hair was looking good too, and her make-up, though still a little sloppy in places, was definitely improving.

'Andee,' she said, brightening as Pamela stood aside to let Andee through. 'I'm all ready, so unless you'd like some coffee first we can go.'

'Perhaps we can stop on the way,' Andee suggested.

'Please take care of her,' Pamela said as she walked out with them, 'and make sure she doesn't do anything rash.'

'You're the one,' Rowzee reminded her, 'that wants Andee to flatten people with her police moves. Now, please mind your own business and go and say hello to your boyfriend.'

Startled, Pamela looked round as Bill Simmonds slowed up in his truck. 'He's not my boyfriend,' she muttered, waving him on. He gave a jaunty wave back and continued to wait, so with an exaggerated sigh Pamela stalked towards him.

'Yet,' Rowzee said quietly behind her.

In no time at all Rowzee and Andee were driving across the heart of the moor, lapping up the mid-morning sunshine as they passed Dunkery Beacon, with the picturesque village of Luccombe glistening enticingly at its feet. Very soon they were at Webbers Post, where the school's natural science teachers often brought young students to begin their treasure-filled nature trails. It was also where Rowzee used to park her 'drama wheels' as the students called her department bus, when they'd come to gain inspiration for a particular piece, or to search out venues to stage *A Midsummer Night's Dream* or a passion play. Thrilling to the memories of the visits, Rowzee described them to Andee, her heart swelling with remembered pride and excitement as if they were happening right now. Along with the kids she'd loved every aspect of the wildlife, from rabbits and squirrels to hares, hedgehogs and mice – to the wild ponies, and more elusive red deer and wild boar. Of course, being the rascals they were the children had pounced on any exotic-looking fungi they could find, wanting to know if it was poisonous and if so could they test it out on some of the less popular members of staff.

'I remember roaming about the moor with Victor during spring.' Rowzee smiled wistfully as they travelled on through endless hectares of wilderness and woodland. 'We'd wade through seas of bluebells, the like of which I'm sure you'd never find anywhere else. He was a big nature-lover. He used to find coming here very inspiring. He'd write for hours as soon as we got home, even if the story had nothing to do with what he'd seen.'

With a smile, Andee said, 'You still miss him?'

'Oh, of course. It hasn't been so long, and besides I think I always will. He and I were soulmates, you see, so I have no problem believing he'll be waiting for me on the other side when the time comes.' Her throat dried as she thought of how soon that might be, and if she really believed it would happen. 'We're meant to be together,' she said softly, 'and every time I come up on to the moor I feel it more deeply than ever.'

Glancing at her fondly, Andee said, 'How did the two of you meet?'

Brightening, Rowzee said, 'We were introduced during an anti-apartheid march back in the seventies. He was at Bath uni, I was at Bristol and busloads of us descended on London one weekend to make our voices heard. We had a fine time of our courtship after that, I can tell you, going back and forth between those two beautiful cities, although Bristol's Waterfront hadn't been developed back then so it definitely wasn't the trendy place it's turned into now. The uni, of course, has always been one of the top in the country, which reminds me, how is Alayna?'

'Actually,' Andee replied, 'she seems OK. We had a chat yesterday, and now she's helping me with something, so I think we might have turned a corner.'

'Oh dear, does that mean you were having difficulties?'

'A few.'

Reminded of Andee's broken marriage, Rowzee said, very gently, 'I don't want to pry, but I'm guessing she's taking your break-up with her father quite hard?'

Andee nodded. 'To be honest, I thought she'd be so wrapped up in student life and her own plans for the summer that she'd hardly concern herself with what was going on at home, which just goes to show how naïve, or even delusional I was.'

'It could very easily have happened that way, you can never tell with children. Just a thought, do you know if everything was good for her before she came home? Any boyfriend problems, or uncertainties about her course?'

Andee frowned. 'What on earth are you going to think of me when I confess that I haven't asked? To be honest, it never even crossed my mind that she might be trying to deal with her own issues. So the situation between her father and me could be making everything worse?'

'I'm not saying that's the case, but from what I remember of Alayna she's a very sensitive and compassionate girl, so it's possible she needed to pour a few things out to you when she came back and then got angry because she didn't have your full attention.'

Andee glanced over at her. 'Why didn't I see it like that?'

Rowzee smiled. 'The bigger picture is often much easier to see from the outside.'

Shaking her head, Andee said, 'It's no wonder all your students loved you. You're easy to talk to and wise and wonderful . . .'

Rowzee gave a shout of laughter. 'Believe me, I'm as capable of getting things wrong as anyone else, and my darling sister would greatly enjoy telling you that if she were here.'

'You're very close, you two,' Andee smiled.

'Yes, we are, and sometimes I wonder if a little too close. I worry that I'm holding her back, stopping her from getting on with her life because she feels she has to take care of me. She likes to have someone to take care of, you see, it gives her an excuse to avoid looking at the things that are missing in her life.'

'You think things are missing?'

'Well, let's just say that she's never met that one special person who recognises just how very special she is. She hides who she really is behind her bossy, overbearing personality, when in actual fact she's as kind and loyal and loving as anyone I've ever known. OK, I'm her sister, so I'm biased, but I know her better than anyone, so I know I'm right. The trouble is, ever since Victor died she's fussed around me like a mother hen, making sure I'm not getting too sad or missing him too much. She even moved in with me, as you know, and

I have to admit I'm quite happy about that because I enjoy the company, even when she's being a cantankerous old bat.' She stopped, puzzled, as it suddenly struck her that Pamela hadn't been quite so irritable lately. She might even be showing signs of becoming more tolerant in her old age – unless there had been outrages and eruptions Rowzee had managed to forget about, or even not notice thanks to the slow but steady breakdown in her brain.

Experiencing a jolt of sadness at the reminder of her condition, she tried to concentrate on what Andee was saying, but it was a while before she was fully focused, and she had no idea how much she'd missed by the time Andee excused herself and took a phone call on her hands-free.

'Hi, Mum, it's me,' Alayna cried excitedly. 'You are so not going to believe this.'

'Try me,' Andee challenged, casting a smile at Rowzee.

'OK, right, so I speak to about twelve different rental agents in West London like you told me to, and I end up talking to this one called Anzel, or something like that. She's half-French, half-Russian, so we spoke in French, which was kind of cool. Anyway, she gave me the number of this other agent who she says operates only on a strictly private basis, if I knew what she meant. I didn't, but I called the number anyway and this other agent – her name's Oleysa and she's also Russian, I think, definitely not English anyway – so she tells me that yes, someone called Yoder did rent a house through her in Holland Park about two years ago. And that's not all, apparently she told the police that three days ago when they called.'

Amazed and fascinated, Andee said, 'You've done a brilliant job, my darling. Now I want you to call Leo at the station and tell him exactly what you just told me.'

'No problem. How's Mrs C? Is she with you?'

'I'm very good, Alayna, thank you,' Rowzee called out. 'It's lovely to hear you.'

'And you. Take care of my mum, won't you – and Mum, take care of Mrs C. Going to call Leo now,' and the line went dead.

Rowzee and Andee exchanged glances.

'Am I right in thinking,' Rowzee said carefully, 'that there's just been a breakthrough in the search for Jessica?'

Cautiously, Andee replied, 'It's sounding like the police in London have made one and decided not to share, which is interesting. Perhaps it's best not to say anything to Blake for the moment. I'd like to hear what the CID officers in London have to say to their colleagues in Kesterly when they're told that we know about the rental.'

Thankful that her and Rowzee's first visit of the day was to Norma Griffiths and her family, since she wanted more time to think before facing Jenny Leonard, Andee followed the satnav directions along Totnes's Western Bypass and turned at the brow of the hill on to Plymouth Road. A few minutes later, just after the council offices, they found themselves in a labyrinth of streets made up of far newer houses than those out on the main road, or in the town's historic centre. Eventually they came to a stop outside a secluded pebble-dash bungalow, tucked into the end of a leafy cul-de-sac with a weeping willow in the front garden and a welcome sign hanging from the gate.

As Andee walked round the car to join Rowzee she could sense how tense Rowzee had become, and put a comforting hand on her arm. 'Are you OK?' she asked gently.

Rowzee was gazing at the heavily netted windows as she nodded. 'I think so. A little nervous, I guess, and wishing Victor was here, but I keep reminding myself that he's probably watching from wherever he is and I know he'd want me to do this.'

Touched by her belief, Andee led the way to the front door but didn't press the bell until Rowzee indicated she was ready.

There was an immediate sound of movement inside, doors opening, footsteps, voices, and a moment later they were being warmly greeted by a friendly, even eager-looking woman with large, violet-blue eyes, a heart-shaped face and copious amounts of silver hair gathered up in a bun and held in place by a chopstick. Andee was immediately struck by how much younger and more glamorous the woman looked than she'd expected – presuming this was Norma Griffiths, but maybe it was a daughter, or friend, or someone they'd yet to hear anything about.

'You must be Rowena,' the woman smiled, taking both of Rowzee's hands in hers. 'I'm Norma. It's so lovely to meet you. Thank you for coming all this way. I hope you managed to track us down OK.'

Finding her voice, Rowzee said, 'Andee's trusty little gizmo did us proud.'

Turning to Andee and still smiling a welcome, Norma said, 'Jason's told me all good things about you. Come in, please. We've been looking forward so much to seeing you. Ever since Jason called to say that you were happy to meet me I've had nothing but positive and joyful feelings about the outcome, and I hope you have too.'

As Rowzee gave an assurance that she had, Andee was surprised and even amused to find herself in a state of optimism too, as though Norma's ebullient nature and belief in good was somehow infectious. It had been right to come here, her instincts were telling her. She'd yet to find out why they'd reached this decision, but there was something so comforting and wholesome about this woman with her twinkly eyes and copious amounts of pretty jewellery that it felt uplifting just to be with her.

Andee watched Rowzee's dear little head in front of her as, still holding Norma's hand, she followed Norma across a dimly lit hall with several closed doors and into a surprisingly large and bright room, given how small the bungalow appeared from the outside. The smell of incense immediately assailed them, while the soothing notes of a harp mingled with the sound of trickling water. Colourful crystals, candles, runes and tiny angels were all around the place, with dreamcatchers and wind chimes dangling from window frames and overhead beams.

The room was clearly double the size it had once been, for the whole of the back wall had been removed to give full and free access into a spacious sun room where water features and Buddhas and yet more crystals glinted serenely in the late-morning sunlight. All the furniture was draped in beautifully embroidered throws and needlepoint cushions, while the floors and walls were home to an impressive collection of what appeared to be handmade rugs and tapestries.

'Jase is just putting the kettle on,' Norma told them, lifting a parrot with one finger and handing it back into its cage. 'He said you like biscuits, so I've made some specially. You don't have to eat them, of course, I shan't be offended, because they never go wasted in this house. People coming and going all the time, wanting readings, or advice of some sort, or a good old chat about whatever's on their minds, which is lovely because it helps keep us all lively and up to date with this world and the next, if that's what they're after.' Her violet eyes followed Rowzee's to the person Andee had only just noticed herself. He was slumped in a wheelchair to one side of the sun room, his carroty hair glinting golden in the sunlight. His head was lolling towards one shoulder, while his thin hands hung loosely in his lap, and his empty blue-grey eyes were staring at nothing at all.

'This is Sean, my son,' Norma told them, going to bring the wheelchair closer. 'Sean, do you remember I told you your stepmother was coming today? Well here she is, and a friend has also come with her. Aren't we lucky to have visitors?'

Andee had seen enough photographs of Victor to realise straight away how this shell of a man resembled him, and of course, Rowzee would be seeing it too. Worrying about the effect it might be having on her, Andee tried to think what to say, but Norma was already answering her own question, speaking as though Sean had in some way responded to her.

'That's right, my lovely, they've had quite a long drive, but Jase is making them some tea – or coffee if you prefer,' she said to Rowzee and Andee.

'Tea's fine,' they replied, almost in unison.

Andee said, 'Jason told us about the accident . . . We hadn't realised . . . Is it how he came to be like this?'

'I'm afraid so,' Norma replied, smoothing a fond hand over Sean's hair.

Hating talking about him as if he weren't there, but having to ask, Andee said, 'Can he hear or speak?'

Still smiling, Norma said, 'He rarely has anything to say, but the doctors are convinced he hears certain sounds so between us we're trying to figure out a system of communication. Music is very good.'

Noticing how pale Rowzee had become, Andee put a hand on her shoulder.

'Ah, here you are,' Norma announced cheerily as Jason came into the room with an overloaded tray. 'Put everything down here next to Dad, there's a love.'

Struck by the incongruity of Jason's razor cut, sleeveless jacket and torn jeans in this mesmerisingly spiritual emporium, Andee watched him set the tray down as expertly as a professional waiter.

'It's lovely to see you,' Rowzee told him huskily, seeming unsure about everything, as well she might.

After giving her a hug, he said, 'Nan, you haven't invited anyone to sit down.'

With a roll of her eyes, Norma said, 'Where are my manners? It's a good job I have this young scallywag to keep me on my toes or who knows where we'd all end up,' and waving Rowzee and Andee to a cosy two-seater sofa, she took an armchair next to Sean while Jason handed round cups of tea before perching on a chair next to the table.

'In case you're wondering,' Norma began, 'we always talk openly in front of Sean so please don't be afraid to ask anything, or say whatever's on your mind.'

Feeling that her own thoughts were largely irrelevant, Andee waited for Rowzee to speak first, but it seemed Rowzee was still finding it hard to say anything.

Coming to the rescue, Norma said, 'I'm going about this all the wrong way round, as usual. I'm the one who should start, of course, by trying to express just how sorry I am for what Sean did to Victor all those years ago. I realise much water has flowed since, but that doesn't make the crime any less serious, or the apology any less necessary or heartfelt. If I'd known where he was going that day I'd have done everything I could to stop him, but he hardly ever confided in me back then so I rarely knew what he was thinking, much less what he was planning to do with his day.'

Deciding to take the lead until Rowzee was ready, Andee said, 'How long before that day did Sean know about Victor being his father?'

'A few months,' Norma replied. 'He kept threatening to go, and I kept telling him that no good would come of it while he was in the state he was in . . . Of course, I realise now that I should have contacted Victor myself to let him know that he had a son who might turn up on him.'

'Why didn't . . .?' Rowzee cleared her throat. 'Why didn't you tell Victor right back when you knew you were pregnant?'

Norma's eyes went to where her hand was holding her son's, and it seemed for a moment that she wasn't going to answer. 'I was a fool not to have,' she replied, her eyes still down, 'and believe me I wish now that I had, but I was very young back then, and selfish and naïve with so many romantic notions in my head . . . I told myself that I'd love my baby so much that he'd never need a father.' Her gentle eyes showed her troubled conscience as she fixed them on Rowzee. 'I couldn't have articulated any of that to myself back then,' she admitted, 'all I knew was that he was mine and I didn't want to share him in case someone tried to take him away. So I never told a soul who the father was, not even my parents who stood by me for as long as they were alive. I realise now, of course, how irrational and unforgivable my actions were, and my only defence is youth and a lack of understanding of myself, never mind the world.'

Since Rowzee didn't seem to have any more questions for the moment, Andee said, 'So what prompted you to tell Sean about Victor when you did?'

Norma shook her head sadly, but before she could answer Rowzee put a hand to her mouth, saying, 'He's crying. Is he crying?'

Tears were indeed running down Sean's sunken cheeks, but Norma was unflustered as she took a tissue from a box beside her to dry his eyes, and another to dab the drool from his chin.

'Why is he crying?' Rowzee asked worriedly.

'We don't know that he is,' Norma replied. 'It could just be the angle that he's holding his head making his eyes run.'

Realising she needed to tell herself that as a way of dealing with his inner distress, if that was indeed what was causing the tears, Andee looked at Jason, who was watching his grandmother, apparently ready to help if needed.

'Now where were we?' Norma asked, sitting back in her chair. 'Oh that's right, why did I tell Sean about Victor when I did? Well, I guess we have to put that down to this one,' she said, nodding towards Jason. 'After his mother ran off and left him when he was twelve and Sean brought him here to me, I got to realise that in their different ways they both needed more than me and what was missing for Sean, most of all, was a father. I'd done my best, I really had, but I couldn't fool myself any longer. Sean wasn't the kind of man I'd hoped he'd be, and I had to accept that the cause of his problems might well have been growing up without a father to teach him the rights and wrongs of the world. I felt sure in my heart that Victor was a good man who'd want to do right by his son and grandson, but even so, I still didn't come clean right away. I thought about it for a long time and prayed for guidance. I was afraid, I suppose, that it wouldn't

224

work out the way I hoped, and now, with the benefit of hindsight, we know I was right to be afraid. I never dreamt it would go the way it did, with Victor ending up in hospital and Sean being arrested on the way back for drunk-driving. I didn't actually know he'd been to see Victor then, he didn't tell me for several weeks, and I'm still not sure if I ever got the whole story. I remember telling myself that if it had been as serious as Sean was making out the police would have come to find him. But no one did, and even though I knew I should be in touch to make sure Victor was all right, I told myself that if he wanted any more contact with Sean he'd do it in his own time, not in mine. I guess you could accuse me of burying my head in the sand, or not wanting to believe the worst of my son in spite of knowing he was capable of some terrible things when he was drunk. And there was Jason to think of too. Life was difficult enough for the lad trying to get over the way his mother had just upped and gone – she used to ring from time to time, but she never came to see him, or invited him to go and visit her. It was a difficult time, and it was all my fault. I knew that then and I know it now. If I'd allowed Victor – and you – to be a part of Sean's life he'd be a very different person today.'

Rowzee was gazing at Sean's glinting thatch of hair and silvery blue eyes as she said, 'Jason told us it was a hit-and-run driver.'

Norma nodded. 'We have our suspicions who was behind it, but we can't go to the police without creating even more problems for ourselves. You see, Sean had got in with the wrong kind of people. He told me before this happened that they were following him and he was afraid, but there was nothing I could do. It was drugs; he was selling them and spending what he got on booze instead of handing it over to the dealers. I only found out after, while he was still in hospital, and they came to see me.' She sighed sadly. 'It was a terrible time. The gangsters – and believe me, they were gangsters – came here wanting money a few weeks after it happened. I was afraid they might do something to harm Jason if I didn't pay up, so I raised the money the only way I could and sold my shop. Luckily it got rid of them.'

'You should have to come to us, we'd have helped you,' Rowzee told her with feeling.

With a smile Norma said, 'I think I knew that, and I was going to get in touch, but then I heard on the news that Victor had died and it seemed just plain wrong to ask for your help when you were going through your own difficult time.'

Rowzee's eyes were solemn and earnest as she said, 'I'd like to help now. So if there's anything you need . . .'

'Not me,' Norma interrupted gently. 'I'm fine, so's Sean, in his way. He's got his mum to take care of him, but it's not right for Jason to be . . .'

'Nan, you promised,' Jason interrupted.

'I know, my love, but you can't go on wasting your life here, trying to make things easier for me when there's a whole world of universities and opportunities out there you should be taking advantage of.'

'I don't want to. I'm all right here.'

Rowzee's eyes moved between the two, as though she might get involved, but in the end all she said to Norma was, 'Do you have help from social services?'

'Actually, they're pretty good,' Norma admitted. 'Someone comes in twice a week so I can go to work in the shop. I enjoy it, it's a busy place and it gets me out for a few hours.'

'Is that where you do your readings?' Rowzee wondered.

'Sometimes. I've got a small room here as well.'

After taking this in, Rowzee said, 'Maybe I could help pay for some private nursing?'

'Oh, no, no,' Norma protested. 'If you want to help Jason that's fine . . .'

'I'm not going anywhere,' Jason informed her belligerently. 'He's as much my dad as he's your son, so if I want to look after him too that's up to me.'

Though Andee might have wondered how Sean had managed to earn himself so much love and loyalty, she could see from the photos around the place of a very young Jason with a very different Sean that there had definitely been a bond once.

Since there seemed to be a bit of a stand-off over Rowzee's offer to help, Andee ventured to say, 'Can I suggest you all take some time to think things over before you reach any decisions?'

After agreeing that this was the most sensible course Rowzee turned to Andee, seeming unsure of what to do next.

Before Andee could speak Norma was getting to her feet. 'I'm sorry,' she said, 'but I have to see to Sean.'

'It's OK, I'll do it Nan,' Jason offered, getting up too.

Realising from the odour that had begun seeping into the musky scent of incense that the poor man must have soiled himself, Andee said, 'Rowzee and I ought to be going. I need to be somewhere.'

With a smile, Norma said, 'Of course.' She watched as Rowzee walked over to Sean and stooped to take his hand.

'I'm sorry this has happened to you,' Rowzee whispered shakily. 'So very sorry.'

There was no reaction from Sean, but she waited anyway, as though expecting it to take some time. In the end, she stood up and turned to embrace Norma.

'Thank you for coming,' Norma murmured against Rowzee's feathery hair.

'I'm glad I did,' Rowzee replied.

Still holding her Norma closed her eyes, and frowned, and for one awful moment Andee was afraid she might be trying to contact someone on the other side. Or perhaps someone there was trying to reach her. *Dear God, don't let it be Victor.*

Seeming unfazed, Rowzee waited and gazed expectantly into Norma's face until eventually Norma said, 'You have a dog?'

Rowzee blinked. 'No.'

Norma simply shrugged. 'I thought maybe you did.'

For a long time after she and Andee had driven away from Norma's bungalow, Rowzee said nothing. The shock of finding Victor's son in such a debilitated state was still resonating profoundly with her, speaking to her in ways she couldn't articulate, only feel. The empathy was like nothing she'd ever known before; the frustration of being unable to reach him, of not knowing how he felt, if he needed to speak, if he wanted to stay as he was simply to remain alive, was so intense it was making her light-headed.

One day, perhaps sooner rather than later, there was every chance she was going to be like that, unable to act for herself, or communicate her needs, or even recognise those she loved. Someone would have to wash and feed her, put her to bed and get her up in the morning. She wondered if Sean did recognise those he loved, if not by sight then by voice or even some kind of extra-sensory perception. Surely to God he didn't want to be as he was, but even if he were desperate to die he couldn't tell anyone. He was being kept alive because medical science had made it possible, not because it was right or what he wanted, if anyone even knew what that was. He could be locked up inside himself, unable to make his voice, his hands, his eyes, or his brain function in a way that could help him to escape the misery and ignominy of a living death.

Feeling absolutely certain now that she must press ahead with her plans to go to Zurich, and soon, probably in the next two to three weeks while the steroids were still working, she refused to allow herself to feel afraid or upset. She simply thought of Sean and what she'd just seen of his tragic existence and his family's devotion. All her instincts were telling her that Victor had been in that room today, showing her his son, and reminding her that it didn't have to be that way for her. He'd be waiting with Edward when she got to the other side, and everyone she loved on this side would understand, once she'd written it all down for them, why she'd chosen to go the way she had.

Eventually breaking the silence, Andee said, 'That was harder than you were expecting?'

Rowzee didn't deny it. 'But it's helped to clarify some things too,' she said, wondering fleetingly if she could ask Norma to go to Zurich with her. She was such a gentle and soothing person, exactly the right sort of presence to help her on her way. But of course it was supremely selfish to think of putting such a burden on dear Norma when she already had so much to contend with. And the last thing she'd need was Rowzee's family blaming her in some way for Rowzee's own decision.

'I wonder why she thought you had a dog,' Andee commented.

Rowzee frowned. 'I've no idea,' she replied, 'but I've just remembered that I'm going to be looking after my niece's dog for the next couple of weeks. I wonder if she was meaning him.'

# Chapter Thirteen

Graeme looked up from the auction site he was browsing as Pamela bustled in through the shop door with her arms full of carrier bags from some of Kesterly's most expensive boutiques.

'Have you heard from Rowzee?' she demanded with no preamble, while dropping her shopping on an elegant mahogany and ivory silk chaise longue.

'I wasn't really expecting to yet,' he replied. 'Were you?'

'I just thought she might have called to keep us in the picture. No word from Andee either, I take it?'

Shaking his head, he nodded towards her bags. 'Robbed a bank?' he teased.

'Actually, most of it's for Rowzee and the girls. I thought they could do with a treat.' She took out her phone to check for messages. 'Are you worried?' she asked.

'You mean about Rowzee? I wasn't.'

'How can you say that when you know she hasn't been herself lately – all these dizzy spells and headaches, and I wouldn't be a bit surprised if they're worse than she's admitting to. You need to talk to her about seeing the doctor. Hello Blake, gosh they're pretty,' she declared, admiring the mid-century Murano glass candlesticks he was bringing through from the workshop. 'I think Rowzee would like these, Graeme, don't you? Shall I get them for her?'

'I'm afraid they're already sold,' Blake told her, 'but we can always look out for more.'

'Yes, I think you should,' she decided. 'They're just her type of thing. And this chaise longue is beautiful. I think she should have that too.'

'Pamela? What's going on?' Graeme asked firmly.

Wide-eyed, she said, 'Going on? In what way?'

'All these gifts. No one has a birthday, and Christmas is still a long way off.'

'I'm just feeling generous, that's all. I hope it's allowed.'

'Of course. It's just . . . unusual.'

'For me, you mean. Well, I've decided to change. Life's too short to stay cross all the time, or to go on beating about the bush when something needs to be said. On which subject, what are you doing about Andee?'

Taken aback, he said, 'What kind of question is that?'

'A direct one. We all know you two had something going a while ago, and she's single again now so . . .'

'That's enough,' he cut in sharply. 'You might have given up being cross, but I see bossy is still featuring large.'

Pamela was about to respond when the door opened behind her and Frankie, the post lady, came in with the mail.

'Recorded delivery for you,' she told Blake, while handing the rest of the envelopes and magazines to Graeme.

As Blake took the large package addressed to him, Graeme saw him look curiously at the brown-paper wrapping tied up with string.

'What is it?' Pamela prompted, seeming to sense some kind of change in the atmosphere.

'There's only one way to find out,' Blake replied, and cutting the string, he tore open the wrapping to find a large shoebox inside. As he removed the lid his face turned white with shock.

'Oh my goodness,' Pamela murmured. 'Is it real?'

Blake looked at Graeme who looked at him.

'Who's it from?' Graeme asked.

'I've no idea,' Blake replied, searching for a card or a note.

'How much is there?' Pamela asked.

Blake looked at Graeme again.

'I'll call Andee,' Graeme said, and picking up the phone he pressed in her mobile number.

'Are you sure you'll be all right here?' Andee was asking Rowzee as she settled her down on the terrace of Dittisham's Anchor Stone café. It was right next to the wonderfully romantic River Dart with plenty of boats and people going by, so full of life, but not so busy as to make it a disconcerting place to be.

'I'll be fine,' Rowzee promised. 'I just need to have a little time to myself, that's all, and if Jenny doesn't know I'm with you she won't be expecting me to come in.'

Though relieved at being able to see Jenny Leonard alone, Andee couldn't help being concerned about Rowzee, for the visit to Victor's son had clearly shaken her up quite a lot.

'I shouldn't be long,' she said, 'then I think we should head home.'

'Oh no,' Rowzee protested. 'Gina's expecting us and I'm so looking forward to seeing her. Please don't let's change our plans.'

Andee regarded her carefully. 'OK, let's see how you feel when I get back.'

A few minutes later she was driving back up the hill to the village's main car park when Graeme rang. Instead of asking about Rowzee, which was what she'd expected, he said, 'Blake's just received a parcel containing a shoebox full of cash. We haven't counted it yet, but it has to amount to several tens of thousands of pounds.'

Stunned, she said, 'Who's it from?'

'We've no idea. There's no sender address, or accompanying note.'

Trying and failing to connect this to the discovery of a rental in Holland Park, she said, 'OK, if you haven't done it already you should call Leo Johnson at the station. Is Blake with you?'

'Yes.'

'I'm about to go and see Jenny. Does he want me to mention this?'

After consulting Blake, Graeme said, 'He'd rather you didn't for now.'

'OK. Understood. I should tell you,' she went on, 'that the police in London have found a house in Holland Park that was rented to someone by the name of Yoder at the time Jessica disappeared.'

There was a moment's shocked silence before Graeme said, 'So there was an oversight?'

'It would appear so, because the letting agent was easy to find. I've no idea yet why she didn't come forward at the time, but I'm hoping to know more by the end of the day. Perhaps you could pass this on to Blake.'

'Of course. Before you go . . . Pamela and I are wondering how Rowzee is? Has she met Norma Griffiths yet?'

'Yes, she has, and I think she's OK, but I have to tell you that seeing Victor's son came as a shock to us both. It turns out he's not just unwell, as Jason put it; the accident he told us about has left his father completely incapacitated. It's impossible to know how compos mentis he is, but there really doesn't seem to be much going on there.'

'Oh God, this is awful. Not what Rowzee would have been expecting at all.'

'He's being very well cared for, but seeing someone like that . . . I don't mind admitting it's shaken me up a bit too. It's so sad, not only for him but for his family. They don't have proper lives any more, which is a tragedy for Jason, being as young as he is. Anyway,

I'm sure Rowzee will call you soon to tell you about it. Needless to say she wants to help in some way.'

'I'm sure she does. You're not with her now?'

'I've left her having a cup of tea while I go and see Jenny Leonard. I'm sorry, but I need to ring off now. If Rowzee can't contact you because she's in a bad reception area I'll get her to call when we're on our way to Gina's.'

After ringing off, she found a space in the main car park and made the connection to Leo Johnson as she walked back along the Level to the address Blake had given her for Jenny's parents. 'You should get a call any minute from Graeme Ogilvie or Blake Leonard,' she told Johnson. 'Apparently a box full of cash has turned up addressed to Blake. No sender address or accompanying note.'

'Surreal,' he murmured. 'I'll go over there myself as soon as I get the call. Any theories on what it's about?'

'None, at this stage, and I don't think Blake has any either. So what's happening in London?'

'Good question. Your daughter's definitely set the cat amongst the pigeons with her findings. I haven't spoken to anyone personally, but DI Gould has and apparently they're furious that we've managed to find out about the rental, which they discovered three days ago, apparently.'

'As a result of you requesting rental information from the initial investigation?'

'*You* requested it, and it's a bit much to be a coincidence.'

'So more likely an oversight than a cover-up?'

'No straight answer to that yet, but I'm told a forensic team has been going over the place for the past two days. Too early yet to know if Jessica was there, and with the amount of time that's passed . . .'

'Is anyone living there now?'

'I don't know. Information's still scant, but we're working on it.'

Marvelling at this turn of events, she said, 'A few phone calls was all it took.'

'So I hear. Tell Alayna from me that she did good. And it's making Gould's day to think of you as part of the team again.'

With a wry smile, she said, 'Just as long as he doesn't get any ideas that it's going to be permanent,' and ending the call she sent a quick text to Alayna saying, *Leo says you did good today, I say you did brilliantly. Please let's talk again soon. I think I'm starting to see the bigger picture.*

Charles had been afraid, terrified, something like this would happen when he returned to Burlingford Hall, yet he'd come all the same. It was as though a macabre compulsion had forced him, and was now holding him here like a prisoner inside his own conscience. He was being mercilessly haunted by the woman's face that would appear out of nowhere, confronting him as he looked from a window, or glanced in a mirror, or turned suddenly at an unexpected sound. He saw it on the horizon, in the gardens, on the stairs, and in his dreams. She stared at him in fear and shock, trapped, unable to move. He saw so many expressions

237

that couldn't be real, only gruesome figments of his imagination. Who was she? How had she come to be there that night? Where was she now? How could he find her?

He was standing at an upstairs window of the Hall, staring blindly across the open fields at the back of the estate towards the ruggedly steep rise of the moor in the distance. It was even further than it appeared from here, two miles or more, with dense woods, streams, swamps, massive swathes of brambles, ancient rocks and overgrown trails all hidden from view. There was even a road that curved around the upper slopes of the hillside to descend, eventually, towards the coast. Did anyone ever use it? He wouldn't know by looking from here.

An email had arrived earlier from his daughter, Lydia, updating him on the progress she and her team were achieving in their fight to help Syrian refugees. She was flying to somewhere in Eastern Europe sometime in the next few weeks, apparently. Meanwhile she'd been invited to the White House, though she hadn't said whether she'd accepted this extraordinary honour, or when it was supposed to be happening. Knowing Lydia, if it coincided with her trip to Europe she'd put the refugees first – self-glory, once-in-a-lifetime photo-ops and the chance of a massively impressive name-drop in the future would carry no weight with her. The invitation's only significance for her would be the power of the contact and what use it might be put to, for she was as dedicated to her work as any terrified exile would be to safety and freedom.

It felt like a slow, terrible crucifixion of his soul every time he thought of her, for it wasn't possible to picture her and feel a surge of fatherly pride without thinking of Jessica Leonard and what she had meant to her father. He wished with all his heart that he had the courage to end Blake's suffering. He could feel the man's helplessness and grief as he imagined Lydia moving inexorably away from him, disappearing from his reach to a place he couldn't go, where he would never be able to find her, as Jessica had moved away from her own father and still no one had found her.

Andee could see from the paintings on the wall of a much younger Jenny Leonard as Modigliani's *Young Woman in a Shirt*, and Picasso's *Nude Seated in a Chair*, that she had always been a fragile-looking woman with a delicate physique and ashen pallor, and she was perhaps even more so now. Still, Andee suspected that today was one of her better days as she focused her large, doe-like eyes on Andee's each time Andee spoke, as though not wanting to miss a word or misunderstand a meaning.

So far, as they'd sat there in Jenny's parents' best room, as they called it, sipping tea and only barely aware of the place becoming darker as clouds drew in, Jenny had told Andee nothing that Andee hadn't already read in the police files. Like Blake and Matt she'd expected Jessica home that day in time to join them for dinner. She'd received no texts or calls to warn her of a delay or change of plan, nor could she throw a single glimmer of light on what might have caused her daughter to go to Notting Hill Gate station instead of Paddington.

Mindful of the rented house in Holland Park, Andee said, 'Are you sure she didn't have any friends in that area, perhaps someone new she'd only mentioned in passing?'

Though Jenny clearly gave it some thought she was already shaking her head. 'I promise, I'd have told the police if anyone had come to mind, but no one did.'

Since there was no record of Jessica performing a gig in Holland Park, or of an upcoming booking, Andee said, 'As you know she was very well paid for her performances, so I'm guessing she was intending to continue with them when she returned to uni in the autumn?'

'I'm sure that was her plan,' Jenny replied. 'She loved to sing, and as you said, she was earning very well from it. It concerned us though that this might be getting in the way of her studies. Blake reminded her of that when she was home during Easter. He told her we were happy to help top up her student loan, but she said she was able to take care of it herself.'

'Did she say how?'

Jenny shook her head. 'We presumed she was going to continue gigging – she was very strong-willed – but we were intending to talk to her again when she came back for the summer.'

Andee said, carefully, 'Her friend Sadie is certain that Jessica was intending to flat-share with her and some other friends when she went back in October. Did Jessica talk to you about that?'

'We knew they'd been to see somewhere and were hopeful of getting it, but we didn't hear until after that their application had been successful.'

'It was an expensive rent and the other girls all come from wealthy families . . . I know you've been asked this before, but I'm afraid I have to ask it again, do you think Jessica had found someone to take care of her financial needs?'

Jenny's eyes drifted as she replied, 'Of course we've considered it, but the police haven't found anyone. They even tried the websites that set students up with people who do those things, but there was no trace of her on any of them.'

Already knowing that, Andee said, 'And the name Kim Yoder means nothing to you?'

'I'd never heard it before she disappeared, and as far as I'm aware the police think it's a false name anyway.'

Wondering if Jessica had known that and gone along with it, or if she'd been misled, even tricked, into trusting someone who'd had only evil in mind, Andee waited for Jenny to continue.

'Like every mother I want to think the best of my daughter, but when something like this happens . . . So many terrible thoughts go through your mind . . . I know Blake thinks them too. You can't help it. I know you're thinking them, because it's your job to, and I don't blame you, I just wish you could have known her . . . More than that I wish you could give us some answers, no matter how terrible they might be, because they'd be so much better than no answers at all.'

Understanding completely, Andee said, 'I promise you, I'm doing my best to find her, but if you and I are sharing the same sort of thoughts you'll know how vital it is that you tell me anything and everything you can, no matter how irrelevant or even shameful it might seem to you.'

Jenny looked away as she nodded. 'I swear I've told you everything I know, but I can't stop thinking about all the rich foreigners at those gigs. Maybe she got herself into something she didn't understand . . . They could have taken her out of the country and if they have, the chances are we'll never find her.'

Andee said, 'There's no record of her leaving the country, but . . .'

'There wouldn't be if someone took her on a private yacht, or aeroplane.' As tears welled in her eyes she put a hand to her head. 'This torture of guessing, the never-ending nightmare of where she might be, who might be hurting her, is she even alive . . . It's impossible to live with, and it doesn't get any easier with time. If anything it gets worse.'

'I know,' Andee said softly.

'It's made me hate myself in ways I can't even begin to admit to anyone. I'm not strong enough to cope with it and I just make things worse for Blake and Matt, that's why I'm here. I love them so much, but I can't stand to see their suffering so I've run away from them, and now I can't find the courage to go back.'

Feeling desperately sorry for her, Andee only wished she could tell her they might be on the verge of a breakthrough, but it would be cruel to raise her hopes until she, Andee, knew exactly what was happening in London. So all she said was, 'I want to find her, Jenny, I really do, so please don't think we've given up on her yet, because we haven't.'

Shock had hit Blake so hard as he'd come into the kitchen that even now, as much as a minute later, he was still experiencing a rapid beat in his heart. He couldn't imagine why he'd thought this girl was Jessica when she looked nothing like her; for a start she was blonde where Jess was dark, and the facial features, pretty as they were, could hardly be more different to his daughter's. It must have been her age, and how desperate he was to walk in one day to find his angel waiting.

'Dad, this is Ellie,' Matt had told him, and the words were still ringing in Blake's ears in spite of the fact that many more had been spoken since.

'What's up?' Matt asked, and Blake's eyes flew to his son's. 'Something's happened,' Matt accused, his voice tripping with alarm.

Blake shook his head.

'Dad! What is it? You have to tell me.'

Ellie got to her feet. 'I should probably go.'

Matt didn't stop her, only went to the door with her and Blake heard him promising to call.

'So what is it?' Matt demanded, coming back to the kitchen.

'I received some money today,' Blake told him. 'It turned up in a parcel.'

'What? I don't understand.'

243

'There was almost a hundred thousand pounds in cash, in a shoebox, addressed to me.'

Matt stared at him, dumbfounded.

'The police have it now,' Blake continued.

'But where did it come from?'

'That's what they're trying to find out.'

Matt's eyes were wide with shock as his mind went into overdrive. 'Do – do they think it's connected to Jess in some way?' he asked incredulously.

'No one knows what to think yet.'

Matt suddenly threw out his hands in anger. 'What the hell?' he growled, clasping his fists to his head. 'Is some sick bastard playing mind games? Is that what's happening here?'

Blake only wished he knew.

'What are you supposed to do with the money?'

Blake had no answer for that either. 'Andee Lawrence was going to see Mum today,' he said. 'I should call to find out how it went.'

'Will you tell Mum about the money?'

'I'm not sure. I'll find out how she is first.'

'It'll completely freak her out. How can it not when it's freaking us out?'

Blake was taking out his phone, then remembering Ellie he said, 'I'm sorry if I interrupted something when I came in.'

Matt shook his head. 'It doesn't matter. We were just talking about a gig she's been offered in London that's paying really well. She wants me to do it with her.'

Feeling the clashing connotations of gigs in London, Blake said, 'Are you going to?'

'I'm thinking about it. It's at a place in Kensington where I'm pretty sure Jess played once,' Matt went on. 'So I was thinking, if I did it, I might be able to ask a few questions, find out if anyone there remembers her.'

Knowing it was a long shot, given how much time had passed and how transient that community was, but ready to grasp at anything, Blake said, 'When is it?'

'The end of the month. They're prepared to put us up in a hotel for the night because of the late finish.'

Blake nodded. 'Before you accept, or before you start asking questions, I think you should talk to Andee to get her advice on the best way to handle it.'

# Chapter Fourteen

It was the middle of the afternoon by the time Rowzee and Andee drove into Dartmouth with its quaintly cobbled lanes, medieval and Elizabethan buildings and of course the glorious estuary with all its romance and history dating back over ten centuries or more. Thankfully the sun had come out again following a heavy downpour earlier, and the way the light was playing on the water made it seem as though it was crackling with stars.

Though Rowzee still couldn't get Sean Griffiths and his tragic existence out of her mind, she was doing a much better job of holding it together now than she had just after the visit. Or at the café after Andee had left her.

Luckily Andee knew nothing about the way a cup of tea had managed to slide right through Rowzee's fingers to spill all over the table. She couldn't think how it had happened. She was sure she'd been holding it firmly enough, but there was no denying the broken and empty cup with her hand still shaped as though it was around it. What a sweet girl the waitress had been, assuring Rowzee that accidents happened all the time and she wasn't to fuss herself about it. Rowzee hadn't fussed, at least not outwardly, but the failure of her grip had upset her. And the way her mind kept going off on panicked searches for what she should do next wasn't helping, for she was getting all tangled up in ideas that would never work, and intentions that must be accomplished. Fortunately she'd remembered to bring her notebook so she'd jotted down lots of reminders, as well as other things that needed careful consideration before she acted. One such project was to seek spiritual counselling from Norma, if Norma provided that service, though she knew already that she couldn't allow herself to become an additional burden for her new friend when Norma already had so much to cope with.

It had occurred to Rowzee to tell Andee about her diagnosis in the hope that she might agree to come to Zurich with her, but she'd soon realised that swearing Andee to secrecy would be selfish in the extreme and grossly unfair. Andee would be sure to want to tell Graeme and Pamela, would probably feel duty bound to, while at the same time she'd be sworn to silence. So telling Andee wasn't an option, and she couldn't tell Norma either for the same reasons she couldn't go to her for counselling. There was always Gina, of course, but Rowzee wouldn't know whether that was a good idea until she had an idea of what was happening in Gina's world these days.

It was noted in her book that she must set up an appointment with her lawyer – she might already have one, if so she hoped to find it in her diary when she got back – to make sure Norma, Sean and Jason were properly taken care of as soon as she set off for the Elysian Fields (not that she considered herself heroic or virtuous, the qualifications necessary for entry into this mythological afterlife, it just had a nice ring). They couldn't argue with the contents of a will and no matter what Norma said to the contrary, having the support of private nurses for Sean would be a godsend for his mother. At least that was how Rowzee was seeing it. She'd never dream of saying this to Norma, but the dear and very attractive (it had to be said) woman wasn't getting any younger. She needed more freedom to go out and live her life while she still could, and who was to say, she might even meet a dashingly romantic kindred spirit to keep her company in her twilight years.

All this was such a whirling confusion in her head as Andee drove them gingerly along a street so narrow that the wing mirrors had to be pulled in, that Rowzee had almost forgotten why they were there. What felt much more important to her quite suddenly was her longing to see Jenny and Blake reunited with their daughter before she, Rowzee, went on her way. What on earth could she do about that? If only she knew. And how was she going to get Pamela properly hooked up with Bill Simmonds, and Graeme rekindling a romance with Andee, before she lost her powers of subtlety and sent them all running for cover? There was so much to do and think about, and so little time, thanks to the devilish roadblock in her brain that was very soon going to stop letting the traffic through altogether.

'Ah, here we are,' Andee declared, slowing up outside a house with the number Gina had given them, then making no less than four attempts to get into the parking space alongside it before success was achieved.

They were barely out of the car before Gina came running out to greet them, all delighted smiles, luxuriant auburn hair and dazzling movie-star looks. Think a sublime mix of Audrey Hepburn and Ginger Rogers, was how Rowzee often described her.

'How are you, how are you?' Gina cried, sweeping Rowzee into a lavish embrace, while holding Andee's hand to show how thrilled she was to see her too. 'I can't tell you how excited I've been since Andee rang to say you were coming. It's been too long, which I know is my fault, but we're going to have some time to catch up now and I can hardly wait to get started.' Leading them up a small flight of steps into the house, she said, 'Can you stay the night, maybe? There's plenty of room. We can go for dinner down in the town, or get fish and chips if you prefer. It's OK, you don't have to make a decision now. I just want you to know that the offer's there. By the way, you know, I'm sure, that this is Anna Shelley's house, and that I'm taking care of it and her gallery while she's away?'

'*The* Anna Shelley?' Rowzee exclaimed, clearly impressed by the name-drop of an artist and actress most of the country had heard of.

'No less,' Gina laughed, squeezing her again.

Once inside it was no surprise to Andee to discover that the nineteenth-century merchant's house with its many crooked floors, polished oak beams and fabulous collection of art was one of the grander dwellings on the hillside. Nor had she expected anything less than the glorious panoramic views from just about every window, taking in the mesmerising waterway where hundreds of sailboats, river cruisers, canoes and ferries were going busily about their day. On the opposite bank with its magnificent harbour, steam railway station and meandering lanes of colourful cottages and town houses, Kingswear appeared almost as a reflection of the old seafaring town.

The first hour or more of their visit was spent on the sitting-room balcony, soaking up the sunshine and inhaling the bittersweet scent of salty sea air as they indulged in one reminiscence after another after another. There were so many plays and projects that had come to fruition, and even more that hadn't, dinners that had been made unforgettable by announcements or outrages or even disasters. Then there were the hilarious coincidences and wonderings of whatever had happened to . . . Rowzee laughed so hard she cried, and Andee found herself relaxing in a way she hadn't in far too long.

'Did I already tell you how amazing you both look?' Gina beamed at them, in her infectiously expansive way. 'Do stay the night, please. We can drink champagne and eat what we like and tell stories until midnight.'

Rowzee and Andee looked at one another with sparkling eyes. Why not? Neither of them had anything to rush back for, and being with Gina was already proving such a tonic for them both that they'd have been crazy to rush off before they had to.

It was while Rowzee was inside calling Pamela to let her know that she wouldn't be back until morning that Gina said gently to Andee, 'Charles told me about you and Martin.'

Having expected as much, Andee merely shrugged.

'If I'm being honest,' Gina went on, 'I'm not surprised. You outgrew him a long time ago, but it still takes courage to move on.'

With raised eyebrows Andee said, 'Most people think I'm mad for leaving him. They see him as a great catch, which of course he is.'

'But so are you, and you have to do what's right for you. Does it feel right?'

'It did when I first left, and it still does. I just hate being the cause of so much heartbreak.'

'Sure you do, but he'll get over it, and so will the kids if they're giving you a rough time. This is something you have to go through in order to get to where you want to be. Any idea where that is?'

Andee laughed. 'Not a clue, but hopefully all will come clear in time. Now tell me about you and Charles. I'm getting a sense of things not being quite right with you two, or am I misreading it?'

With a sigh, Gina stretched out her long legs as she said, 'Charles has been unwell, as you know, which coming hard on the heels of my own health issues and of course the election defeat . . . Let's just say that after all the pressure and stress it felt a good idea to spend some time apart.'

'So when Anna asked if you'd be interested in taking care of things here, you jumped at it?'

'Precisely. Not too far from Charles, but far enough to allow us some space to breathe. Sometimes I find observing things from a distance can give you a better perspective. Do you find that too?'

Admitting that she did, whenever she remembered to do it, Andee said, 'I guess you both miss Lydia.'

'Oh we do. More than we'd ever tell her, that's for sure. Charles has been finding it especially difficult, but I can't get him to talk about it, so I guess I just have to wait until he's ready.' Though the shadows and misgivings were invisible, Andee could sense them darkening Gina's thoughts while her words remained tender and light.

Continuing, Gina said, 'I think he's done with politics. Something changed in him when he lost his seat. He's never really known failure before, I guess, so I think it came as a far bigger blow than he was prepared for. He didn't know how to deal with it. And there was a power struggle at the company, brought on, I'm sure, by his health issues. Josh Stevens, his number two, has been running things for the past year or so.' She sighed sadly. 'He's been in a kind of shutdown since, at least where I'm concerned, which I know I'm to blame for . . . It was why I needed to get away. It's very stressful living with someone who doesn't communicate any more, or who's hiding things.'

Wondering if Gina knew about Charles's 'friend' and the blackmail, Andee said, 'So what do you think he's hiding?'

Gina's lovely eyes came to hers. 'Always the detective,' she teased.

Andee grimaced as Rowzee returned to the balcony saying, 'Does that mean she's told you she's helping us to find Jessica Leonard?'

Gina's eyes returned to Andee. 'You are?' she said, seeming more concerned than surprised. 'And have you come up with any new leads?'

'Not that I can discuss at the moment,' Andee admitted.

'Meaning there is something?' Gina prompted.

'Possibly. I'm waiting to hear.'

Clearly deciding not to press her, Gina said to Rowzee, 'Charles tells me that he met Jessica's father at your birthday party.'

'It was Pamela's party, actually, but yes, Blake was there. He's been working for Graeme since they moved to the area, his wife did too until Jessica disappeared. It's totally broken her, him too in its way.'

'How could it not?' Gina murmured. 'Losing a daughter like that . . .' She was quiet as she seemed to be visualising the fear and horror of Jessica's parents.

Rowzee said, echoing Jenny as though she'd been there earlier, 'It's possible, even probable that someone took her abroad.'

Apparently intrigued, Gina said, 'Why do you say that?'

'Because it makes the most sense. You'll have read in the press about the kind of parties she gigged at.'

Gina nodded. 'Of course. A lot of rich foreigners. You know, I've often wondered if Charles and I might have been at one of those parties. We used to go to a good many functions back then, thanks to Charles's contacts

253

in the City. I can't say I remember seeing Jessica at any of them, but of course I didn't know what she looked like then. Am I allowed to ask if our names came up during the police investigation?' She turned to Andee.

'If they had,' Andee replied, 'you'd have been interviewed.'

With a mischievous twinkle Gina said, 'But there are names that we'd know, I'm sure?'

'There are names that most of the country would know, but they've all been questioned and cleared, so the question still remains: who was she on her way to see the day she disappeared? Or, put another way, who is Kim Yoder?'

'The sixty-four thousand dollar question,' Rowzee muttered.

Andee was watching Gina. 'Are you all right?' she asked. 'You've gone quite pale.'

Dismissing it with a wave of her hand, Gina said, 'A side effect of one of the drugs I have to take. I'm fine, honestly. So Rowzee, was Pamela OK about you staying here tonight?'

'Actually, she said it was a lovely idea and that I should stay as long as I like. This immediately makes me suspicious, so I think I should go home right away.'

Since it was clearly a joke, Andee and Gina laughed and after deciding they'd like more tea they went downstairs to the kitchen. The subject stayed with Pamela and how, Gina insisted, Bill Simmonds had had a thing for her for years. Seizing the chance of help with her plans to further the romance, Rowzee started coming up with various strategies that were actually more hilarious than feasible, while Gina and Andee's suggestions only added more raucous merriment to the mix.

By the time the topic of conversation changed it was clear that Rowzee was starting to flag, so it was no surprise when she said she hoped no one would mind if she sat in a shady part of the garden for a quick forty winks. 'It's been quite an exhausting day,' she confessed to Gina, 'but I'll spare you the details of my new family until later.'

'New family?' Gina echoed in amazement.

'Later,' Rowzee promised.

After settling her under a pergola on the patio Gina offered to show Andee to a guest room where she could freshen up, or lie down, or make calls, whatever she might need to do. 'Or you can just drop off your things and we'll carry on chatting,' she added. 'Everything's possible.'

Having not heard back from Leo Johnson yet, Andee said, 'If you don't mind, there is a call I need to make. I'll come to find you in about ten minutes?'

'Perfect.'

Finding herself connecting to Leo Johnson's voicemail, Andee tried her old detective inspector instead and got through straight away.

'All we've been told so far,' Gould informed her, 'is that six months' rent was paid up front on the Holland Park house, in cash, two months before Jessica disappeared. The agent didn't meet Kim Yoder in person – she says it's not rare for properties of that type to be rented sight unseen, usually by foreigners, or for the transactions to take place over the phone or Internet. Don't let's get into the money-laundering issue here, that's for the Met to deal with.'

'Were no references taken up?'

'My guess is they probably weren't even asked for, but no word on that yet either.'

'Does the place have any security cameras?'

'Something else we're waiting on an answer to. What I can tell you is that the agent didn't come forward sooner because she and her company are big on safeguarding their clients' confidentiality, so they took the decision that if the police didn't come to them, they wouldn't go to the police.'

Appalled, though not surprised, Andee said, 'It never fails to amaze me how some people come here and seem to think it's OK to operate outside the law just because they have money.'

'Indeed. I can also tell you,' Gould continued, 'that the place was rented to a Peruvian couple after the six-month prepaid period ran out. They're still there, and are being quite helpful apparently, but obviously it's making it a nightmare for forensics.'

'I can imagine. Anything else?'

'Not right now.'

'What about the money Blake received?'

'All I can tell you about that is the parcel was sent from a post office in Dorchester. Someone locally is talking to the staff there to try to find out what they remember.'

'Do you think it's connected to Jessica in some way?'

'I do, but in what way . . . Well, there you have me. Where are you?'

'In Dartmouth, back tomorrow, but if you hear any more on either issue I'd appreciate a call.'

After ringing off Andee wandered back upstairs and found Gina in a spacious studio at the top of the house with a wide, low bed in one corner, a collection of easels and blank canvases, a large centre table and an entire wall full of garish landscapes.

'No prizes for guessing this is where Anna does most of her work,' Gina declared as Andee took in the bohemian surroundings. 'She has another studio, above the gallery in town, which is generally rented out to visiting artists. Please excuse all the parcels over there. They're about to head off to Anna's dealer in the States. He's in Dartmouth, Massachusetts, and does a roaring trade in works from here, it being the original so to speak. If you're ever in that part of the world it's worth dropping in if only to hear him talk about old Dartmouth's fabulous history from the bloody crusades, to the Pilgrim Fathers' brief stopover, to the part the naval base played in aiding the French Resistance during the Second World War. He's a natural when it comes to bringing the past to life, has his listeners all rapt and no one ever questions how tall the tales might be, they just lap them up.'

'Are they tall?'

'Actually not as far as I know, although I'm sure he adds a little embellishment here and there. I'll have to get these off to him tomorrow, or they won't arrive in time for his next presentation.'

'Is there anything I can do to help?'

'Thanks, but they're mostly already sealed up and addressed. Jonno, Anna's assistant, will come and help

257

me carry them to the gallery in the morning ready for the courier.'

Minutes later, while Gina went back down to the kitchen to fetch lemonade, Andee returned to the sitting room and was idly browsing the coffee-table books when she came to a sudden stop. The shock of what she was seeing was making it difficult to think straight; too much was happening at once, and not seeming to make any sense. Picking up the small, battered paperback, she turned it over, opened it up and even, in a distracted way, started to read.

'Ah ha, you've unearthed my guilty pleasure,' Gina laughed as she came into the room.

'Seriously?' Andee asked, turning to look at her.

'Not really, but it can be quite calming in its way. It belonged to my great-grandmother.'

'Was she Amish?'

'Oh yes, until she met my great-grandfather and decided to leave the Church. Such a scandal, especially for the time. She wrote about it, how hard it was being shunned by her family and the rest of the community; it's what happens to everyone who turns their back on that life, even now. Can you imagine, even her own mother wouldn't see or speak to her again, or her father, and they'd been very close. It would have broken her heart if she hadn't loved her husband so much. Of course, if it weren't for loving him so much she'd never have left.'

'Do you still have what she wrote?'

'My mother does, in Pennsylvania. She's keeping it for Lydia. Meanwhile, I get the prayer book.'

Setting it back on the table, Andee took the glass of lemonade Gina was offering and followed her out to the balcony, barely registering the sounds of gulls shrieking overhead while a steam train hooted merrily across the water. She needed to think this through, go over it carefully, because too many thoughts were coming at her at once, scenarios that hardly seemed likely, connections refusing to be made, but whether by her, or by implausibility, she had no idea.

'Everything OK?' Gina asked curiously.

Andee's eyes went to hers. 'Yes, of course,' she smiled. 'Sorry, I was miles away.' Thinking fast, she said, 'I've been wanting to ask how you really are? Of course you don't have to talk about it if you don't want to, but Charles tells me there's been no return of the cancer . . .'

Touching the wooden balustrade, Gina said, 'I'm doing great, thanks. But being minus one breast and an entire womb, and going through an early menopause wasn't much fun. Actually, it's why Charles and I aren't as close as we used to be, I'm sure of it. Until my diagnosis we always had a very healthy sex life, but once the treatment was over . . . To be honest, I find intimacy quite painful and as my libido is about as active as a dead fish, there's nothing to drive me.'

'You've sought help, obviously?'

'Believe me, I've tried everything.' She sighed sadly. 'So we rub along, still loving one another, and enjoying each other's company as long as we're not together for too long, but there's no physical bond between us now. And do you know, what's surprised me the most since it happened to me, is how many other couples are hiding the same thing. It's the great untalked-about horror that some menopausal women face, and could very well be the reason why so many older men go off and find themselves younger models.'

'But not Charles?'

Gina's eyes drifted across the estuary as she shook her head. 'None that he's ever admitted to.'

'But you suspect there is someone?'

'Was. Past tense. I don't think she's around any more, but losing her, giving her up, whatever happened, has affected him deeply.'

'Do you have any idea who she was?'

Gina nodded. 'Yes, I know. He's told me in ways he's not even aware of. I guess you could say I tricked it out of him, and now I wish I hadn't because it's put me in the same sort of hell.'

Confused, Andee waited for her to expand, but all she said was, 'Marriages. They're never what they seem from the outside, are they? They're so full of secrets and guilt and lies, all mixed up with love and loyalty and God only knows what else.' Turning to Andee, she said, 'Have you spent much time with Charles since he went back to the Hall?'

Andee shook her head. 'Not really. I can tell he's stressed, though. There's obviously something on his mind.'

Gina nodded. 'Did he mention anything to you about being blackmailed?'

'As a matter of fact he did, but he said it was happening to a friend of his.'

Not contradicting that, Gina said, 'I'm guessing he's asked you to try to find out who it is. The blackmailer, I mean, not the friend.'

'Yes, he has.'

'And you said?'

'That until I know what it's about there's nothing I can do.' After a pause she added, 'Do you know what it's about?'

For a long time it seemed as though Gina wouldn't answer as she gazed out to sea, watching erratic sparks of sunlight on the waves, until eventually she said, 'I don't know everything, but what I do know . . .'

Andee waited.

'I wish I didn't.'

# Chapter Fifteen

It was around lunchtime the following day when Rowzee arrived home to find Pamela in the kitchen, clearly in tears, and being comforted by . . . *Bill Simmonds*?

'What on earth is it?' Rowzee cried, rushing straight to Pamela's side. 'What's happened?'

Woefully, Pamela said, 'You're not going to believe this, but Bill's just offered me a job.'

Stunned, Rowzee turned to Bill. What kind of a job could make Pamela cry and Bill look so pleased with himself?

'He's asked me to go and run his caravan park over at Paradise Cove,' Pamela explained, dabbing her eyes.

Rowzee blinked. 'You have a caravan park?' she exclaimed in amazement. 'How marvellous. I had no idea.'

'I just closed the deal,' he smiled. 'It's next door to my nursery.'

'I didn't know about it either, until he told me,' Pamela said, blowing her nose.

'Well, a bloke can't go round telling girls all his secrets now, can he?' Bill retorted. 'Or he'll lose all his mystery and what's the use of a bloke without mystery?'

At that, Pamela's eyes sparkled. 'Or a mower,' she added, making herself giggle.

Deciding she rather liked the way this was going, Rowzee said, 'So when do you start this new job?'

'As soon as she wishes,' Bill replied. 'The old manager's still running the show, but he'll be happy to hand over as soon as Pammy's ready.'

*Pammy!*

Rowzee looked at her sister, who seemed about to speak when she burst into tears again. 'I'm sorry,' she wailed as Rowzee folded her into a tender embrace. 'I'm feeling very emotional today. So much seems to be happening and I don't understand why I'm upset when I'm thrilled by the offer, really. I haven't had a job in so long, and to think someone would trust me . . .'

'Of course someone would trust you,' Rowzee cried with feeling. 'You're a very good manager.'

'I used to be, but I will be again,' she promised Bill. 'It'll be a really good start for the new me.'

Frowning, Rowzee was about to ask when Bill said, 'I keep telling her, I didn't mind the old her, not one bit.'

Doing her best to keep up, Rowzee blinked as Pamela suddenly got up.

'I have presents for you,' Pamela declared, going to collect an armful of carrier bags and bringing them back to Rowzee. 'It's the kind of things you like, scented candles, expensive bubble bath, a lovely silk scarf, a cashmere sweater . . . You'll see when you open them.'

Becoming more bemused by the second, Rowzee looked at the bags and back at her sister. 'It's not my birthday,' she pointed out unnecessarily.

'I know that. It's not the girls' birthdays either, but I've got things for them too,' and to Rowzee's astonishment she started to cry again.

'There, there,' Bill soothed, fondly patting her back. 'It'll be all right, you just wait and see.'

Rowzee wanted to sit down, or wake up, or go out and come in again. She couldn't make out what was going on, and was afraid to ask in case her own inadequacies were causing the confusion.

'I haven't cried this much since I was a child,' Pamela confessed. 'Or not that I can remember.'

'It's good to get it all out,' Bill gently informed her. 'You know what the therapist said, no holding back.'

*Therapist? Pamela was seeing a therapist?* Did Rowzee know this and had forgotten? In the end she had to ask.

'I didn't tell you,' Pamela replied, 'because I wanted to be sure it would work. I think it has, in a way, but it's making me a bit of an emotional wreck. Actually, it's your fault,' she told Bill. 'You shouldn't be nice to me.'

'It won't happen again,' he promised.

Ordinarily Rowzee would have laughed at that, but she was so perplexed that she wasn't even sure she was hearing right. 'You've been going to therapy?' she asked Pamela.

Seeming both embarrassed and defensive, Pamela said, 'I've been trying to turn myself into a nice person, like you.'

Rowzee didn't know what to say, but eventually the right words managed to trip out, almost of their own accord. 'But you are a nice person. You're lovely . . .'

'No I'm not,' Pamela snapped impatiently. 'I'm bad-tempered, resentful, always critical, snobbish . . .'

'Oh, I'm coming over all unnecessary,' Bill cautioned.

With a splutter of laughter, Pamela said, 'You fool.'

Looking from one to the other and certain she must be dreaming, Rowzee said, 'We all love you the way you are . . .'

'But I don't,' Pamela cut in quickly. 'It's horrible being so angry and uptight all the time. I want to be calm and happy and kind, like you. So I thought, if I went to see someone, they'd help me to find out why I'm so querulous and hostile, and if I could find out why I might be able to change it.'

Rowzee glanced at Bill, clocked his suspiciously benign smile, and turned back to Pamela. 'So did you find out why?' she asked.

'Oh there are a lot of things that came up from the past,' Pamela admitted, 'most of it to do with you, as a matter of fact. I always thought you were the favourite, you see . . . Well, you were, which is why I've always felt so second best and angry with the world, because our parents never loved me as much as they loved you.'

Shocked, Rowzee cried, 'That is absolutely not true. I don't know why you're telling yourself that when Mummy and Daddy adored you. You were the one with all the character, the feisty, gutsy one who wasn't afraid to take on anything or anyone to make sure the right thing was done. They were so proud of you, and I always wished I could be more like you.'

Pamela appeared bewildered.

'Coffee, anyone?' Bill offered cheerily.

Rowzee said, 'Yes, please,' and holding out her arms she went to wrap them around her sister. 'I can't believe you've been having therapy to try and change yourself. You're perfect as you are . . .'

'I'm angry and negative and that's not good. It's like lots of demons are all locked up inside me, and I don't expect I'll ever get rid of them all, but the therapist has encouraged me to start being kind to myself and to those I love, so that's what I'm trying to do. I have to appreciate myself more, he said, and feel good about myself when I look in the mirror. I need to think about what I'm saying to others to make sure it isn't hurtful or offensive or meant to make them feel small.'

'And you're doing marvellously,' Bill assured her. 'You only bit my head off twice when we had dinner last night, mind you, I thoroughly enjoyed both times.'

Rowzee blurted, 'You two had dinner last night?'

With a sigh, Pamela explained, 'When you rang to say you weren't coming home . . . I'd already bought salmon steaks for our supper, and it seemed a shame to waste them.'

'So you rang Bill?'

'Actually he was already here,' Pamela said irritably. 'And I thought it would be a good opportunity, as a part of my therapy, to be nice to someone I might have wronged.'

'I told her,' Bill put in, 'I have no objection to her experimenting on me.'

Rowzee looked from him to the carrier bags full of presents, to the dear, dear sister struggling to be a better person, and suddenly felt so overwhelmed that she couldn't collect any thoughts at all.

'. . . I thought she'd have come in with you,' Pamela was saying.

'Who?' Rowzee asked.

'Andee. Didn't she bring you back?'

*Andee? Back from where?*

'Are you OK?' Pamela asked, peering at her. 'You look a bit . . . glazed.'

Oddly it was exactly how she felt.

'Are you going to tell us about your stepson?' Pamela urged. 'What's his mother like? I hope they didn't try to get any money out of you.'

'Andee's trying to find Jessica,' Rowzee heard herself mumble.

Frowning, Pamela said, 'I know she was going to see Jenny. Did you see Jenny too?'

Rowzee shook her head. 'That poor, dear girl. What on earth has happened to her?'

Glancing worriedly at Bill, Pamela said, 'It's what we'd all like to know.'

'I can't stop thinking about her,' Rowzee confided.

Carefully, Pamela said, 'How long has she been missing now?'

Rowzee looked at her, not sure what to say. Everything seemed so tangled and unreachable, with small flickers of light sparking in the darkness. Pamela had asked about Victor's son. 'His name's Sean,' she said, 'and he looks just like Victor.'

Pamela's eyes were narrowed as she regarded her closely. 'What did he have to say for himself?' she asked. 'Whatever it was, I hope it started with an apology.'

'He's in a vegetative state,' Rowzee responded. 'His mother's taking care of him, and his son. It was very shocking and upsetting to see.'

Pamela looked at Bill as he set down a pot of coffee and fresh cups. 'Are you sure,' she ventured tentatively, 'they weren't trying it on? You know, pretending he was out of it to try and get your sympathy?'

Rowzee felt sure, but couldn't find the words to convince Pamela.

'Did Andee go in with you?' Bill asked.

Rowzee nodded. 'Yes, she was there. She's gone to see Charles now.'

As Pamela started to speak again there was a knock at the door, and moments later Lucie was bounding into the kitchen with Teddy, her adorably daft and excitable Wheaten terrier.

'Oh Teddy,' Rowzee smiled in delight, clasping his eager face in both hands as he came straight to her. He was so soft and fluffy, with curly champagne-coloured fur, irresistible brown eyes and a tail that never stopped wagging. 'I'd forgotten you were coming today,' she crooned, planting a kiss on his head. 'Isn't this lovely?' she gushed to Pamela and Bill. 'We've got him for a whole two weeks.'

'Are you OK, Mum?' Lucie asked, going to embrace Pamela. 'You look as though you've been crying.'

'Don't be daft,' Pamela scolded. 'What have I got to cry about?'

Eyeing her suspiciously, Lucie turned to Bill. 'How are you?' she smiled, hugging him too. 'You know, the guy you recommended to take over our garden is an absolute genius. I can't thank you enough.'

'Glad he's working out,' Bill responded. 'Are you staying for coffee? I've just made some.'

Lucie was apparently unfazed by him playing host. 'I'd love to, but I have to rush . . . What's all this?' she asked, as Pamela handed her half a dozen carrier bags.

'A few things I picked up for you,' Pamela told her. 'You don't have to open them now. Remind me, is Katie going away with you?'

'No, she's already in Cornwall with Bob's parents. *Mum!* I hope you're not getting Alzheimer's. Wow! What have I done to deserve all this?' she exclaimed, peeking into one of the bags. 'My God, this is seriously expensive stuff . . .'

'Just enjoy it,' Pamela interrupted crossly.

Lucie turned to Rowzee as if she might offer an explanation.

'I've cashed in some Premium Bonds,' Pamela told her impatiently, 'and I thought we might as well all benefit.'

Though clearly thrown, it was with a mischievous twinkle that Lucie said to Bill, 'So what did she get you?'

Drily, he replied, 'You mean apart from all excited?'

As Lucie's eyes widened and Rowzee laughed, Pamela snapped, 'Take no notice of him, he's weird and delusional.'

'Mum's going to be working for Bill,' Rowzee told her. Did she have that right? She hadn't just imagined the last half an hour, had she?

Amazed, Lucie said, 'How come?'

Loftily, Pamela said, 'Bill needs someone to run his caravan park so I'm going to take it on.'

'Wow! This is great news. You and Bill . . .'

'All right, that's enough,' Pamela cut in before Lucie could go any further. 'Do you have Teddy's food and everything else he needs?'

'It's in the car. I'll go get it.'

As she disappeared, Pamela turned back to Rowzee. 'You're acting strange,' she accused her firmly. 'So what happened in Devon? Something obviously did, and I want to know what it was.'

'Nothing happened,' Rowzee assured her, still fondling the dog and loving the way he was pressed against her. 'Or not in the way you're meaning it.' She was remembering how Norma had seemed to think she had a dog. Well, she did now, at least for the next couple of weeks, and it was going to be a joy taking him for long walks on the moors and the beaches, the way she had in the past . . .

'I think I need to speak to Andee,' she heard Pamela mutter to Bill.

'Here we are,' Lucie declared, dumping Teddy's bed full of toys, dry food, towels, lead and shrink-wrapped treats on the floor.

Though Teddy watched her he didn't move from Rowzee's side. Apparently he was more than happy to be here.

'Are you OK, Rowzee?' Lucie asked, concerned. 'You seem a bit quiet today.'

'I'm fine,' Rowzee assured her. 'Just a little tired.'

'She's been gallivanting around Devon since yesterday morning,' Pamela explained, 'and if I know Gina Stamfield more than a few glasses of wine came Rowzee's way last night, and you know she can't take it.'

Though she'd had no more than two glasses at the most, Rowzee decided to seize the excuse to go upstairs and lie down for an hour. Better they thought she was suffering with a hangover than have Pamela start going on about anything else. She wasn't up to fending her off right now, nor was she very sure about what was happening to her. She'd felt so well yesterday, at least for most of the day, and had been sure that the dexamethasone was doing its thing. Now she could only feel a dark, dragging ache at the back of her skull as she tried her best to remember what Andee had been talking about on the way back. It was important, she knew that, and because of it she'd decided that she must look something up when she got home, something to do with dear Jessica, she thought, but with all the distractions of Pamela and Bill, and now Teddy arriving, she simply couldn't remember what it was.

\* \* \*

As Andee drove back into Kesterly she was trying once again to make some sense of what she'd discovered the day before. Actually it was more of a suspicion that was attempting to settle in her mind, the way suspicions sometimes did before enabling one to form a logical conclusion. Yoder was an Amish name, Gina's great-grandmother had been Amish – the coincidence couldn't be ignored, and yet it hardly seemed credible that there could be a connection between this mystery person and Gina's American ancestry.

Although Andee had decided not to bring it up with Gina again until she'd had more time to think, she'd got up early this morning to take another look at the prayer book in the hope it might give her some assistance. She'd found no mention of the name Yoder either in print or in the handwritten inscriptions on an inside page. Gina, or someone, had bookmarked a couple of prayers, the first seeming to be about shame, and the second apologising to the Father for not being true. If there were anything to be read into either Andee had had no idea what it was then, and she still didn't now. However, feeling terrible that she was doing this to a friend, she'd photographed them both just in case they turned out to have some relevance.

During the drive home she'd asked Rowzee what she knew about the Amish people, but apart from being able to tell her about Gina's great-grandmother, Rowzee had seemed as much in the dark about this particular community as Andee was.

After dropping Rowzee at the Coach House Andee had driven on to the Hall in the hope of finding Charles at home, but there had been no sign of him. The fact that Gina knew about the blackmail was something else that was bothering her. Though Gina hadn't confirmed the existence of a friend as the victim, she hadn't denied it either, which had left Andee more convinced than ever that Charles himself was being subjected to extortion. Even as she thought it, she was aware of physically shaking her head. It was like trying to connect two live wires, Yoder and Jessica's disappearance on the one hand; Charles's blackmail on the other. It just didn't fit. She was leaping to conclusions without having anything tangible or credible to back them up, only a name and a situation that on the face of it, at least, couldn't possibly have anything to do with each other. However, her instincts were telling her that there was more, if she'd just allow herself to see it.

Not for the first time Andee found herself reflecting on closed doors and what happened behind them, particularly those belonging to families. As a detective she'd come across countless tragedies and crimes that no one would ever have dreamt their neighbour, or friend, or colleague capable of. It hadn't made her so much cynical as sad to be shown, time after time, that even good people could be guilty of the worst imaginable offences. And she knew how far some would go to protect their secrets, or loved ones, and though she hated even to think it, she had to ask herself if this was why Charles was trying to find out the identity of his tormentor. Did he have plans for this person that could end him up in an even worse place than he already was?

After leaving her car in the parking spot opposite her building, she collected the mail and climbed the stairs to her apartment. Finding the place hot and stuffy inside she opened the windows, letting in a flood of warm sea air and holiday noise.

Though she had plenty of calls to make she went to make coffee first, and smiled with affection when a text turned up from Rowzee.

*Thank you for being such a good friend to me yesterday. I really enjoyed our chat on the way back. I hope to see you again very soon. With love Rowzee xxx*

Texting back, Andee said, *Having you as a friend has brought a lot of sunshine into my life at a time when it seems full of (self-inflicted?) clouds. Let's make sure to get together again very soon. With love xxx*

No sooner had the message gone than the phone rang, and seeing it was Graeme she quickly clicked on.

'Is Rowzee still with you?' he asked after enquiring how she was.

'I dropped her about half an hour ago. I think she enjoyed seeing Gina, in fact I know she did, but finding Victor's son in such a dreadful way has definitely taken its toll on her.'

'I'm not surprised. She's always been a very sensitive soul, taking things to heart that aren't even anything to do with her. In this instance, she'll no doubt feel it her duty to find a way to help him, and provided you can persuade me that there was no deception involved I'll be happy to support it.'

'I really don't think there was,' Andee assured him. 'If you'd seen the poor man . . . It was heartbreaking to watch a fellow human being suffering such a hopeless and undignified existence.'

'How long has he been like it?'

Andee frowned as she tried to remember. 'I'm not entirely sure,' she replied, 'I don't think we asked, but long enough for a house to have been found and suitably adapted for his mother to take care of him at home. She's an exceptional woman. Quite New Agey, and very young-looking when she can't be far off seventy. Rowzee warmed to her greatly, and I've no doubt the feeling was mutual.'

'This is good to hear. It's putting my mind at rest and it'll give me something positive to tell Pamela when we speak. I expect we'll want to go and visit the family ourselves. So now, what do I ask next? I have so many questions, about Jenny, the money Blake received, the investigation in London . . . I'm sure you're too busy to indulge me, but if you're free to have dinner with me tonight . . .?'

As a jolt of surprise hit her heart, Andee found herself saying, 'I'd love to.' Was she supposed to be doing something else? Maybe she'd arranged to meet Alayna. She should have checked first.

'Great, I was hoping you'd say that. So shall we save this chat until then? I'll book the Crustacean for 7.30, unless you'd rather . . .'

'The Crustacean sounds lovely.' It was a restaurant her family often used, but she wasn't going to bring that up now, and later she'd just keep her fingers crossed that they didn't run into Martin.

After ringing off she checked her last message from Alayna, which said, *Can't wait to see this big picture!! Will text at weekend after Flo goes back to Derby.* Flo? Presumably a friend from uni. *Was happy to help with the search. Let me know if anything else I can do. Xxx*

Relieved there was no clash for the evening, Andee took a coffee through to the sitting room and sat at the table in front of the window to start making her calls. The first turned into another failed attempt to get hold of Charles, the second was to Blake who was still waiting to hear back from the police about the money, and the third was to Leo Johnson at the station.

Since there was nothing new to tell him following her meeting with Jenny, and he had nothing significant to report from his colleagues in London, she decided to call Gina to thank her for last night.

'Actually, there's something I need to tell you,' Gina confessed before the call ended. 'I should have told you yesterday, or before you left this morning, but I couldn't bring myself to. I'm not even sure I can now.'

Andee said, very carefully, 'Would you like me to come back to Devon?'

'No. No, I wouldn't dream of asking you to do that. I'll come there. It won't be today; I've got commitments here. I'll call when I'm on my way. Have you spoken to Charles since you left here?'

'No. I can't get hold of him and he wasn't at the Hall when I called in earlier.'

'Maybe he's gone back to London. I'll try to find him. Meantime, thanks for bringing Rowzee. She's always such a delight, isn't she? It's people like her who make the world a wonderful place to be.'

'She loved seeing you too. It gave her a much-needed lift after the shock of finding Victor's son in such a bad way.'

'That's so awful, isn't it? I can hardly stop thinking about it. Poor man. Listen, I'm sorry, I have to go. If you hear from Charles before I do please ask him to call me,' and forgetting to say goodbye she rang off.

'And you still haven't heard from him?' Graeme was saying later, after approving the wine for a waiter to pour.

'Actually, he texted about an hour ago,' Andee replied, 'to tell me he was in London, but should be back in the next couple of days.'

'And you're seeming so relieved about that because?'

Shaking her head, she said, 'I'm pretty sure he's got himself into some sort of trouble, and I'm afraid of what he might do to get out of it.'

Graeme's eyebrows rose in a way that made her worry again about how stable Charles might be. 'Is there anything I can do?' he offered.

Loving the kindness, she said, 'I don't think so, at this stage.' Should she tell him about the blackmail? It would be breaking a confidence, but did that really matter when they were all such good friends? She decided it didn't.

When she'd finished relating what she knew he remained silent for a while, clearly trying to figure out what could be behind the extortion. In the end, he said, 'And he's never mentioned any names, or given any indication of what kind of trouble he might be in?'

'I wish he had so I'd have more to go on,' she replied. 'But I guess as long as he's in touch . . .' She decided to leave it there. After all there was nothing either of them could do tonight to bring Charles back to the Hall, any more than they could force him to tell them what was really going on.

After taking a sip of wine she found her eyes meeting Graeme's, and felt the pleasure of being with him eddying through her. It was rare, she reflected, to find someone who really listened the way he seemed to, so effortlessly and yet attentively. Over cocktails earlier she'd told him as much as she knew about what was happening in London, and about Blake's money, but as it hadn't amounted to any more than she'd known that morning, they'd soon moved on to other things.

And so it was now, as with an unspoken agreement, that they allowed themselves to set aside the issues of friends and families, and drift into the enjoyment of simply being together. They talked about the religious paintings Blake had discovered inside an ivory box that Graeme had bought at auction for twenty pounds. They thought it probably dated from the sixteenth century and could easily be Greek Orthodox, or perhaps Eastern European. It was unusual and potentially valuable enough to end up in a museum, which was why Graeme was meeting a contact of his from the Ashmolean the following day.

She asked more about his business, enjoying the way he recreated the drama of auctions, or described the oddities of collectors, or took her on searches for missing pieces that sometimes turned up on the other side of the globe. There was so much to his profession that she found fascinating that she'd have encouraged him to go on talking all night if he hadn't insisted they change the subject to her.

From there the conversation seemed to grow wings, carrying them from one topic to another, moving around the world, or through their lives, or randomly out to the future and the realm of dreams. The wine flowed, the candlelight flickered and their banter grew more adventurous and flirtatious. Andee especially enjoyed hearing about Graeme growing up with the challenges and joys of having Rowzee and Pamela as sisters. Since knowing they were related she'd never doubted how much he loved them, and their closeness as a family filled her with a deep affection for them all.

'I've often thought,' she dared to confess as he walked her along the promenade towards home, 'about the day I came to tell you I'd decided to marry Martin.'

'As I recall,' he said sardonically, 'I was the one who told you you were going to marry him.'

It was true, he had, because she'd been unable to form the words. 'I felt terrible, so torn and hardly myself. There was so much going on, I was quitting my job, we'd just found Sophie Monroe, do you remember the missing fourteen-year-old?'

He nodded soberly. It had been a tragic end for the poor girl, killed, as it transpired, by her own father and stepmother.

'Then Martin was turning on the charm, not only with me, but with the whole family . . .'

279

'You did what you felt was right at the time,' he reminded her gently.

'That's the trouble, it never did feel right, even then. I kept trying to tell myself it did, but it didn't.' She remembered only too well how wretched and even cheated she'd felt when she'd walked away from Graeme that day, how deeply she'd regretted not being able to go with him to Italy as they'd planned, or how often she'd longed for it since. It was something she'd tried not to think about, but it had always been there, like a dream that wouldn't fade with the dawn.

'How are things with Martin now?' he ventured.

She shook her head. 'I haven't seen or heard from him this week. He could be trying to worry or punish me, or hopefully he's getting on with his life.' She turned to look at him. 'Please tell me he hasn't been in touch with you.'

With a smile he assured her that her fears were groundless. 'I can't help sympathising with him,' he confessed. 'I know how it feels to be in his shoes.'

Remembering that his wife had left him, she decided he could be referring to that rather than to her, and came to a stop outside her apartment building. 'This is where I live now,' she told him, feeling absurdly proud of having her own place.

He looked up at the freshly painted stucco façade and nodded. 'A good spot,' he declared. 'Do you have a view of the bay, or are you at the back?'

'I have a view.' Her mouth was turning dry and her nerves began fluttering as she heard herself saying, 'You're welcome to come and see it for yourself.'

As his eyes came to hers in the lamplight she knew instinctively that he was going to turn her down and immediately regretted asking. Taking her hand, he said, 'I want you to be absolutely sure about Martin and where you want to go from here before we consider committing to one another again.'

Of course he was right to say that, even though she was sure – at least about Martin.

Touching his mouth gently to her forehead, he looked at her again with those droll, knowing eyes and after walking her to her front door, he went off down the street.

# Chapter Sixteen

Rowzee was sitting on a padded bench in the corridor of Kesterly Infirmary's neurosurgery wing, waiting to be called into Mr Mervin's office. It would appear, given the hour and the fact that no one else was around, that hers was the last appointment of the day. She could easily imagine how busy Mr Mervin was with so many people's brains to take care of, but it had been quite a busy day for her too so she was glad of this little sit-down. Not that her commitments could be considered anything like as important as the surgeon's, but they mattered to her, and they'd matter to Norma, Sean and Jason too when she was gone.

Her lawyer, the delightful Jamie Flood whose dad had been on the Kesterly cricket team with Victor, had been very understanding about the reasons why she wanted to change her will, and had even offered advice on how to make things more tax-efficient for her beneficiaries. Unfortunately, it seemed she'd have had to live another seven years in order for them to avoid the clobber of inheritance tax, but she hadn't admitted to Jamie that this was a problem. She'd simply gone along with his suggestions while sending a silent sorry to Norma, Pamela, Graeme and her nieces for the deprivations that would be made by Her Majesty's Government. Before leaving Jamie's office she'd added a small bequest for Andee of an amethyst brooch that had belonged to her mother, and a garnet pendant for Gina that had come from Victor's aunt and Gina had once admired. Pamela and the girls wouldn't mind those two trinkets going elsewhere, she was sure, and she hoped Andee and Gina wouldn't be embarrassed. Maybe she should leave them each a note urging them not to be.

As soon as her appointment with Jamie was over she'd returned to the house intending to walk Teddy for an hour before having to go back into Kesterly, but it turned out he'd already taken off on adventure with Bill.

'We weren't sure what time you'd be back,' Pamela explained, 'and that dear dog needs more exercise than a flimsy little thing like you can give it. So where have you been and why didn't you take your car?'

'I told you earlier I was going to see Jamie Flood,' Rowzee replied, 'and I get into such a flap about parking around his offices that I decided to take a taxi. What are you doing home? Aren't you supposed to be running Bill's campsite?'

'I shan't be taking over officially until the week after next. Meantime, I'm only going in for a few hours a day to learn the ropes. What's that book you're always carrying about with you?'

Spotting it at the top of her bag, Rowzee tucked it in more tightly saying, 'I'm making notes for a novel, if you must know.' What a good answer and right off the top of her head! Somehow it had escaped the mental tangles it might have encountered.

Pamela's eyes widened. 'What's it about?'

'I haven't quite decided yet, but don't worry, you'll be heavily disguised as someone who's never nosy or bossy or shamelessly overbearing.'

'Then it'll be based on the new me. How lovely. Does she have a sister who's hopeless at trying to hide things, even though she thinks she's very good at it?'

Alarmed, Rowzee said, 'What do you think I'm trying to hide?'

'Shall we start with the fact that you've been to see Jilly Ansell without telling me?'

Even more alarmed, Rowzee said, 'How do you know?'

'I ran into Julia Granger who works at the pharmacy. She saw you come in with a prescription and wanted to know if you were all right. So are you?'

'You know I am.'

'I know nothing of the sort. So what did Jilly say about all the headaches and dizzy spells? I hope you remembered to tell her how forgetful you can be too.'

'Oh, funnily enough I forgot that.'

'Ha ha.'

'She said it's normal for a woman of my age to have memory lapses and to feel a bit under the weather sometimes, but if things haven't got better in a couple of weeks she'll send me for tests. Does that satisfy you?'

'No. I think you should be going for tests now, and I'd have told her that if I'd been with you.'

'I'm sure you would, and I'm equally sure that she knows her job better than you do.'

'I wouldn't disagree, provided she's working with all the facts. Did you fess up to getting lost when you were out with Teddy yesterday?'

'I didn't get lost. We were just having a lovely time so I decided to stay out for a bit longer.'

She had got lost, and it had been rather worrying for a while, until she'd started recognising the landscape again and it turned out they weren't so far from home. However, it would probably be safer to stick to the Burlingford Estate and dog-friendly beaches from now on, because no one would ever forgive her – nor would she forgive herself – if anything happened to Teddy.

Glancing at her watch she saw that there were still ten minutes to go before her appointment, provided Mr Mervin was running to time, so she took out her notebook to try once again to find a reminder of what she needed to tell Andee. She felt certain it was about Gina and her great-grandmother being Amish, or at least she was sure it had entered her head while she and Andee were talking about that. The trouble was, they'd been in the car at the time so Rowzee hadn't been able to jot anything down. And now here she was probably connecting the wrong dots . . . Speaking of which, she hadn't had any before her eyes for a couple of days, which was a blessing indeed, and her headaches weren't seeming to last as long, so maybe the steroids were properly out of the starting gate now and beginning a nice smooth run.

Radiotherapy. Mr Mervin would undoubtedly try to persuade her to have it, but once she explained about Sean, and how Norma wouldn't take her money unless it came through a will when she'd have no choice, he might understand why she was so keen to go on her own terms. In other words, sooner rather than later.

Suspecting Mr Mervin might not find that a very good argument, she decided to try and think of another, but there was no time now because his secretary had just told her to go in.

'Ah, Rowzee,' David Mervin greeted her warmly, getting up from his desk to come and show her to a chair. He was a tall, elegant man in his early fifties with a shock of silvery hair and the kind of laughing blue eyes she wouldn't have expected of someone with such a serious job. However, she always felt welcome and safe when she was with him, which was what counted. Such a shame he couldn't operate on her. She was sure if anyone could make a success of it he could. 'I hope I didn't keep you waiting too long,' he smiled as she sat down.

'Oh no,' she assured him, 'my early arrival is just a measure of how keen I am to see you.'

Laughing, he returned to his chair and folded his hands on the blotter as he looked at her. 'So how are you?' he asked, sounding as though he really wanted to know. Well, she supposed he did, after all it was the point of her being here.

'You mean apart from fed up about being on my way upstairs?' she joked. 'I'd say I'm not too bad. How are you?' Funnily enough she'd really like to know. It would be quite interesting to find out whether he was married and had a family; what sort of things he enjoyed when he wasn't being a top surgeon.

However, he seemed to be having none of it, because after a brief 'Very well thank you,' he swiftly moved on. 'Jilly Ansell tells me that you are in touch with Dignitas, and that you would like me to provide the necessary medical proof that you are an acceptable candidate.'

'If you don't mind. That would be very kind of you.'

He nodded thoughtfully. 'Jilly also tells me that you haven't discussed this decision with your family.'

Feeling herself colour, she said, 'That's correct. They would only try to stop me from doing it, so I've decided it's best to make it a fait accompli.'

Sitting back in his chair, he made a bony steeple with his fingers. 'Everything I hear about you, Rowzee, tells me that you're a very loving and considerate woman. I also know how courageous you are.'

Courageous enough to die, that was right, except she was terrified really, especially of doing it alone, but it was the only way, and she mustn't cry or he'd think she was weakening.

'I understand,' he continued, 'that it takes an enormous amount of courage to carry through the decision you've made, and I believe you have that courage. Yet you don't seem able to find it to share the decision with your loved ones.'

Startled that he should see it that way, she tried to think how to correct him, but wasn't sure that she could given that he might have a point. 'I told you,' she said, 'they'll try to stop me and I don't want to be a burden to them. It's not fair on them or me.'

'But don't you think they should be allowed to speak for themselves? You might find that they are willing, after some discussion, to respect your wishes.'

She was suddenly finding it very hard indeed to hold back the tears. It was the thought of Pamela and Graeme being with her, holding her hands and saying a final goodbye. She couldn't bear the idea of not seeing them again.

Attempting to gather herself with the reminder that Victor and Edward would be waiting for her, she accepted a tissue from Mr Mervin as she said, 'If they do respect my wishes they'll want to come with me to Switzerland and I'm afraid when we get there that I won't be brave enough to leave them so it would be a wasted journey and I'll end up hating myself for putting them through it, and then we'll all have to come home again and we won't be any better off than we were before, but I'll still have the tumour and before you know it I'll start talking gibberish, or shouting at them and falling over in the street. I already have difficulty staying focused, I keep forgetting things that I know are important, and I can't find a way to bring them back.' Time to take a breath, Rowzee, she told herself.

Turning his computer terminal around, he positioned it so she could see the screen. She realised right away that she was looking at MRI scans of her brain – unless it was someone else's and this was all a big mistake.

Dream on, Rowzee.

'As you know,' he said, enlarging one of the images, 'your tumour is on the left-hand side of the brain.' Did she know that? Probably someone had told her, but if they had she'd obviously forgotten. 'This is it.' He was pointing to a fuzzy sort of mass that didn't look all that bothersome to her. 'Because it's up against the middle cerebral artery,' he continued, 'there's a grave risk of causing damage to this artery during surgery, which could trigger a major stroke. If this happens it would leave you paralysed down the right-hand side of your body and it would also affect your speech. This is the reason, together with it being a secondary cancer, that we've decided not to operate. However that doesn't mean it's untreatable. I know that's already been explained to you, and I know you've started taking dexamethasone . . . How are you finding it so far?'

'Yes, good, I think. I mean, I still have odd moments of not quite being myself, but the headaches aren't as bad.'

'Jilly's told you that a course of radiotherapy will also help?'

'Yes, but I don't want to go through all that. I really don't. Treating it is just putting off the inevitable, and we might as well get on with it or it'll be too late and Dignitas won't take me.'

Swivelling his computer back to its original position, he regarded her steadily before finally saying, 'It might come as a surprise to you to hear me say this, but I'm afraid I'm not at all convinced that you've thought this through. Being the kind of person you are I'd have expected you to be out there fighting while you can for the right to die, not running straight to it without a thought for those you love.'

Her face fell. 'But I do think about them,' she protested, appalled that he could think she hadn't. 'They're the reason . . .'

'Yes, I understand that you don't want to be a burden . . .'

'They have their own lives. I don't want them to put everything on hold for me.' Should she tell him about Sean and Norma now, and how eager she was for Norma to have some proper backup, and for young Jason to go to uni, or find himself a good apprenticeship? The sooner she was dead, the sooner they'd inherit, and they couldn't argue with an inheritance, could they?

'Rowzee, don't you see that you're playing straight into the hands of those who don't believe in the right to die? One of their biggest fears, and it's justified, is that people will feel obliged to go before their time . . .'

'But it's not before my time. The tumour proves that. You said yourself that it's inoperable, so that means I'm going to die.'

'But not for at least another six months provided you have the radiotherapy, and is that so very long to ask your family to take care of you when you know in your heart that they'll want to do everything possible to make the time you have left as special as they can?'

Rowzee was staring at him, dumbfounded. She only had six months to live? She'd assumed, based on heaven only knew what, that she was going to fumble on for a year or two at least, getting progressively more dependent and annoying and smelly and disgusting . . . If she only had six months, did that mean she was heading for that dreadful state as soon as the next week or two? She needed to ask.

'I shouldn't think for one minute that you'll be incapacitated by the end of the month,' he replied gently. 'In fact there's nothing to say that you'll become incapacitated at all. If you'll just let us treat you . . .'

She wasn't listening; she was shaking her head, trying to catch up with the thoughts that seemed to be going off in all directions. In the end, she said, 'You're right, I need to think about this some more. I hadn't realised my time was going to be so short. I guess it changes things, but I need to work out how and what's best to be done.' After a pause, she went on. 'I should be doing something to help people in my position, not turning tail and running away from it. Did you already say that?'

With a smile, he said, 'I want you to come and see me again in a week, and I hope by then that you'll be ready to bring someone from your family with you, so that I can explain things to them in a way that will help them and you to come to the right decision.'

It was Monday evening when Charles drove past the Coach House where Bill and Pamela were tending some colourful urns of flowers, and carried on along the drive to Burlingford Hall. He wondered if they thought him rude for not stopping. Should he go back to say hello? Though he was in no mood to be sociable, he felt he ought, considering how long he'd known them. However, his foot remained on the accelerator, taking him on through the leafy arch of limes, over the humpback bridge and around the mermaid fountain, only moving to the brake as he reached the Hall's front steps.

Suddenly deciding he didn't want to go in that way, he drove on to the back and pulled up next to Bill's quad bike outside the garages.

The place was as deserted as he'd expected it to be. The housekeeper was away until tomorrow, and there were no garden tours on weekdays. There was nothing, no one, to disturb him, apart from the face, the guilt that followed him wherever he went. Whether he was asleep or awake, talking to someone on the phone, attending a meeting, travelling in a taxi, or standing at a window staring at nothing, the face was there. A hideous flash of shock and terror, followed by a scream and the kind of noise that made him feel as though he was drowning.

Going to let himself in through the kitchen, he moved quickly through to the library, poured himself a Scotch and went to open the French windows. He needed the alcohol as much as the air, and yet neither felt soothing. Nothing ever would again. He'd made such terrible choices, had done something no decent human being ever would, and no saint or God could ever forgive.

It was as impossible for him to live with himself as it was for him to confess, yet how could he end his life without giving Gina and Lydia a reason why? What kind of man would shatter their world with an unexplained suicide? A better man, maybe, than one who'd force them to live with the truth. He should just go, and leave them in what they'd never realise was blissful ignorance. He could do it now, tonight, not here in the house, but out there in the distant reaches of the estate, the swamp in Valley Woods, invisible from the fields and from the jagged clifftop above. No one ever went there, most didn't even know it existed, so no one would ever find him.

How could he even be contemplating disappearing without a trace, the way Jessica Leonard had? How much did the blackmailer actually know? Would he or she come forward afterwards to tell what Charles Stamfield had done? Having no way of knowing the answer to that was what kept him alive. The dilemma was terrible and all-consuming. For his own family's sake he couldn't admit to what he'd done, and yet he couldn't allow Blake Leonard and his family to carry on suffering the way they were.

Taking out his mobile he scrolled to Andee's number, but didn't press to connect. There was nothing she could do to save him from this; maybe she wouldn't even want to try.

Andee knew very well that she had to tell the police about Gina's Amish great-grandmother, and Charles's blackmail situation, and she would, just as soon as she'd spoken to Charles and/or Gina. However, in spite of saying, independently of each other, that they were coming to Kesterly, she'd still not heard from either.

Earlier in the day Leo Johnson had called to let her know that new CCTV footage had apparently come to light in London, showing Jessica going into a garage at the back of the Holland Park residence leased by Yoder. (Had anyone told Blake that, yet? She needed to check.) According to those examining the footage it wasn't possible from the camera's angle – apparently it was affixed to a neighbouring property – to see if there was a car in the garage, and the door had closed behind Jessica without revealing signs of anyone else being inside. However, Jessica's response as she'd walked in – clasping her hands to her face in what? Joy? Shock? Laughter? It was impossible to tell, apparently, because her back was to the camera – strongly suggested that someone was there. Whoever it was, whatever had been happening, there was still nothing to give them a link to Kim Yoder or his/her identity – unless more video turned up of a car leaving the premises that they might be able to trace.

Putting her hands to her head, Andee tried to think what to do next. She knew she wouldn't be hesitating at all if Charles and Gina weren't friends, or if Gina hadn't said on the phone that she had something to tell her.

Getting up from her computer where the name Yoder was displayed large on the screen, she went to pour herself a glass of wine and started at the sound of the doorbell. She wasn't expecting anyone – unless it was Gina, arrived in Kesterly at last. Had she given her this address?

'Hi, it's me,' a voice at the other end of the entry-phone told her.

Andee's eyes closed as she released the door, then remembering what was on her computer she returned to the sitting room to shut down the screen.

It was early on Tuesday morning. A damp, silvery mist was rolling across the countryside turning it into a kind of Elysian paradise, Rowzee thought, as she and Teddy started out on their walk. It was hard to see much beyond twenty yards ahead, and as though sensing the need to stay close Teddy was holding on to his ball instead of urging her to throw it. However, the spotting of a deer as they crossed into the estate soon sent him hurtling off into the bushes.

Knowing he'd give up the chase soon enough Rowzee kept going, enjoying the way sunlight was sparkling through the haze, making it seem as though the cob-webby grass was littered with diamonds. The air was still, yet invigorating, the birds were chirping merrily. She could hear a woodpecker somewhere close by, but was unable to spot it through the mist. On mornings like this she and Victor had always enjoyed getting up early for a stroll, and on a level she was finding easier to connect with now that her own life was soon to end, she could feel him with her today.

In her mind she was speaking to him, asking him to help her find the courage to tell Pamela and Graeme her news. She could hear him assuring her that Graeme would be supportive in every way; Pamela would be too, he was saying, but she'd be angry that Rowzee hadn't told her sooner, and frustrated with Mr Mervin that there was nothing he could do to cure the cancer.

'I don't want Pamela to be rude to Mr Mervin,' Rowzee said out loud.

Victor's reply came instantly into her mind. 'She won't be,' he said silently. 'Remember she's a new person, thanks to her therapy.'

Feeling disloyal, but saying it anyway, Rowzee couldn't help pointing out that it hadn't completely worked. 'Not that I want it to,' she went on hastily, 'because I love her the way she is. We don't want her turning into a sweet-natured, uncomplaining old soul who sees nothing but good in everything. It wouldn't be her.'

'Don't worry, it won't happen. Leopards don't change their spots.'

Victor was right, it wouldn't happen and Bill would be glad of it, because he was clearly besotted with the feisty old bat he'd finally managed to hook. Or so it seemed. 'The main difficulty,' she told Victor, 'is not Pamela changing into somebody else, it's not knowing how much longer before I stop being me.'

'You'll always be you, Rowzee.'

'I knew you'd say something like that, but you have to take this seriously, my love. I want to do the right thing for everyone before I go, including Norma, Sean and Jason. They're your flesh and blood, well Sean and Jason are, and that means a great deal to me. I hope you've forgiven Sean for what he did to you. It was terrible, I know, and he shouldn't have got away with it, but we know now that he didn't.'

'Do you think what happened to him was a punishment for what he did to me?'

'Yes, I think I do, and that's what makes it so sad, because I know you'd never wish anything so awful on him. I wish I could ask him if he'd like to come with me when I go to Dignitas so we could come to you together.'

'So you're still intending to do that?'

Sighing, she said, 'I'm not sure. Since talking to Mr Mervin yesterday I haven't been able to make up my mind about anything.'

'You know, you have a lot more to give to the world before you come to me.'

Welling up, Rowzee said, 'Do you think so?' She was so torn, longing desperately to be with Victor and Edward, yet wanting to stay where she was for as long as she could with Graeme and Pamela and now Jason, her dear, sweet grandson.

'I know so, and you do too. You can make yourself a cause célèbre.'

Wryly she replied, 'With Pamela as my spokesman when I can't speak for myself any more?'

'That could be interesting, because if anyone knows how to fight a corner she does. But I was thinking more of Sean and what someone in your position could do for people in his.'

Taking this in, Rowzee looked around for Teddy and spotted him sniffing about a marshy patch in the grass a short way ahead. 'Tell me, Victor,' she whispered, filling up with emotion, 'will you be waiting for me when I get there?'

'You know I will.'

'And Edward?'

'He's here too.'

'Can he hear me now?'

'If you want him to.'

'Eddie, my darling, Mummy's coming to you soon and we'll all be together again. Won't that be lovely?' To Victor she said brokenly, 'Is he still five years old?'

'Not in the way you understand it.'

She walked on, certain they were still there, watching her, caring for her and wanting to help her in any way they could. In the end, in a tiny voice she said, 'I'm afraid, Victor.'

'I know, my love, but there's nothing to be afraid of. Everyone will take good care of you, and if things get really bad they'll find a way to let you go.'

She couldn't be sure of that, but it was what she wanted to believe so she decided she would.

'I think I feel ready to come now, Victor.'

'You mustn't say that. It's like giving up.'

'But what difference will six months make? I think it might be even less if I don't have radiotherapy.' Mr Mervin hadn't said so, but she was sure he'd implied it.

'You'll never know unless you stay around to find out, and who knows, you might do something amazing in that time that will make a huge difference to everyone.'

'Like what?'

'Mm, let me see, I'm thinking solving the theorem of quantum gravity.'

Rowzee had to laugh. Such a typical Victor answer. 'I hate forgetting things,' she told him. 'It makes me feel like one of those cheeses with holes in it. Lots of substance and then suddenly nothing but air.'

'What are you trying to remember?'

'I only wish I knew.'

Victor laughed, and so did she.

She missed him so much and wanted desperately to be with him, but now the possibility was drawing close she wasn't sure how well her faith was holding up. She could hear him in her mind, feel him right next to her as she walked across the fields, but she knew very well that it was all imaginary. If it really were possible to speak to the dead they'd know everything they needed to about the afterlife, and probably lots more about this one too. Such as whether it was necessary to be afraid of dying, and what the point was of everything. Was there some divine purpose behind what had happened to Sean; to taking small children from their parents the way Edward had been taken from them, or making others, like Jessica, simply disappear? If it were possible to understand these things they might be easier to accept, but sadly it didn't work that way, and she could feel a Pamela-like frustration coming over her for how randomly cruel and nonsensical life could be.

Using the thrower to scoop up Teddy's ball she hurled it as far as she could into the next field, and tramped along after him, climbing the stile and wading on through the long grass, wellies soaked in dew and plastered with buttercup petals. In the distance she could just make out the woods, a kind of C.S. Lewis dreamland in the rising mist.

She'd tried calling Andee last night, after Pamela and Bill had gone out. They'd invited her to go along too, but she'd had too much to think about to be able to carry off the pretence of enjoying herself. She'd felt disappointed when she'd been directed to Andee's voicemail, but Andee would have lots of things to do, people to see, and Rowzee felt foolish now for thinking she might have wanted to come and spend the evening with her. So she'd rung Norma instead and they'd had a lovely long chat about Jason and how clever he was underneath it all, and how much they both enjoyed rereading Jane Austen's *Northanger Abbey* and watching *Strictly Come Dancing*. They'd talked about Norma's brief relationship with Victor, how the two of them had met and how they'd never really been suited. Apparently Norma had been a different sort of person back then, so it seemed that sometimes a leopard could change its spots.

By the time they'd rung off Norma had recommended some books for Rowzee to read, mostly spiritual guides as though she'd sensed Rowzee might need them, and as soon as she'd put the phone down Rowzee had gone online to order them. No point hanging around, or she might not get to finish them.

How awful the timing had been for Sean's accident that hadn't been an accident at all. If Victor hadn't died so soon afterwards Norma would have got in touch to ask for help, and Rowzee knew Victor would have willingly given it. There was another inexplicable tragedy flung out by fate, that father and son had never been reconciled in this lifetime. She could only hope that it was on the cards for the next or there really would be no point to anything at all.

She'd crossed several more fields and followed a few more ragged trails by now, and was becoming aware of Teddy barking somewhere up ahead. Since she wasn't familiar with this part of the estate it was hard to think of where he might be, unless he was in the horribly dark woods huddling round the foot of the cliffs like a towering bunch of demons.

That certainly seemed to be where the barking was coming from, and starting to worry that his collar might have got caught up in brambles she began picking her way through the densely packed pines, stepping gingerly over the tangled mass of undergrowth, and sliding on the wet leaves underfoot.

'Teddy, sweetie, please come,' she cried. 'I'm not sure I can get to you.'

Teddy carried on barking, sounding more urgent and excited by the second.

'Where are you?' she called out, still trying to get through. She might have to go back and get Bill at this rate, but it would seem so unkind to leave Teddy if he was trapped. He wouldn't understand that she was coming back, so she had to try harder to get to him.

Eventually the snaking brambles and twisted garlands of ivy seemed to shrink from the trees, and to her surprise she found herself in a sort of clearing with a grimy lake, more like a swamp, at its heart. Teddy was close by, up to his shoulders in mud as he barked like crazy, seeming to want to jump in the water, but then, as though sensing danger, pulling back again. He ran to the broken trunk of a fallen tree that was providing a kind of bridge towards the far side of the swamp. Rowzee looked across to where an immense jagged wall of rock soared up, as high as forty feet or more, to a cluster of trees at its summit and something metallic below them. Realising it was a road barrier, she decided they must be beneath one of the seldom-used back lanes into Kesterly.

Teddy was still barking like fury.

'What is it, sweetie?' she asked, going towards him. If he'd dropped his ball in the mud it had clearly sunk because there was no sign of it, and love him as she did she wasn't about to start fishing around for it. Any closer and they'd probably both get sucked into the quagmire. That would be an awful end, drowned in mud and probably never found.

'Come on, Teddy, we should go,' she said, not liking the feeling she was getting here. It was cold and sinister, like some dreadful netherworld that existed out of sight and time and might at any minute suck her and Teddy into some ghastly strangeness they could never escape from.

'That's a good boy,' she murmured as Teddy came towards her, but as she reached for him he moved quickly away, still barking at the swamp.

Finally realising he was trying to tell her something, she looked at the slimy water again, and this time she frowned as she noticed that the fallen tree was resting on something midway across. It took a moment for her to figure out what it was, and as she did her heartbeat started to slow.

'Oh my goodness, Teddy,' she murmured, trying to tell herself that the light was playing tricks on her eyes. 'Oh my goodness. What have you found?'

## Chapter Seventeen

It was just before ten o'clock when Andee drove out of Kesterly, heading for Burlingford Hall. Charles had texted late last night asking her to come, and offering an apology for not being in touch sooner. For some reason she'd found the apology a little odd, but that was nothing to what she was finding her own wild imaginings, which had Jessica being held by an Amish community somewhere in the American Midwest. Or maybe she'd gone voluntarily, which really didn't add up at all.

It had been her intention to try calling Gina again last night once Martin had gone, but she'd been unable to persuade him to leave. She'd ended up giving him a blanket so he could sleep on the sofa, and taken herself off to bed. She didn't want to think about the ugly scene that had followed when he'd tried to join her, it was best to wipe it from her mind, and considering how much he'd had to drink hopefully he wouldn't remember it either.

After coaxing him back to the sofa she'd returned to the bedroom, put a chair against her door and done something she hadn't in so long, she'd rung her mother in tears. It must have been the hour that had made everything seem so overwhelming, although there wasn't any other time of day when she didn't feel a terrible sense of guilt for causing so much hurt to someone she actually loved. She'd even wondered if perhaps she should do as Martin asked and try again, but her mother had put her foot down about that. 'You'll only end up doing the same thing further down the line,' she'd said firmly, 'so you might as well carry on and finish what you've already started.'

Ever practical, ever supportive, that was Maureen Lawrence, and Andee couldn't have loved her more if she'd tried. She'd even babbled on for a while about Graeme and how wary they both seemed about trying again, and was it what she wanted anyway? If she was being totally honest she didn't think he wanted it at all, was just being polite and friendly because she was so much in his world at the moment, what with her search for Jessica Leonard and new friendship with Rowzee. She'd forgotten now exactly what she'd said to make her mother laugh, she was only aware of how uplifting she had found that moment.

'So was that him you were on the phone to during the night?' Martin had demanded sourly when she'd taken him a coffee before leaving the flat just now.

She hadn't bothered to answer, nor, thankfully, had he pursued it.

'Where are you going?' he'd growled as she'd headed for the door.

'To see Charles Stamfield.'

His eyes darkened suspiciously. 'Why?'

'There are some things we need to discuss. I'd appreciate it if you weren't here when I get back.'

'Would you? Well, maybe it would suit me better to stay.'

Biting down on her frustration, she'd simply picked up her bag and left.

Now, as she approached the Coach House and spotted Pamela waving out to her, she pulled over to say hello.

'I don't suppose you've seen Rowzee on your travels?' Pamela asked worriedly as Andee lowered the driver's window.

'There was no sign of her on the road coming up here,' Andee replied. 'Why? What's happened?'

'Nothing, I hope. It's just that I thought she'd have been back in time for breakfast.'

'Where did she go?'

'To walk Teddy. I heard her leaving about seven o'clock, and silly thing hasn't taken her phone. I'm afraid she might have got lost, or had a fall and knocked herself out. Bill's gone up to the Hall to get his quad bike so he can search the estate. He said I should wait here in case she comes back, and I suppose he's right, but I'm next to useless, pacing up and down frightening myself to death. Do you think I should call Graeme? Yes, I should. I'll do it now,' and before Andee could respond she'd disappeared inside.

Carrying on to the Hall, Andee kept a lookout for Rowzee as she went, but the grounds were as still and tranquil as a painting in the mid-morning sunlight.

Three hours was a long dog walk, she was reflecting worriedly to herself, especially when Rowzee had clearly been expected home after not much more than an hour.

Spotting Charles and Bill in front of the Hall, she circled the fountain and was just getting out of her car when both men suddenly turned away from her. Realising they were responding to Rowzee stumbling across the grass and calling out to them, Andee moved quickly, getting to her just as Bill did and holding her steady as she tried to catch her breath, with Teddy running around them in circles.

'It's OK,' Andee soothed, as Rowzee struggled to speak. 'Just take a breath.'

Rowzee was bruised and scratched, her hair was full of brambles and leaves, but finally she found her voice. Looking at Bill, she gasped, 'You have to come. There's a car . . . in the swamp.'

'What swamp?' Bill demanded urgently.

'Over that way.' She was pointing across the flowing expanse of fields. 'At the back of Valley Woods. I came as fast as I could. I got lost, looking for Teddy, but . . . Oh Bill, I think – I'm sure, someone's *in* the car.'

As Bill took off towards the fields on his quad bike with Rowzee in a helmet riding pillion and Teddy in hot pursuit, Andee's eyes returned to Charles. She'd noticed the instant Rowzee had told them about the car how pale he'd gone, and there was still no colour to him now.

Surely to God this wasn't what she was thinking, but she had a horrible feeling it was.

'You'd better come in,' he said quietly.

Following him up the front steps and across the vestibule into the library, she wondered if Gina was around, but there was no sign of her.

'There's coffee,' Charles said, stopping at a table in front of his desk. 'I made it myself ready for your visit, so I don't know how warm it still is.'

'I'm sure it's fine,' she responded. A part of her was desperately wishing this wasn't happening; she didn't want him, or Gina, to be involved in whatever had happened to Jessica, they were friends whom she cared for deeply, but simply being here now, like this, was enough to convince her that her suspicions were correct.

*What the hell had they done?*

He didn't speak again until they were seated in wingback chairs either side of the Byzantine fireplace with an enormous portrait of his grandfather towering over them, and hazy bands of sunlight streaming through the south-facing windows. 'The police will be here soon,' he said bleakly. 'Bill will call them once he reaches the lake, but I'd rather speak to you.'

Her mouth was turning dry as she watched him. Never, in a million years, when Blake had asked her to take this case on, would she have imagined that it would end up here. In spite of her instincts, she was still finding it hard to accept. 'You realise you'll probably have to repeat it all to them?' she said softly.

He nodded in a way that seemed both vague and yet almost impatient, as though he were trying to maintain, or even establish, a train of thought. She watched him closely, and as his eyes seemed to cloud she could sense him moving away from where he was to a place, a time, a circumstance that only he could see. 'I should begin by telling you how Jessica and I met,' he said quietly, and the confirmation of her fears turned her heart inside out.

He took a breath that shook on a sob, and for a moment she could see how hard he was struggling. Whatever he was about to tell her was clearly causing him such immense anguish that putting it into words was almost too much to bear. In the end he spoke coherently, his voice low as he said, 'It was at one of the parties there was so much talk about. I can tell you which one if you like, but as what happened after had nothing to do with the hosts, or anyone else who was there, I'd rather keep them out of it.'

Knowing that would have to be a decision for later, Andee simply waited for him to continue.

'My name wasn't on the guest list,' he told her, 'because I went along at the last minute with a friend whose partner couldn't make it. The friend left early but I stayed. Jessica was singing that night and I know this is going to sound clichéd, delusional, maybe even sick given the difference in our ages, but I felt a connection with her even before we spoke. I found her mesmerising; I couldn't take my eyes off her, and the whole time she sang she seemed to be singing to me. I didn't ask anyone to introduce us when she'd finished; I simply went up and introduced myself. She said she knew who I was because her parents lived in Kesterly-on-Sea. We didn't talk for long, she said she

309

had to leave, so I asked if I could see her again and to my amazement she said yes.'

It was a measure of his modesty, Andee was thinking, that he'd find a young girl's attraction to him surprising, for he was, and always had been, an exceptionally attractive man. He was also very rich.

'She knew I was married, of course,' he continued, 'so she understood the need for discretion. Even so, I was aware I was taking a risk; girls of her age can rarely keep things to themselves, but over time it turned out that she could. I'd go as far as to say that the secrecy of our relationship was something that excited her.' He swallowed drily. 'It was after our first couple of meetings, at a hotel in Knightsbridge where I took two rooms to disguise the fact we were together, that I decided to rent a place. We needed somewhere to go where we could spend as much time as we wanted to, and where we wouldn't be seen by other hotel guests, or staff. So I contacted a rental agent I knew about who finds places for people who don't want to be on the record, mostly foreigners who want to keep a low profile in London for whatever reason, and everything went through without me having to meet anyone, or formally state a source of funding. Jessica fell in love with the house the minute she saw it, and she never seemed to mind that we couldn't invite anyone round, or go out together in public. She said she was happy for us to spend whatever time we could just the two of us, not sharing it with anyone else, or even thinking about them.' He paused for a moment, lowering his eyes as he dealt with another build-up of emotion.

'None of it would have happened if things had been right between me and Gina,' he continued hoarsely, 'but that sounds as though I'm trying to blame her, and nothing about this was anyone's fault but mine. Gina couldn't help what happened to her after the cancer, I knew she felt terrible about it, and she tried so many ways to put it right, but nothing ever seemed to work. It got to a point where I was afraid to touch her in case she recoiled, and she felt so bad about always rejecting me that our marriage was in danger of collapse. It was an attempt to keep us together that made Gina offer to turn a blind eye if I wanted to have an affair, on the proviso I didn't allow it to get serious. At the time I had no intention of carrying it through, I loved Gina, I still do, but then I met Jessica and ... And I realised how much I'd been missing that part of my life. Please don't think I'm only talking about sex, although I won't deny it was a big part of our relationship, I'm talking about the fun and laughter that goes with that sort of togetherness, the joy of discovering what gives someone else pleasure, feeling so close to them that it's as though you're inside their skin. Young as she was, that's how it was for me with Jessica, and I believe it was the same for her.'

Trying to remain detached as she watched him struggle for control, Andee allowed several moments to pass before saying, 'Would I be right in thinking that the house was in Holland Park?'

He didn't appear surprised that she knew, seemed in a way hardly to be listening. 'Yes, you would,' he said. 'It wasn't large, but it was ours and we spent

311

as much time there as we could. I told her she could
live there if she wanted to, but she insisted it would
be best if she carried on with her plans to share with
her friends when she returned to uni after the summer.
That way no one would wonder where she was getting
the money from to rent somewhere in one of the most
expensive parts of town – and besides she didn't want
to feel obliged to invite her friends to her home when it
was our special place.' He swallowed hard, pressed his
fingers to his temples and forced himself to continue. 'I
wanted to help her financially, with tuition fees and the
rest of it so she wouldn't start out life in debt, and she
was willing to let that happen provided I didn't think
it was the reason she was with me. Whether or not it
was I suppose we'll never know for certain, but I truly
believe that her feelings for me were as strong as mine
were for her.' As he lost his words Andee could see how
desperately he wanted that to be true, and because she
knew him so well she didn't doubt that it was. He was,
and always had been, very easy to love. 'I used to fan-
tasise about leaving Gina for her,' he confessed, 'about
being able to live our lives openly, I even used to imagine marrying her and starting a new family . . . I never
told her that, I didn't want to frighten her. She was so
young, with her whole life ahead of her . . .' He broke
off as harsh, despairing tears overwhelmed him.

Andee waited quietly, sensing he didn't want her to
touch him, but feeling as sorry for him as she always
did for someone who had no clear understanding of
how things had turned out the way they had. 'So what
happened to her?' she asked gently.

His eyes closed as he shrank from the need to continue, until finally he managed to accept it.

'She was going home to Kesterly that day for the summer,' he said shakily. 'We'd already arranged a secret rendezvous place on the moor so we could keep seeing one another. I could see how intrigued and excited she was by the idea of clandestine meetings in a remote place in the outdoors. She wanted . . . She wanted to make love in the open air . . .' He broke off as his voice was swallowed by another surge of grief.

'When I rang her,' he finally continued, 'she was already on her way to Paddington. I told her I had a surprise for her that I'd like her to have before she left. So we arranged to meet at the house. There was a private garage at the back where you could enter, close the door behind you and go into the house without going outside again. It was the way we always went, so it was where I waited for her. And when she saw her surprise . . .'

Jessica's hands flew to her face. 'Oh my God, oh my God, oh my God,' she murmured, unable to believe it. Her eyes went to Charles, fearfully, expectantly, delightedly, as though checking to make sure she wasn't seeing things.

He was smiling and holding out the key for her to take.

'Is it mine?' she asked, seeming almost afraid to look at the brand-new Mini again in case she was wrong.

'Of course,' he replied, knowing he'd treasure this precious moment for ever. Nothing, but nothing gave him as much pleasure as making someone happy, especially her. 'Your dream car, I believe?'

Suddenly she was shrugging off her heavy backpack and running towards him, leaping into his arms and wrapping her entire self around him.

Laughing, he held her tight as she showered him with kisses.

'I didn't mean for you to get me one, you know that, don't you?' she insisted, clasping his face in her hands to gaze earnestly into his eyes.

'But I did,' he twinkled, and he couldn't remember ever feeling so happy as they embraced again and again until the car was forgotten, and they went into the house to celebrate its arrival.

'I'm going to call her Milly,' she declared, when they eventually returned to the garage. 'Milly the Mini. She's so beautiful. I want to drive her right away.' Her eyes came mischievously to his. 'Can I?' she dared him.

Having expected it, he said, 'Of course. She's yours so you can take her anywhere you like.'

'But what about insurance?'

'It's in my name with you as an additional driver. I had to do it that way to get it here, but we'll change it when you're ready.'

Running a hand over the gleaming paintwork as though smoothing an exotic cat, she said, 'How am I going to explain it to my parents?'

'Well, I was thinking you might say you'd saved up the fees from your gigs,' he suggested, not sure whether that would work or not.

Her eyes narrowed as they came to his. 'It would have to make me extremely well paid,' she pointed out.

'Some of those people are extremely rich, and nothing less than extravagant with tips, especially when drunk.'

Apparently dismissing the concern for the moment, she opened the driver's door and slipped in behind the wheel. 'Oh Charles,' she sobbed and laughed as she inspected the instrument panels and adjusted the seat to suit her height, 'I want to drive it home, today. Can we do that? Will you come with me?' Getting out again, she wrapped her arms around him. 'Please say you'll come. I want you to be with me the first time I drive it.'

How could he refuse her? Was there anything he'd rather do than be with her? He'd never told her, yet, that he'd composed poems to her, love sonnets that he thought, self-consciously but hopefully, she might one day set to music. 'We can put all your belongings in the boot, if you like,' he suggested.

'Yes, yes, and we can raid the fridge for a picnic to have at our special place on the moor,' she added excitedly. 'You need to show me where it is, remember, so why don't we do it today?'

Andee could see how lost he was to the memory of that day, to the power of feeling he'd known for a girl less than half his age, and clearly still had.

'I had a meeting to go to that afternoon,' he went on quietly, not looking at Andee, still staring into the past, 'but I rang my assistant and got her to reschedule.' His eyes closed as he was swamped by the memory. 'I said

I was going to be in Kesterly for the next few days,' he resumed, 'and so Jess and I loaded up her car and set off on the journey west, going via the M3 so we could get to our rendezvous point on the moor more quickly. I don't think I'd ever seen her so happy. She kept looking over at me and grinning, or she'd reach for my hand and kiss it. I suppose I'd been just as happy in my time, obviously I had, but on that day she was all that mattered.

'We didn't stop until we reached our nook, as she instantly dubbed it. The picnic didn't happen right away, I guess you could say we were too hungry for each other. It was a sunny afternoon and we ended up staying far longer than we'd intended. I was having trouble persuading her to put her clothes back on, but I guess I didn't try very hard.' His eyes flickered as he seemed to sense this was the kind of detail Andee wouldn't want. 'If it had been possible we might have stayed there all night,' he continued, 'but she'd told her family to expect her home and the battery was dead on her phone so she couldn't call them. Of course, she could have used mine, but they would have wondered about the number, so we returned to the car and set off for Kesterly. It was starting to get dark by then, and because we were late I directed her along the back roads of the estate . . .' He stopped, took a breath and put a hand to his head. For a while he seemed unable to speak, or even breathe, and Andee could almost feel the depth of his suffering. 'I'm not sure what we were laughing at as we went round Drayman's curve,' he said, his voice fractured by emotion, 'I only remember that we were laughing then suddenly, out of nowhere, someone was standing in the road.' He shook his head, as though still unable to believe it. 'How could someone be standing in the road? It didn't make any sense. It was so remote and dark. No one ever went there, but there was a woman, and she didn't move, just stared like she was trapped in the headlights. As soon as we saw her Jessica screamed and spun the wheel, but it was too late, we'd already hit her, and I think instead of slamming on the brake she accelerated and the next thing we were flying off the edge of the road . . . There's a barrier in place now, but there wasn't then . . .' He stopped, trying to catch his breath as the horror of it all overcame him. 'I keep thinking of how quiet everything seemed as the car descended,' he said, 'and yet it couldn't have been because I'm sure Jess was still screaming . . . I have no recollection of hitting the water, none at all. It's as though minutes, maybe even days, except it wasn't that long I know, just vanished from the world. I can only tell you that when I came round I was on the bank, half in and half out of the mud, and there was no sign of Jessica or the car. For one bizarre moment I thought she'd somehow driven on, but of course that couldn't have happened. I knew the only place she could be was in the water, trapped in the car, but when I tried to get to her it was hopeless. The Mini was too far down and the swamp was trying to drag me in. I kept trying and trying until in the end I knew she couldn't possibly have survived. Too much time had passed. If she hadn't been killed outright then she'd have drowned by now. I didn't know what to do, my phone was in the car, as was hers.' He started to sob, the huge wrenching sounds of a man in terrible torment. 'I left her there,' he choked. 'Oh God, oh God, I left her there.'

As she watched him trying to deal with the horror and shame of his actions, Andee knew that there would never be any excusing what he'd done. Nothing in the world could ever justify allowing Jessica's family to suffer and wonder and hope for two long years, when all the time Charles Stamfield had known their daughter was dead.

In the end, because she had to, she said, 'Didn't someone see you when you got to the Hall?'

He shook his head. 'I don't think so. I still have no recollection of that part of it. The truth is I didn't remember any of it for several weeks. I realise now that I must have suffered a concussion in the crash, because for a long time I couldn't even remember knowing her.'

'But you must have realised, through the media, that she was missing. Didn't that trigger something for you?'

'I kept feeling that it should, but I had no idea how, and when they said that she had been last seen in the Holland Park area . . . I had no memory of the house at that time . . . I didn't remember anything about the car, or what we'd meant to one another . . . It was as though that part of my memory had been wiped clean. It only started to come back later. Not all of it, only parts, until eventually I remembered enough to know what had happened to her, and even where she was.'

He began sobbing again, and though Andee wasn't beyond feeling pity she was thinking of the election and wondering, with a cynicism she didn't much like, if it had played a part in his amnesia. It wouldn't have done him, or the Party, any good for him to have become embroiled in the case of a missing girl at such a crucial time.

'I wanted to tell someone,' he pressed on, 'but so much time had gone by . . . I was sure no one would believe in my memory loss, they'd think I'd deliberately left her there and maybe . . . Maybe I had, because I remember thrashing about the swamp in the darkness, sobbing and begging her to forgive me, so I knew then where she was. It was only after that my mind went blank.'

Abruptly he got up from his chair and started to pace, his long limbs trembling, his anguish and shame as apparent as the tears on his cheeks. His memories, Andee realised, were as torturous as they deserved to be.

'What about the person you hit?' she finally ventured.

Several seconds passed before he seemed to connect with the question. 'I think . . . I don't know, but I think it's who's been blackmailing me.'

Puzzled by that, she said, 'Have you never tried to find out who it was, if they even survived?'

'I thought, if I showed an interest, the police would want to know why, and, if she'd survived, she'd end up telling them what she'd seen.'

At a loss to see how this could have got any worse for him, she said, 'But the lake, or swamp, from what I can gather, is on your estate. It wouldn't be unusual for you to enquire about an accident that had happened on the road above it.'

He didn't seem to have heard her; she couldn't even be sure that he was still aware of her being in the room.

In the end she said, 'Does Gina know any of this?'

He swallowed hard as he shook his head. 'I think she knows I had an affair with someone,' he replied, 'but no more than that.'

Remembering that Gina had told her she knew who it was, Andee got to her feet. 'I have to call the police,' she said, wishing with all her heart it was to tell them that Jessica was somewhere with an Amish community. 'I realise Bill might already have done it by now, but they'll need to know everything you've just told me.'

He didn't argue, he didn't even seem to connect with the meaning of her words.

'Then,' she added, 'I'm going into Kesterly to break the news to Blake Leonard.'

At that his eyes came to hers, and in that moment she could see quite clearly that he would never, in his entire life, get over this.


An hour later, after a lengthy conversation with Detective Inspector Gould, Andee was with Blake Leonard in the sitting room of his home in the old town. The walls were like a gallery of brilliant copies, with Jenny, Jessica and Matt featuring in famous portraits. As a family they'd obviously had fun with this over the years, and the photographs, mostly of the twins, showed how very close they all were. Andee was finding them difficult to look at without a lump forming in her throat.

Blake was perched on the edge of an armchair, staring at Andee as he struggled to take in the enormity of what she'd just told him. She could sense how desperately he wanted to reject it, to shut out the images she'd been careful not to make too graphic while at the same time giving him the truth, from Jessica's affair with a much older and married man, to the gift of a car, to the crash that had led to her death.

He'd said nothing since inviting her to sit down, and she wasn't sure he was going to speak now. He needed time, obviously, to assimilate the unthinkable horror of where his precious daughter had been these past two years, so much closer to home than anyone had ever imagined. Maybe, once he grasped that terrible reality, he'd be able to connect with the relief of finally knowing what had happened to her, dreadful though it was. Finding a body should bring the closure the family needed for a proper time of grieving to begin.

At last he spoke, clutching randomly at a smaller issue, evidently still unable to confront the bigger one. 'Do you believe in the amnesia?' he asked hoarsely.

Not sure whether she did or not, she said, 'I'm not going to make excuses for Charles; his actions are indefensible.'

He nodded, but she could see he was hardly listening. After a while he said, 'He's a father himself. How could he have let us go through this when he must

321

have known . . .' As his words failed, all he could do was shake his head in stunned disbelief.

More minutes ticked by before he spoke again. 'Should I go there?' he asked. 'Will they expect me to?'

'Do you want to go?'

He clearly didn't know.

Thinking of the awful condition Jessica's body would be in after so long in the swamp, Andee said, 'From what I hear it's not an easy spot to get to, so it's probably best to let the police do their job. They'll contact you when they're ready.'

Seeming to accept that, he appeared suddenly alarmed as he said, 'Will I have to identify her?'

'I wouldn't advise it,' she replied. 'There are other ways for the coroner to get what he needs.'

Huskily, he said, 'We'll want to remember her how she was before she died, not how she is . . . how she is now,' and as the horrific imagining of it overcame him he covered his eyes.

Knowing there were no words to make this any easier, Andee sat quietly, lending an unspoken support that she hoped he could sense.

Eventually he got to his feet, seeming agitated. 'I need to tell Matt,' he said, 'and then we'll go to see Jenny.'

Standing too, Andee regarded him sadly. She knew there would be many more questions later, and a lot of vengeful feelings directed towards the man who could have spared them so much pain. For now, he only seemed able to go from one moment to the next, trying to find his way forward and constantly getting lost in the maelstrom of shock.

As they walked to the door, Andee said, 'We guessed you'd want to go to Devon, so the police are doing their best to keep things from the media until you've had time to get there.'

He made no response to that, though she felt sure he appreciated it.

'Where's Matt?' she asked.

'On his way home. He was out with his friends, but I texted him when I knew you were coming.'

Realising instinct had warned him that the news wasn't going to be good, Andee put a hand on his arm as she said, 'Call me any time, day or night.'

He nodded and thanked her and as she started to leave he suddenly embraced her, so tightly she could feel the raw power of his despair. 'Thank you,' he whispered brokenly. 'Thank you for coming, and thank you for caring.'

Her eyes were still wet with tears as she reached her car. Jessica's death wasn't the outcome any of them had wanted, nothing like the one that cruel trickster called hope had constantly promised, yet she'd known since becoming involved that it was the most likely one. She'd known too how it would bring back all the grief of losing her sister, make those terrible times feel real and present again in spite of how long ago it had happened. It simply wasn't possible that Penny was still out there somewhere, and yet she couldn't stop telling herself that it wasn't impossible either.

Reminding herself that she'd have time later for her own tears, she drove out of the street and was about to connect to Graeme when he rang.

'Bill Simmonds just called me,' he said, the solemnity of his tone telling her that he knew the worst – or part of it anyway. She still wasn't sure how much Bill knew.

'So you know they found a car?' she said carefully.

'And who was in it.'

Wondering if he was aware yet of Charles's involvement, and suspecting not, she said, 'How's Rowzee taking it?'

'I'm on my way there now. She's very upset, apparently. Pamela says she's had one of her turns. She wants to call the paramedics, but Rowzee's having none of it. Where are you?'

'I've just left Blake's. He's going to tell Matt, then drive to Devon to break it to Jenny.'

'Oh God, poor man. I didn't want to call until I was sure he knew. How is he?'

Since there were no words to describe it, she said, 'He'll appreciate hearing from you.'

'OK. I'll offer to drive him to Devon. He shouldn't have to do it himself. He won't be in any fit state.'

Not disagreeing, she said, 'If you're going to do that, then unless you already know I need to tell you about Charles Stamfield's involvement.'

He listened in silence as she gave him the unembellished facts, and even when she'd finished it was several moments before he spoke. 'Blake knows all this?' he said soberly.

'Yes, but going by what I'm picking up from you I don't think Rowzee and Bill do yet.'

'No, they don't. Maybe you'll let me know when I can tell them?'

'Of course.'

'So where are you now?' he asked.

'On my way to see my mother. She finds this sort of news quite difficult to cope with, so I want to break it to her myself.'

'Do you want to get together later?' he offered.

Thinking of how much she'd like that, she said, 'If my mother's OK, and you're back from Devon . . .'

'I'll call you,' he promised, and as the line went dead she found herself welling up again. Kindness often did that to her, and he was being so kind not only to her, but to Blake and Rowzee . . . Maybe she shouldn't take up his time later, Blake's or Rowzee's needs would be greater.

She was almost at her mother's when to her dismay Martin rang. Though tempted to let him go to voice-mail, she reminded herself that to him the issue of their break-up was paramount; he had no idea what else was going on in her world, how much greater the loss of Jessica felt right now than the regret for hurting him.

'Hello,' she said evenly.

'Where are you?' he asked, his tone more clipped than friendly.

'On my way to Bourne Hollow.'

'If you're intending to see your mother I can save you a journey. She's with mine in Westleigh.'

Where she usually was on Tuesdays, Andee remembered. 'Thank you,' she said. 'Are you still at the flat?'

'We need to talk.'

'You need to leave.'

'I'll see you when you get here,' and he rang off.

Deciding to put him out of her mind for now, she turned the car around and twenty minutes later she was pulling up outside her mother-in-law's. Alayna came bounding out to greet her.

'Hey Mum,' she chirped happily, and Andee's heart contracted. Alayna was almost the same age as Jessica had been when she'd fallen for Charles and ended up losing her life.

Quickly sensing her mother's low spirits, Alayna said, 'Are you all right? What's happened?'

Andee's eyes went briefly to hers, and for one dizzying moment, feeling she was looking at her teenage sister, the deeply suppressed grief almost escaped her.

'Mum?' Alayna prompted worriedly.

Putting an arm around her, Andee walked her over to a wooden bench and sat holding her hands as she told her what had happened to Jessica.

'Oh no, oh no,' Alayna murmured, her eyes closing over her tears. 'I'm so sorry. I didn't want it to end like this. I thought we . . .' She broke off on a sob. 'I really thought she might still be alive.'

'So did I,' Andee admitted, only realising now how desperately she'd wanted it to be true. Because it would have given her hope for her sister? Or because it would have been what Blake's family deserved?

Both, of course.

As though reading her mind, Alayna gave her a hug. 'I know how hard this is for you. I wish there was something I could do.'

Loving her tenderness and understanding, Andee said, 'It's harder for Blake and his family.'

'Maybe, but at least they know where Jessica is now.'

Andee nodded absently.

After a while, Alayna said, 'I wish I'd known Aunt Penny.'

Andee smiled as she touched Alayna's cheek. 'I do too.'

Resting her head on her mother's shoulder, Alayna said, 'Do you think we should try again to find her?'

Though a part of Andee wanted to, more than anything, she said, 'I wouldn't know where to start now, after all these years.'

'But you still miss her?'

Andee swallowed. 'I miss what we should have had,' she whispered.

Curling her fingers around her mother's, Alayna said, 'What would you say if you could speak to her now?'

Andee smiled sadly. 'What I always say to her in my mind, that I'm sorry for not being a better sister and not realising how much pain she was in. I could have helped her, changed things for her, but I was a selfish teenager back then who couldn't see any further than herself.'

'I can't imagine you being like that.'

'I was, I'm afraid.'

More minutes ticked quietly by as Andee pictured her sister the way she'd last known her, a fourteen-year-old girl with worried eyes and curly dark hair. It was as though no time had passed; if she reached out she might touch her, grab her, hold her back from the terrible fate life had planned for her. But there was no way of doing that; time had moved inexorably on, more than thirty years had passed, separating them in ways that had no rhyme or reason, no substance or meaning. What would she be like now, if she was still alive? Would she have grown tall, would she still be worried, afraid, unsure of herself, or loved and happy, a mother like Andee, a wife, a daughter and sister to somebody else?

'Tell me,' Alayna said, 'in your heart, do you really believe she killed herself? I know the letter she sent made it look that way, but do you think there's a chance she might still be out there somewhere?'

Taking a breath, Andee said, 'I think it all the time, but I've no idea whether that's due to instinct or hope. If she is alive . . . I don't understand why she's never come back.'

'Maybe she can't. If someone's holding her . . . I know it doesn't seem likely after so many years, but no one's ever found a body, and like you say, it doesn't make sense for her not to be in touch.'

'I know it doesn't to us, but if she has made another life . . . Maybe she just doesn't want to come back.'

'If that's true it would be so cruel, when she surely has to know how much you've all suffered.'

Andee couldn't deny it. 'What's really cruel,' she murmured, 'is the not knowing.'

\* \* \*

Rowzee was much calmer now. Not that she'd panicked earlier, when she was by the swamp with Bill or lost her head in such a way as to embarrass herself or alarm the police. She'd just got so upset when she'd heard one of the officers take a call and then tell another officer that it seemed they'd found Jessica Leonard that she'd ended up coming over very strange indeed. Fortunately, only Bill had noticed, so he'd sat her down next to a tree and urged her to breathe deeply while he patted her hand and tried to stop Teddy from licking her.

It seemed everything had gone a bit haywire then, because apparently she hadn't known who Bill was for a while, which had spooked him, he'd claimed, and she hadn't seemed to know where they were either, or what was happening around her.

'I need to get her home,' she'd heard Bill telling a policeman. 'I'm not sure she can make it on the bike.'

'I'm fine,' Rowzee had made herself insist, feeling nauseous as things swam in and out of focus. 'I just felt a bit faint for a moment.' She'd tried to get up, but then she'd remembered about Jessica and the reason they were there and suddenly she started to cry, huge racking sobs as she thought of Blake and Jenny, dear Matt, and Edward her own sweet little son whom she still missed every single day.

Eventually, she'd been ferried back through the estate in a police car to a waiting Pamela beside herself with worry and fear, and ready to box her ears – she'd actually said that – for not taking her phone.

Bill had arrived a few minutes later with Teddy, and when he'd told Pamela about Jessica Rowzee had felt herself coming over all peculiar again.

'Oh my God, look at her,' Pamela cried in horror. 'She doesn't have any colour in her cheeks and she keeps swaying. I'm calling the paramedics.'

'Don't,' Rowzee protested. 'I'm fine. I just need to lie down.'

Pamela turned to Bill, clearly needing him to decide.

'She should lie down,' he declared.

So Pamela had helped Rowzee upstairs to bed where they'd cried together for Jessica and her family and Edward and Victor and their dear, saintly parents, talking at length about the happy family life they'd shared.

'Does Blake know yet?' Pamela asked Bill when he brought in some tea.

'I'm not sure,' he replied. 'Rowzee and I have been asked not to say anything, but I rang Graeme just now. I thought he ought to know, because of Rowzee finding her and everything.'

Seeming to approve of that, Pamela turned back to her sister. 'How are you feeling now?' she asked, her eyes showing tenderness while her tone was daring Rowzee to admit to anything but perfectly fine.

*Not right*, was the answer, but what Rowzee said was, 'Stop worrying about me. We have to think of Blake and Jenny . . .'

'We are,' Pamela insisted, 'but you've had a shock . . . Oh no, you didn't see Jessica, did you?' she groaned in horror.

'Not her face,' Rowzee replied shakily, 'but I could see something was in the car and it looked like it might be a person. I never dreamt for a minute . . . I didn't even know that Jessica had a car. No one's ever mentioned it, have they?'

Once again Pamela turned to Bill.

'Not that I'm aware of,' he replied, checking his phone as it rang. 'Graeme,' he told them clicking on. 'He's on his way. Are you here?' he asked Graeme, going to the window.

Rowzee and Pamela waited as Bill listened to their brother, making the occasional sound of agreement, or simply nodding, until finally he said, 'Why don't you talk to her?' and bringing the phone to Rowzee he handed it over.

'How are you?' Graeme asked her worriedly, 'and I want the truth.'

'I'm fine,' she assured him, 'just reacting a bit to the shock, but it's nothing to get worked up about.' She suddenly felt like crying again, and wished he was there already because she always felt better when he was around, but she had to get a grip or they'd all start making a fuss and that was the last thing she wanted. 'Have you spoken to Blake?' she asked. 'Does he know yet?'

'Yes, Andee's been to see him, and if you're sure you're fine I'm going to offer to drive him to Devon.'

'Oh yes, you must do that,' she insisted. 'He shouldn't be allowed to drive himself, not today. Do you know how he took it?'

'Andee didn't go into detail, but I think we can work it out.'

331

Since she could, she said, 'You must tell him that we're here for him, and if there's anything we can do he has only to ask.'

'Of course. And please tell Pamela that she's to call me if she's worried about you . . . Better still, let me speak to her myself.'

Reluctantly passing the phone over, Rowzee met Pamela's meaningful glare as Pamela assured their brother that she'd be taking no more nonsense from stubborn old women who shouldn't have been out walking the dog for so long in the first place; the instant she detected anything close to a funny turn coming over the tiresome baggage again she'd be dialling 999.

Fortunately Pamela hadn't carried out her threat yet, but there was still time and without Bill to stop her – he'd gone to see if there was anything he could do over at the woods – Rowzee could almost feel her sister's fingers itching.

Deciding that the only way to get some peace was to feign sleep, Rowzee closed her eyes and attempted a little snore to make it more convincing.

'You don't fool me,' Pamela told her crisply. 'I know you want me to leave you alone, so I will, but only for a few minutes while I go downstairs to ring Charles.'

'He'll probably be at the woods himself by now,' Rowzee reminded her.

Agreeing that he probably would, Pamela said, 'Then I'll fix you something to eat, because I don't think you've had anything yet today.'

Rowzee hadn't, but she was a very long way from hungry, and even further, she had to concede, from being ready to tell Graeme and Pamela about her cancer. She'd decided she would though, mainly because of what Mr Mervin had told her, but it couldn't happen while all this was going on. Blake and his family had to come first; she was determined about that. In a week or two, maybe after the funeral, which they'd all want to go to, she'd sit her brother and sister down and tell them about her situation and what she intended to do. Not the Dignitas thing, she knew she couldn't tell them about that yet, but she'd had another idea that was starting to grow on her.

'Mrs C's cunning plan,' her students used to cry jubilantly when she'd come up with an often wild solution to getting them what they needed for a play, or a trip, or on one memorable occasion a sleepover in a haunted theatre.

In this instance her idea wasn't so much wild as drastic, maybe even dangerous, but if she presented it the right way she liked to think that Pamela and Graeme would be up for it too.

# Chapter Eighteen

It was early the next morning when Andee parked in the leafy quadrant outside Kesterly police station before going inside to meet her old boss, Detective Inspector Gould.

Though she felt tense and unrested following a near sleepless night at her mother's, her mind was alert as she greeted her ex-colleagues on the way through, many of whom appeared eager to chat, but she didn't have the time. There was a lot to get through today, and already, before any unforeseen circumstances arose, she couldn't imagine achieving even half of what she'd like to before the sun went down.

'First and foremost,' she'd told Graeme when they'd met at a bar in the old town last night, 'I need to find out who Jessica's car hit before it went off the road, because Charles thinks that's who's been blackmailing him.'

'So someone else has known about the accident all this time and not come forward?'

'It would seem so.' She had yet to speak to Gina, who might also have known, but she still couldn't get hold of her.

'Do the police know about the blackmail?'

'Charles told them himself. He's got nothing to hide now it's all about to come out anyway. Incidentally, I had a call from Leo Johnson. Apparently Charles has been charged with failing to report an accident, and they've let him go on police bail.'

'Will it get any more serious than that?'

'I'm not sure that it can. In a legal sense it's the only offence he's committed. From a moral standpoint . . . Well, that's a whole other story.'

'So is he still at the Hall?'

'As far as I know. I tried calling a while ago, but he's not picking up.'

Seeming as unsurprised by that as she was, Graeme said, 'The sky was alive with helicopters when I was at the Coach House earlier. I guess it was mainly press, trying to get shots of the swamp. I believe the police are having trouble lifting the car out.'

'Yes, they are, but apparently Jessica's body has already been taken to the mortuary. Did Blake know that by the time you left him?'

'Yes, he did, but neither he nor Jenny want it to be the last time they see her. They'd prefer to remember her how she was before it happened.'

'A wise decision. Did Jenny come back with Blake and Matt?'

'Yes. She was very quiet during the journey, but unless I'm mistaken I think finally knowing what happened, terrible though it is, is better than what they've been going through these past two years.'

Certain it would be, Andee said, 'What time did you get back?'

'Around six. Jenny's parents followed in their car. They're staying at my place until after the funeral.'

Able to imagine how well they'd be taken care of, she said, 'We need to make sure the family has all the help they need during the arrangements.'

'I believe my sisters are on it, but obviously we should find out from Blake and Jenny if they actually want any help.'

'I don't expect they have much idea what they want at the moment.'

'Apart from Charles's head on a spike?'

'They'll no doubt have the rest of the nation behind them on that, once the news breaks about his involvement.' She watched him signal to the waiter for the bill, and found herself wishing it weren't quite so late so the evening could go on a while longer. 'How's Rowzee after the discovery?' she asked as he paid.

Frowning, he said, 'She didn't seem too bad when I left to come here, but apparently there was an episode earlier when she appeared to lose contact with what was happening.'

'Shock can do that. I've seen it many times.'

He nodded slowly. 'But something's not right with her, that's for sure. She keeps saying it's nothing, and that if the doctor's not worried then there's no need for us to be, but like Pamela, I have to wonder if she's telling the doctor the whole story.'

Carefully, Andee said, 'Maybe she is and it's you she's holding back on?'

The way his eyes came to hers told her she'd just voiced his main fear. 'We'll get to the bottom of it,' he assured her, 'whether she wants us to or not.'

Certain he would, Andee went ahead of him out into the night and liked the way he took her hand as they walked to her car.

As she recalled those moments now, on her way up in the lift to Gould's office, she could only feel thankful that tiredness hadn't made her blurt out something inappropriate, such as asking him to help get Martin out of her flat, or find a way to make him accept that she wasn't going to respond to pleading or bullying.

'Andee, there you are,' Gould declared as she entered his office with its half-glass walls and endless performance charts. 'How are you?'

Always pleased to see him now he was no longer ruling her world with his ferocious bark and even fiercer bite, she said, 'I'm OK, considering. How are things this end?'

'I'm afraid our main focus has switched from your case to a fatal stabbing during the early hours. Three kids and their mother, the father's in custody, still high as a kite.'

'So he did it?'

'Not according to him, but the evidence isn't in his favour. However, it's not why you're here. I've got the information you asked for, though I'm not sure how much good it's going to do you.'

Going to look at his computer screen, she quickly scanned the report he'd displayed, and for a bewildering moment she thought he'd either made a mistake, or misunderstood her request.

'Not what you were expecting?' he asked, knowing very well that it wasn't.

She shook her head. No, this wasn't what she'd been expecting at all; however there was no getting away from the fact that the date and time on the accident report checked out exactly, as did the location. It was the victim's name that had completely thrown her.

Quickly thanking Gould, she took out her phone as she headed back to the lift. 'Hi, it's me,' she said, when Graeme picked up, 'can you meet me at Rowzee and Pamela's in half an hour? I've just found out who Charles and Jessica hit before the car went off the road.'

As Rowzee listened to what Andee was telling them about Charles she was aware of a memory trying to stage a breakthrough, like a tentative ray of light being blocked by clouds. She remembered the first time this memory had tried to claim her attention; it was when she and Andee had been driving back from Devon in the car. It had proved too elusive for her to capture then, but here it was again, like a nervous player peeking shyly from the wings, wanting to make itself heard and understood, but still not quite able to summon all its lines.

What was it?

She glanced down as Pamela's hand reached for hers and squeezed it hard. Andee's words were registering again; she could feel Graeme's eyes watching her. It seemed that Charles Stamfield, their dear friend and

338

erstwhile MP, had been having an affair with nineteen-year-old Jessica Leonard. Now the shock of it was passing, Rowzee realised that the truth was not so very hard to comprehend; she could see why they'd find one another attractive, in spite of the difference in their ages.

Since when did age ever dictate to love?

Did Gina know, she wondered.

Andee was telling them now how Charles had bought Jessica a car, and how Jessica had driven them from London the day she'd disappeared.

Quite suddenly Rowzee blurted, 'Yoder is an Amish name.'

Andee's eyes narrowed curiously. 'Yes, it is,' she confirmed. 'Why do you mention that?'

'Gina's great-grandmother was Amish,' Rowzee explained, though she wasn't entirely sure of the point she was trying to make. Hadn't the name Yoder come up during the investigation?

Andee said, 'Charles used the name when he registered a phone to call Jessica. And when he rented the house.'

'So the police already know that it's Amish?' Rowzee asked.

'Yes, they do,' Andee replied.

Relieved that her muddle over vital information wasn't hampering things, Rowzee said, 'I'm sorry. I didn't mean to interrupt. You were telling us that Charles bought Jessica a new car. That was very generous of him, I must say.'

'Which is hardly the point,' Pamela murmured.

Realising it wasn't, Rowzee fixed Andee with atten-
tive eyes and over the next few minutes, as the full story
unfolded of that fateful day, she felt her heart starting
slowly to break at the horror of the journey's end. What
a dreadful, cruel thing to happen. She hardly knew
what to say, or do. She wanted to rush to Blake and
Jenny to try and console them, or to Charles in spite
of the terrible thing he'd done. Had he really just left
Jessica there? Gina must be devastated, and how was
poor Lydia taking it? Did she even know yet? Andee
had said that Charles had lost his memory after the
accident and that surely had to be true, because Rowzee
couldn't imagine the man she knew and admired, even
considered family in a way, consciously abandoning
dear Jessica and leaving her parents to suffer the way
they had.

'Are you listening, Rowzee?' Graeme asked gently.

Rowzee's eyes went to his as she nodded.

Pamela's grip tightened on her hand.

'We've just found out,' Andee told her, 'the identity
of the person the car hit before going off the road.'

'You said it was a woman,' Pamela reminded her.

Andee nodded, her eyes travelling between the sisters, her expression troubled and grave.

Rowzee was watching her carefully. Her lips were
moving, forming words that seemed to be causing shock and alarm, but Rowzee wasn't sure what
they were. Pamela had clasped her hands to her face;
Graeme was coming to sit with Rowzee, putting an
arm around her. 'Did you hear what Andee said?' he
prompted kindly.

Rowzee nodded. Yes, the words had reached her now, but she couldn't make any sense of them.

She looked up as Pamela began saying something angrily to Andee. Then suddenly Pamela was shouting at Rowzee. 'I told you not to trust them,' she cried, 'what were they doing . . .'

'Pamela, stop!' Graeme cut in firmly. To Rowzee he said, 'What do you want to do?'

Rowzee looked at him and touched a hand to his handsome face. 'We have to go and see Norma,' she said, as if it were the most natural thing in the world, and leaving Pamela to go and meet Blake and his family at the church this morning, she went to get into the back of Graeme's car.

A little over two hours later Andee and Graeme were listening to Rowzee explaining to Norma what the police now knew about Jessica Leonard and Charles Stamfield. Considering how distracted Rowzee had seemed at home earlier, and how long she'd slept during the journey to Devon, it was surprising Andee, though pleasing her, to see that she was experiencing no memory lapses now, nor was she wandering from the point.

As she listened Norma was appearing puzzled and concerned, clearly grasping the importance of what she was being told though as yet unable to work out how it was relevant to her. Beside her, slumped in his wheelchair, head on one shoulder, hands bunched loosely in his lap, Sean apparently had no understanding of what was going on, while Jason, listening as attentively as his grandmother, seemed to be growing paler by the minute.

In the end, when Rowzee had finished telling how Charles had thought he and Jessica had hit a woman that fateful night, but Andee had now discovered that it wasn't a woman at all, Norma looked from her, to Andee and then to Graeme, with such bewildered eyes that Andee could see she needed to step in.

'It was Sean that they hit,' she said gently.

'Yes, Sean,' Rowzee echoed.

Norma looked as though she'd been struck.

Jason could only stare at them as though they'd suddenly turned into strangers.

Rowzee reached for Norma's hand as Andee said, 'It would have happened very fast, and I'm guessing that Sean's hair back then . . .'

'Was quite wild and long,' Norma finished for her. 'Very bushy, like his father's, though I think Victor always kept his short.'

'Usually,' Rowzee confirmed.

Breaking out of his silence, Jason said, 'So it wasn't those gangsters who hit him and drove off?'

Andee shook her head. 'Apparently not.'

He seemed unable to take it in.

'It was still a hit and run,' Norma mumbled, 'but just not the kind we thought.' Her hand was trembling as it went to her mouth. 'Oh my goodness, that poor girl. To think that the whole time the police and ambulance services were seeing to Sean, she was right there . . . Didn't they realise a car had gone off the road?'

Andee said, 'Charles thinks the shock made Jessica hit the accelerator instead of the brake, so there wouldn't have been any signs of a car leaving the road.'

Clearly still flummoxed by the news, Norma started to shake her head, needing more time to assimilate.

Continuing the story, Andee said, 'A passing driver spotted Sean in his headlights, lying on the side of the road. He called the police and they found Sean's car close by.'

'He'd stopped to relieve himself,' Norma explained. 'That's what they told us at the time. They said his urine was all over a bush. That was why he was out of the car.'

After a while, Graeme said, carefully, 'The accident spot is only a few miles from where Rowzee lives, so we were wondering if Sean might have been to see Victor that day? Or perhaps he was on his way there?'

Norma blinked as she looked at him. 'I've no idea,' she replied, appearing as mystified as they did. To Rowzee she said, 'I hadn't realised it was so close to you. I mean, I knew it was on the edge of Exmoor, but Sean had friends up around that way. Not anyone I knew, but he'd go there sometimes . . . Oh my goodness,' she suddenly gasped, 'you think he saw Victor and something awful happened between them to cause Victor's heart attack.'

'No, that's not what I think,' Rowzee quickly assured her, though Andee knew it must have crossed her mind. 'If Victor had seen him again he would have told me,' Rowzee asserted, 'and the heart attack didn't happen until at least three days after the accident. Maybe it was even longer than that.'

'You remember the accident?' Andee asked curiously.

Rowzee was frowning. 'Only vaguely. We knew something had happened on one of the back roads, but then Victor collapsed . . .' Suddenly surprising them, she left that subject and said to Norma, 'Did they tell you which direction Sean's car was pointing in when they found it?'

Norma shook her head apologetically.

Realising where Rowzee was probably going with this, Andee said, 'I'm sure we can find out,' and after sending a quick message to Leo Johnson, she asked Norma, 'Did the police at the time never make the connection between Sean and Victor?'

'There wouldn't have been any reason for them to,' Norma replied. 'He has a different name, and when they asked me what he was doing up around that way I'm not sure what I told them . . . Probably about his friends . . . It had just happened and we had no idea if he was going to live or die . . .'

'But later,' Graeme put in, 'when you realised how close he was to Kesterly . . .'

Meeting his eyes, Norma said, 'I remember wanting to contact Victor when I knew how serious things were for Sean, not to ask for anything, just to tell him . . .' She broke off as Andee's phone received a text.

After reading it, Andee said, 'The car was on the left-hand side of the road, pointing west, towards Kesterly.' She watched Norma and Rowzee look at one another, apparently making their own deductions and coming to the same conclusion.

'He might have been on his way to see Victor,' Rowzee said softly.

344

'But he never got there,' Norma added.

Jason watched them, seeming lost and a little afraid.

After a while Rowzee said, 'I'd like to think Sean was coming to try and make things up with his father.'

Norma regarded her uncertainly.

Andee said nothing, nor did Graeme.

'Why shouldn't we think that?' Rowzee demanded. 'We have no reason to think anything else, unless we want to torture ourselves.'

The shadows of angst in Norma's lovely eyes started to fade as she said, 'I often tell people in situations like this, I mean where there are no clear answers, that it's OK to create your own truth, just as long as no one can be harmed by it.'

Rowzee got to her feet and pulled Norma into an affectionate embrace. 'I'm very glad we met,' she told her, 'and I think we shall again.'

'Yes, we shall,' Norma assured her, and Andee could see that neither woman was in any doubt of it.

Going to Sean, Rowzee pressed a kiss to his forehead and smoothed a hand over his coarse carroty-gold hair. Though he made no response, Jason got up to hug her.

'I feel very lucky having two such lovely grans,' he told her, holding her tight.

'Blessed is the word,' Norma informed him with a twinkle.

Twinkling too, Rowzee said, 'I'll be in touch,' and after brushing a hand across Sean's cheek again, she led the way out to the car.

\* \* \*

Charles was staring at Gina. Since confessing to Andee, then to the police, it was as though all his nightmares were becoming reality and reality was stretching endlessly into a living hell.

And now this.

'Are you saying you knew?' he asked, certain he must have misunderstood her.

'Yes, I knew,' she confirmed, her beautiful face as blanched and strained as his own. He could see the fine bones beneath the skin.

He had to look away, but then his sore, haunted eyes returned to hers.

How easily loved ones could become strangers, how disturbing when strangers were those you loved.

'Not at first,' she admitted. 'I suspected, but I didn't find out for certain until you told me.'

He wasn't following her. He had no recollection of telling her anything, he was sure they'd never mentioned Jessica at all, and yet she seemed so definite. 'When did I tell you?' he asked, his parched voice scraping the depths of his conscience.

Her eyes remained on his as she said, 'I knew you were having problems around that time . . . You weren't yourself, I could tell something was wrong, but I put it down to the stress of the election, the bruising defeat, the problems building up at the company . . . While all that was going on I was aware of the search for Jessica, obviously, it was all over the news, and I took an interest because of her connection to Kesterly. Then they revealed the name, Yoder, and I . . . I tried not to believe it. It seemed such a remote and unlikely connection, but I couldn't get it out of my mind. Then you began falling apart physically and mentally . . . I kept waiting for you to tell me what had happened, where she was, what had been done to her . . . I was sure someone else was involved, that they were the ones who'd taken her. I was afraid for you, and I could see that you were terrified for yourself.'

All this she'd been thinking, but had never said. It was almost as incredible to him as the fact that they were having this conversation at all.

'I had to find out if I was right,' she continued, 'but I couldn't make myself ask, because if I was wrong and it had nothing to do with you . . . How were we ever going to get past that? Or maybe I was too afraid of the answer. I didn't want details; I just wanted to know if you were involved. So I sent you a letter.'

A letter? He had no memory of a letter from her concerning Jessica. They never wrote to one another at all these days, unless by text or email.

'It was anonymous,' she told him. 'In it I said I knew you'd had an affair with Jessica Leonard and that you were with her on the day she disappeared. Of course, I didn't know that, I had no idea where you were that day, but I said if you wanted me to keep what I knew to myself it would cost you twenty-five thousand pounds.'

Charles had tensed with disbelief. His wife was his blackmailer? All those ugly letters, all that money, the fear, the thoughts of suicide . . . Was that what she'd wanted, to push him into ending his life?

'When I received the cash,' she went on, 'my worst fears were confirmed. You were clearly involved in whatever had happened to her. I still had no idea how, but the fact that you were willing to pay to keep it a secret . . . That was when I realised I couldn't go on living with you. I didn't want you to lose everything, and I knew if it came out that you would, but if you found a way to sort it out . . . If she was still alive and you could persuade those holding her to let her go . . . I created so many scenarios for myself, I was desperate for you to work something out . . . I should have confronted you of course, but I still had no idea if anyone else was involved . . . I kept telling myself they had to be, because you'd never allow her family to go through so much suffering unless there was some kind of threat hanging over me or Lydia . . . I've waited all this time for you to act, but you never did . . . I stepped up the blackmail as a way of putting on the pressure, but it didn't work, because you sent the money every time . . .'

Charles was silently reeling. He had no idea what he wanted to say, or do. Her reasoning, her actions were beyond his powers of comprehension.

She was still speaking. 'I sent all the money to Blake Leonard,' she told him. 'I don't know what he's done with it, but I do know that no amount of what we can give them will ever make up for what they've lost.'

As the awful truth of her words curdled the air between them, Charles turned away and went to stand at the window. He had no idea what to do now, how to repair any of the damage he'd caused to his own family as well as the Leonards. He felt the responsibility of making amends as deeply as he felt the shame of his cowardice, but all he could think to say for the moment was, 'I need to speak to Lydia before she finds out through someone else.'

'She knows. She's on her way here.'

He turned around, shaken. 'You told her? When?'

'This morning. I was afraid that you wouldn't, so I did it myself.'

Hating that she'd had no faith in him, while understanding it, he almost asked how his daughter had taken it, but he'd find out soon enough.

Coming to him, Gina stared hard into his eyes as though searching for the man she used to know and love. He could tell she thought he was still there, but he had no idea himself how to find him.

'I'm glad you told Andee,' she said eventually. 'I was going to. I meant to, but you're the only one who knows the truth. Do we have it now? Is there any more?'

'No,' he said quietly, 'there's no more.'

Apparently willing to believe him, she said, 'Why Yoder? What made you choose that name?'

He shook his head absently. 'I can't remember.'

'If you'd used Smith . . .' She stopped as he turned to her.

'If I had she might never have been found,' he stated.

Gina looked away. After a while she said, 'I feel partly responsible. If you hadn't felt the need for an affair . . .'

'It's not your fault,' he came in quickly. 'Please, for God's sake, don't blame yourself.'

She didn't argue, only continued to look at him, but he knew her conscience well, she wouldn't be able to forgive herself for never telling what she had known any more than he would. 'You loved her?' she said softly.

He wouldn't, couldn't deny it.

'You know it couldn't have lasted.'

Yes, he'd known that.

'I'm sorry,' she whispered, and slipping her arms around him, she held him close. He stood staring across the fields in the direction of the woods and marshy lake where Blake and his family were due to visit what had been their daughter's watery grave for the past two years.

Charles had been asked to stay away.

Blake could hardly believe how many flowers had already been left on this remote country road, so many that the police had been forced to move some aside to make room for him and his family to get through to the barrier that marked the edge of the sheer drop. They were now standing in the midst of the blooms, with Jenny one side of him and Matt the other. It was cool, up here on the hill, where a dense canopy of trees blocked out the sun and a wayward breeze blew carelessly by, taking the heady scent of flowers with it. The officers policing the scene were keeping their distance, not wanting to intrude on the family's private grief, but keen to provide support or information if it was needed.

As close as they were to the cliff edge there was little chance of them going over, unless they climbed the solid metal barrier first. It had been installed, someone had told Blake, less than a month after Jessica had driven her car off the road. It wasn't her accident that had triggered the work – no one had known about it, so it couldn't have happened that way – it had been part of a scheduled road safety programme for the county.

What a bitter, tragic irony that it hadn't been carried out a month earlier, although there was no knowing if it would have saved her life. Hitting a barrier at a tremendous speed would inevitably have produced its own disastrous results.

Feeling Jenny's slight figure move in more closely to him, he tightened his arm around her and pressed a kiss to her head. This discovery, this awful, nightmarish tragedy, had, perversely, brought his beloved wife back to him, and she was here, she said, to stay.

Matt was standing slightly apart, staring down at the boggy pit of a lake. The lifting paraphernalia that had been brought in to recover the body and the car had gone now, leaving no trace. The machinery had been swallowed up by the past, just like Jessica.

Blake could feel his son's grief as palpably as he could feel his own. It was a powerfully genetic force that joined them together. He wondered what Matt was seeing in his mind's eye, what he was saying or hearing in his heart. He was surely connecting with his sister, drawing her to him as she would draw him to her. Death couldn't put an end to that, could it? Their souls were surely as linked as their DNA.

Still holding Jenny close he looked down at the sludgy lake himself, and became aware of a horrible, terrifying sense of being sucked into its murky depths.

His eyes closed as bile rose to his throat and he started to sway.

'Are you OK?' Jenny whispered.

'Yes,' he whispered back. 'Are you?'

After a while she said, 'I don't know. It feels strange, as though we're not really here.'

Understanding what she meant, he turned to look at Matt again. He wanted to reach out for him, but didn't. Matt would come when he was ready; as a family they would bond even more tightly than before to get themselves through this. At least the journey from here would be unhampered by false hopes and debilitating fears.

His eyes closed again as, out of nowhere, he heard Jessica laughing down the phone. 'I'm OK, Daddy, I promise. You have to stop worrying.'

'I'm not worried,' he'd lied, 'I just want to know that you're settling in all right and making friends.'

'I have lots of friends and I love it here. Does that make you happy?'

'Everything about you makes me happy.'

'Oh Dad, that is such a corny thing to say. I know this is hard for you to get your head around, but I'm a grown-up now. I've left home, I'm at uni, I'm loving it and I can take care of myself.'

As his heart filled with the unstoppable pain of her not taking care, of her making mistakes that he should have saved her from, of being led astray by a man who should have known better, he kept hearing her, over and over, louder and yet softer as though trying to soothe him. 'I'm OK, Daddy, I promise. You have to stop worrying. I'm OK, Daddy, I promise. You have to stop worrying.'

Was she OK? There was no reason to worry any more: the worst had happened, it couldn't happen again.

Since being told about her affair with Stamfield and how Stamfield had hidden what he'd known for so long, Blake had been waiting for a terrible rage and hatred to consume him. He felt sure it was there, biding its time like a beast of prey, choosing the deadliest moment to strike, but if it was he could feel none of its power yet, not even a hint of its cold, steely need for a terrible revenge.

He'd been told that Stamfield was willing to see him, but he didn't feel ready for that yet, wasn't even sure he'd ever be. He only knew that he didn't want to remember his daughter as the mistress of a much older and, until now, highly respected and powerful man. He wanted to see her the way she'd been for him, a musician, a gifted student, a fearless, radiant teenager with her whole life ahead of her. Allowing Stamfield's part in her death to consume him would only end up destroying him, and his family needed him now more than they ever had.

Aware of Matt coming to stand next to him, he hooked an arm through his son's and drew him closer. Nothing about the experience of coming here was proving easy. They hadn't expected it to be, but already they were realising that finding Jessica, even like this, was better than the torture of not knowing.

The funeral was to be held next Friday at St Monica's on the Hill. They'd decided on a small, family affair to try to avoid the press, since the news would have broken by then of Stamfield's involvement. Though Blake was dreading that, he was trying to see it simply as something else to be got through, another step along the very difficult road to recovery. Somehow they'd survive it, of course they would, though whether Stamfield would was another story. The police might only be able to charge him with failing to report an accident, but the media and the public would no doubt subject him to a whole other kind of trial. There would be the man's punishment, if Blake were seeking it, for the scandal, the disgust and well-deserved derision were likely to ruin him.

Matt said, 'I think she'd want a bigger funeral than the one we're planning.'

Jenny stooped to gather up the cards that had been left with the flowers. 'So many people have been in touch,' she said, 'even some of our old friends from the north. They want to come if they're invited.'

'So do her mates from uni and school,' Matt added. 'I think she'd want them there.'

Feeling certain she would, Blake's heart swelled with the love people were showing for his daughter, and for them. He'd heard from Andee this morning that her son Luke had already returned from Cornwall to be there for Matt, and apparently Graeme's sons were on their way for the same reason. It seemed that all the town's young people were gathering to support and pay respects to two of their own. Even those who hadn't really known them were rallying, like Andee's daughter Alayna who'd texted him, Jenny and Matt the night before, offering to do anything she could to help. Today, along with her mother and Pamela, Alayna was visiting the Victoria hotel with Jenny's parents to act as the young persons' representative in the decision of where to hold the reception.

If it was going to be a bigger affair he'd better call now to let them know.


It was feeling eerily quiet, almost other-worldly, as Andee drove along the avenue of limes towards Burlingford Hall. No one was around; the grounds staff had taken the day off to attend the funeral, and were now at Jessica and Matt's favourite beach bar for the celebration of her life.

The church service had proved memorable in every way with so many young people taking part, reading poems they'd chosen specially, or even written themselves, and joining with Matt to perform some of Jessica's favourite songs. Somehow Andee had managed to hold it together, desperate not to break down in front of her mother, who'd insisted on coming, but then something had happened that she knew she would never forget. Matt had been partway through performing a duet with a recording of Jessica singing 'Fields of Gold' when he'd suddenly found himself unable to continue. He took a breath, but nothing seemed to help, until his parents came to stand either side of him and together the three sang, with Jess, to the end of the song. Andee had never seen anything so brave or so moving. Even the minister had wiped away a tear, while the rest of the gathering broke into a spontaneous repeat of the chorus before Blake and his family returned to their seats.

After the service Andee's mother had intended to return home, but Blake and Jenny had persuaded her to attend the celebration, and when Andee had last seen her she, Rowzee and Pamela, much to the youngsters' delight, had been showing off their skills on the dance floor. She'd have willingly joined in, along with Jenny and Graeme's nieces who were frantically waving her over, had she not promised to go and see Charles and Gina before they left this evening.

'I'll call when I'm leaving the Hall,' she'd told Graeme as he walked her outside, 'and if the party's still going I'll come back.'

'Andee,' Blake called out, coming up behind her. 'Can I have a word?'

Clearly sensing that Blake wanted to talk privately, Graeme excused himself and returned to the party.

'I couldn't imagine giving up on her,' Blake said when they were alone. 'As her father, it just wasn't something I was able to do, even when the police seemed to.'

Remembering how it had been for her own father, for her and her mother too, Andee squeezed his hand. 'You were right not to give up,' she told him. 'I'm glad you didn't.'

Looking deeply into her eyes he asked softly, 'Does there ever come a time when you do?'

She nodded. 'For the sake of your own sanity you have to, but two years wasn't so very long. In my family's case it's been over thirty, so we've had to let go.'

Not always successfully, she didn't add, because it was something he didn't need to know.

'Thank you for not turning me away,' he said. 'I wouldn't have known how to carry on alone, and whatever you say about Rowzee finding her, which of course she did, it was you who connected the name Yoder to Stamfield, and you who he finally confessed to.'

Guessing the police had told him that, Andee watched him kick a stray football back to a group of children and smiled as he looked at her again.

'Have you seen Stamfield since?' he asked.

'No,' she replied.

He turned to gaze at the blinding sunlight on the waves, the swoop and soar of gulls over the bay. 'Is that where you're going now?' he finally managed, bringing his eyes back to hers.

Deciding not to deny it, she said, 'I know it probably doesn't help, and you'll say he deserves it, but he's suffering terribly for what he did. We've all seen how viciously he's been attacked by the media, but even they won't be making him feel as bad as he's made himself feel since it happened.'

He swallowed hard as he said, 'Maybe it does help to know that. If she hadn't mattered to him, if he'd gone on living his life as though nothing had happened . . .' There was a tightness to his features, an edge to his voice that did more to express his feelings than the words he was struggling to find.

Understanding, she glanced back to the bar as she said, 'I think they're calling for you.'

Still holding on to her hand, he said, 'Tell Stamfield from me . . .' He broke off, shaking his head. 'I have nothing to say to him. Nothing at all.'

Now, as Andee pulled up outside the Hall, she was recalling those words and understanding their meaning – there could be no forgiveness at this time, and probably none later either.

By the time she got out of the car the main front door was opening, and to her surprise it was Lydia who came to greet her. She was a tall, arrestingly attractive young woman with her mother's striking colouring and her father's deep-set intelligent eyes. Her air of confidence and sophistication had always made her seem a good ten years older than she was, but today, with so much grief and confusion in her heart, she looked much closer to her actual age of twenty-five.

'Thank you for coming,' she said, throwing her arms around Andee. 'It's been awful here with the two of them. I hardly know what to do.'

Certain it couldn't be easy, Andee said, 'It'll mean a lot to them that you're here.'

Lydia nodded. 'You're right, I think it does. You've been told, I take it, that my mother is just as much to blame for keeping it to herself?'

Yes, Andee had been told, though apparently Gina hadn't actually known where Jessica was. She'd also learned that Gina was the mysterious blackmailer who'd sent the money on to Blake and his family. Since she wasn't sure if that part of it had reached Lydia yet she decided not to mention it.

'I can't imagine what they were thinking,' Lydia ran on emotionally. 'Clearly not about the poor girl, or her family who they were completely destroying. It goes to show that you never know anyone as well as you think you do, because never in my life would I have imagined my own parents doing something like that.'

'How are they?' Andee asked gently.

Lydia's eyes closed as she took a breath. 'No better than you'd expect. I'm worried for Dad. He could be heading for another breakdown, and though some might say it's no less than he deserves he's still my father and I can't help caring.'

'No one would expect you not to.'

Lydia's eyes remained bleak as they travelled out across the gardens where she'd spent so many happy times as a child. 'They're selling up,' she stated. 'Four generations this place has been in our family, but no one will want them here now.'

Saddened by the truth of that, Andee said, 'Where will they go?'

'To London, tonight. They'll leave for the States as soon as they can after his court hearing, provided he doesn't go to prison, but the lawyer doesn't seem to think that'll happen. A suspended sentence at worst, is what they're predicting. Imagine what an uproar the press will get into over that. They'll probably make it look like he's managed to get away with murder.'

Suspecting she was right, Andee said, 'And what about you? What are you going to do now?'

Steadying herself with a breath, Lydia said, 'I'm staying on here for a while to take care of things. What a nightmare it's going to be, working out some kind of marketing strategy to make the place saleable.'

'And after?' Andee prompted.

Lydia's eyes came back to hers. 'I shall return to the refugees in crisis, if I can. The Stamfield scandal's made front pages in the States too, it's gotten more coverage than anything I can drum up for our relief efforts, so I've no idea if my job will still be open. As for a future in politics . . .' She shrugged, as if there were no hope of that at all.

'I hadn't realised you had ambitions in that direction.'

Lydia's smile held no humour. 'I'm now revising them.' After a beat she said, 'Have you seen the drop in Dad's company's share price? Fifteen per cent already. They've asked for his resignation, naturally, so there goes his job along with his reputation, his health, his home, his heritage even.'

Feeling for her anger and helplessness, Andee said, 'Things will die down, you know . . .'

'Until they're dragged up again to throw in his face, or mine, or Mum's every time one of us raises our head . . . It's like a repeat of Chappaquiddick, only worse. My father let two years go by before telling any-one he'd gone off the road with a girl in the car, at least Ted Kennedy fessed up the next day.'

But it had still ended his presidential hopes, and the scandal had dogged him for the rest of his life. There was no denying that, and the similarities of the two cases hadn't passed Andee by, even if the Stamfield family wasn't quite as high profile as the Kennedys.

In a softer tone, Lydia said, 'How was the funeral?'

'Very moving,' Andee replied, knowing she would have expected no less.

Lydia swallowed as her eyes filled with tears. 'I wish I could reach out to the Leonards,' she said brokenly, 'but I realise I'm the last person they'd want to hear from.'

Wishing she wasn't right, Andee said, 'Everything changes over time.'

Appearing unsure whether to believe that, Lydia seemed to pull herself together as she said, 'We should go inside. They're waiting for you.'

Though really not looking forward to this, Andee followed her into the vestibule, taking out her mobile as it rang with the intention of turning it off. However, seeing it was Graeme she excused herself and clicked on.

'Is everything all right?' she asked, sensing already that it wasn't.

'It's Rowzee,' he told her. 'We're on our way to A & E.'

# Chapter Nineteen

A whole week might have gone by since they'd carted her off to hospital in a panic, but Rowzee was still feeling quite impatient with everyone. Fancy creating all that fuss on such an important day for Blake and his family, when everything should have been about them and Jessica and nothing else. She felt dreadful about it now and she hoped Pamela did too. She'd only had a little absence attack, for heaven's sake, nothing to get so excited about. However, Pamela excelled at turning a drama into a crisis, even though she, Rowzee, had been perfectly all right by the time she'd been stuffed into a wheelchair to get her into A & E. So what if she hadn't been able to smile when she'd first gone floppy, or properly raise her arm, she'd soon got the hang of it, and at least it had made Graeme laugh when she'd kept grinning at him like a Halloween pumpkin the whole time they were waiting to be seen.

Pamela hadn't seen the funny side at all, and realising how frightened she was, Rowzee had stopped acting up and held her hand instead, squeezing it regularly to show her own was working.

It turned out she'd probably had an ischaemic transient attack (she wasn't sure it was that way round, but it probably all amounted to the same thing), which was a kind of mini-stroke, and not very serious. So they'd given her a quick check over, had a good laugh at some trips down memory lane since two of the nurses were ex-students, and then they'd sent her off home with the recommendation that she pop to see her GP in the next couple of days. The only mention made of Mr Mervin was when a very young doctor had said she'd be contacting him about the episode and he would probably be in touch. Fortunately neither Graeme nor Pamela had been in the cubicle at that point – she'd already banished them just in case her history was brought up – so she'd had no awkward questions to answer on that front. She'd also been able to inform the young doctor that she already had an appointment scheduled with Mr Mervin for the following Monday.

That appointment had now happened, and had gone on for much longer than she'd expected, thanks to all her questions and the careful notes she'd made of the surgeon's answers to make sure she wouldn't forget what she was being told. He was such a patient man, giving her all the time she'd needed, and the way he explained things made them sound so straightforward – which they probably were for him – that she hadn't felt worried at all. Well, that wasn't true, she'd felt worried out of her mind if the truth were told, and still did, but thankfully her acting skills remained well honed so no one would ever know.

Now, with all her ducks in a row, so to speak, she was ready to have a sit-down with Pamela and Graeme to tell them about her cancer. She'd invited Bill to join them, since he had a knack of calming Pamela down when she started going off the deep end – something Graeme was quite gifted at too, but considering the nature of her news Rowzee had decided that Graeme shouldn't be trying to deal with both sisters at once. She'd also thought of inviting Andee, as a kind of ally, until she'd remembered that no one was her enemy and much as she'd like Andee to feel a part of their family, there were probably better ways of going about it.

'You're making me nervous,' Pamela accused irritably as Bill carried a tray of coffee to the table and set it down.

'Who, me?' he retorted, amazed.

'No, Rowzee. What's all this about?' she demanded, glaring at Rowzee's notebook. 'Are we here for a reading of your new novel?'

As Rowzee's eyes met Graeme's they both smiled, but she could tell he was anxious too, and in response to that she felt a scurry of butterflies in her tummy. 'How long are the boys staying?' she asked him. 'It meant a great deal to Matt, you know, that they came back for the funeral. Are they still spending a lot of time with him?'

'Quite a bit,' Graeme replied. 'There's been a noticeable bonding between the town's young people since Jessica was found, which has been a tremendous help to Matt.'

She wanted to ask how Blake and Jenny were too, but she realised she couldn't keep putting off the inevitable, so she took the coffee Bill was passing and opened her notebook. Blake and Jenny were already back at work, she remembered, Blake restoring the antiques, with Jenny helping out in the shop again and teaching piano three evenings a week. How brave they were, and how marvellous that Jenny was finally getting help for her depressions. There was a lot Rowzee needed to discuss with them, but she'd best not dwell on that now, since Pamela had just reminded her again that they were waiting.

'OK,' Rowzee began, putting on a smile, and feeling tempted to say *Once upon a time*, to try and lighten things. Refraining, she said, 'There's not really an easy way of telling you this, so I thought I should come to the point right away. I'm afraid I have a tumour in my brain, which they've discovered is a secondary cancer, so there isn't a cure.' There, as nutshells went, that was a pretty good one, she thought, as Graeme's face paled and Pamela's collapsed in shock.

Realising stupid tears were blurring her eyes, Rowzee quickly blinked them back and said, 'It's not really as bad as it sounds . . .'

Pamela suddenly exploded. 'You've got a tumour? In your brain? And you're only just telling us? How long have you known?'

Since there was no point in lying, Rowzee said, 'A few weeks.'

Pamela looked as though she'd been struck. 'So you've been to the doctor, had all the tests and not once did you ask me to go with you? I can't believe you'd do that.'

'I didn't want to worry you.'

'I was already worried,' Pamela shouted angrily. 'I've been telling you for months that there's something wrong with you. If you'd gone straight away they might have caught it in time.'

Quietly Rowzee said, 'I don't think they would have . . .'

Pamela suddenly shot to her feet. 'This is all nonsense,' she raged tearfully. 'I'm not having it, do you hear me? You need a second opinion, maybe even a third, because no way am I just sitting here accepting what one person says.'

'Pamela, sit down,' Graeme said gently.

Pamela only looked at him.

Rowzee said, 'I've already had a second opinion and both surgeons have said that the tumour is inoperable.'

Clearly about to erupt again, Pamela rashly satisfied the urge with a slap to Bill's face.

Though startled, Rowzee and Graeme couldn't help laughing, while a bemused Bill rubbed his cheek and picked up his coffee.

'We need to speak to these *surgeons*,' Pamela informed Graeme, as though she doubted their credentials, or even existence.

Though Rowzee could see Graeme agreed, she was grateful to him for not saying so just yet. Presumably he wanted to hear everything she had to tell them before making up his mind about what should be done.

Since she'd already made up her own mind, and since her brother was usually a sane and rational human being, Rowzee was hopeful that her decisions would end up chiming with his. So, continuing under the force of Pamela's frightened glare, she said, 'They've given me about six months, maybe nine . . .'

'No!' Pamela gulped desperately. 'I'm telling you no, Rowzee. You've got it confused, you don't understand . . . It can't . . . It . . .' As she broke down sobbing, Rowzee went to fold her in her arms.

'It's all right,' Rowzee whispered softly. 'I promise. Everything's going to be all right, because I have a plan.'

Grabbing a tissue from the box Bill was offering, Pamela dabbed her eyes and tried to look at her sister. 'What do you mean, you have a plan?' she asked warily.

'I'm about to tell you,' Rowzee replied. Once they were all sitting down again, she said, 'The reason the tumour is inoperable is because it's so close to,' she checked her notes, 'the cerebral artery, and if that gets damaged during surgery it could cause a major stroke.'

Pamela looked so afraid – and hopeful for the plan – that Rowzee quickly continued. 'I had a long chat with the surgeon yesterday,' she told them, 'and I've decided to risk having the surgery. No, please don't interrupt, not yet. I really don't want to leave either of you, obviously, but there's Jason, my grandson, to think about as well. Life might have been cruel in the way it took Edward away, but it's given me Jason now,

367

and I want to be here for as long as I can to do my very best for him.'

Pamela's hand went to her mouth as more tears flooded her eyes.

Pressing on, Rowzee said, 'I'd like to have your solemn promises, Pamela and Graeme, that if I do suffer a major stroke during the op you will not do anything to overturn the instruction I shall give for non-resuscitation. I don't think you can, actually, but I don't want you to try.'

Pamela could only stare at her.

Graeme swallowed as he said, 'Of course you have our promise, if that's what you want.'

Rowzee reached for his hand and squeezed it. 'I'm not afraid of dying,' she lied, 'I'm only afraid of not being me any more, of becoming a helpless burden on my family . . .'

'OK, you can stop that right now,' Pamela blurted. 'I'm not killing you off just so you can avoid . . .'

'Pamela, shush,' Graeme interrupted.

'Well, I'm not,' she told him hotly. 'I don't care if she can't feed herself, or go to the bathroom on her own, I'm not letting her die . . .'

'But it isn't about you,' Graeme reminded her. 'It's about Rowzee and the quality of her life after the surgery.'

'And it might be successful,' Rowzee added, trying to sound cheerful, while knowing the chances were extremely slim. However, she'd rather go this way then have it drag out over months and months getting steadily worse, maybe even turning into the kind of person who shouted abuse at people in the street, or tried to beat up her family.

Feeling certain she hadn't finished yet, she consulted her notebook again and said, 'Even if I do come through with no adverse side effects, we mustn't forget that this is a secondary cancer so I'll be playing out the last act anyway. They'll give me treatment to help me live as normal a life as I can for as long as I can, but as soon as that changes and there's no longer a way of reversing the decline, I want to end my life in a humane and dignified way.'

'But you're not an animal,' Pamela sobbed angrily, 'and I don't understand why you're so intent on killing yourself when you're supposed to have a cancer that's doing it for you. Why can't you let things take their own course? You are such a control freak.'

Rowzee had to smile at that. 'If I let them take their course I probably don't have much more than six months,' she reminded Pamela, 'and my decline will be quite rapid from here on.' She wasn't going to tell them about her plans for Dignitas, since they were no longer relevant at this stage. Later, they might be, but they'd deal with that then. 'If I have the operation and it works we can probably add as much as a year to that six months, maybe more, depending on how many miracles are looking for homes at the time.'

Graeme asked, 'How soon can you have the operation?'

Rowzee's mouth turned dry as she said, 'Apparently they can make room for me in the next couple of weeks.'

Pamela said, testily, 'But if you have the operation and it brings on a major stroke you want us to let you die, which means we could lose you as soon as next week? I have to wonder why we're bothering to wait so long?'

Understanding her fear, and feeling it herself, Rowzee looked at Graeme.

'I'd like to have a chat with the surgeon,' he told her.

'Yes, you must do that,' Pamela agreed. 'She's probably got it all wrong. You know what you're like,' she said to Rowzee, 'always forgetting the most important parts, or missing out something crucial to the story.'

'That's not true,' Rowzee protested. 'I've always been very good at remembering my lines.'

'In fact,' Pamela ran on undeterred, 'I wouldn't be at all surprised if you don't have cancer at all. You've probably been reading about someone who does and you've got things all mixed up. Or they have. It happens, you know.'

Rowzee didn't argue, or remind Pamela that she was the one who'd been pointing out for months that something was wrong. Pamela knew it, and if it was helping her to take refuge in denial for now then Rowzee wasn't about to force her out of it.

Getting to his feet Graeme came to put his arms round Rowzee, dwarfing her little frame in the size of his embrace. 'Whatever happens,' he said softly, tilting her face up to his, 'you know we'll always be here for you and we'll support your wishes in every way.'

Rowzee could see Pamela was about to protest, but it seemed the feel of Bill's hand sliding into hers was enough to stop her.

A few days later, with her surgery now scheduled for the end of the following week, Rowzee went to meet Andee at the Seafront Café. She'd been very busy since her chat with Pamela and Graeme, and had lots of things she needed to discuss with someone before putting herself into Mr Mervin's hands. Since it would be too hard for her brother and sister to remain objective when they were emotionally involved, she'd decided that Andee was both wise and rational enough to give opinions or advice without attaching them to an agenda of her own.

'I know Graeme's told you,' Rowzee said, as Andee came into the café and embraced her warmly, 'so please don't feel awkward, or think you have to trot out any appropriate words. I don't think there are any, actually, or none that I can think of, but even if you can shall we just skip over them?'

'If that's what you want,' Andee smiled tenderly.

'Oh, it is. I can't bear pity and anyway, I don't need it when I've got so much of it for myself. Will you have a coffee?'

'Americano,' Andee told the waiter.

'Make that two,' Rowzee added, and as he went away she opened up her notebook to the list she'd made before coming. Then suddenly realising how self-involved she was being, she closed the book again, and said, 'How is your dear mother? It was lovely to see her at the funeral, though we could have wished for better circumstances, obviously.'

'She's fine,' Andee assured her. 'It did her good to let her hair down with you, and she's liking having me under the same roof again.'

Rowzee's eyes widened.

With irony, Andee said, 'Martin has moved into the flat I rented in town, so I've returned to Bourne Hollow.'

Tentatively, Rowzee said, 'Oh dear, I'm not sure whether that's a good or a bad thing.'

'Mostly good,' Andee replied. 'Mum and I get along very well, and Martin's less likely to create a scene if she's around.'

'Does he create many scenes?'

'He never used to. Incidentally, I haven't told Mum your news because Graeme said you didn't want anyone to know yet.'

Rowzee smiled. 'I'm trying not to make too much fuss,' she confided, 'but I do have some things to ask of you. I hope they won't be too much trouble,' and opening her notebook again she turned it so Andee could see, 'but in case I don't make it through the operation, these,' she was pointing to a roughly scrawled list, 'are my dying wishes.'

Andee's eyes filled with alarm.

'Don't worry about not being able to read my writing,' Rowzee continued, 'I'll feed everything into the computer later and print it out. I just wanted to discuss things with you first, and make any amendments or additions that we might decide on.' Her eyes came anxiously to Andee's. 'I hope you don't mind me asking you to make sure they're carried out, but you're the only person I can think of, apart from Norma, who could do this, and she already has enough to be coping with. Besides, she's on the list, and if no one's checking she might quietly take herself off it and that just won't do.'

As thrown as she was moved, Andee said, 'I'm honoured that you would ask me, and I promise, provided it's in my power, I'll make sure your wishes are carried out.'

Rowzee beamed. 'I knew asking you was the right decision,' she declared, 'but please don't think you have to take responsibility for everything. A lot of this is in my will, but just in case I don't die next week, I shall still want to see a lot of these things happen before I go and I might need your help to bring everyone on side.' With a twinkle she added, 'Pamela calls me a control freak and I'm beginning to think that maybe I got the genes too.'

Certain she had, albeit in a slightly more subtle version, Andee waited for her to continue.

Turning businesslike, Rowzee said, 'OK, let's start with Norma, because she'll probably be the most difficult. I know she says she doesn't need help taking care of Sean, but I'm afraid she does. You see, she won't live for ever, and there's no knowing how long he might go on for, so I've set up a trust to cover his needs once Norma can't do it any more. That's all in the will, but here, on this list, which will come into operation if I don't die right away, is an instruction to give her a letter I've already written and will give to you before I go into hospital, telling her that she is to accept the financial help I'm offering so she can have more of a life before it's too late. She deserves it, and so does Jason. I know she won't have a problem accepting funding for him to go to uni, or to take up an apprenticeship, because she wants it as much as I do. I'm quite clear in my letter about these being my dying wishes, so hopefully she won't put up a fight.'

Having no idea what to say to that, Andee simply reflected that she'd probably never met a more determined or adorable human being in her life.

'OK, next wish,' Rowzee went on. 'I don't think there'll be too much of a problem with this, but if I'm not strong enough to get Blake properly on board myself, I'd like you to lend some muscle. He's had an idea, you see, that I think is brilliant, and I promised to help him bring it to fruition, but only if he would oversee it himself. As it involves the school he's reluctant to take a lead, but no one will be able to run it as well as he can, not even me, especially not me, given how scatty I am these days and we know that's not going to improve. His idea is to start up a collaborative project between the students of art, literature and music. Actually, I think it started out as Jessica's idea, which is why I'm referring to it as the Jessica Project. I'm in the process of writing letters for the heads of each of these departments, reminding them of the conversations we've already had on the subject. They won't have forgotten, but if they understand that it's my dying wish to get the project off the ground with Blake, I'm sure they'll do it.'

Finding herself wanting to laugh, Andee said, 'I can see you've got a lot of faith in the power of a dying wish.'

'Haven't you?' Rowzee replied in surprise.

Deciding that yes, she probably had, Andee gestured for her to continue.

'Right, next on the list is Blake again,' Rowzee told her. 'I want him to put on an exhibition of his own paintings, probably at the Guild Hall. I have contacts there who I hope you'll give one of my letters to – I could use Royal Mail, of course, but if it's hand-delivered by you I think that will carry a lot more clout.'

'So is Blake keen to have this exhibition?' Andee asked carefully.

'He says no, but Jenny and Matt say yes, so I think we should listen to them. He shuns the limelight because of what happened at the school up north, but hopefully we'll get him over that.'

Eager to know who the next instruction was for, Andee looked at the list as an encouragement for Rowzee to continue.

'Bill and Pamela,' Rowzee stated. 'I'm leaving Pamela the Coach House in my will, naturally, but if I make it through the op I'd love Bill to feel welcome to move in with us. I know he already has a lovely home of his own, but he'll be a tremendous support to Pamela if he's with us as we navigate our way through the rough seas ahead.' Mischievously she added, 'I'm being a bit selfish here, because if I am around I'm going to need some help dealing with Pamela myself. She's very cross with me about this, you know?'

'Cross?' Andee echoed.

'It's her way of trying to cope. Cover it all up with a show of chagrin and outrage and no one will know how she's really feeling. Of course I can see right through it, we all can, and I suppose it's a part of what makes us love her so much.' As her eyes filled with tears, she said, 'I know how I'd feel if the shoe was on the other foot, but I probably wouldn't be quite so loud or bossy about it.' Laughing, she added, 'I think this list is about as bossy as you can get, so it just goes to show how similar we are. Anyway, I'd like you to assure Bill that I am very happy for him to live with us if he can bear it. I'll tell him myself, of course, but if you can add your voice to mine he'll be more inclined to believe it.'

Having no problem with that Andee sat back as their coffee arrived, and was about to take a sip of hers when she noticed Rowzee having difficulty lifting her cup. 'Are you all right?' she asked worriedly.

Rowzee stared at her trembling hand. 'It'll pass,' she replied.

'Can I get you something?'

By way of an answer Rowzee lifted the weakened hand and broke into a smile. 'Just making sure,' she explained.

Realising she was testing herself for signs of a stroke, Andee said, 'Why don't you let me drive you home?'

'But we haven't finished, and I promise you, I'm fine. Maybe another ITA.'

Realising she meant TIA, Andee watched her closely as she blinked a few times, as though clearing her eyes, and took a couple of breaths.

'Charles is next,' she declared, after consulting her book. 'I haven't finished writing to him yet, but I will. I know what he did was terrible, but I want him to know that he's always had a special place in my heart, and that I understand even good people are capable of doing bad things, and not always intentionally. Of course, I've no idea what was really going on his mind all that time, only he can tell us that, and only he has to live with his conscience. I just don't think it's my place to sit in judgement when we have a Maker to do that for us. Do you believe in God?'

Startled, Andee said, 'I'm not sure. Probably when it suits me.'

Rowzee smiled. 'I've always been a bit like that, ambivalent one day, at church the next. I find myself more willing to believe now, probably just in case.'

Wondering just how brave she was really feeling, and suspecting not very, Andee reached for her hand.

Seeming grateful, Rowzee met her eyes for a moment, allowing their unexpected but nonetheless special bond a silent recognition before she returned to her notes. 'As I said, I'm in the middle of writing a letter to Charles. I'll do a separate one for Gina, I think, and if you don't mind making sure they get them . . . Have they gone to the States yet?'

'No, they won't be able to leave until after the trial and . . .'

'Trial?'

Realising the latest news had either slipped her mind, or somehow passed her by, Andee said, 'Charles has received an additional charge of failing to notify the coroner, so the case has to go to Crown Court.'

Rowzee blinked. 'Will he go to prison?' she asked worriedly.

'Possibly, but whether he does or doesn't, it's going to be difficult for him to go to the States once he has a criminal record.'

Rowzee nodded slowly as she digested the problems facing the Stamfields. 'It's going to seem strange not having them at the Hall,' she remarked sadly. 'Do you think they'll really sell it?'

'That certainly seems to be the intention, but I guess only time will tell.'

Coming out of a kind of reverie, Rowzee said, 'And maybe I'll never know, so I don't think I'll trouble myself with it,' and she returned to her list.

Finding her remarkable in so many ways, Andee drank more coffee as the notebook pages were turned and consulted, until Rowzee finally closed it. 'I think that's all for now,' she declared.

Wondering if she'd had a change of heart about something, or if she was running out of energy, Andee said, 'I hope you're not forgetting about yourself as you make plans for everyone else.'

Appearing surprised, Rowzee said, 'But this is all about me and what I want.'

Smiling as she conceded the point, Andee said, 'No dying wishes for Graeme?'

A twinkle immediately lit Rowzee's eyes. 'Where my brother's concerned I shall have to come at things a different way, but never fear, I have it all worked out.'

Laughing, Andee watched her unlock her phone to read a text.

With a sigh, Rowzee said, 'Graeme's just left the surgeon's office. I know he didn't doubt what I was telling him, the way Pamela did, but I think it's a good thing that he's had a chat with Mr Mervin himself. He'll want to understand more about the procedure. Men do, don't they?'

Not disagreeing, Andee continued to watch her, and suddenly felt bold enough to ask if she was afraid.

As Rowzee's gaze drifted off towards the bay, she said, '*Nothing in his life became him like the leaving it.*' After a while her eyes returned to Andee. 'A line from *Macbeth*,' she told her, 'spoken by Malcolm. I find myself surprised by some of the things I remember, and I wonder why they come floating up to the surface when they do, either in parts or sometimes even as a whole.' She smiled tenderly. 'To answer your question, I don't feel afraid today, but I'm sure I will when it comes time to go under and I have no idea whether I'll be coming back. I just hope I don't do anything to upset anyone or to disgrace myself. I really wouldn't like that.'

The following week Graeme drove Rowzee to the Infirmary where she was to undergo a series of pre-surgery scans, blood tests, and all sorts of other health checks before her appearance, as she'd taken to calling it, in the operating theatre the next morning. There were no lines to learn for this performance, no moves, no anything to tax her dramatic skills at all. Mr Mervin was going to take the lead with his support cast of doctors and nurses, and all sorts of medical props and paraphernalia (they might even have an audience somewhere in a gallery), and all she had to do was put her trust in them and try to let go of everything else.

'Deep breaths and positive thinking,' had been Norma's advice on the phone last night. 'And if you can manage a little meditation you should find it very soothing.'

'You're darned well going to get through this or I'll come in there and box your silly ears,' were Pamela's parting words this morning as she squeezed Rowzee to within an inch of her life.

'Are you sure you understand about not coming today?' Rowzee had asked her gently.

'Yes, of course,' Pamela promised tearfully. 'I know I'll just get stressed and cross and start upsetting people, and that's the last thing any of us needs. I'll be there tomorrow though, when they put you under, and I won't be leaving again until I can take you with me.'

'Hopefully not in a box,' Rowzee tried to joke, and immediately wished she hadn't.

'That's not going to happen,' Pamela told her tenderly. 'You're darned well going to get through this, or I'll never speak to you again.' That was before she'd threatened to come and box Rowzee's silly ears, or maybe it was after. It hardly mattered, but silly ears? What was silly about her ears, other than the fact that she was even wondering about it now when there was so much else to be thinking about?

'Did Mr Mervin tell you about his satnav for the brain?' she said chattily to Graeme, her words feeling like high-strung piano notes over booming chords of dread. 'That's what's happening today, I think. They're doing scans for him to use with this special navigation system so he'll know exactly where to go and how to get there. Apparently he was one of the surgeons who got the funding for this system at Frenchay Hospital in Bristol. It was the first hospital in the country to have it and the fourth in the world, and it's saved so many lives.' Had he said that? Yes, she was sure he had. 'So, he's top in his field, he's even taught surgeons from all over the world how to use it so we mustn't worry about him being able to do his job, because if anyone can weed out this tumour without damaging the artery he can.'

'I have every confidence in him,' Graeme stated firmly, 'and in you.'

Not sure about herself, Rowzee did her best to fight down an onslaught of dragons – butterflies had been defeated long ago – and tried taking one of Norma's steadying breaths as they turned into the hospital grounds.

'You'll be fine,' Graeme assured her, taking her hand as she suddenly sobbed. 'And you know I'm never wrong.'

Spluttering a laugh, Rowzee said, 'It's lucky, isn't it, that they don't have to shave my head, only the part where they're going in, so at least I won't be bald when

I come out,' *or when I go to see Victor and Edward*, she didn't add. Her beloved husband and son. They were waiting for her in heaven, and if she knew for certain she was going to join them this wouldn't be half so bad.

Finally finding a parking space, Graeme came round to open the door for her and pulled her into his arms.

'You know the weirdest thing,' she said, her voice muffled by his shoulder, 'is that I don't feel ill at all.' She pulled back to look up into his eyes. 'Will you stay with me for a while after they've checked me in?' she asked.

'Of course,' he promised. 'I'll be here for as long as you want me to be.'

There was something else she wanted to say to him, but with so much going on inside her – fear and worry, hope and even a strange sort of intrigue and excitement at the prospect of possibly seeing Victor and Edward – she couldn't reach through it to all the reminders she'd given herself. Not to worry, she was sure they were written in her notebook, and even if they weren't, Graeme was going to be with her for as long as she wanted him to be, and that was all that really mattered.

It was just after ten the next morning when Andee brought coffees and pastries to the hospital waiting room where Rowzee's entire family, apart from her great-nephew Alfie, was already gathered. Even Jason was there, looking worried and unsure of himself and relieved to see Andee. She knew Norma would have come too had there been anyone to take care of Sean, but she'd promised to call her as soon as there was some news.

It was lucky no one else wanted to use the waiting room for there wasn't a single spare seat, though Bill and Graeme were quick to get up to make a space for Andee.

'I'm so glad you came,' Pamela murmured, hugging her. 'You might keep us all from going to pieces.'

Hugging her too, Graeme said, 'It came to her just before I was leaving last night, that she wanted you to be here today if you could spare the time.'

'Of course I can,' Andee assured him, suspecting that Rowzee had wanted someone to be there for her brother if things didn't go well. He'd be strong for his sons, naturally, and his sister and nieces, but it would matter a lot to Rowzee that he'd have someone to turn to himself.

Graeme was saying, 'She asked if you could use one of your police holds on Pamela should she decide to give Bill another biff.'

Having been told about Pamela's burst of frustration, Andee couldn't help but smile as Graeme explained it to the others and Bill blew a kiss to his slap-happy sweetheart. 'Did you see her before she went in?' she asked, after embracing Pamela's daughters and Graeme's remarkably unalike sons, whom she'd met for the first time at Jessica's funeral.

'Briefly,' Pamela replied, 'and she was high as a kite – or fabulously chillaxed, as she informed us, like she'd gone back to being a hippy. She told the surgeon that she hoped he was a good hairdresser, because she was very particular about looking her best at all times, and even before he could answer she was gone. Well, not gone in that sense, just out of it, you know, and I didn't get the chance to tell her I love her, none of us did and I can't bear that she might think we don't . . .'

'Don't be daft, Mum,' Katie chided. 'She knows very well how much we love her.'

'But I wanted her to hear it.'

'Then you can tell her as soon as she comes round,' Lucie put in firmly.

Pamela looked at her younger daughter and smiled through her tears. 'That's a lovely thing to say,' she told her. 'Yes, I'll tell her when she comes round.'

'Have they given you any idea of how long the surgery's likely to take?' Andee asked.

Graeme said, 'Between three and four hours. After that she'll be in the recovery room for two to three hours before they move her to the high-dependency unit overnight.'

'We probably won't be able to see her until tomorrow morning,' Pamela added, 'provided the worst hasn't happened, of course. Oh please God, don't let them damage that artery and cause her to have a stroke, please, please, please.'

Graeme said, 'If it doesn't happen during surgery, which obviously we're praying it won't, it'll be about twelve hours before they'll feel confident that the operation has been a success. If it is she should be ready to come home in about a week.'

Already knowing that an intensive course of radiotherapy would then follow, possibly chemo too, Andee sent her own silent prayer for success and sat down on the chair Bill was insisting she take to begin the long

wait. The longer the better, she realised, for if anything disastrous occurred they'd probably be notified
straight away.

For the next hour or more, led by Pamela and Graeme,
everyone told their favourite Rowzee story, leading
to far more laughter than seemed right for a hospital
waiting room, yet everyone knew it was exactly what
Rowzee would have wanted. Naturally, there were
tears too, and even the odd argument when Pamela
insisted someone had got something wrong.

It was just after one o'clock when the waiting-room
door opened and a stocky, pale-faced nurse came to
summon Graeme outside. Since the surgery wasn't
due to be over yet, fear struck deep into everyone's
heart. They'd lost her; she'd gone and wasn't coming
back . . .

How could there be a world without Rowzee?

# Chapter Twenty

Six weeks later Andee was helping her mother to pack up parcels of old clothes to take to the charity shop when her mobile rang. Seeing it was Graeme she quickly clicked on. 'Hi, how are you?' she asked softly.

'I'm OK,' he replied. 'I was just wondering if you were going to be in town today?'

'We'll be heading that way in about half an hour. Is there something you need?'

'Would you have time to call into the shop?'

'Of course. Mum's got a hairdresser's appointment at three, so I'll come then if that suits.'

'It's perfect. See you then.'

After loading up the car, Andee waited for her mother to lock the house and was about to start driving down the hill when Martin rang. After showing her mother who it was, she let the call go to messages, feeling terrible for the way she was avoiding him, but all he ever did these days was threaten her with the bitterest of divorces or even the grisliest of suicides, which she could blame herself for when they dragged his body out of the sea, or from a wrecked car.

'It's not getting any easier, is it?' her mother murmured.

'He doesn't help himself by drinking so much,' Andee replied.

'I just hope he doesn't call the children when he's in that state.'

'If he did I'm sure they'd tell us.'

In fact, she wasn't sure who Martin was talking to these days, apart from the menacing calls he made to her. Apparently he was rarely in touch with his mother, or sister, and he hadn't been going into the office much either. Although she felt wretched for having caused him so much pain, she couldn't help wondering how much of it was about the breakdown of their marriage, and how much to do with the blow to his ego.

Deciding not to think about it now, she turned her thoughts to Graeme and what he might want to see her about. Though she could hazard several guesses, it wasn't until three o'clock when she entered the shop to find him alone that she discovered how way off the mark she was with them all.

As he greeted her she could see that he was trying, and failing, to sound solemn. 'It's about Rowzee,' he told her.

Loving the fact that almost everything had been about Rowzee since she'd come safely through the surgery, and the intensive course of radiotherapy that had followed, Andee encouraged him to continue.

'She has a dying wish,' he told her.

Andee's eyes sparkled with laughter. 'Another?'

'Another,' he confirmed.

The last one, put forward just over a week ago, had been to go to London for Charles's trial. Graeme had flatly refused, saying she still wasn't strong enough, no matter what she said, so she'd persuaded him and Andee to go 'on her behalf' to show support for Lydia, even if they didn't feel they could for Charles.

Although their feelings towards Stamfield were ambivalent, to say the least, they'd let Lydia know they were coming, and had sat with her and Gina during her father's sentencing. Since the Crown Prosecution Service had added the charge of Preventing a Lawful Burial to the Failure to Report an Accident, it had meant that the likelihood of Charles receiving a custodial sentence had greatly increased, so it hadn't come as a big surprise when he'd received an eighteen-month term. It wasn't long enough as far as the press was concerned, that much was obvious, but watching him being led away, bowed with shame, and hearing Gina's sobs as she tried to follow, Andee had felt her heart breaking for them both.

'He'd been expecting it,' Lydia told them over a drink in a wine bar afterwards, 'and to be honest I think Dad almost welcomed it. He feels he needs to be punished, and trying to survive in prison will be hard for him. Nothing like as hard as these past two years have been for Jessica's family, of course, he'll never be able to make up for what he did to them and he knows it.'

'What's your mother going to do while he's away?' Andee asked.

'Visit him, I guess, and find a place to rent in the Caribbean for when he comes out. They've decided they won't be able to stay here, and his criminal record will prevent him from returning to the States, so their plan is to live a quiet life away from the limelight.'

'And you?' Graeme prompted.

'My job is safe, apparently, so I'll go back to it just as soon as Burlingford Hall is properly on the market.' She paused awkwardly, gazing down at her drink and seeming lost for a moment. 'We were hoping,' she said, bringing her eyes back to Graeme, 'that you'd handle the sale of the furniture for us. I've made a list of the pieces we want to keep, but the rest of it can go to auction.'

Thinking of Blake and how he'd feel about being involved in the sale, Andee looked at Graeme as he said, 'I'm about to make Blake Leonard a full partner in the company, so I'll have to consult him before I can give you an answer.'

Flushing, Lydia said, 'Of course, I understand. Am I allowed to ask how he is?'

With a sardonic smile, Graeme said, 'Currently being bulldozed by the mighty force called Rowzee into setting up all sorts of projects. She's wearing herself out with excitement over them, while we, including Blake, are all so happy she's still with us that we'll do anything she asks. I could call it shameless manipulation, in fact I think I will, because that's exactly what it is. We're starting a crusade for the right to die next week, with her leading the way.'

'It was such a relief when we heard she'd pulled through,' Lydia told him earnestly. 'I hope you got our card and flowers.'

'We did,' Graeme confirmed, 'and they meant a lot to her. She's always been very fond of your parents, and she's not someone to condemn old friends out of hand for something she believes they deeply regret.'

'They do,' Lydia assured him. 'Nevertheless, she's far more forgiving than they deserve. I'm afraid I can't get there myself, but I can't abandon them either. Dad asked me to give you a message,' she said to Andee. 'He understands, of course, why the Leonards don't want to accept the money Mum sent them, but he's hoping you might be able to persuade them to donate it to a charity of their choice.'

'I'll certainly try,' she promised.

As it turned out, Blake and Jenny were willing for the money to go to a missing persons charity, so there had been no problem on that front. Nor, it seemed, did they have any objection to Graeme handling the contents sale from Burlingford Hall, just as long as they weren't obliged to visit the place themselves.

To say Blake was delighted by his new role as Graeme's business partner was an understatement indeed. It was just what he'd needed to help get him started again, while Jenny, with ready assistance from Rowzee and Pamela, was overseeing Blake's exhibition at the Guild Hall, due to open in a month's time. The Leonards had also had an offer accepted on one of the sprawling old thatched cottages in Bourne Hollow, close to Andee's mother, and Matt had apparently settled back into uni.

'So with the Jessica Project under serious discussion at Kesterly High,' Andee said to Graeme now, 'and

Norma and Jason accepting all the help they've had pressed on them, and Bill happily ensconced at the Coach House, and our first campaign meeting for the right to die scheduled for Wednesday, what on earth can the next dying wish be?'

With no small irony, Graeme said, 'She wants me to take her and Pamela to Italy so she can have a say in how we go about renovating the villa.'

Impressed, Andee said, 'She's got a real knack for dying wishes, you have to give her that. I take it you've already booked?'

'Not quite yet, because that's not the actual wish. That's just a request, apparently, the wish . . . wait for this . . . is for you to come with us.'

Andee's eyes opened wide as her heart skipped a beat.

'It's a dying wish,' he reminded her, his face alight with humour.

Starting to laugh, Andee said, 'She wants *me* to come too?'

He nodded. 'That's what she wants.'

Still laughing, and shaking her head at Rowzee's shameless matchmaking skills, Andee said, 'Then how could I possibly refuse?'

Out of view in the workshop, but not out of earshot, Rowzee turned to Blake, and raising their hands they gave a silent, jubilant, high five.

# Acknowledgements

The biggest thank you of all must go to neurosurgeon Professor Hugh Coakham who so patiently and expertly helped me through Rowzee's diagnosis and treatment. If anything seems awry, or on an unusual timeline, this will be me taking poetic licence for story purposes.

My thanks also go to Ian Kelcey for his expert legal advice, and without whom it would seem that no book of mine can be completed!

And to Ian Chaney, Antique and Furniture Restorer extraordinaire. Thank you for showing me around your workshop and answering all my questions.

Also with love and thanks to my dear friend Ryno Posthumus. Hope to see you again one of these days!

# Susan Lewis

# The Moment
# She Left

Bonus Material

# Susan Lewis

## on
### *The Moment She Left*

Dear Reader

For those of you who've read my previous books, I hope you enjoyed this return to Kesterly-on-Sea. For new readers a very warm welcome to this quirky west-country resort; I hope very much that you enjoyed your time there, and were happy to meet some of the characters.

While I was keen for Andee Lawrence (*Behind Closed Doors*, *The Girl Who Came Back*) to lead us through this story, I was also keen to introduce a new ensemble of characters. It's both exciting and challenging to have several plots running at once, and to find myself taking on so many different roles in the course of storytelling. Thanks to Rowzee and Pamela I had plenty of laughs, but with the laughter came tears as Rowzee's condition became clearer. My heart always ached for Blake and his family, so torn apart by the mysterious disappearance of their beloved Jessica. And then there was poor, mixed up Charles whose wealth, position and conscience were all but killing him.

While trying to help each one of her friends, Andee was facing emotional battles of her own, thanks to a broken marriage and the blame heaped on her by her children. I'm sure that, like me, you find the quiet courage and strength of women who support others selflessly, while hiding their own challenges, unfailingly impressive and inspiring. For Andee, becoming involved in the search for Jessica was especially difficult given the way her sister, Penny, disappeared at the age of fourteen. No one has ever been able to explain what happened to Penny. Knowing how hard that reality is to live with is what motivates Andee to try and discover what became of Jessica, who vanished quite suddenly and without trace at the age of nineteen. The harrowing emotions of loss, fear, confusion and self-blame became real to Andee all over again, even after so many years.

It felt important to try to acknowledge the stoicism and empathy of women who put others before themselves, whether facing a terminal illness as in Rowzee's case, or their own unending nightmares as in Andee's.

Thank you so much for the time you have given this book. I hope you came to love Rowzee as much as I did, and that you felt this latest journey with Andee to have been worthwhile. For another journey with Andee look out for *Hiding in Plain Sight*, due for publication later this year.

With my warmest wishes

Susan

# Coming February 2017
## *You Said Forever*

The much anticipated new novel that follows on
from *No Child of Mine* and *Don't Let Me Go*

Charlotte Goodman is living the dream.

Surrounded by family, friends and a stunning vineyard
overlooking the ocean, it would be difficult for anyone to believe
that she has a troubled past.

However, haunted by the theft of a young girl, Charlotte begins
to realise the enormity of something she did many years ago, and
soon finds herself having to make the most harrowing decision
any woman would ever have to face.

**Available in Hardback and ebook from 9th February**
**ORDER NOW**

Turn over to find out more from Susan. . .

# Susan Lewis

## On writing *You Said Forever*

When I began little Ottilie's story in *No Child of Mine*, and continued it when she became Chloe in *Don't Let Me Go*, I never imagined that there would be a third book in the series. It was amazing and incredibly moving to receive so many requests for more of this little girl's story; this little girl that everyone has taken so tenderly to their hearts.

I admit, when I finished *Don't Let Me Go* it was very hard to say goodbye. But I felt Chloe's story had reached a natural end, and it was time to let her be for a while.

Now, a few years have elapsed. Chloe is eight and living on a vineyard in New Zealand, just as *Don't Let Me Go* promised. And that is just the beginning of this next stage of her journey.

Thank you so much to everyone who wrote to me after the first two books; not only for the wonderfully supportive messages and often courageous confidences you shared, but for persuading me to return to New Zealand to check on Chloe.

I really didn't expect what I found! I hope you enjoy *You Said Forever* and why not revisit or read *No Child of Mine* and *Don't Let Me Go* before dipping in to the new novel.

Susan

# Read and revisit
## *No Child of Mine* and
## *Don't Let Me Go*

Available in paperback and ebook

# About

## Susan

I was born in 1956 to a happy, normal family living in a brand new council house on the outskirts of Bristol. My mother, at the age of twenty, and one of thirteen children, persuaded my father to spend his bonus on a ring rather than a motorbike and they never looked back. She was an ambitious woman determined to see her children on the right path: I was signed up for ballet, elocution and piano lessons and my little brother was to succeed in all he set his mind to.

Tragically, at the age of thirty-three, my mother lost the battle against cancer and died. I was nine, my brother was five.

My father was left with two children to bring up on his own. Sending me to boarding school was thought to be 'for the best' but I disagreed. No one listened to my pleas for freedom, so after a while I took it upon myself to get expelled. By the time I was thirteen, I was back in our little council house with my father and brother. The teenage years passed and before I knew it I was eighteen … an adult.

I got a job at HTV in Bristol for a few years before moving to London at the age of twenty-two to work for Thames. I moved up the ranks, from secretary in news and current affairs, to a production assistant in light entertainment and drama. My mother's ambition and a love of drama gave me the courage to knock on the Controller's door to ask what it takes to be a success. I received the reply of 'Oh, go away and write something'. So I did!

Three years into my writing career I left TV and moved to France. At first it was bliss. I was living the dream and even found myself involved in a love affair with one of the FBI's most wanted! Reality soon dawned, however, and I realised that a full-time life in France was very different to a two-week holiday frolicking around on the sunny Riviera.

So I made the move to California with my beloved dogs Casanova and Floozie. With the rich and famous as my neighbours I was enthralled and inspired by Tinsel Town. The reality, however, was an obstacle course of cowboy agents, big-talking producers and wannabe directors. Hollywood was not waiting for me, but it was a great place to have fun! Romances flourished and faded, dreams were crushed but others came true.

After seven happy years of taking the best of Hollywood and avoiding the rest, I decided it was time for a change. My dogs and I spent a short while in Wiltshire before then settling once again in France, perched high above the Riviera with glorious views of the sea. It was wonderful to be back amongst old friends, and to make so many new ones. Casanova and Floozie both passed away during our first few years there, but Coco and Lulabelle are doing a valiant job of taking over their places – and my life!

Everything changed again three months after my fiftieth birthday when I met James, my partner, who lived and works in Bristol. For a couple of years we had a very romantic and enjoyable time of flying back and forth to see one another at the weekends, but at the end of 2010 I finally sold my house on the Riviera and am now living in Gloucestershire in a delightful old barn with Coco and

Lulabelle. My writing is flourishing and over thirty books down the line I couldn't be happier. James continued to live in Bristol, with his boys, Michael and Luke – a great musician and a champion footballer! – for a while until we decided to get married in 2013.

It's been exhilarating and educational having two teenage boys in my life! Needless to say they know everything, which is very useful (saves me looking things up) and they're incredibly inspiring in ways they probably have no idea about.

Should you be interested to know a little more about my early life, why not try *Just One More Day*, a memoir about me and my mother and then the story continues in *One Day at a Time*, a memoir about me and my father and how we coped with my mother's loss.

# Memoirs by

## *Susan Lewis*

Read the true story of Susan Lewis and her family and how they coped when tragedy struck. *Just One More Day* and its follow-up *One Day At A Time* are two memoirs that will hopefully make you laugh as well as cry as you follow Susan on her journey to love again.

Available in paperback

# 5 minutes with

## *Susan*

**Where does the inspiration for your books come from?**

I often write about difficult issues, as you well know.
I don't necessarily write from experience in these cases but
I rely on listening and seeking the experience of others
who might have witnessed or been through challenging
situations. It's important as a writer to imagine how you'd
feel if it happened to you. I enjoy doing it but sometimes it
can be quite distressing – sometimes I cry, which tells me it's
working. This is how I really bring my characters to life.

**Do you have any peculiar writing rituals or habits?**

Nothing too peculiar! I'm very strict about the hours I write,
starting at 10 in the morning and going through until 5pm
or 6pm, usually six days a week. Then, I love to have a glass
of wine at the end of the day as I read back over what has
happened in 'my fictional world' over the last seven or eight
hours, socialising with the characters and often wanting
to gossip about them with someone else.

**What advice would you offer to aspiring writers?**

Remember to listen: listen to the way people speak,
to the rhythm of the words you are writing  (you're most
likely to do this in your head), and always give your characters
room to be themselves. They'll have plenty to say if you
just let them chatter on to one another, often giving
you ideas you hadn't even thought of!

**What is the last book you bought someone as a gift?**

A variety of children's books for the recipients of the
Special Recognition Award that I'm sponsoring for the local
secondary school. They've chosen the titles themselves and what
a fascinating selection they've made – from *The Diary of a
Wimpy Kid* to *The Curious Incident of the Dog in the Night Time*
(one of my own favourites).

**What's the best piece of advice you've ever been given?**

If you want to be a producer you'd better write. I was
working in TV drama and this was what I was told to get
me out of the Controller's office! I took him at his word
and the rest, as they say, is history.

**If you had a superpower, what would it be?**

If I had a superpower I'd rescue all the children
and animals being subjected to cruelty.

**What literary character is most like you?**

Definitely Emma from Jane Austen's wonderful novel.

**If you were stranded on a desert island what song would
you choose to listen to, which book would you take and
what luxury item would you pack?**

That's a hard one. Song choice would have to be Just My
Imagination by the Temptations. Book choice . . . *How to Survive
on a Desert Island* by anyone who's been thoughtful enough to
write such a useful guide. Luxury item: A double-ended stick
with a toothbrush at one end and a knife at the other . . .
I could give Bear Grylls a sure run for his money!

# Have you read them all?

For a full list of books please visit
**www.susanlewis.com**

Connect with

# Susan Lewis

online

Sign up to Susan's newsletter for
exclusive content, competitions and
all the latest news from Susan.

Want to know more? Visit

**www.susanlewis.com**

Connect with other fans and join in the
conversation at

**f/SusanLewisBooks**

Follow Susan on

**🐦 @susandlewis**